UNDISCOVERED COUNTRY

VOLUME ONE

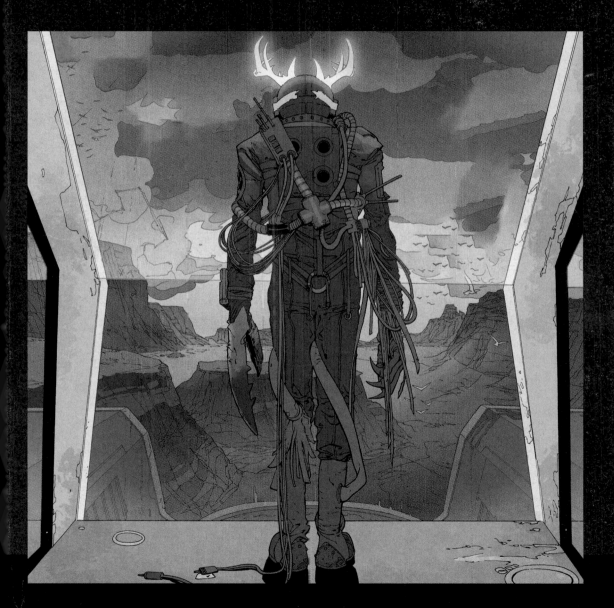

DESTINY

UNDISC
cot

VOLUME ONE

DESTINY

Production & design by **RYAN BREWER**
Cover design by **DREW GILL**
Logo design by **MAURO CORRADINI**

IMAGE COMICS, INC. • Robert Kirkman: Chief Operating Officer • Erik Larsen: Chief Financial Officer • Todd McFarlane: President • Marc Silvestri: Chief Executive Officer • Jim Valentino: Vice President • Eric Stephenson: Publisher / Chief Creative Officer • Jeff Boison: Director of Publishing Planning & Book Trade Sales • Chris Ross: Director of Digital Services • Jeff Stang: Director of Direct Market Sales • Kat Salazar: Director of PR & Marketing • Drew Gill: Cover Editor • Heather Doornink: Production Director • Nicole Lapalme: Controller • IMAGECOMICS.COM

OVERED NTRY

Written by
SCOTT SNYDER & **CHARLES SOULE**

Layouts by
GIUSEPPE CAMUNCOLI

Finishes by
DANIELE ORLANDINI (issues 1-4)
LEONARDO MARCELLO GRASSI
(issues 4-6)

Colored by
MATT WILSON

Lettered by
CRANK!

Edited by
WILL DENNIS

CHAPTER ONE

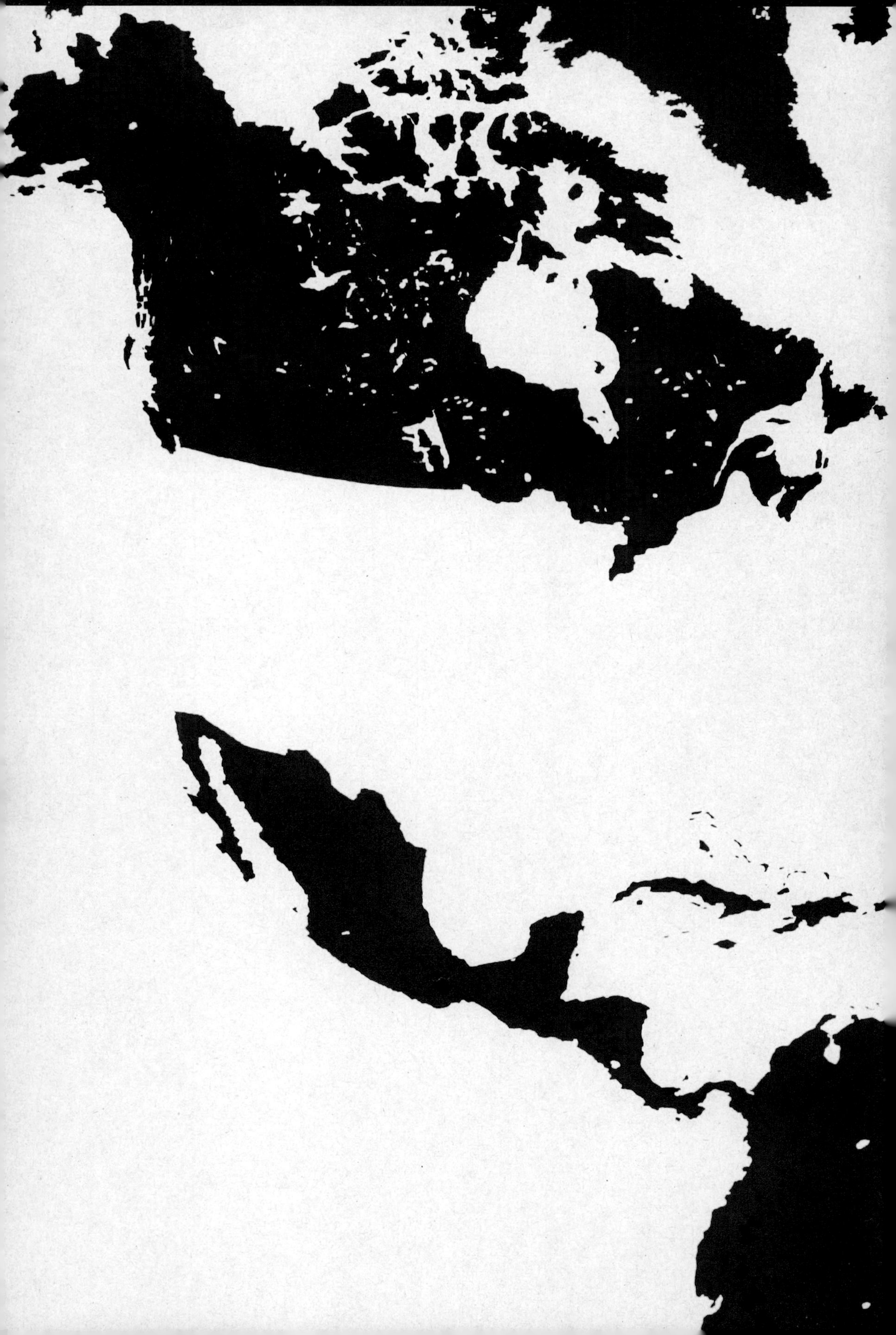

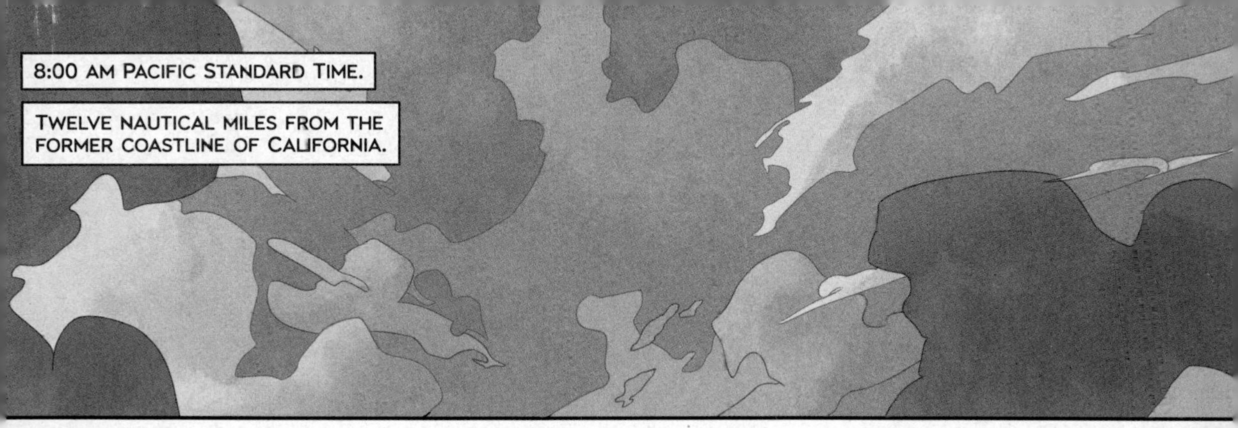
8:00 AM Pacific Standard Time.
Twelve nautical miles from the former coastline of California.

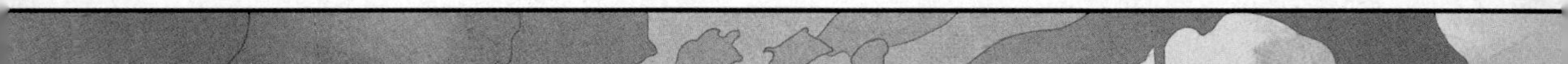
COMMAND, IF YOU CAN STILL HEAR US, WE'RE VECTORING IN AS PER APPROVED COORDINATES.
WE'LL CROSS OVER IN ONE MINUTE...

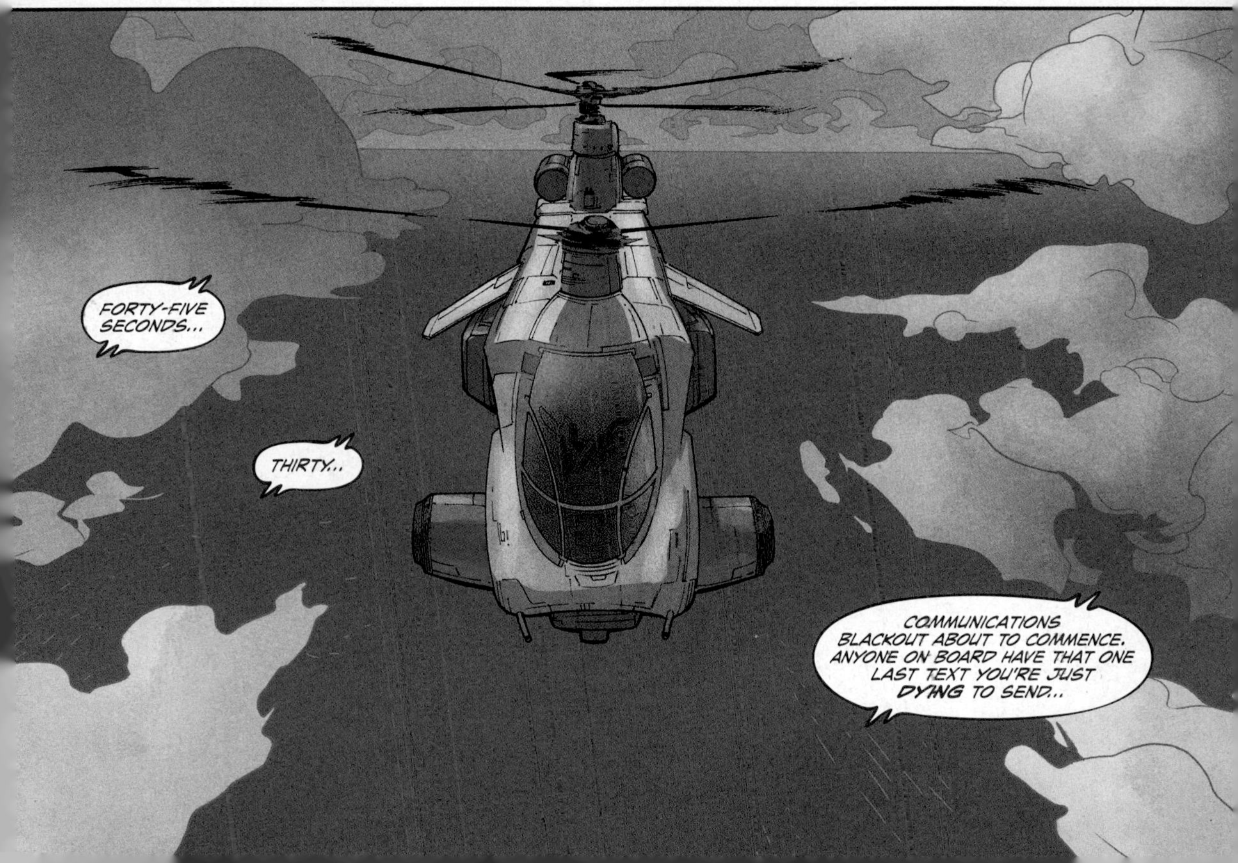
FORTY-FIVE SECONDS...
THIRTY...
COMMUNICATIONS BLACKOUT ABOUT TO COMMENCE. ANYONE ON BOARD HAVE THAT ONE LAST TEXT YOU'RE JUST DYING TO SEND...

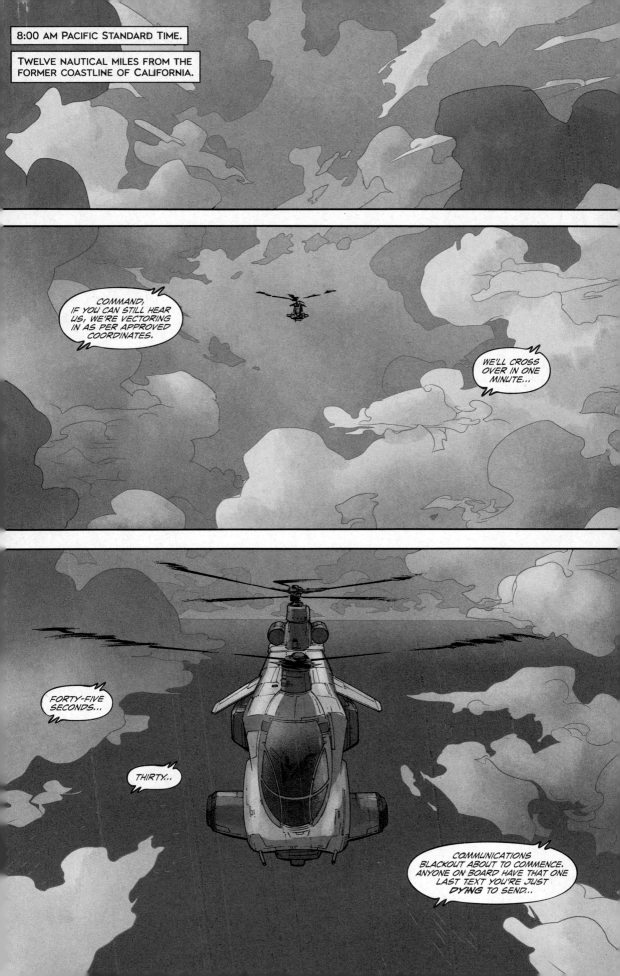

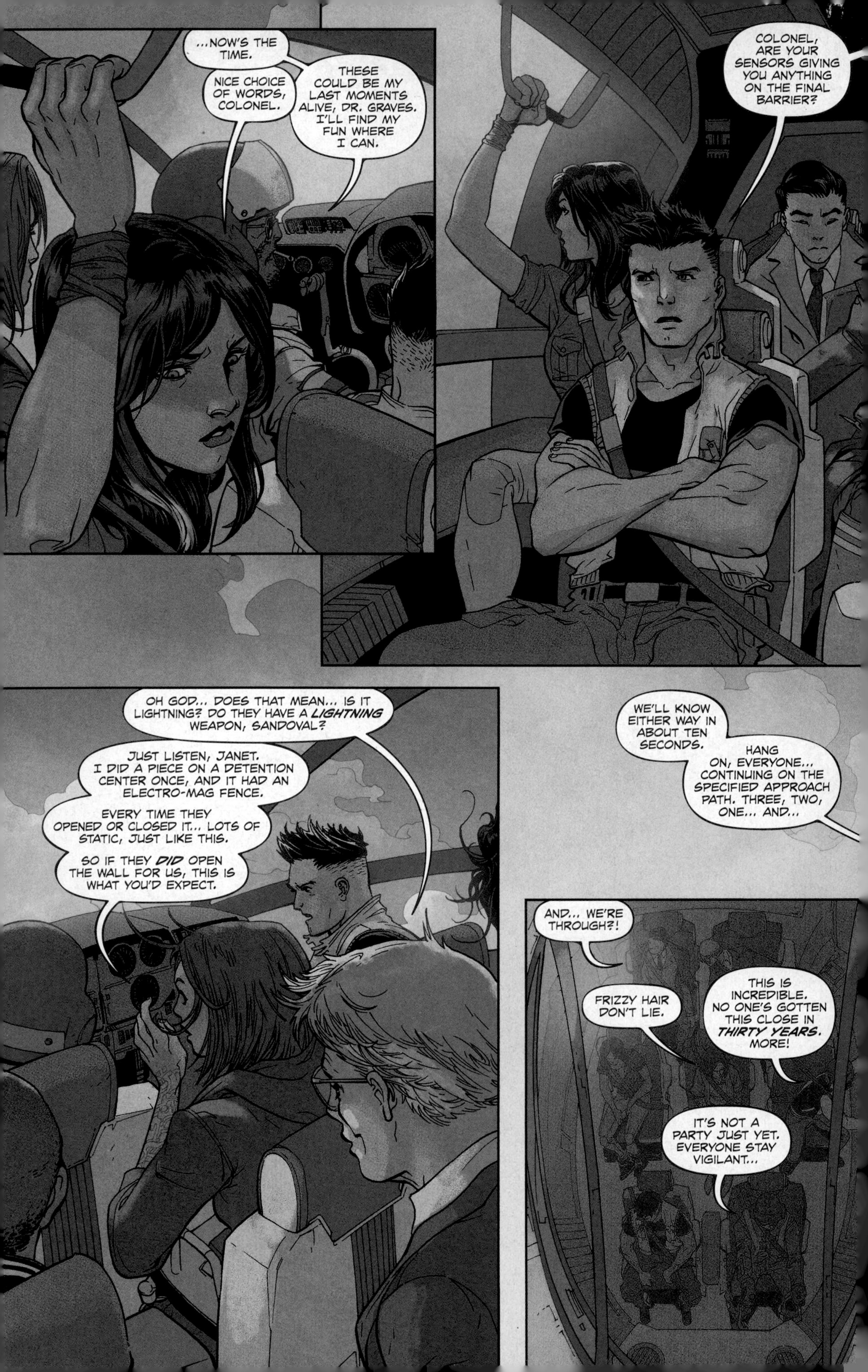
...NOW'S THE TIME.
NICE CHOICE OF WORDS, COLONEL.
THESE COULD BE MY LAST MOMENTS ALIVE, DR. GRAVES. I'LL FIND MY FUN WHERE I CAN.
COLONEL, ARE YOUR SENSORS GIVING YOU ANYTHING ON THE FINAL BARRIER?
OH GOD... DOES THAT MEAN... IS IT LIGHTNING? DO THEY HAVE A *LIGHTNING* WEAPON, SANDOVAL?
JUST LISTEN, JANET. I DID A PIECE ON A DETENTION CENTER ONCE, AND IT HAD AN ELECTRO-MAG FENCE.
EVERY TIME THEY OPENED OR CLOSED IT... LOTS OF STATIC, JUST LIKE THIS.
SO IF THEY *DID* OPEN THE WALL FOR US, THIS IS WHAT YOU'D EXPECT.
WE'LL KNOW EITHER WAY IN ABOUT TEN SECONDS.
HANG ON, EVERYONE... CONTINUING ON THE SPECIFIED APPROACH PATH. THREE, TWO, ONE... AND...
AND... WE'RE THROUGH?!
FRIZZY HAIR DON'T LIE.
THIS IS INCREDIBLE. NO ONE'S GOTTEN THIS CLOSE IN *THIRTY YEARS*. MORE!
IT'S NOT A PARTY JUST YET. EVERYONE STAY VIGILANT...

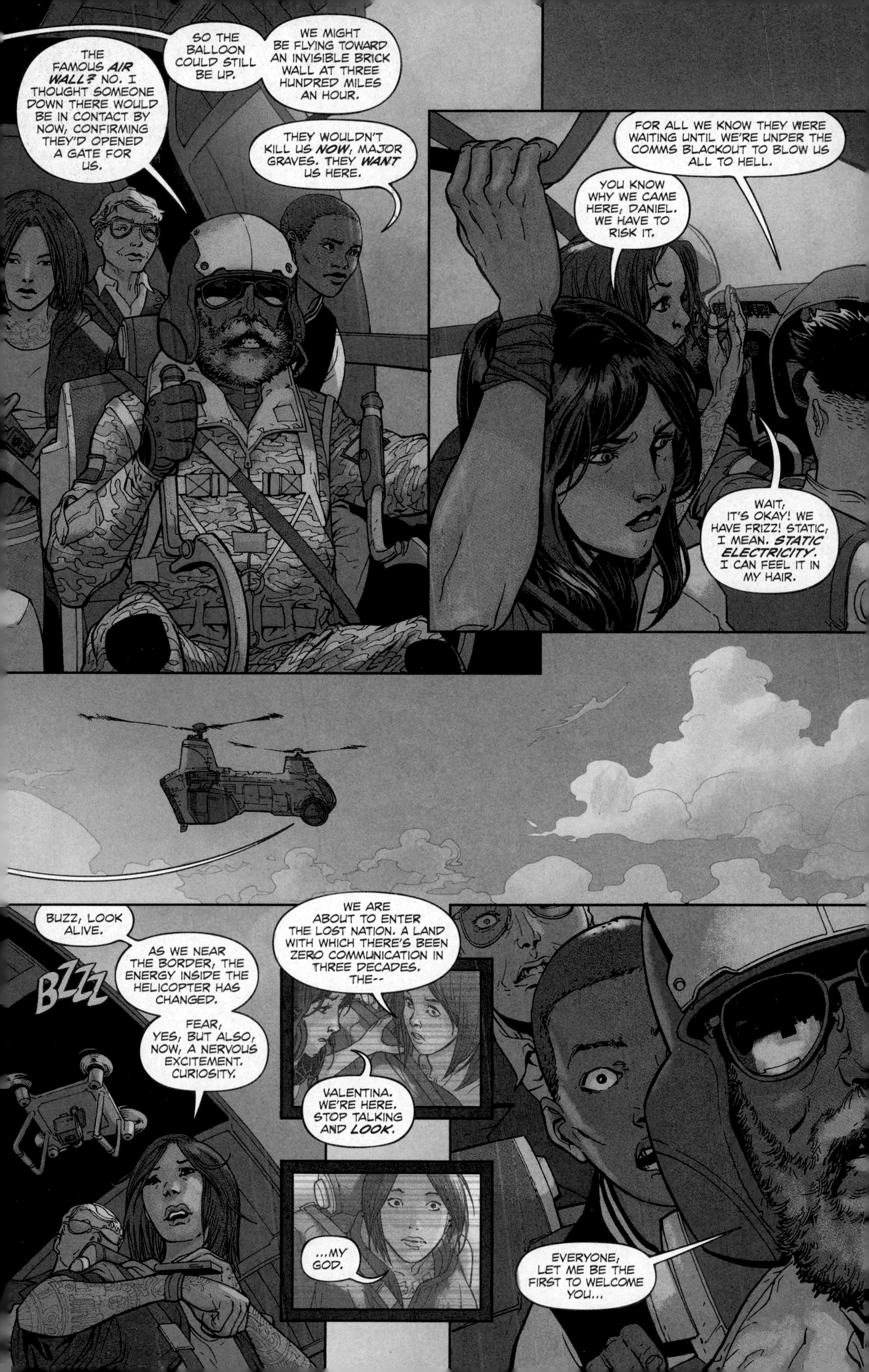
THE FAMOUS AIR WALL? NO. I THOUGHT SOMEONE DOWN THERE WOULD BE IN CONTACT BY NOW, CONFIRMING THEY'D OPENED A GATE FOR US.
SO THE BALLOON COULD STILL BE UP.
WE MIGHT BE FLYING TOWARD AN INVISIBLE BRICK WALL AT THREE HUNDRED MILES AN HOUR.
THEY WOULDN'T KILL US NOW, MAJOR GRAVES. THEY WANT US HERE.
FOR ALL WE KNOW THEY WERE WAITING UNTIL WE'RE UNDER THE COMMS BLACKOUT TO BLOW US ALL TO HELL.
YOU KNOW WHY WE CAME HERE, DANIEL. WE HAVE TO RISK IT.
WAIT, IT'S OKAY! WE HAVE FRIZZ! STATIC, I MEAN. STATIC ELECTRICITY. I CAN FEEL IT IN MY HAIR.
BUZZ, LOOK ALIVE.
BZZZ
AS WE NEAR THE BORDER, THE ENERGY INSIDE THE HELICOPTER HAS CHANGED.
FEAR, YES, BUT ALSO, NOW, A NERVOUS EXCITEMENT. CURIOSITY.
WE ARE ABOUT TO ENTER THE LOST NATION. A LAND WITH WHICH THERE'S BEEN ZERO COMMUNICATION IN THREE DECADES. THE--
VALENTINA. WE'RE HERE. STOP TALKING AND LOOK.
...MY GOD.
EVERYONE, LET ME BE THE FIRST TO WELCOME YOU...

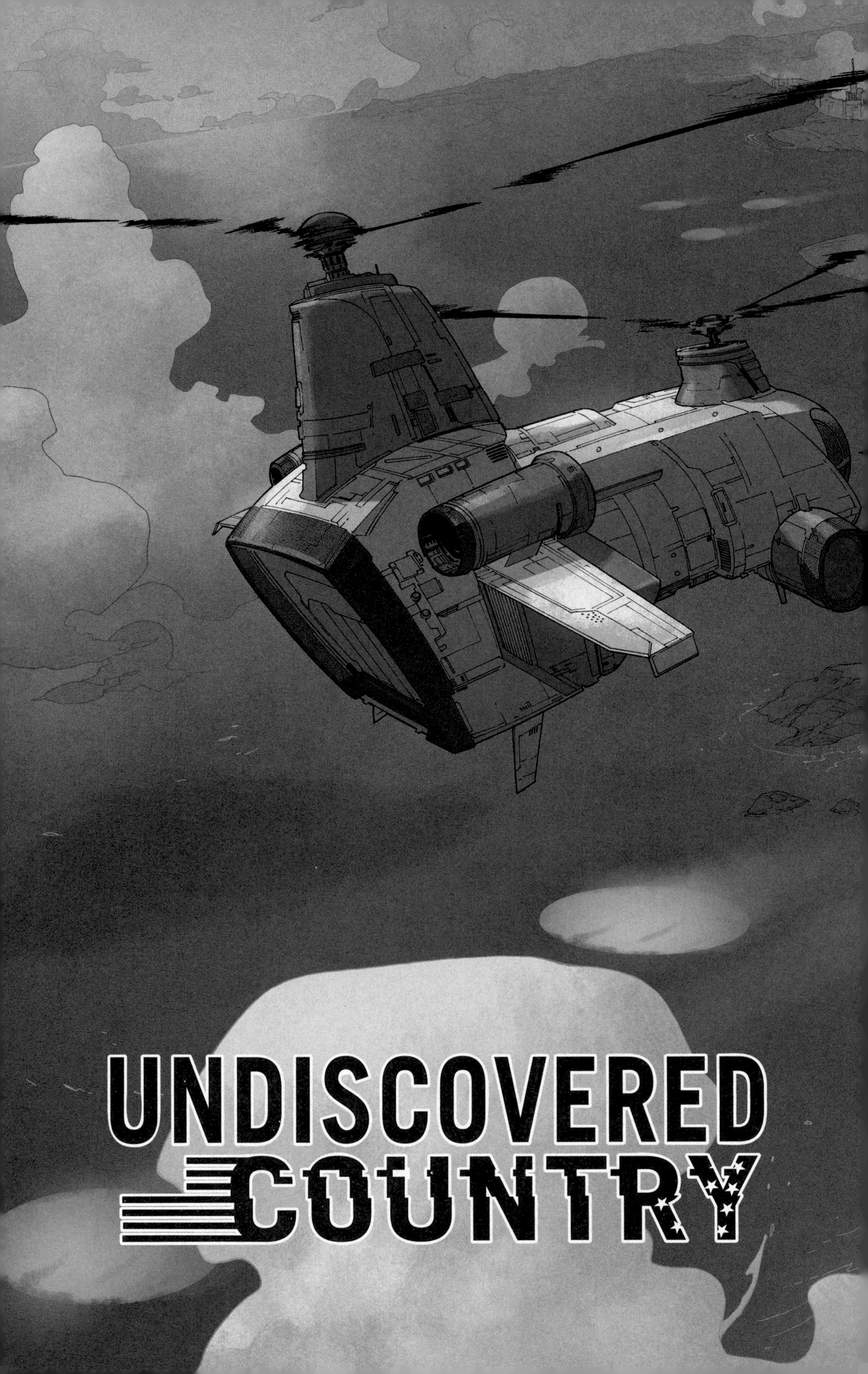
UNDISCOVERED
COUNTRY

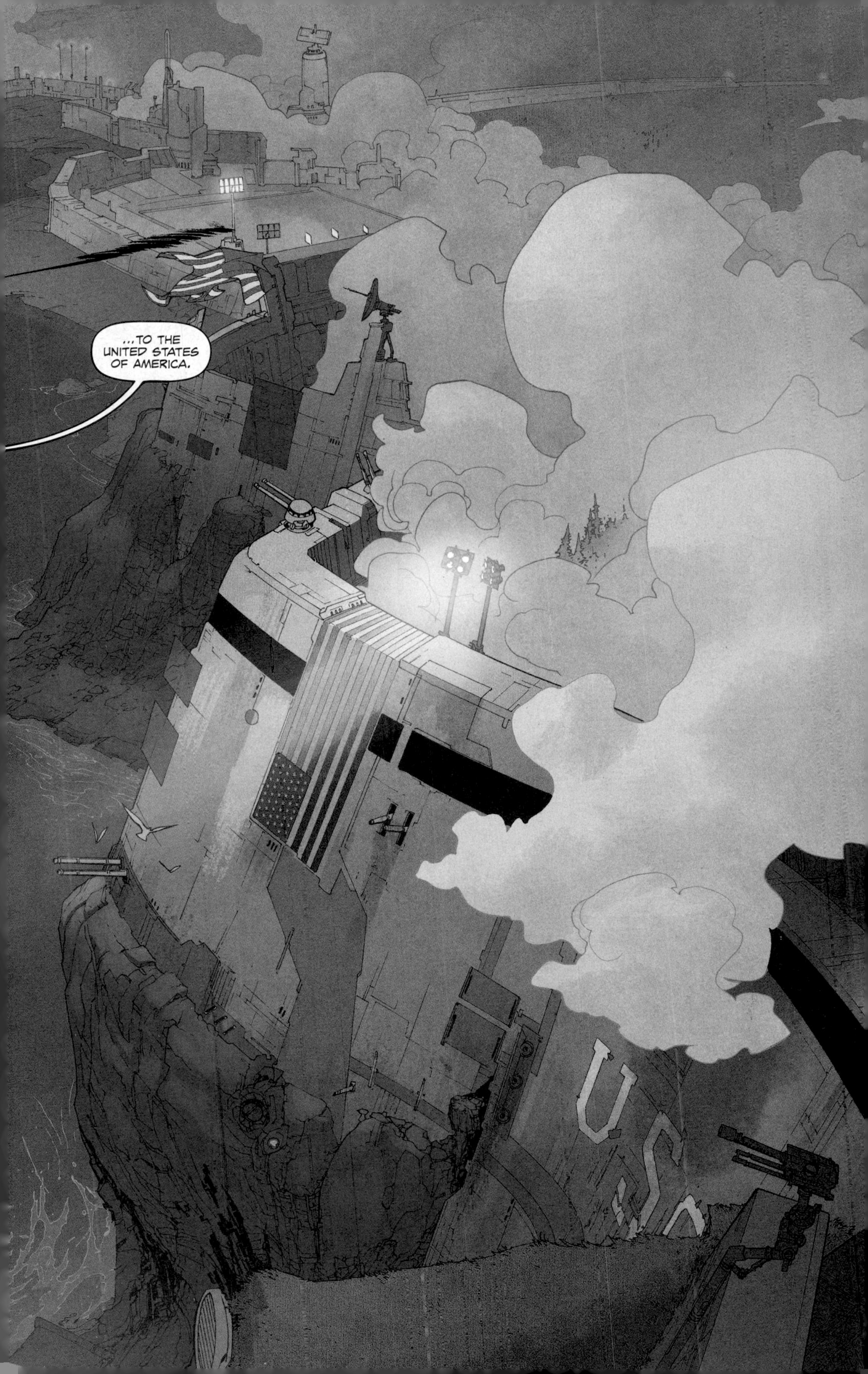
...TO THE UNITED STATES OF AMERICA.

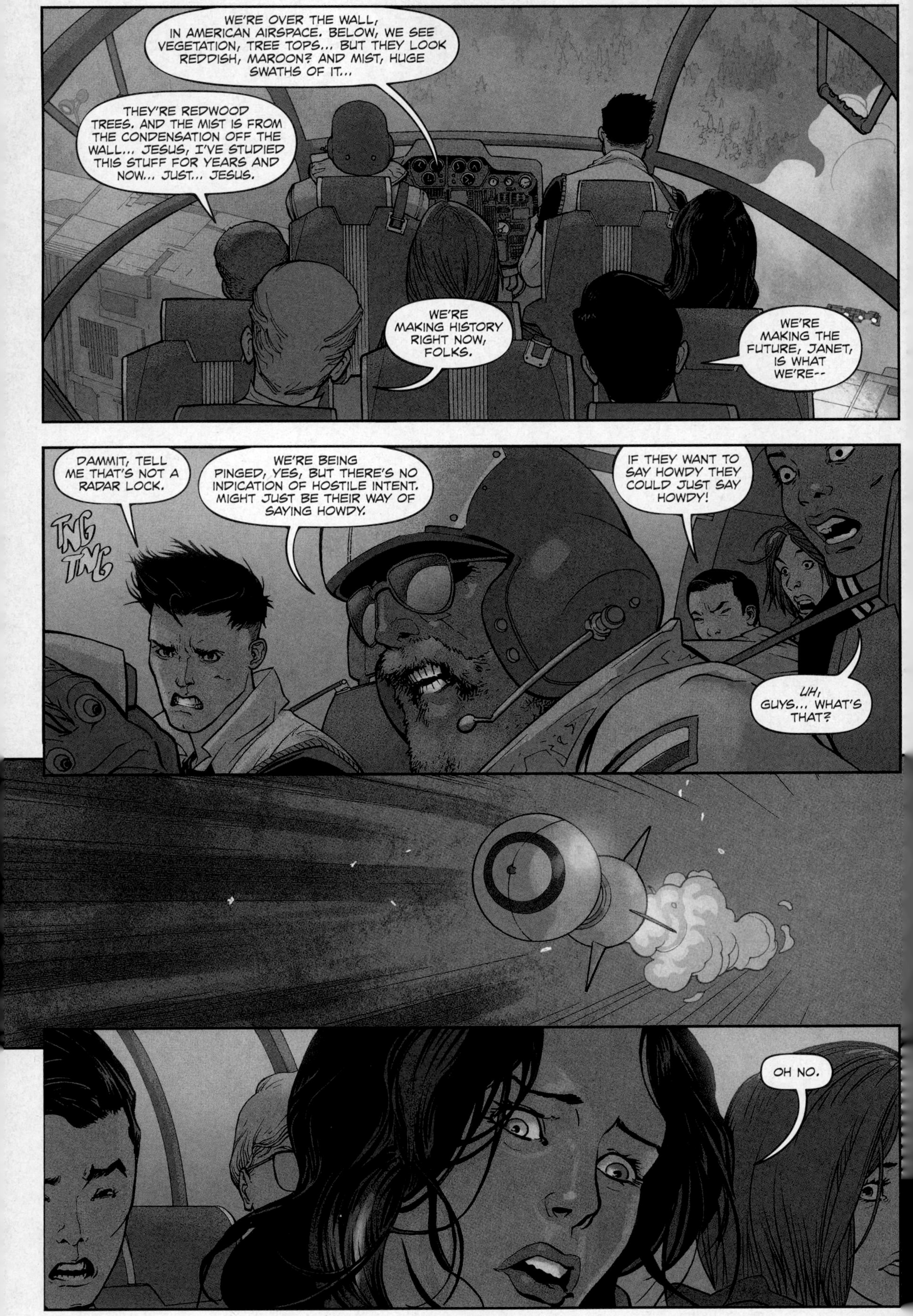
WE'RE OVER THE WALL, IN AMERICAN AIRSPACE. BELOW, WE SEE VEGETATION, TREE TOPS... BUT THEY LOOK REDDISH, MAROON? AND MIST, HUGE SWATHS OF IT...
THEY'RE REDWOOD TREES. AND THE MIST IS FROM THE CONDENSATION OFF THE WALL... JESUS, I'VE STUDIED THIS STUFF FOR YEARS AND NOW... JUST... JESUS.
WE'RE MAKING HISTORY RIGHT NOW, FOLKS.
WE'RE MAKING THE FUTURE, JANET, IS WHAT WE'RE--
DAMMIT, TELL ME THAT'S NOT A RADAR LOCK.
TNG TNG
WE'RE BEING PINGED, YES, BUT THERE'S NO INDICATION OF HOSTILE INTENT. MIGHT JUST BE THEIR WAY OF SAYING HOWDY.
IF THEY WANT TO SAY HOWDY THEY COULD JUST SAY HOWDY!
UH, GUYS... WHAT'S THAT?
OH NO.

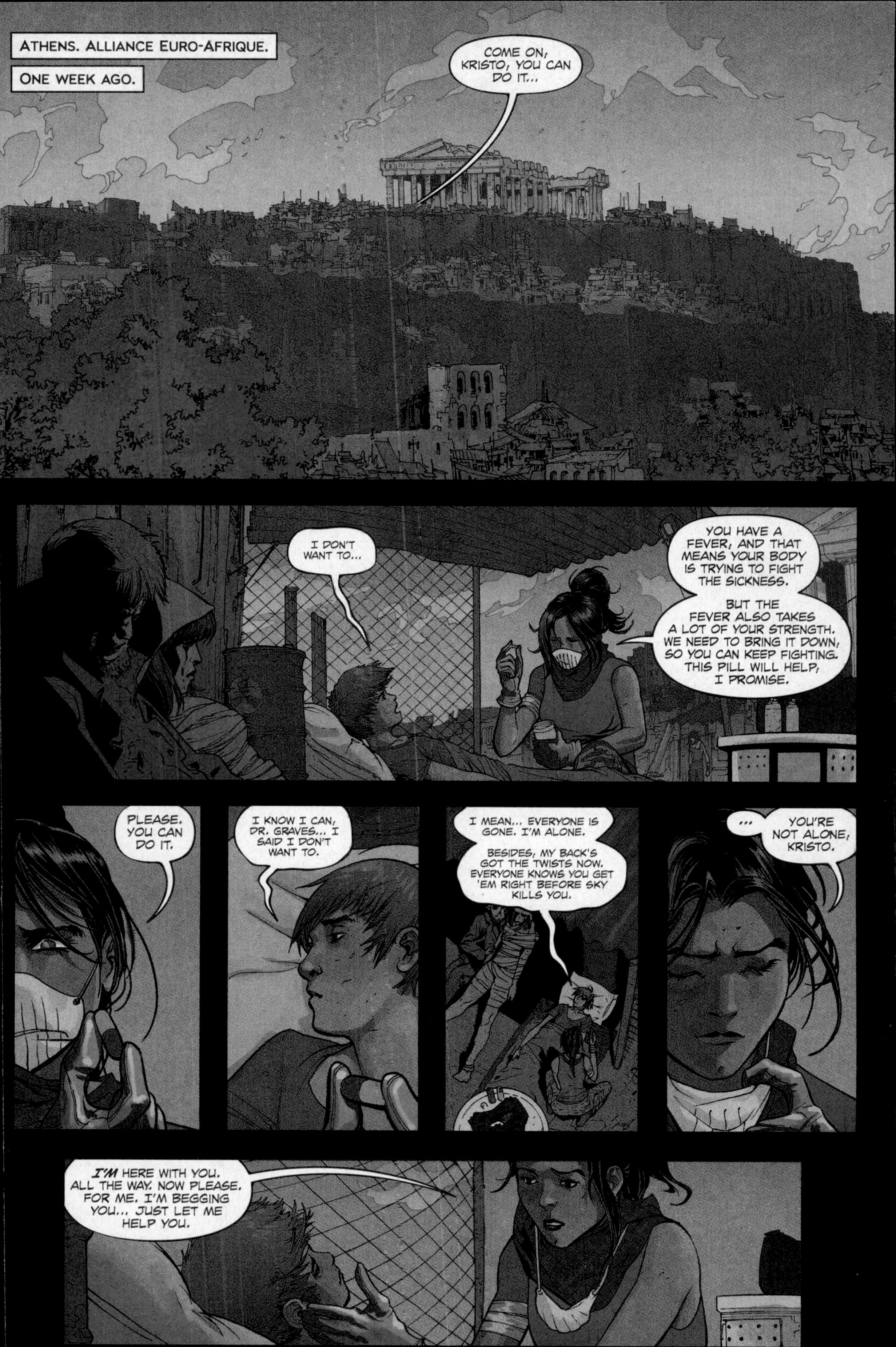

ATHENS. ALLIANCE EURO-AFRIQUE.
ONE WEEK AGO.
COME ON, KRISTO, YOU CAN DO IT...
I DON'T WANT TO...
YOU HAVE A FEVER, AND THAT MEANS YOUR BODY IS TRYING TO FIGHT THE SICKNESS.
BUT THE FEVER ALSO TAKES A LOT OF YOUR STRENGTH. WE NEED TO BRING IT DOWN, SO YOU CAN KEEP FIGHTING. THIS PILL WILL HELP, I PROMISE.
PLEASE. YOU CAN DO IT.
I KNOW I CAN, DR. GRAVES... I SAID I DON'T WANT TO.
I MEAN... EVERYONE IS GONE. I'M ALONE.
BESIDES, MY BACK'S GOT THE TWISTS NOW. EVERYONE KNOWS YOU GET 'EM RIGHT BEFORE SKY KILLS YOU.
...
YOU'RE NOT ALONE, KRISTO.
I'M HERE WITH YOU. ALL THE WAY. NOW PLEASE. FOR ME. I'M BEGGING YOU... JUST LET ME HELP YOU.

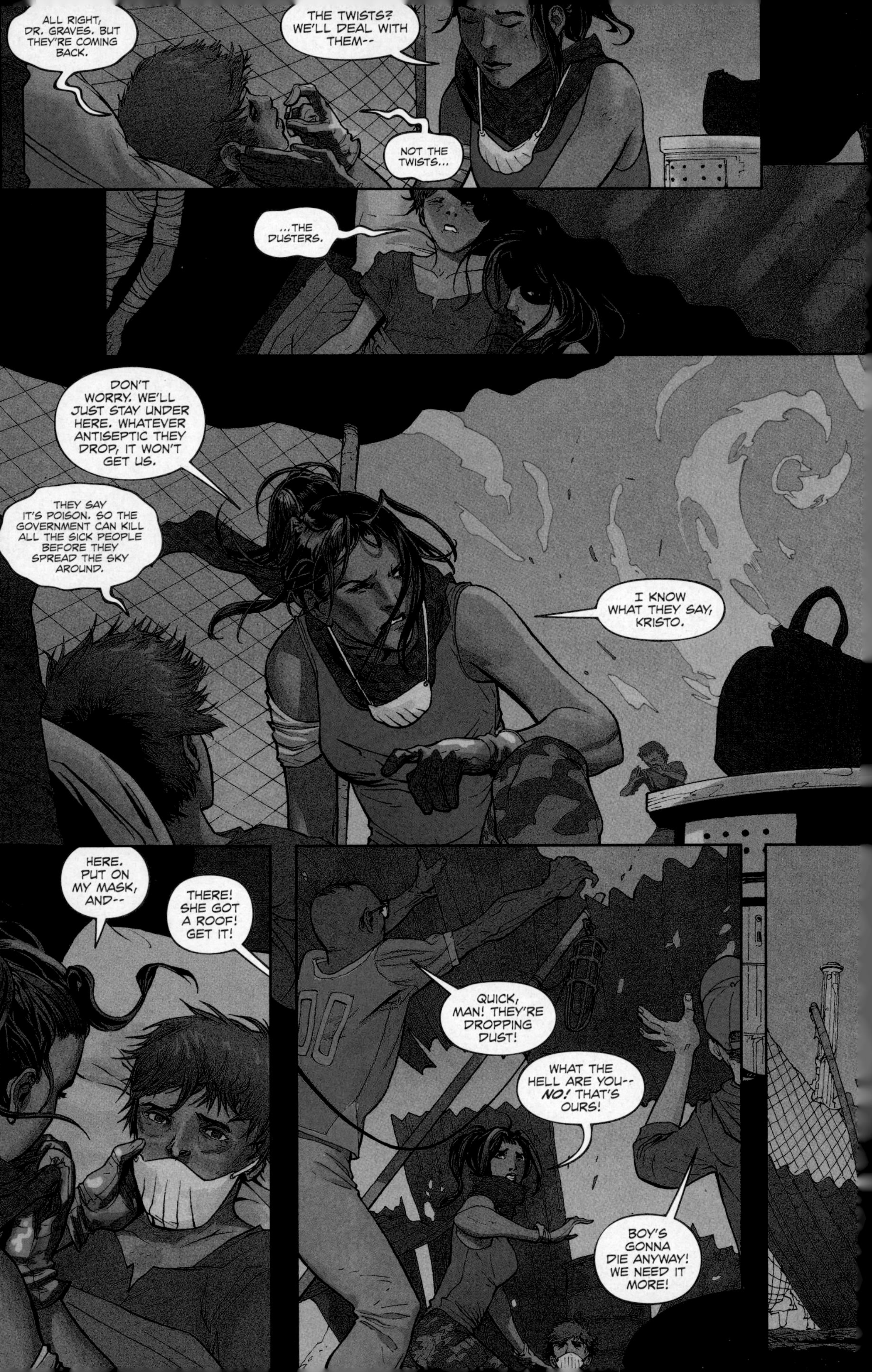
ALL RIGHT, DR. GRAVES. BUT THEY'RE COMING BACK.
THE TWISTS? WE'LL DEAL WITH THEM--
NOT THE TWISTS...
...THE DUSTERS.
DON'T WORRY. WE'LL JUST STAY UNDER HERE. WHATEVER ANTISEPTIC THEY DROP, IT WON'T GET US.
THEY SAY IT'S POISON. SO THE GOVERNMENT CAN KILL ALL THE SICK PEOPLE BEFORE THEY SPREAD THE SKY AROUND.
I KNOW WHAT THEY SAY, KRISTO.
HERE. PUT ON MY MASK, AND--
THERE! SHE GOT A ROOF! GET IT!
QUICK, MAN! THEY'RE DROPPING DUST!
WHAT THE HELL ARE YOU-- NO! THAT'S OURS!
BOY'S GONNA DIE ANYWAY! WE NEED IT MORE!

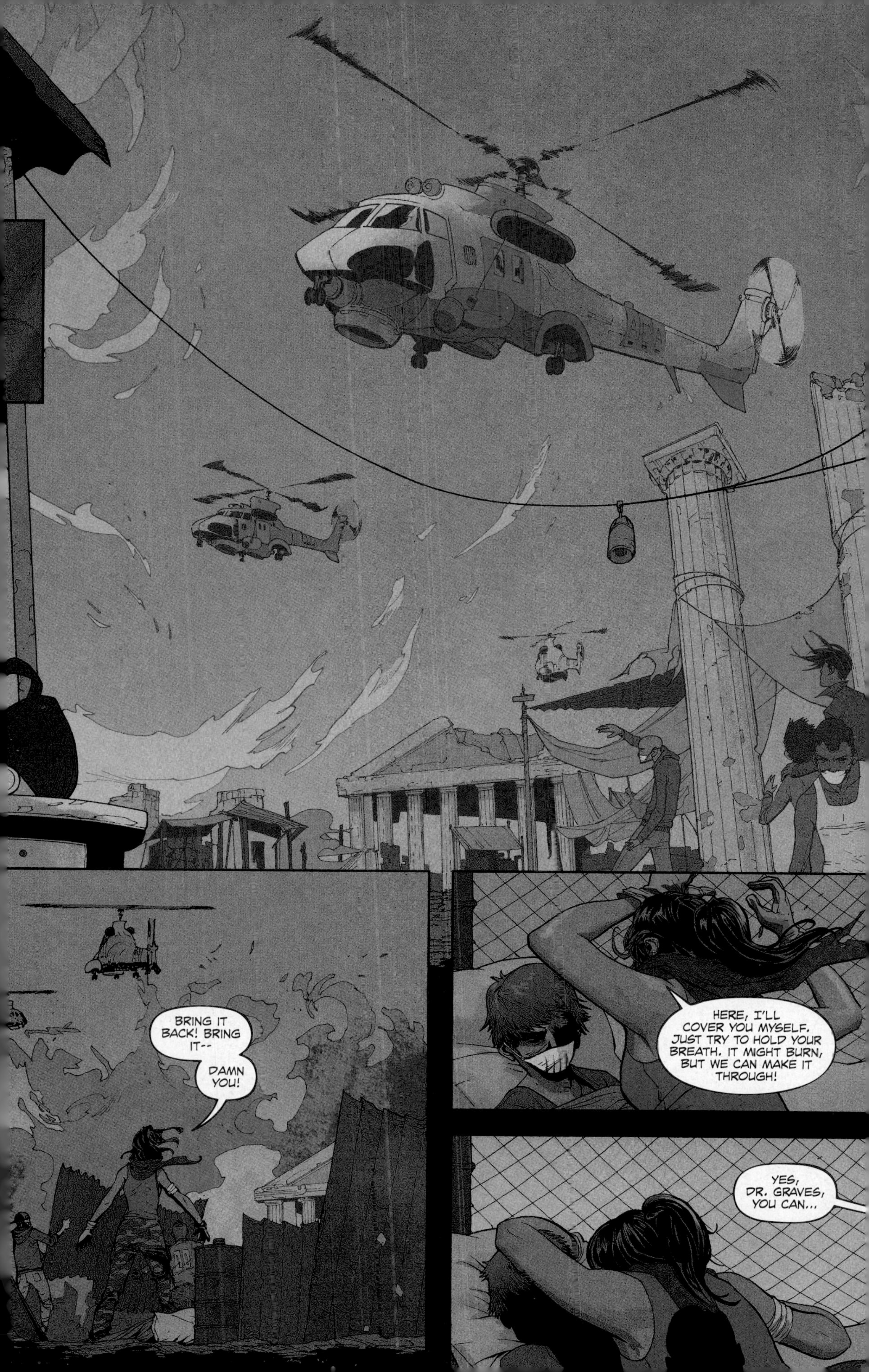
BRING IT BACK! BRING IT--
DAMN YOU!
HERE, I'LL COVER YOU MYSELF. JUST TRY TO HOLD YOUR BREATH. IT MIGHT BURN, BUT WE CAN MAKE IT THROUGH!
YES, DR. GRAVES, YOU CAN...

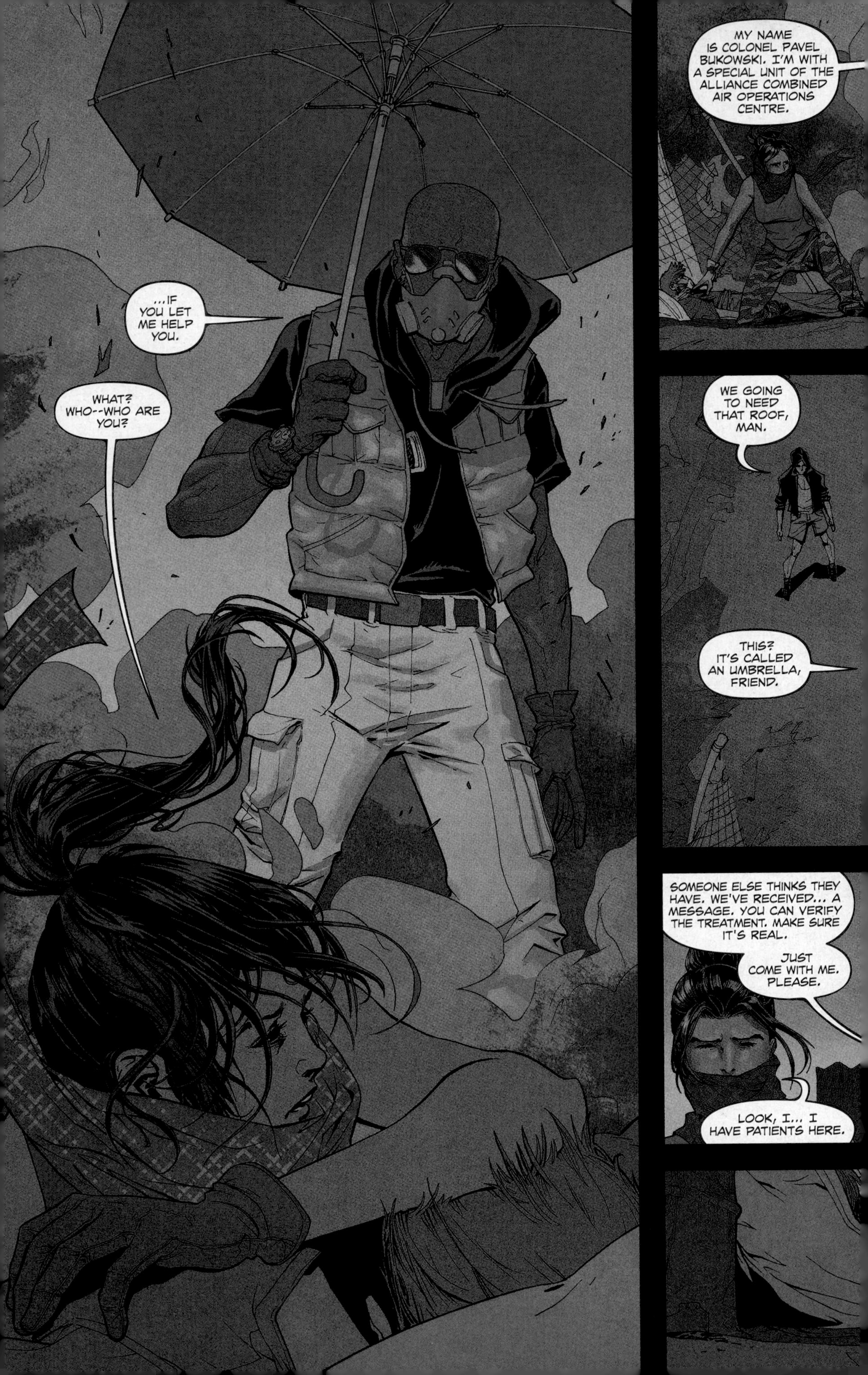
...IF YOU LET ME HELP YOU.
WHAT? WHO--WHO ARE YOU?
MY NAME IS COLONEL PAVEL BUKOWSKI. I'M WITH A SPECIAL UNIT OF THE ALLIANCE COMBINED AIR OPERATIONS CENTRE.
WE GOING TO NEED THAT ROOF, MAN.
THIS? IT'S CALLED AN UMBRELLA, FRIEND.
SOMEONE ELSE THINKS THEY HAVE. WE'VE RECEIVED... A MESSAGE. YOU CAN VERIFY THE TREATMENT. MAKE SURE IT'S REAL.
JUST COME WITH ME. PLEASE.
LOOK, I... I HAVE PATIENTS HERE.

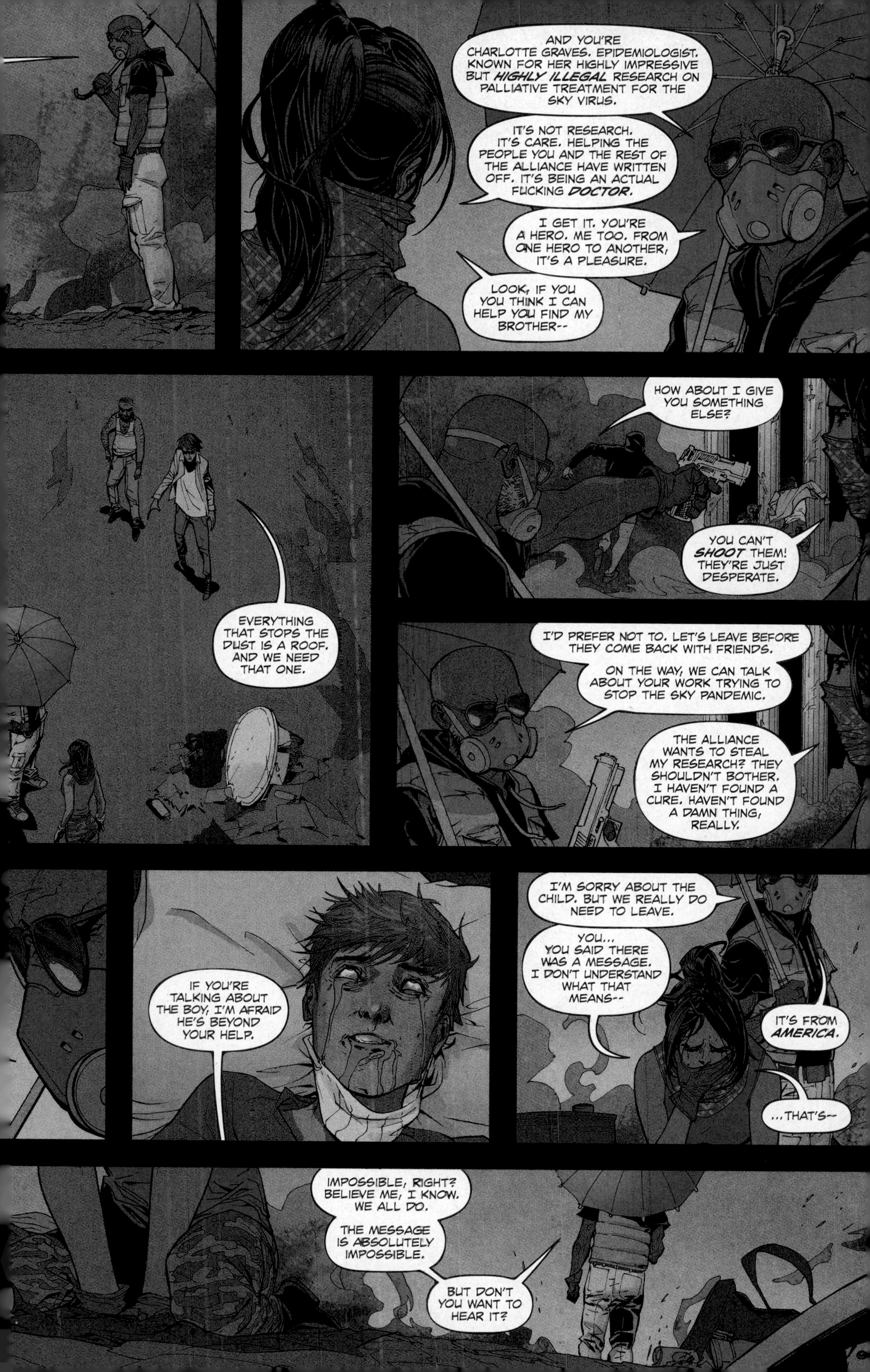

AND YOU'RE CHARLOTTE GRAVES. EPIDEMIOLOGIST. KNOWN FOR HER HIGHLY IMPRESSIVE BUT HIGHLY ILLEGAL RESEARCH ON PALLIATIVE TREATMENT FOR THE SKY VIRUS.
IT'S NOT RESEARCH. IT'S CARE. HELPING THE PEOPLE YOU AND THE REST OF THE ALLIANCE HAVE WRITTEN OFF. IT'S BEING AN ACTUAL FUCKING DOCTOR.
I GET IT. YOU'RE A HERO. ME TOO. FROM ONE HERO TO ANOTHER, IT'S A PLEASURE.
LOOK, IF YOU YOU THINK I CAN HELP YOU FIND MY BROTHER--
EVERYTHING THAT STOPS THE DUST IS A ROOF. AND WE NEED THAT ONE.
HOW ABOUT I GIVE YOU SOMETHING ELSE?
YOU CAN'T SHOOT THEM! THEY'RE JUST DESPERATE.
I'D PREFER NOT TO. LET'S LEAVE BEFORE THEY COME BACK WITH FRIENDS.
ON THE WAY, WE CAN TALK ABOUT YOUR WORK TRYING TO STOP THE SKY PANDEMIC.
THE ALLIANCE WANTS TO STEAL MY RESEARCH? THEY SHOULDN'T BOTHER. I HAVEN'T FOUND A CURE. HAVEN'T FOUND A DAMN THING, REALLY.
IF YOU'RE TALKING ABOUT THE BOY, I'M AFRAID HE'S BEYOND YOUR HELP.
I'M SORRY ABOUT THE CHILD. BUT WE REALLY DO NEED TO LEAVE.
YOU... YOU SAID THERE WAS A MESSAGE. I DON'T UNDERSTAND WHAT THAT MEANS--
IT'S FROM AMERICA.
...THAT'S--
IMPOSSIBLE, RIGHT? BELIEVE ME, I KNOW. WE ALL DO.
THE MESSAGE IS ABSOLUTELY IMPOSSIBLE.
BUT DON'T YOU WANT TO HEAR IT?

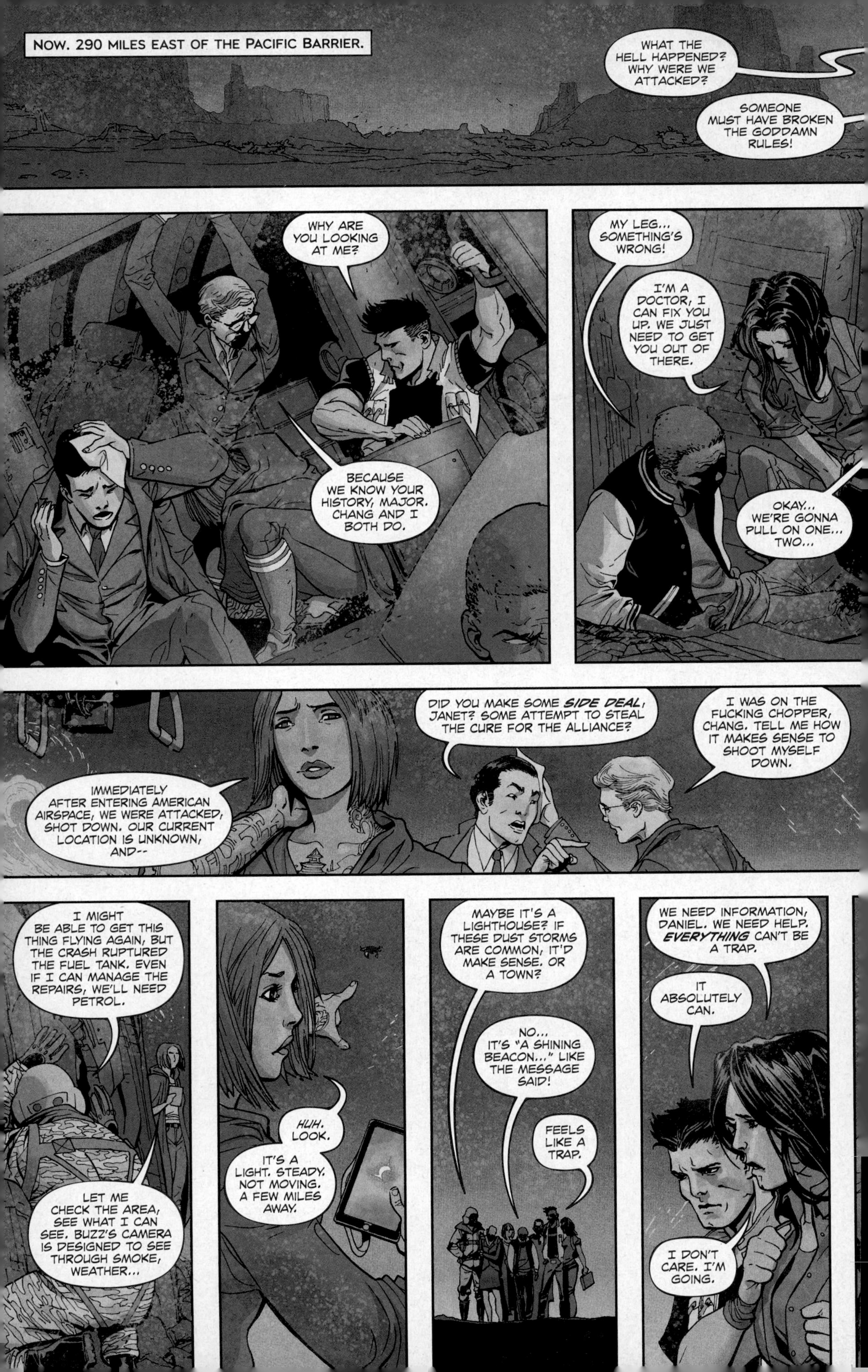

NOW. 290 MILES EAST OF THE PACIFIC BARRIER.
WHAT THE HELL HAPPENED? WHY WERE WE ATTACKED?
SOMEONE MUST HAVE BROKEN THE GODDAMN RULES!
WHY ARE YOU LOOKING AT ME?
BECAUSE WE KNOW YOUR HISTORY, MAJOR. CHANG AND I BOTH DO.
MY LEG... SOMETHING'S WRONG!
I'M A DOCTOR, I CAN FIX YOU UP. WE JUST NEED TO GET YOU OUT OF THERE.
OKAY... WE'RE GONNA PULL ON ONE... TWO...
IMMEDIATELY AFTER ENTERING AMERICAN AIRSPACE, WE WERE ATTACKED, SHOT DOWN. OUR CURRENT LOCATION IS UNKNOWN, AND--
DID YOU MAKE SOME *SIDE DEAL*, JANET? SOME ATTEMPT TO STEAL THE CURE FOR THE ALLIANCE?
I WAS ON THE FUCKING CHOPPER, CHANG. TELL ME HOW IT MAKES SENSE TO SHOOT MYSELF DOWN.
I MIGHT BE ABLE TO GET THIS THING FLYING AGAIN, BUT THE CRASH RUPTURED THE FUEL TANK. EVEN IF I CAN MANAGE THE REPAIRS, WE'LL NEED PETROL.
LET ME CHECK THE AREA, SEE WHAT I CAN SEE. BUZZ'S CAMERA IS DESIGNED TO SEE THROUGH SMOKE, WEATHER...
HUH. LOOK.
IT'S A LIGHT. STEADY. NOT MOVING. A FEW MILES AWAY.
MAYBE IT'S A LIGHTHOUSE? IF THESE DUST STORMS ARE COMMON, IT'D MAKE SENSE. OR A TOWN?
NO... IT'S "A SHINING BEACON..." LIKE THE MESSAGE SAID!
FEELS LIKE A TRAP.
WE NEED INFORMATION, DANIEL. WE NEED HELP. *EVERYTHING* CAN'T BE A TRAP.
IT ABSOLUTELY CAN.
I DON'T CARE. I'M GOING.

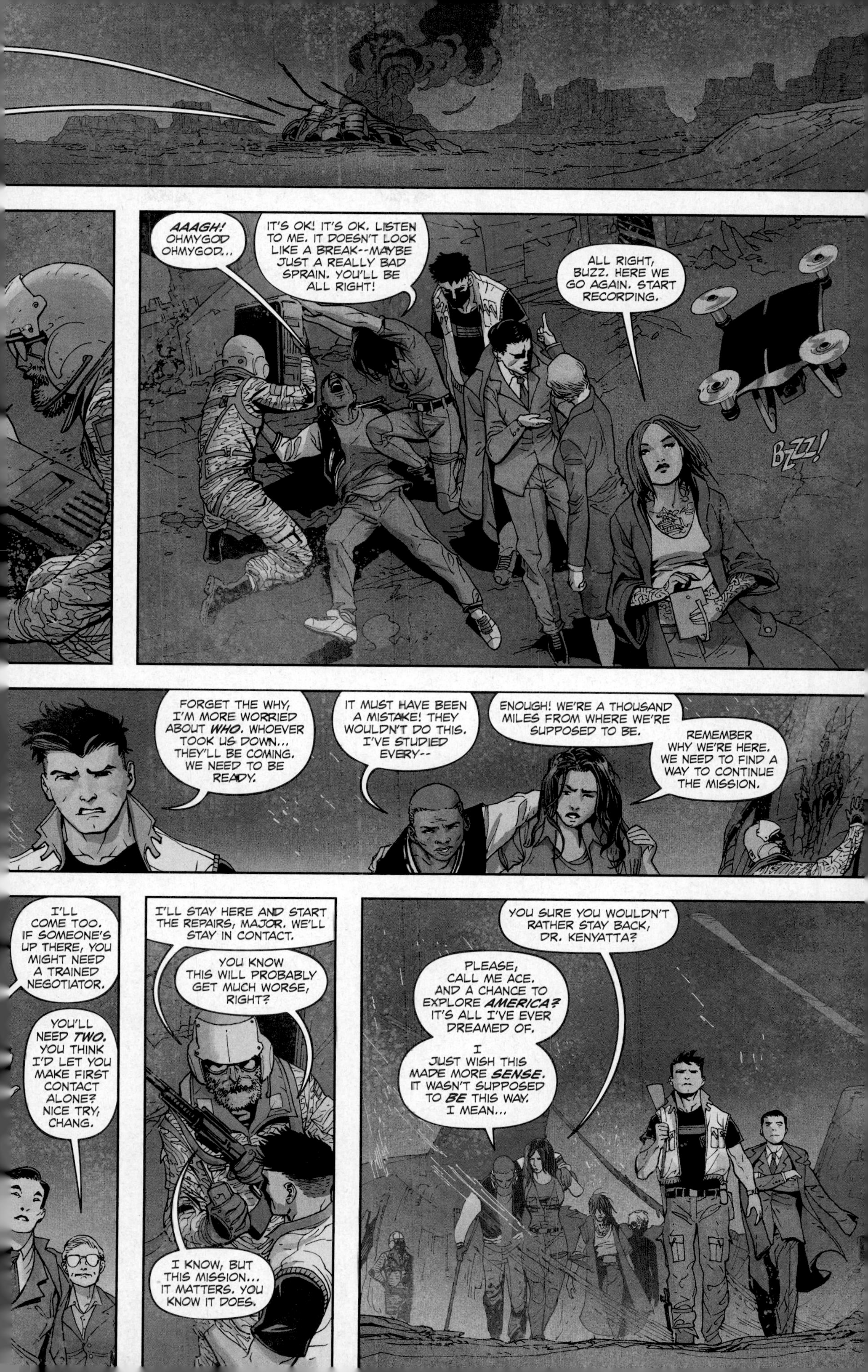
AAAGH! OHMYGOD OHMYGOD...
IT'S OK! IT'S OK. LISTEN TO ME. IT DOESN'T LOOK LIKE A BREAK--MAYBE JUST A REALLY BAD SPRAIN. YOU'LL BE ALL RIGHT!
ALL RIGHT, BUZZ. HERE WE GO AGAIN. START RECORDING.
BZZZ!
FORGET THE WHY, I'M MORE WORRIED ABOUT WHO. WHOEVER TOOK US DOWN... THEY'LL BE COMING. WE NEED TO BE READY.
IT MUST HAVE BEEN A MISTAKE! THEY WOULDN'T DO THIS. I'VE STUDIED EVERY--
ENOUGH! WE'RE A THOUSAND MILES FROM WHERE WE'RE SUPPOSED TO BE.
REMEMBER WHY WE'RE HERE. WE NEED TO FIND A WAY TO CONTINUE THE MISSION.
I'LL COME TOO. IF SOMEONE'S UP THERE, YOU MIGHT NEED A TRAINED NEGOTIATOR.
YOU'LL NEED TWO. YOU THINK I'D LET YOU MAKE FIRST CONTACT ALONE? NICE TRY, CHANG.
I'LL STAY HERE AND START THE REPAIRS, MAJOR. WE'LL STAY IN CONTACT.
YOU KNOW THIS WILL PROBABLY GET MUCH WORSE, RIGHT?
I KNOW, BUT THIS MISSION... IT MATTERS. YOU KNOW IT DOES.
YOU SURE YOU WOULDN'T RATHER STAY BACK, DR. KENYATTA?
PLEASE, CALL ME ACE. AND A CHANCE TO EXPLORE AMERICA? IT'S ALL I'VE EVER DREAMED OF.
I JUST WISH THIS MADE MORE SENSE. IT WASN'T SUPPOSED TO BE THIS WAY. I MEAN...

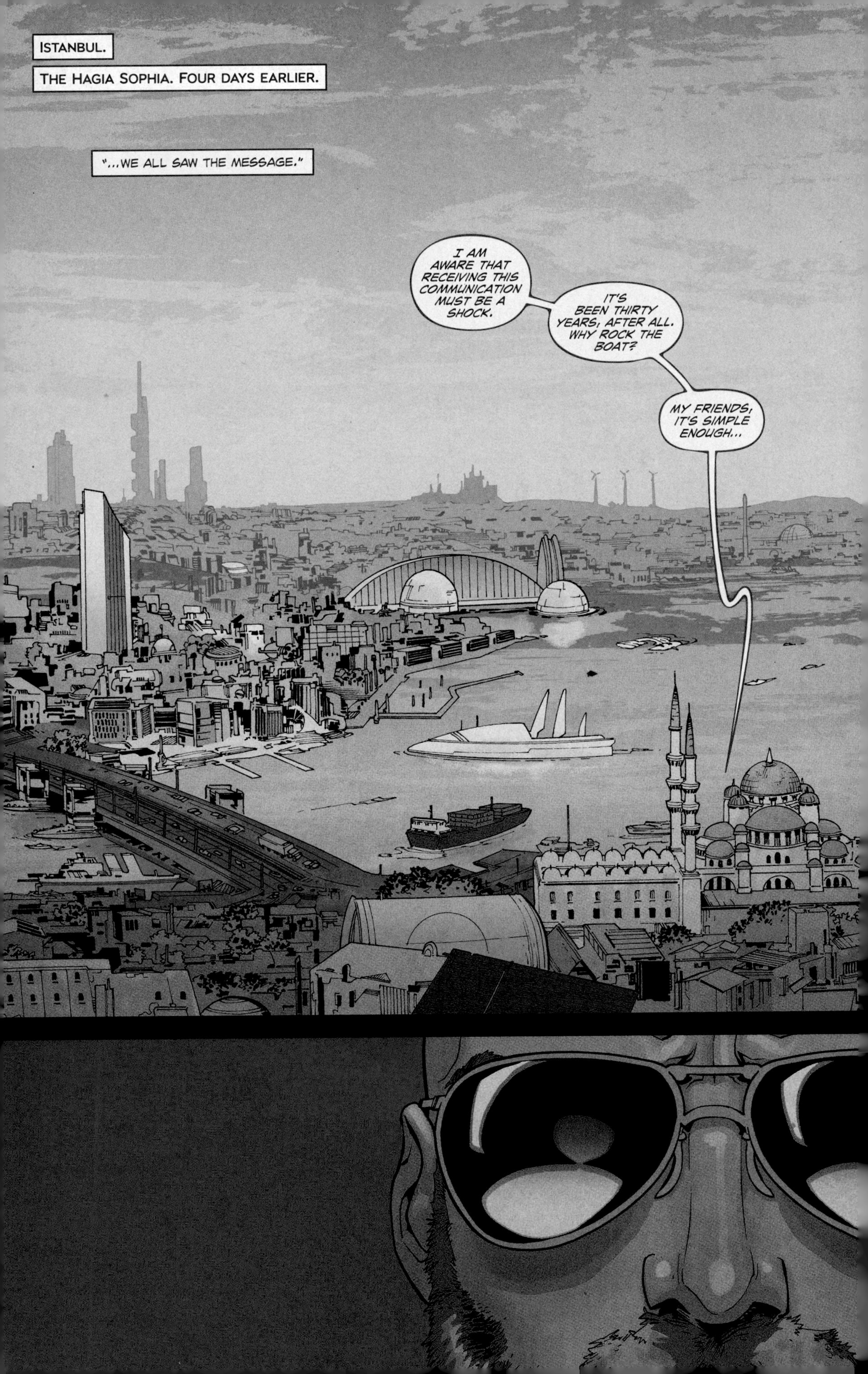
ISTANBUL.
THE HAGIA SOPHIA. FOUR DAYS EARLIER.
"...WE ALL SAW THE MESSAGE."
I AM AWARE THAT RECEIVING THIS COMMUNICATION MUST BE A SHOCK.
IT'S BEEN THIRTY YEARS, AFTER ALL. WHY ROCK THE BOAT?
MY FRIENDS, IT'S SIMPLE ENOUGH...

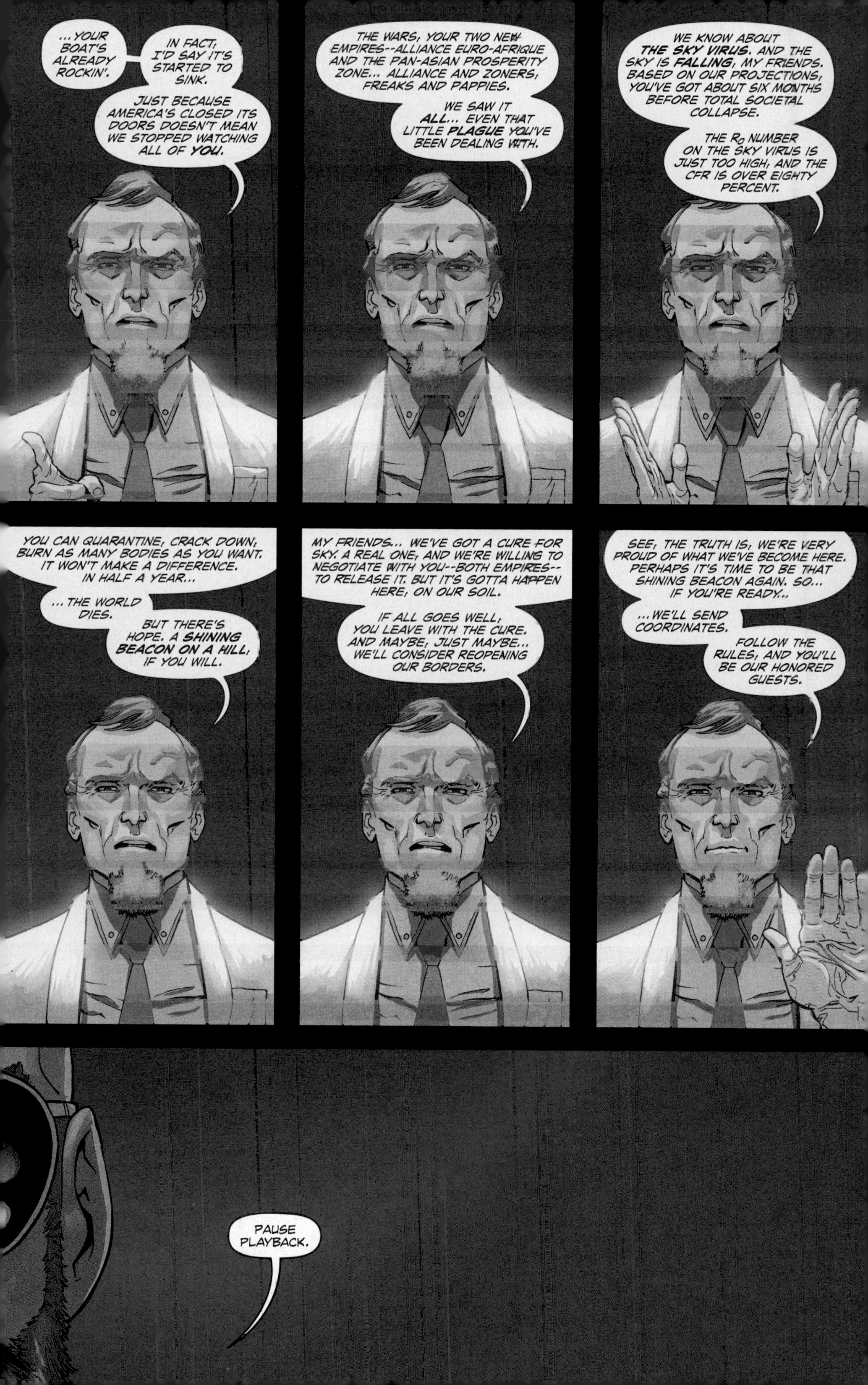
...YOUR BOAT'S ALREADY ROCKIN'.
IN FACT, I'D SAY IT'S STARTED TO SINK.
JUST BECAUSE AMERICA'S CLOSED ITS DOORS DOESN'T MEAN WE STOPPED WATCHING ALL OF **YOU**.
THE WARS, YOUR TWO NEW EMPIRES--ALLIANCE EURO-AFRIQUE AND THE PAN-ASIAN PROSPERITY ZONE... ALLIANCE AND ZONERS, FREAKS AND PAPPIES.
WE SAW IT **ALL**... EVEN THAT LITTLE **PLAGUE** YOU'VE BEEN DEALING WITH.
WE KNOW ABOUT **THE SKY VIRUS**. AND THE SKY IS **FALLING**, MY FRIENDS. BASED ON OUR PROJECTIONS, YOU'VE GOT ABOUT SIX MONTHS BEFORE TOTAL SOCIETAL COLLAPSE.
THE R_0 NUMBER ON THE SKY VIRUS IS JUST TOO HIGH, AND THE CFR IS OVER EIGHTY PERCENT.
YOU CAN QUARANTINE, CRACK DOWN, BURN AS MANY BODIES AS YOU WANT. IT WON'T MAKE A DIFFERENCE. IN HALF A YEAR...
...THE WORLD DIES.
BUT THERE'S HOPE. A **SHINING BEACON ON A HILL**, IF YOU WILL.
MY FRIENDS... WE'VE GOT A CURE FOR SKY. A REAL ONE, AND WE'RE WILLING TO NEGOTIATE WITH YOU--BOTH EMPIRES--TO RELEASE IT. BUT IT'S GOTTA HAPPEN HERE, ON OUR SOIL.
IF ALL GOES WELL, YOU LEAVE WITH THE CURE. AND MAYBE, JUST MAYBE... WE'LL CONSIDER REOPENING OUR BORDERS.
SEE, THE TRUTH IS, WE'RE VERY PROUD OF WHAT WE'VE BECOME HERE. PERHAPS IT'S TIME TO BE THAT SHINING BEACON AGAIN. SO... IF YOU'RE READY...
...WE'LL SEND COORDINATES.
FOLLOW THE RULES, AND YOU'LL BE OUR HONORED GUESTS.
PAUSE PLAYBACK.

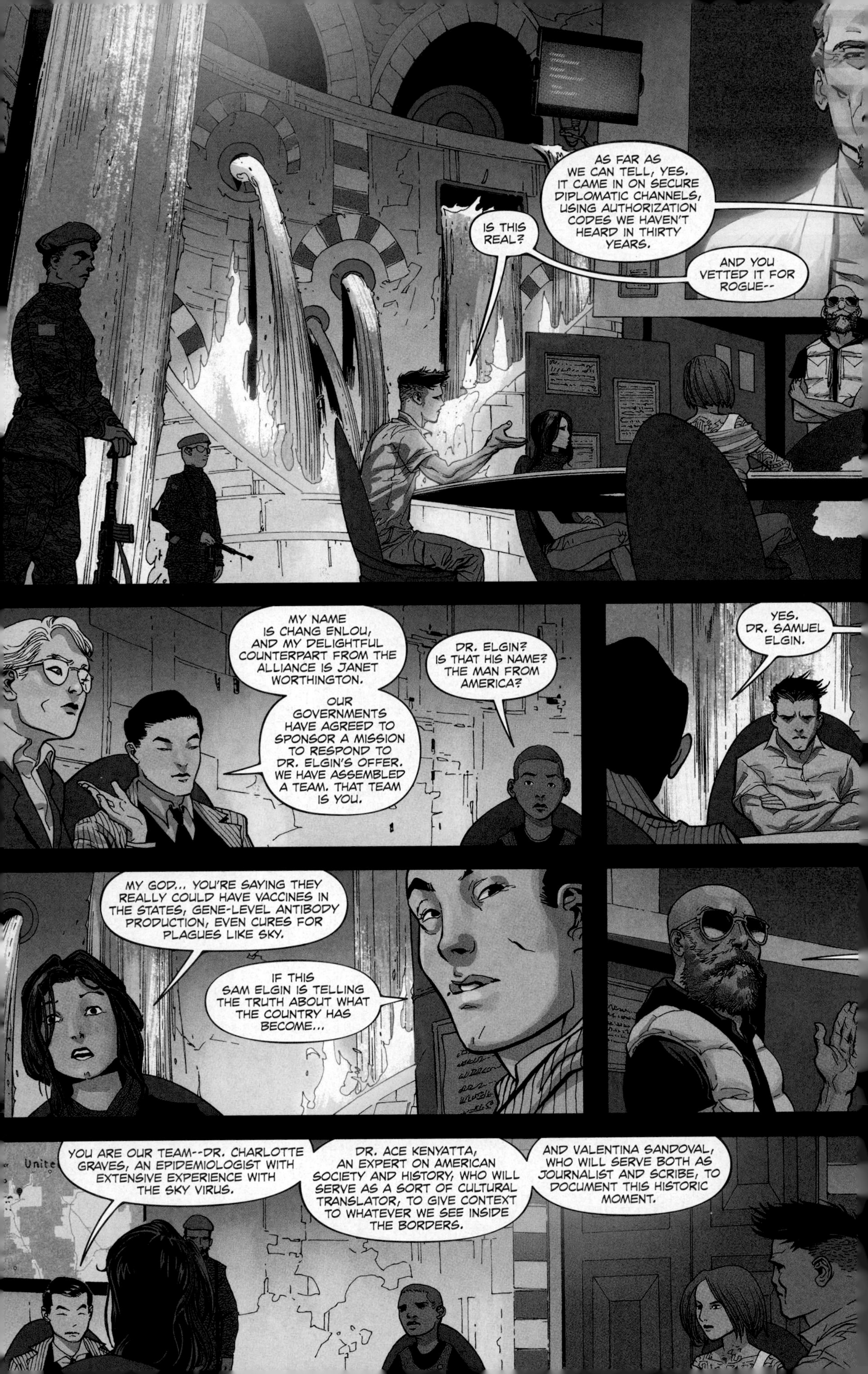
IS THIS REAL?
AS FAR AS WE CAN TELL, YES. IT CAME IN ON SECURE DIPLOMATIC CHANNELS, USING AUTHORIZATION CODES WE HAVEN'T HEARD IN THIRTY YEARS.
AND YOU VETTED IT FOR ROGUE--
MY NAME IS CHANG ENLOU, AND MY DELIGHTFUL COUNTERPART FROM THE ALLIANCE IS JANET WORTHINGTON.
OUR GOVERNMENTS HAVE AGREED TO SPONSOR A MISSION TO RESPOND TO DR. ELGIN'S OFFER. WE HAVE ASSEMBLED A TEAM. THAT TEAM IS YOU.
DR. ELGIN? IS THAT HIS NAME? THE MAN FROM AMERICA?
YES. DR. SAMUEL ELGIN.
MY GOD... YOU'RE SAYING THEY REALLY COULD HAVE VACCINES IN THE STATES, GENE-LEVEL ANTIBODY PRODUCTION, EVEN CURES FOR PLAGUES LIKE SKY.
IF THIS SAM ELGIN IS TELLING THE TRUTH ABOUT WHAT THE COUNTRY HAS BECOME...
YOU ARE OUR TEAM--DR. CHARLOTTE GRAVES, AN EPIDEMIOLOGIST WITH EXTENSIVE EXPERIENCE WITH THE SKY VIRUS.
DR. ACE KENYATTA, AN EXPERT ON AMERICAN SOCIETY AND HISTORY, WHO WILL SERVE AS A SORT OF CULTURAL TRANSLATOR, TO GIVE CONTEXT TO WHATEVER WE SEE INSIDE THE BORDERS.
AND VALENTINA SANDOVAL, WHO WILL SERVE BOTH AS JOURNALIST AND SCRIBE, TO DOCUMENT THIS HISTORIC MOMENT.

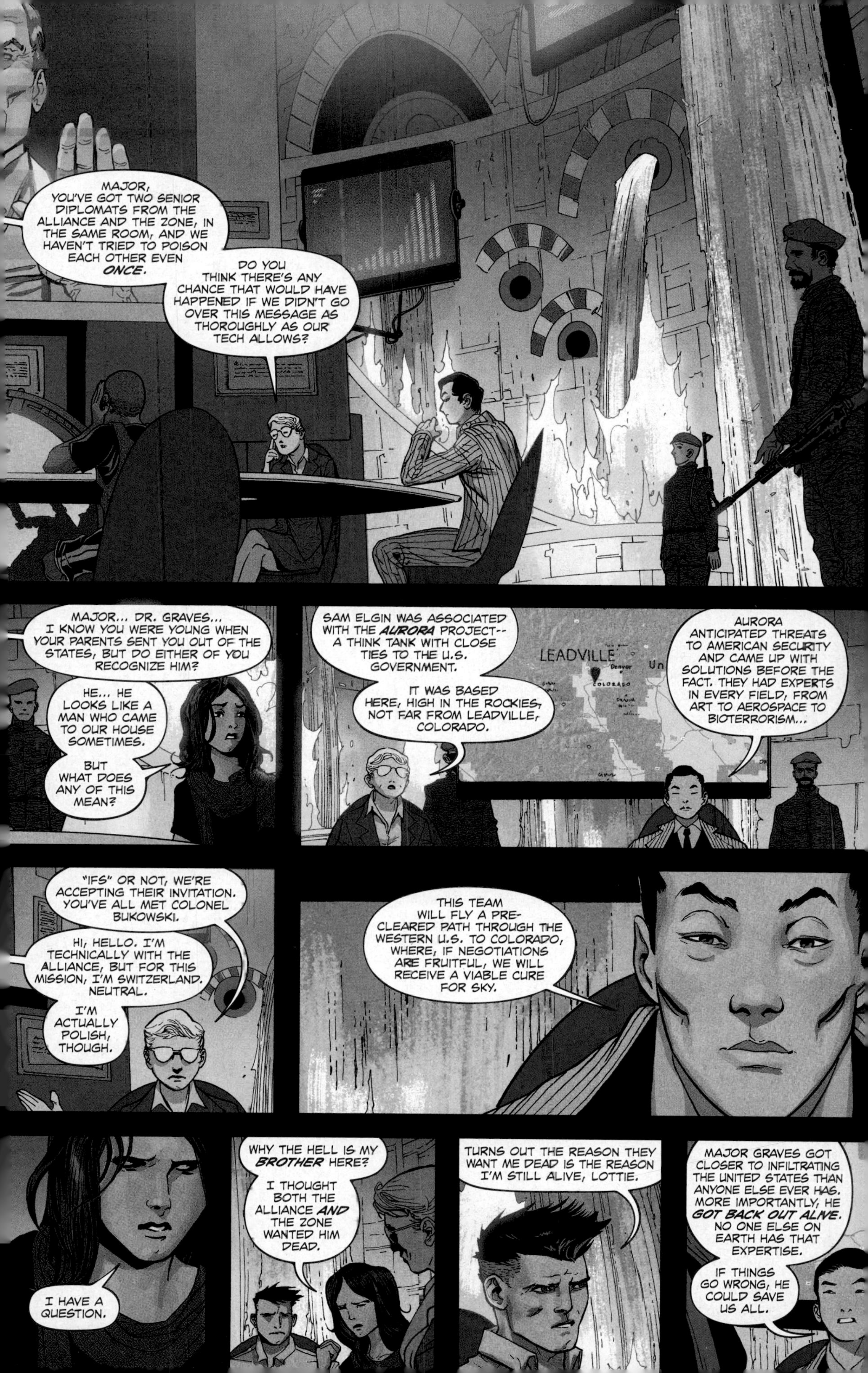
MAJOR, YOU'VE GOT TWO SENIOR DIPLOMATS FROM THE ALLIANCE AND THE ZONE, IN THE SAME ROOM, AND WE HAVEN'T TRIED TO POISON EACH OTHER EVEN ONCE.
DO YOU THINK THERE'S ANY CHANCE THAT WOULD HAVE HAPPENED IF WE DIDN'T GO OVER THIS MESSAGE AS THOROUGHLY AS OUR TECH ALLOWS?
MAJOR... DR. GRAVES... I KNOW YOU WERE YOUNG WHEN YOUR PARENTS SENT YOU OUT OF THE STATES, BUT DO EITHER OF YOU RECOGNIZE HIM?
HE... HE LOOKS LIKE A MAN WHO CAME TO OUR HOUSE SOMETIMES.
BUT WHAT DOES ANY OF THIS MEAN?
SAM ELGIN WAS ASSOCIATED WITH THE AURORA PROJECT-- A THINK TANK WITH CLOSE TIES TO THE U.S. GOVERNMENT.
IT WAS BASED HERE, HIGH IN THE ROCKIES, NOT FAR FROM LEADVILLE, COLORADO.
LEADVILLE
Denver
COLORADO
AURORA ANTICIPATED THREATS TO AMERICAN SECURITY AND CAME UP WITH SOLUTIONS BEFORE THE FACT. THEY HAD EXPERTS IN EVERY FIELD, FROM ART TO AEROSPACE TO BIOTERRORISM...
"IFS" OR NOT, WE'RE ACCEPTING THEIR INVITATION. YOU'VE ALL MET COLONEL BUKOWSKI.
HI, HELLO. I'M TECHNICALLY WITH THE ALLIANCE, BUT FOR THIS MISSION, I'M SWITZERLAND. NEUTRAL.
I'M ACTUALLY POLISH, THOUGH.
THIS TEAM WILL FLY A PRE-CLEARED PATH THROUGH THE WESTERN U.S. TO COLORADO, WHERE, IF NEGOTIATIONS ARE FRUITFUL, WE WILL RECEIVE A VIABLE CURE FOR SKY.
I HAVE A QUESTION.
WHY THE HELL IS MY BROTHER HERE?
I THOUGHT BOTH THE ALLIANCE AND THE ZONE WANTED HIM DEAD.
TURNS OUT THE REASON THEY WANT ME DEAD IS THE REASON I'M STILL ALIVE, LOTTIE.
MAJOR GRAVES GOT CLOSER TO INFILTRATING THE UNITED STATES THAN ANYONE ELSE EVER HAS. MORE IMPORTANTLY, HE GOT BACK OUT ALIVE. NO ONE ELSE ON EARTH HAS THAT EXPERTISE.
IF THINGS GO WRONG, HE COULD SAVE US ALL.

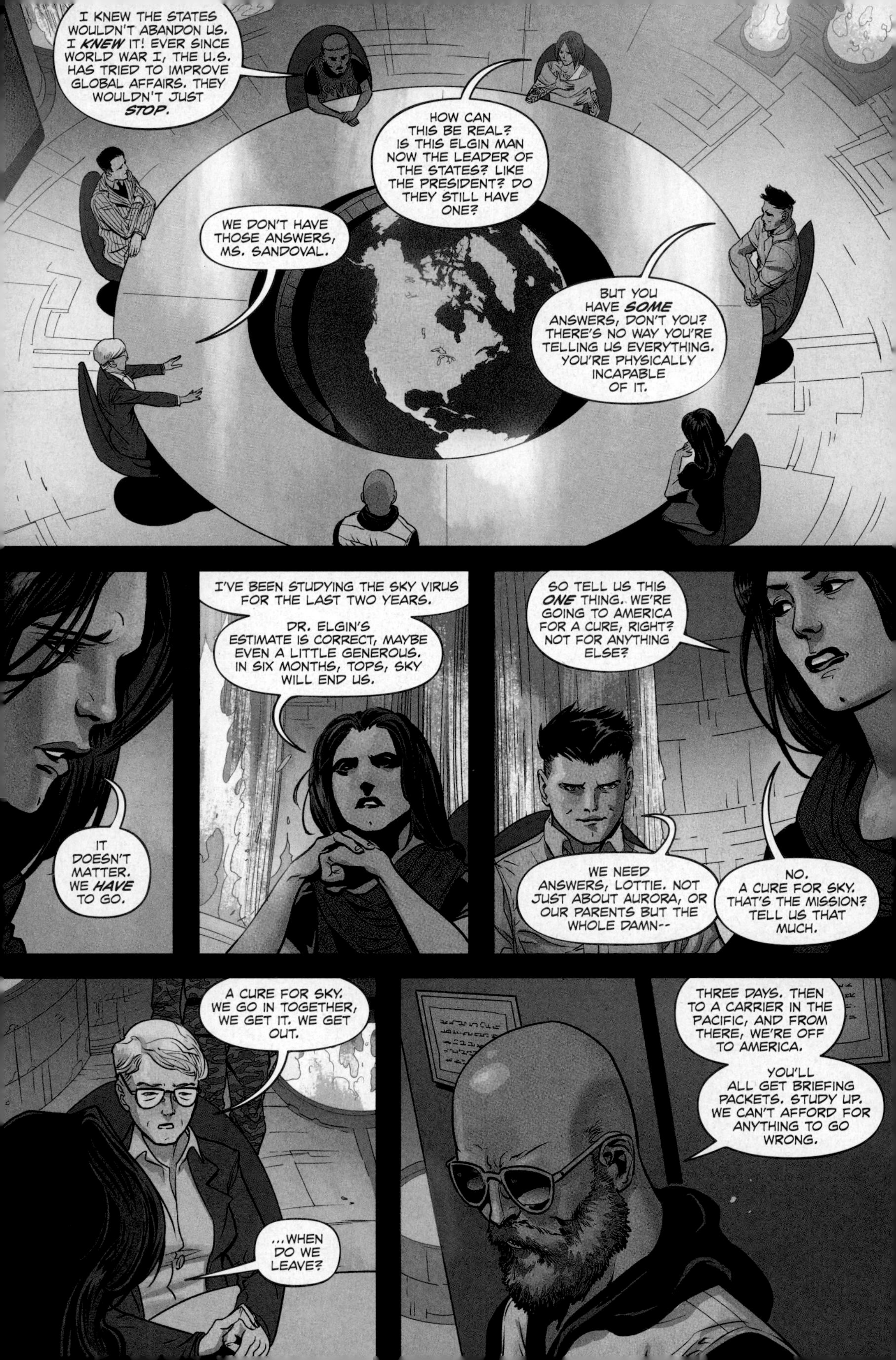
I KNEW THE STATES WOULDN'T ABANDON US. I *KNEW* IT! EVER SINCE WORLD WAR I, THE U.S. HAS TRIED TO IMPROVE GLOBAL AFFAIRS. THEY WOULDN'T JUST *STOP*.
HOW CAN THIS BE REAL? IS THIS ELGIN MAN NOW THE LEADER OF THE STATES? LIKE THE PRESIDENT? DO THEY STILL HAVE ONE?
WE DON'T HAVE THOSE ANSWERS, MS. SANDOVAL.
BUT YOU HAVE *SOME* ANSWERS, DON'T YOU? THERE'S NO WAY YOU'RE TELLING US EVERYTHING. YOU'RE PHYSICALLY INCAPABLE OF IT.
IT DOESN'T MATTER. WE *HAVE* TO GO.
I'VE BEEN STUDYING THE SKY VIRUS FOR THE LAST TWO YEARS.
DR. ELGIN'S ESTIMATE IS CORRECT, MAYBE EVEN A LITTLE GENEROUS. IN SIX MONTHS, TOPS, SKY WILL END US.
SO TELL US THIS *ONE* THING. WE'RE GOING TO AMERICA FOR A CURE, RIGHT? NOT FOR ANYTHING ELSE?
WE NEED ANSWERS, LOTTIE. NOT JUST ABOUT AURORA, OR OUR PARENTS BUT THE WHOLE DAMN--
NO. A CURE FOR SKY. THAT'S THE MISSION? TELL US THAT MUCH.
A CURE FOR SKY. WE GO IN TOGETHER, WE GET IT. WE GET OUT.
...WHEN DO WE LEAVE?
THREE DAYS. THEN TO A CARRIER IN THE PACIFIC, AND FROM THERE, WE'RE OFF TO AMERICA.
YOU'LL ALL GET BRIEFING PACKETS. STUDY UP. WE CAN'T AFFORD FOR ANYTHING TO GO WRONG.

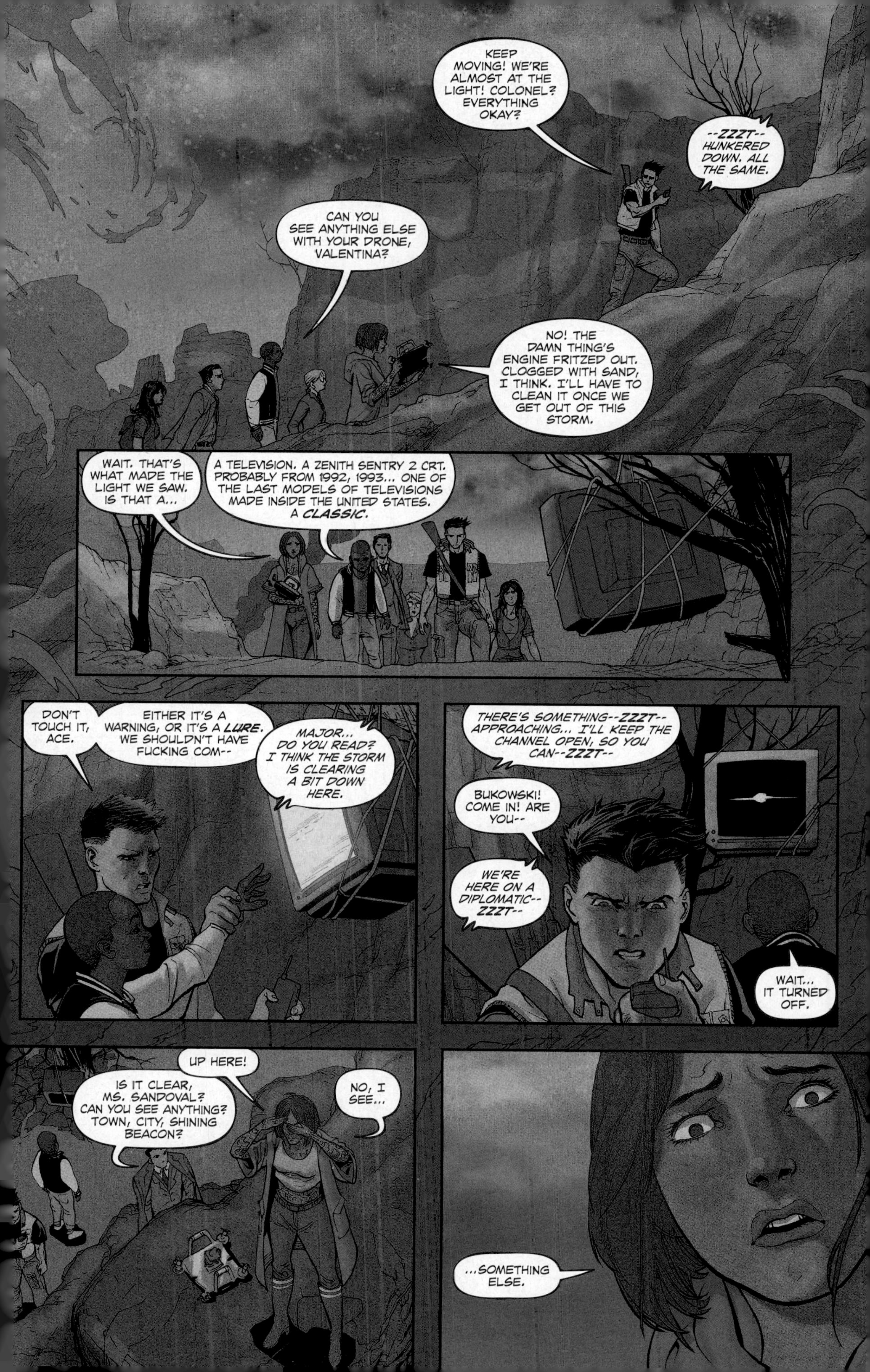

KEEP MOVING! WE'RE ALMOST AT THE LIGHT! COLONEL? EVERYTHING OKAY?
--ZZZT-- HUNKERED DOWN. ALL THE SAME.
CAN YOU SEE ANYTHING ELSE WITH YOUR DRONE, VALENTINA?
NO! THE DAMN THING'S ENGINE FRITZED OUT. CLOGGED WITH SAND, I THINK. I'LL HAVE TO CLEAN IT ONCE WE GET OUT OF THIS STORM.
WAIT. THAT'S WHAT MADE THE LIGHT WE SAW. IS THAT A...
A TELEVISION. A ZENITH SENTRY 2 CRT. PROBABLY FROM 1992, 1993... ONE OF THE LAST MODELS OF TELEVISIONS MADE INSIDE THE UNITED STATES. A *CLASSIC*.
DON'T TOUCH IT, ACE.
EITHER IT'S A WARNING, OR IT'S A *LURE*. WE SHOULDN'T HAVE FUCKING COM--
MAJOR... DO YOU READ? I THINK THE STORM IS CLEARING A BIT DOWN HERE.
THERE'S SOMETHING--ZZZT-- APPROACHING... I'LL KEEP THE CHANNEL OPEN, SO YOU CAN--ZZZT--
BUKOWSKI! COME IN! ARE YOU--
WE'RE HERE ON A DIPLOMATIC-- ZZZT--
WAIT... IT TURNED OFF.
UP HERE!
IS IT CLEAR, MS. SANDOVAL? CAN YOU SEE ANYTHING? TOWN, CITY, SHINING BEACON?
NO, I SEE...
...SOMETHING ELSE.

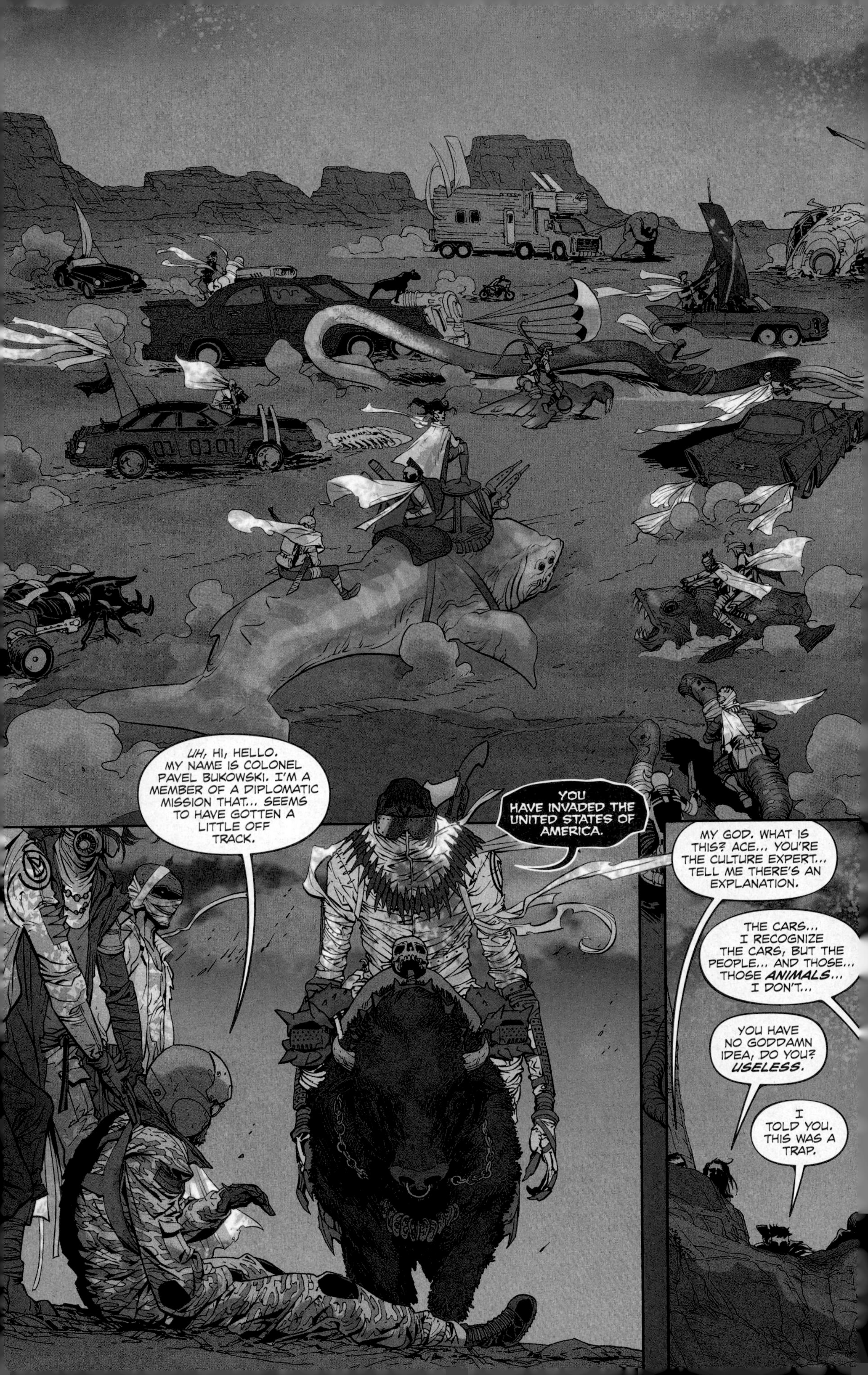
UH, HI, HELLO. MY NAME IS COLONEL PAVEL BUKOWSKI. I'M A MEMBER OF A DIPLOMATIC MISSION THAT... SEEMS TO HAVE GOTTEN A LITTLE OFF TRACK.
YOU HAVE INVADED THE UNITED STATES OF AMERICA.
MY GOD. WHAT IS THIS? ACE... YOU'RE THE CULTURE EXPERT... TELL ME THERE'S AN EXPLANATION.
THE CARS... I RECOGNIZE THE CARS, BUT THE PEOPLE... AND THOSE... THOSE ANIMALS... I DON'T...
YOU HAVE NO GODDAMN IDEA, DO YOU? USELESS.
I TOLD YOU. THIS WAS A TRAP.

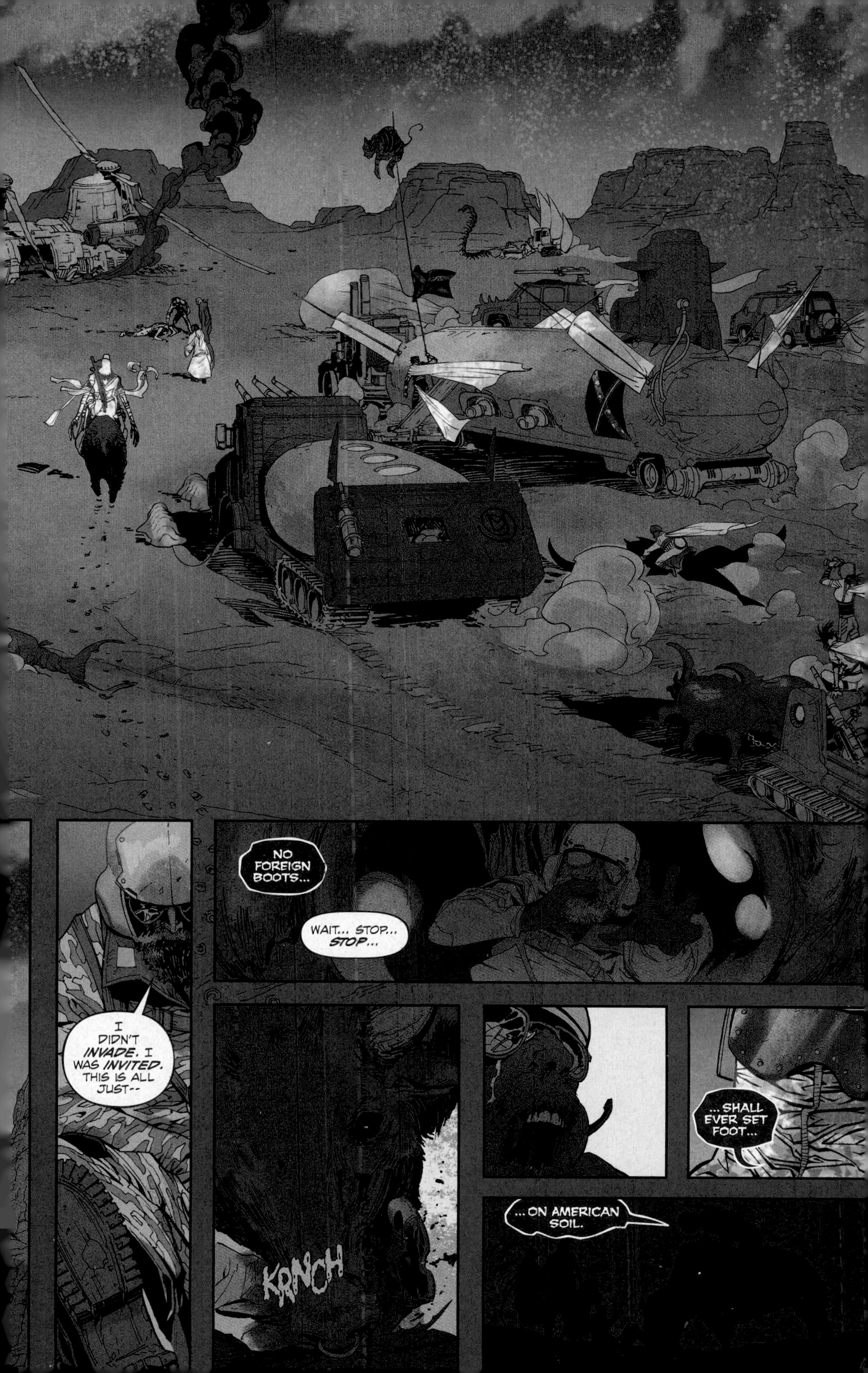
NO FOREIGN BOOTS...
WAIT... STOP... STOP...
I DIDN'T INVADE. I WAS INVITED. THIS IS ALL JUST--
KRNCH
...SHALL EVER SET FOOT...
...ON AMERICAN SOIL.

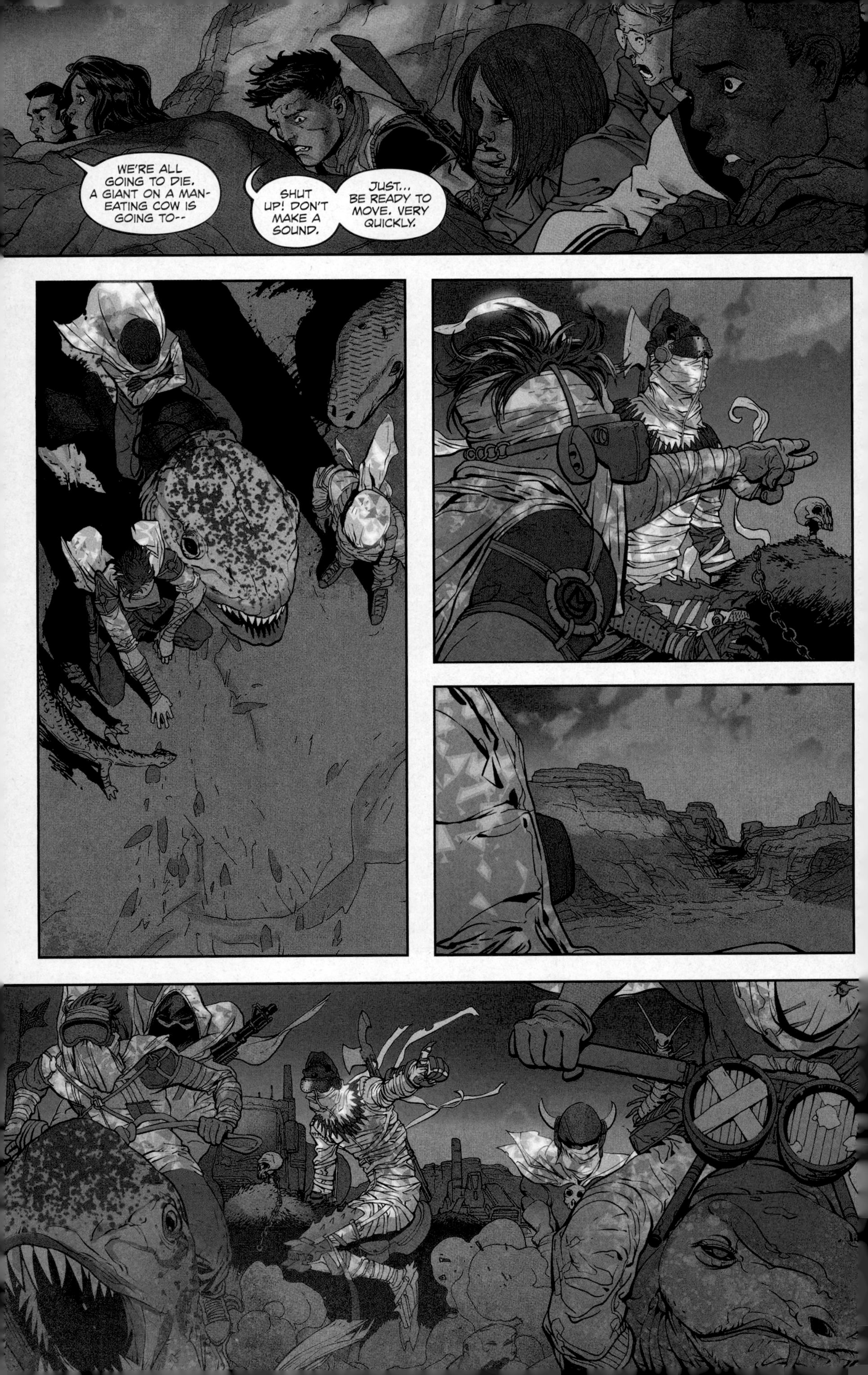
WE'RE ALL GOING TO DIE. A GIANT ON A MAN-EATING COW IS GOING TO--
SHUT UP! DON'T MAKE A SOUND.
JUST... BE READY TO MOVE. VERY QUICKLY.

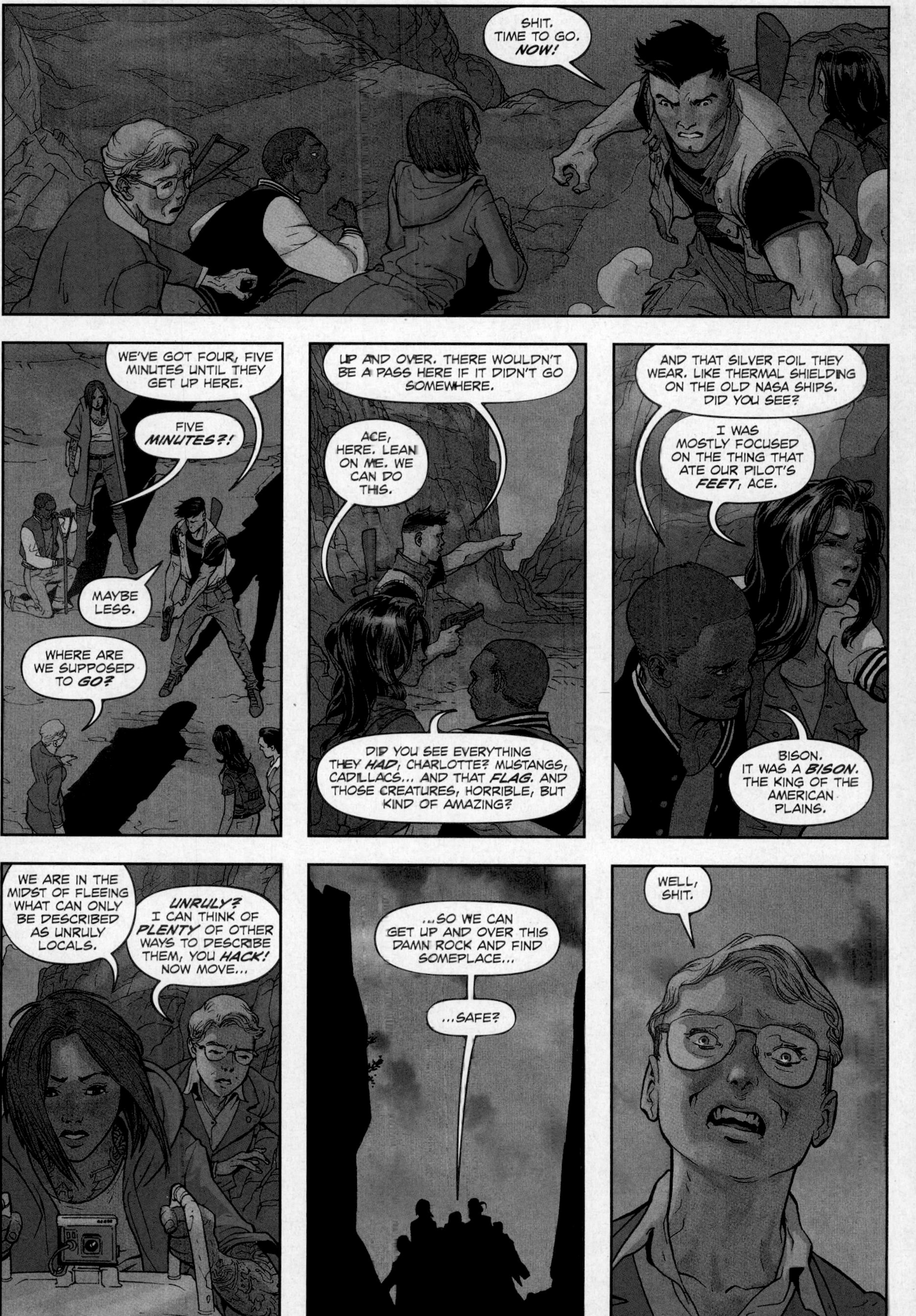
SHIT. TIME TO GO. NOW!
WE'VE GOT FOUR, FIVE MINUTES UNTIL THEY GET UP HERE.
FIVE MINUTES?!
MAYBE LESS.
WHERE ARE WE SUPPOSED TO GO?
UP AND OVER. THERE WOULDN'T BE A PASS HERE IF IT DIDN'T GO SOMEWHERE.
ACE, HERE. LEAN ON ME. WE CAN DO THIS.
DID YOU SEE EVERYTHING THEY HAD, CHARLOTTE? MUSTANGS, CADILLACS... AND THAT FLAG. AND THOSE CREATURES, HORRIBLE, BUT KIND OF AMAZING?
AND THAT SILVER FOIL THEY WEAR. LIKE THERMAL SHIELDING ON THE OLD NASA SHIPS. DID YOU SEE?
I WAS MOSTLY FOCUSED ON THE THING THAT ATE OUR PILOT'S FEET, ACE.
BISON. IT WAS A BISON. THE KING OF THE AMERICAN PLAINS.
WE ARE IN THE MIDST OF FLEEING WHAT CAN ONLY BE DESCRIBED AS UNRULY LOCALS.
UNRULY? I CAN THINK OF PLENTY OF OTHER WAYS TO DESCRIBE THEM, YOU HACK! NOW MOVE...
...SO WE CAN GET UP AND OVER THIS DAMN ROCK AND FIND SOMEPLACE...
...SAFE?
WELL, SHIT.

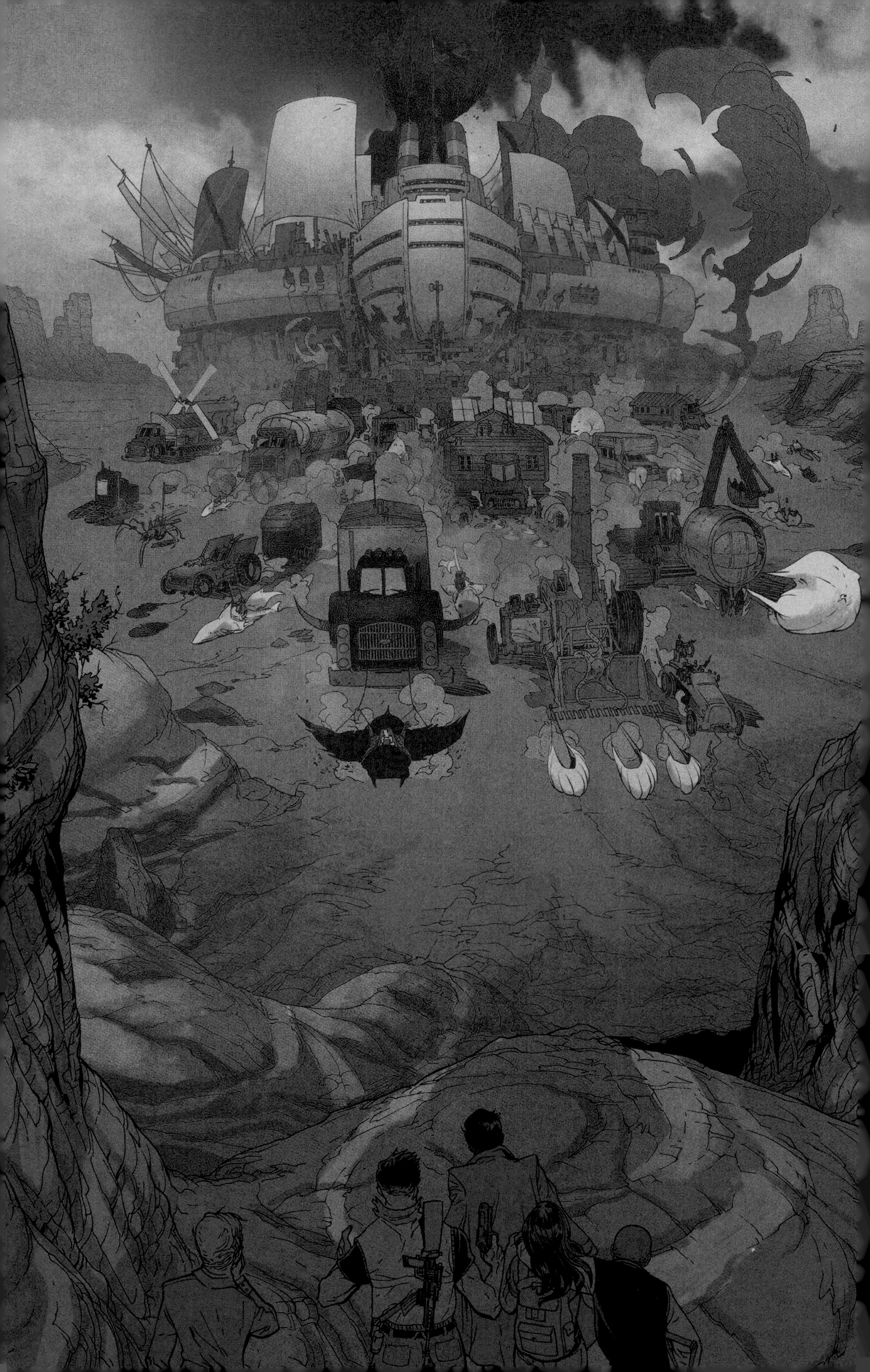

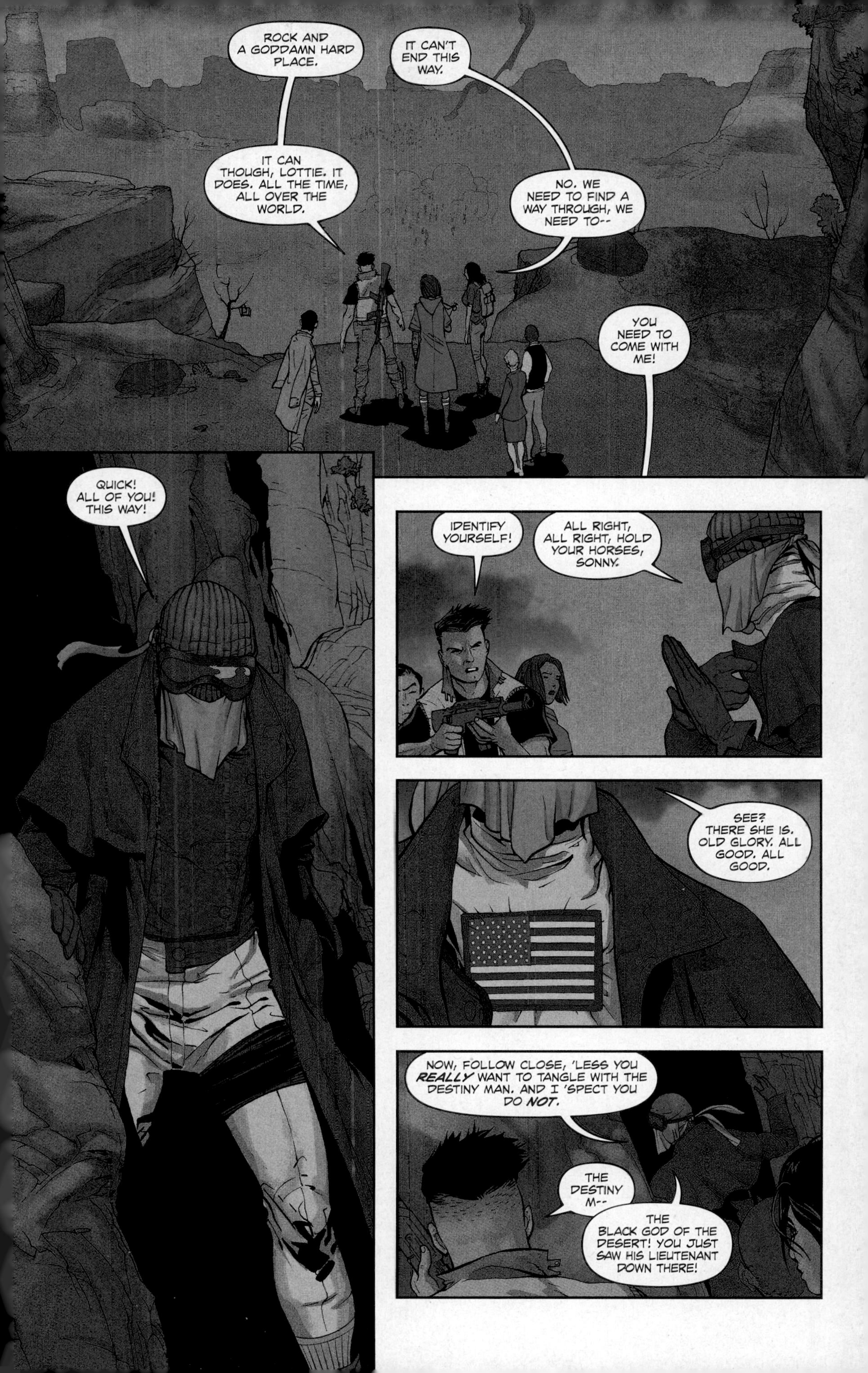
ROCK AND A GODDAMN HARD PLACE.
IT CAN'T END THIS WAY.
IT CAN THOUGH, LOTTIE. IT DOES. ALL THE TIME, ALL OVER THE WORLD.
NO. WE NEED TO FIND A WAY THROUGH, WE NEED TO--
YOU NEED TO COME WITH ME!
QUICK! ALL OF YOU! THIS WAY!
IDENTIFY YOURSELF!
ALL RIGHT, ALL RIGHT, HOLD YOUR HORSES, SONNY.
SEE? THERE SHE IS. OLD GLORY. ALL GOOD. ALL GOOD.
NOW, FOLLOW CLOSE, 'LESS YOU *REALLY* WANT TO TANGLE WITH THE DESTINY MAN. AND I 'SPECT YOU DO *NOT*.
THE DESTINY M--
THE BLACK GOD OF THE DESERT! YOU JUST SAW HIS LIEUTENANT DOWN THERE!

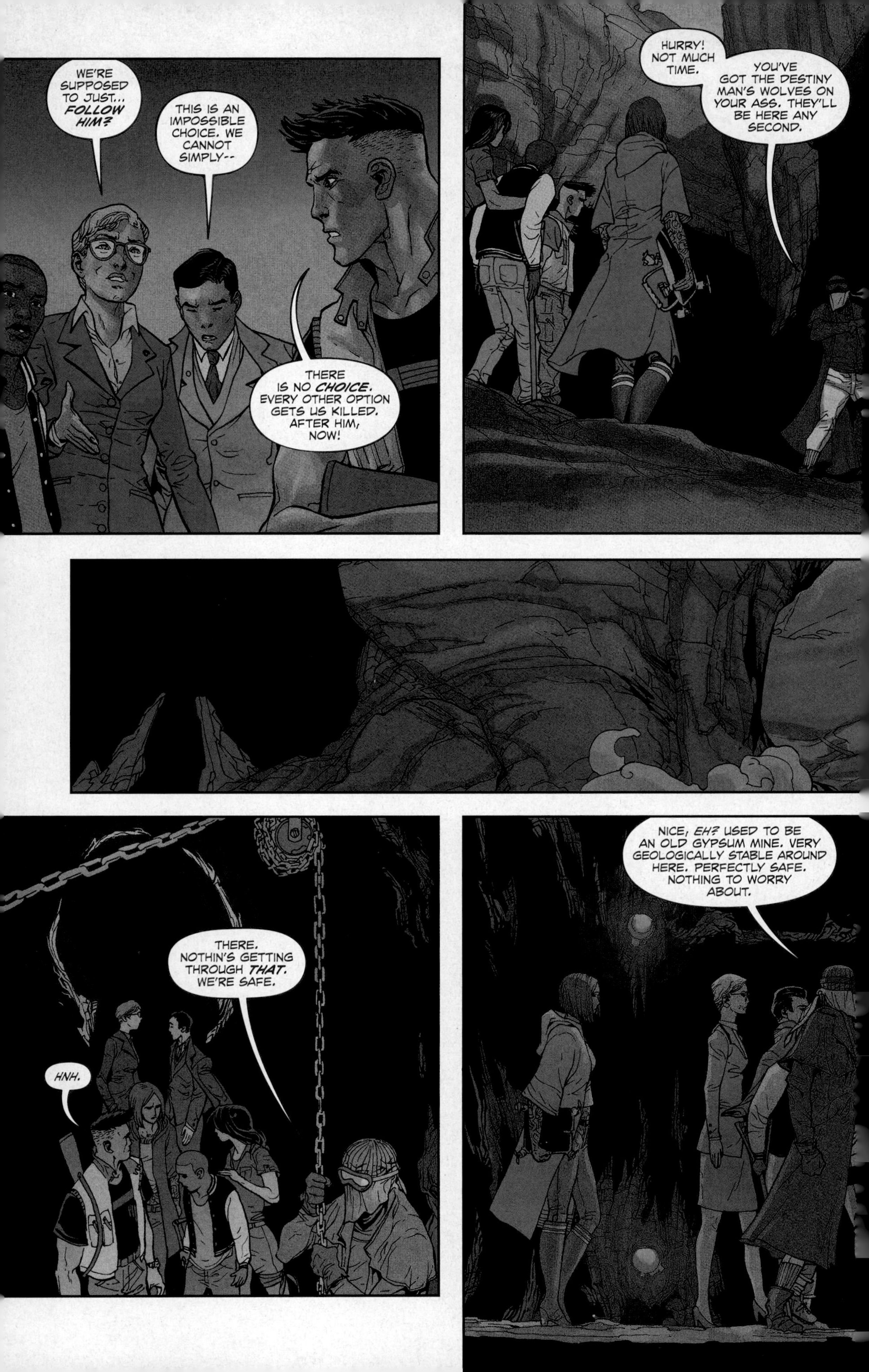
WE'RE SUPPOSED TO JUST... FOLLOW HIM?
THIS IS AN IMPOSSIBLE CHOICE. WE CANNOT SIMPLY--
THERE IS NO CHOICE. EVERY OTHER OPTION GETS US KILLED. AFTER HIM, NOW!
HURRY! NOT MUCH TIME.
YOU'VE GOT THE DESTINY MAN'S WOLVES ON YOUR ASS. THEY'LL BE HERE ANY SECOND.
HNH.
THERE. NOTHIN'S GETTING THROUGH THAT. WE'RE SAFE.
NICE, EH? USED TO BE AN OLD GYPSUM MINE. VERY GEOLOGICALLY STABLE AROUND HERE. PERFECTLY SAFE. NOTHING TO WORRY ABOUT.

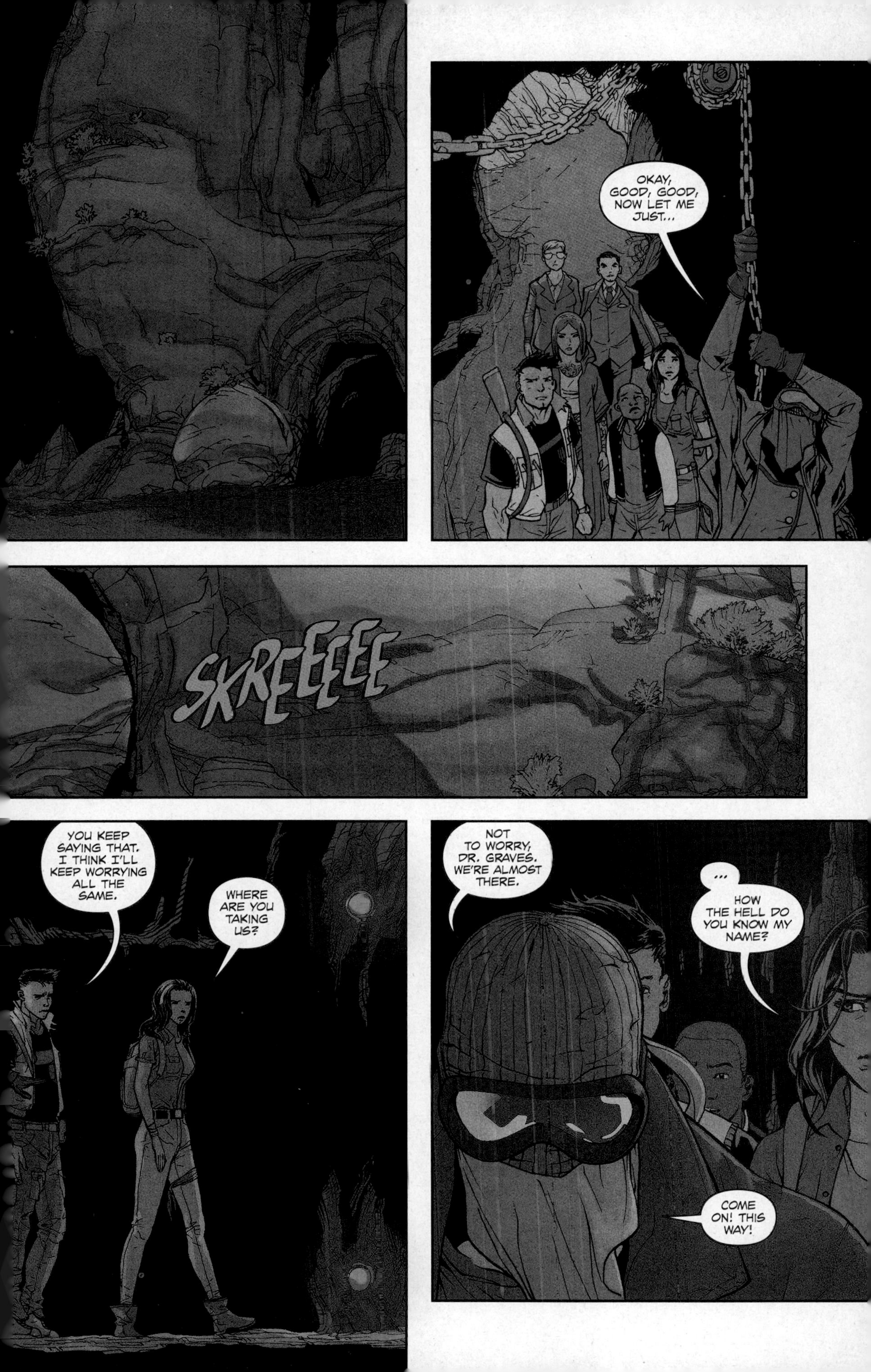
OKAY, GOOD, GOOD, NOW LET ME JUST...
SKREEEEE
YOU KEEP SAYING THAT. I THINK I'LL KEEP WORRYING ALL THE SAME.
WHERE ARE YOU TAKING US?
NOT TO WORRY, DR. GRAVES. WE'RE ALMOST THERE.
...
HOW THE HELL DO YOU KNOW MY NAME?
COME ON! THIS WAY!

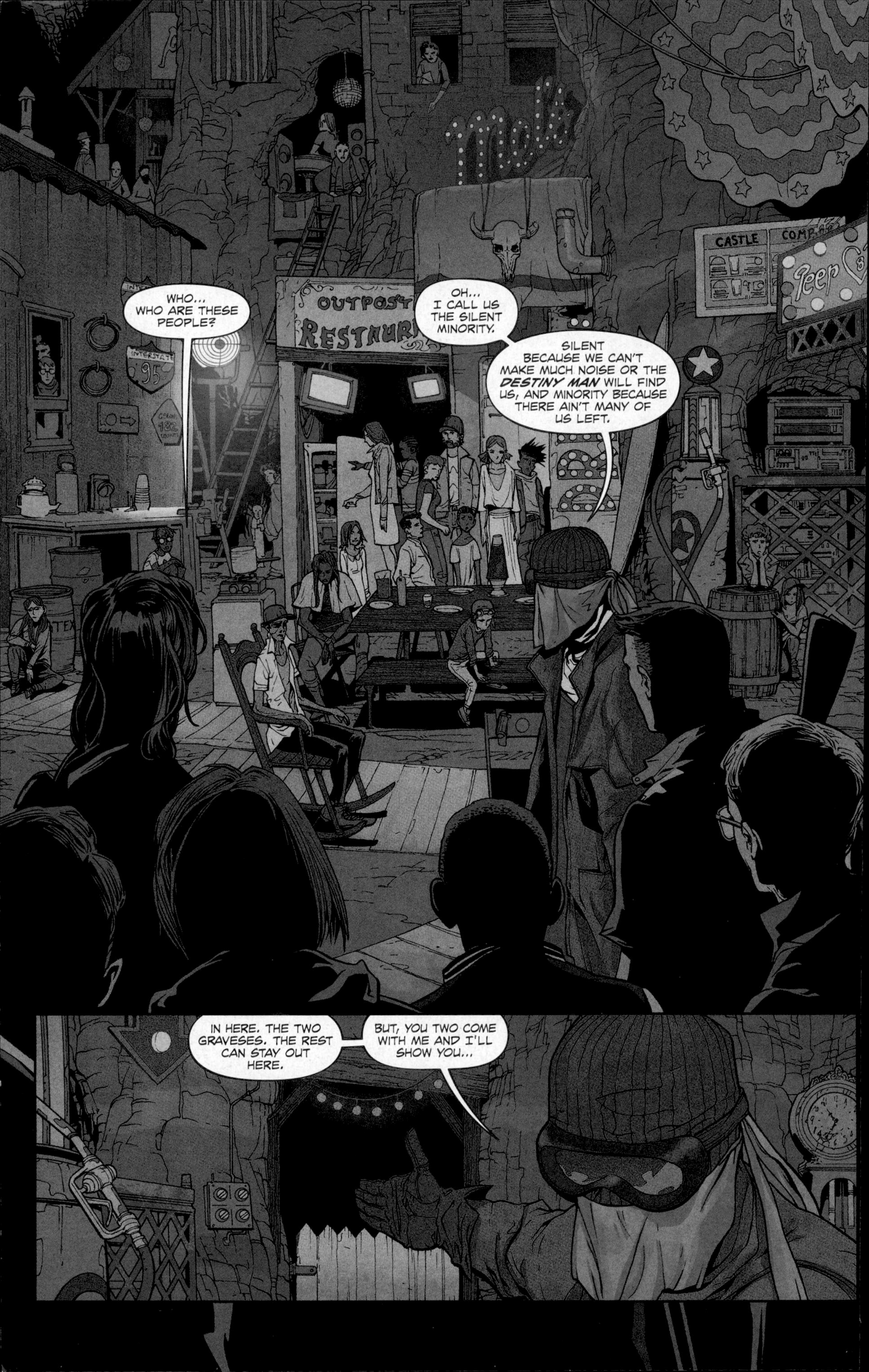
WHO... WHO ARE THESE PEOPLE?
OH... I CALL US THE SILENT MINORITY.
SILENT BECAUSE WE CAN'T MAKE MUCH NOISE OR THE **DESTINY MAN** WILL FIND US, AND MINORITY BECAUSE THERE AIN'T MANY OF US LEFT.
IN HERE. THE TWO GRAVESES. THE REST CAN STAY OUT HERE.
BUT, YOU TWO COME WITH ME AND I'LL SHOW YOU...

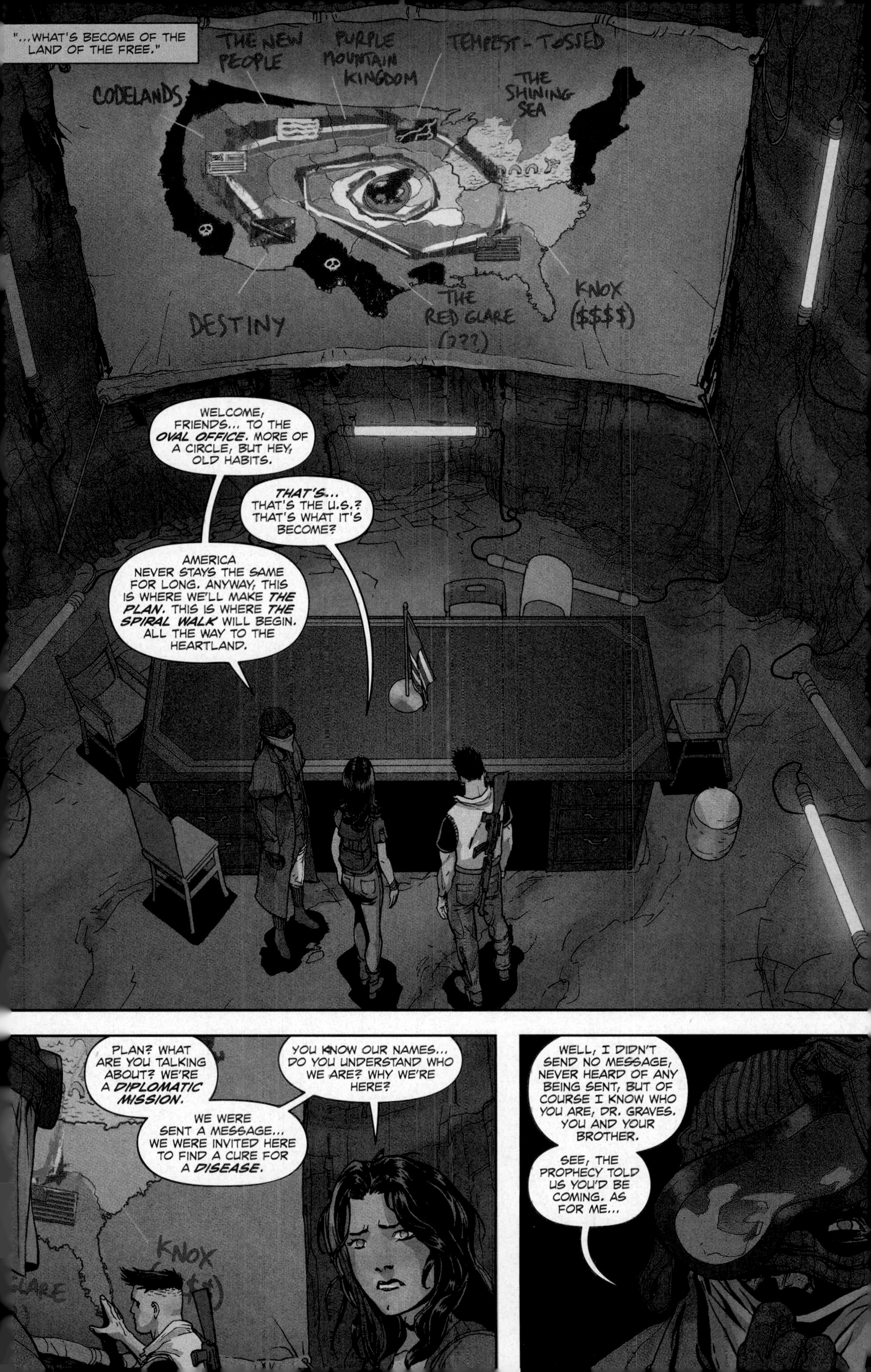
"...WHAT'S BECOME OF THE LAND OF THE FREE."
THE NEW PEOPLE
PURPLE MOUNTAIN KINGDOM
TEMPEST-TOSSED
CODELANDS
THE SHINING SEA
DESTINY
THE RED GLARE (???)
KNOX ($$$$)
WELCOME, FRIENDS... TO THE OVAL OFFICE. MORE OF A CIRCLE, BUT HEY, OLD HABITS.
THAT'S... THAT'S THE U.S.? THAT'S WHAT IT'S BECOME?
AMERICA NEVER STAYS THE SAME FOR LONG. ANYWAY, THIS IS WHERE WE'LL MAKE THE PLAN. THIS IS WHERE THE SPIRAL WALK WILL BEGIN. ALL THE WAY TO THE HEARTLAND.
PLAN? WHAT ARE YOU TALKING ABOUT? WE'RE A DIPLOMATIC MISSION.
WE WERE SENT A MESSAGE... WE WERE INVITED HERE TO FIND A CURE FOR A DISEASE.
YOU KNOW OUR NAMES... DO YOU UNDERSTAND WHO WE ARE? WHY WE'RE HERE?
WELL, I DIDN'T SEND NO MESSAGE, NEVER HEARD OF ANY BEING SENT, BUT OF COURSE I KNOW WHO YOU ARE, DR. GRAVES. YOU AND YOUR BROTHER.
SEE, THE PROPHECY TOLD US YOU'D BE COMING. AS FOR ME...

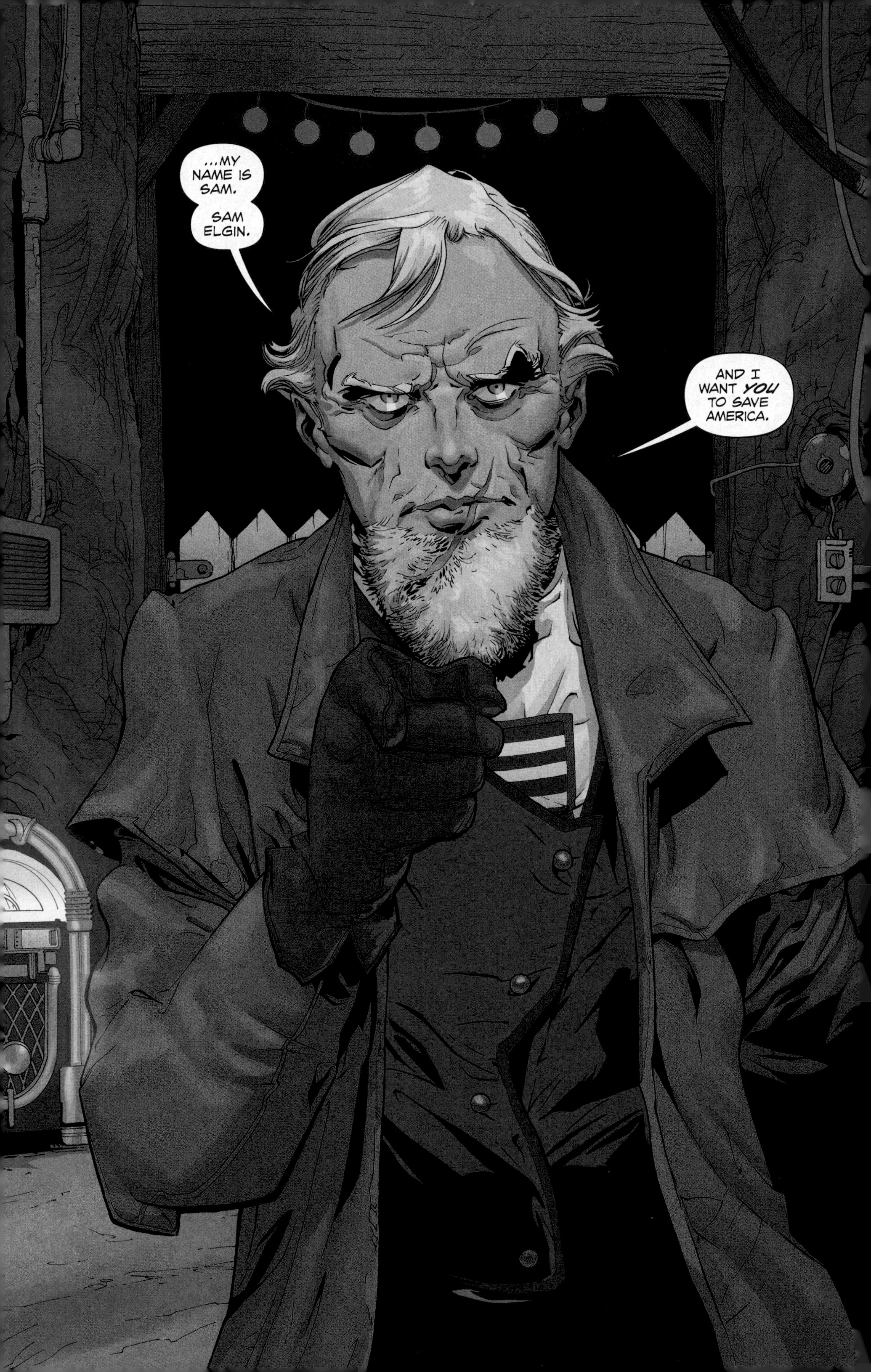
...MY NAME IS SAM.
SAM ELGIN.
AND I WANT YOU TO SAVE AMERICA.

"It didn't seem possible. People die. Countries don't— at least
not like that. But that's what happened. One day to the next, the
United States was gone from the world. I was on a date when
I heard. I remember. It ended up going very well. We were in
shock. A little comfort seemed like just the thing. The whole
world was in shock, really.

It stayed that way for a long, long time."

—Madeleine Leveux, 53, primary school teacher.
Paris, Alliance Euro-Afrique.

"Seemed out of character. The States always liked to poke its
nose in every other country's business. And then, they just...
stop? Didn't make sense. Still doesn't, really."

—Johnny Bautista, 61, software engineer.
Manila, Pan-Asian Prosperity Zone.

Quotes from *The New World: An Oral History of the Sealing* by Valentina Sandoval.

CHAPTER TWO

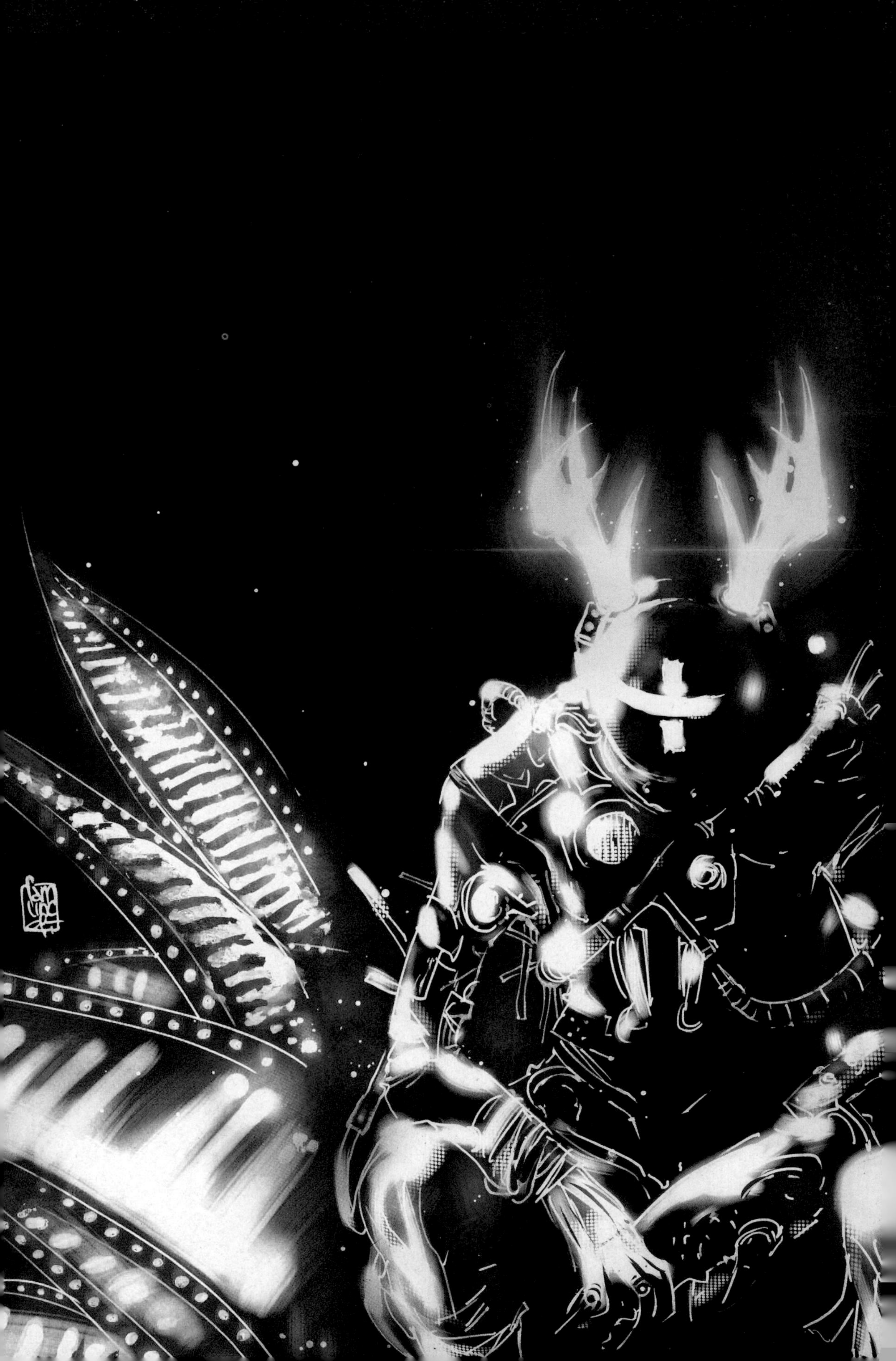

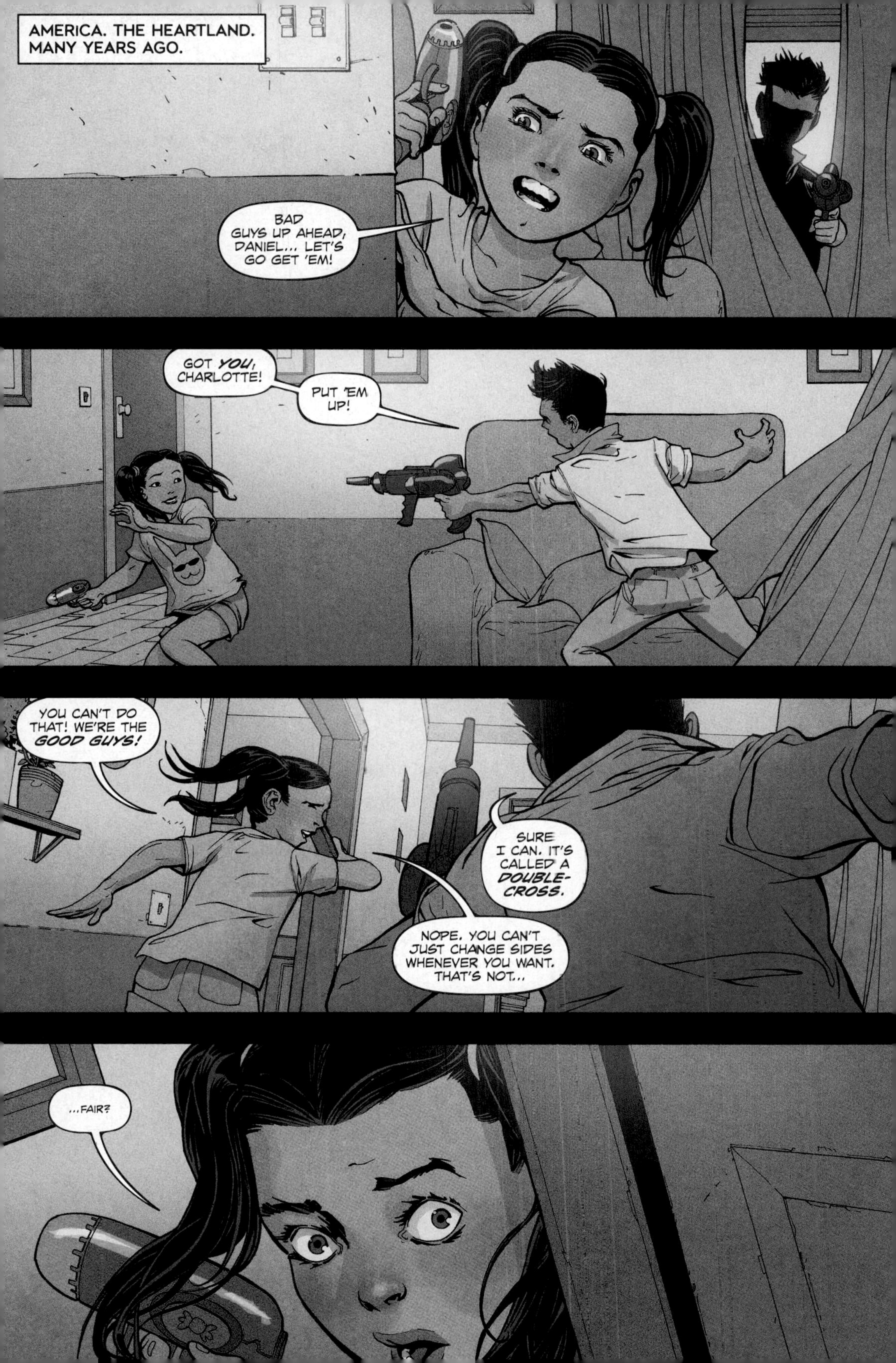

AMERICA. THE HEARTLAND. MANY YEARS AGO.
BAD GUYS UP AHEAD, DANIEL... LET'S GO GET 'EM!
GOT YOU, CHARLOTTE!
PUT 'EM UP!
YOU CAN'T DO THAT! WE'RE THE GOOD GUYS!
SURE I CAN. IT'S CALLED A DOUBLE-CROSS.
NOPE. YOU CAN'T JUST CHANGE SIDES WHENEVER YOU WANT. THAT'S NOT...
...FAIR?

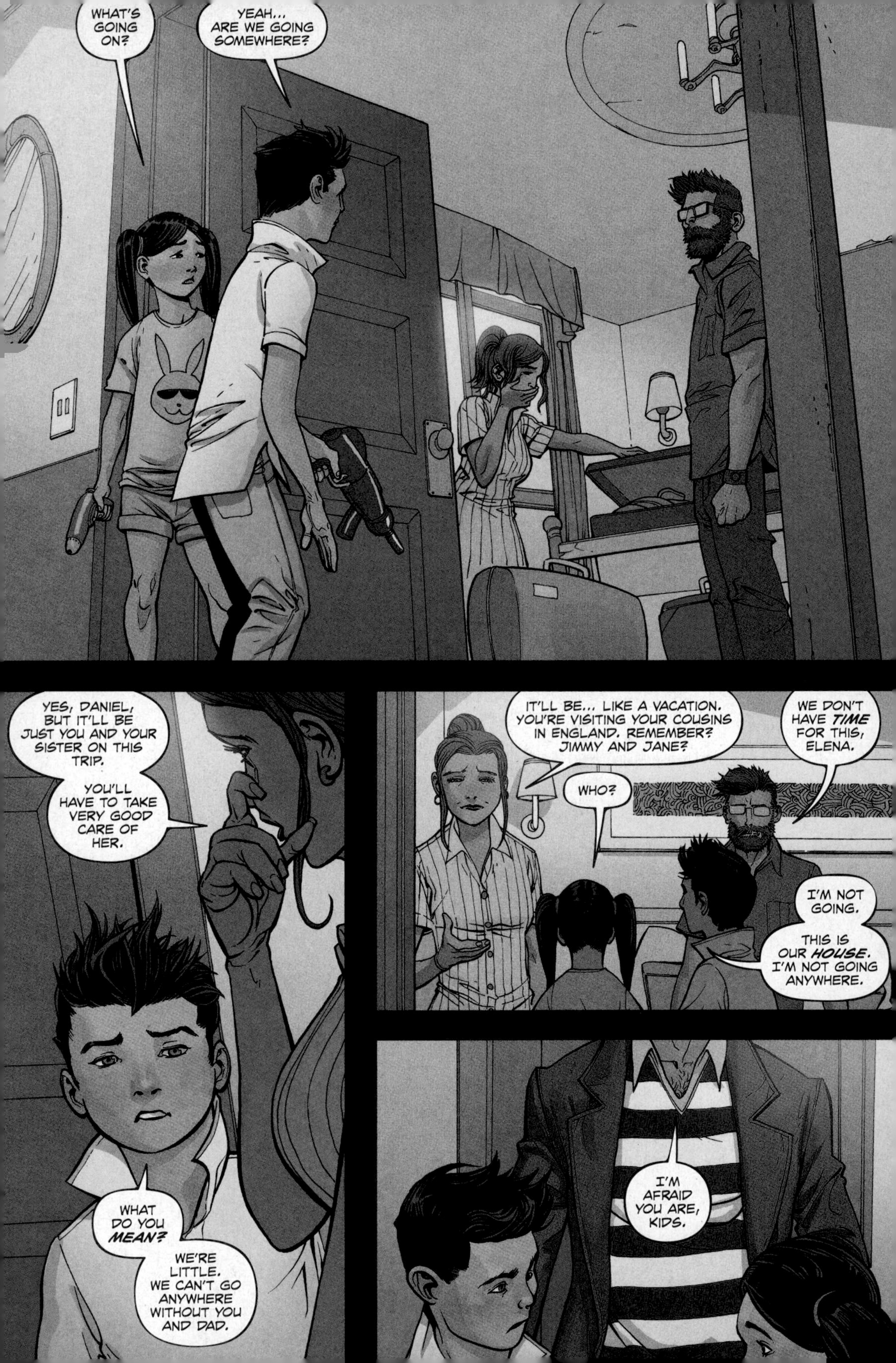

WHAT'S GOING ON?
YEAH... ARE WE GOING SOMEWHERE?
YES, DANIEL, BUT IT'LL BE JUST YOU AND YOUR SISTER ON THIS TRIP.
YOU'LL HAVE TO TAKE VERY GOOD CARE OF HER.
WHAT DO YOU MEAN?
WE'RE LITTLE. WE CAN'T GO ANYWHERE WITHOUT YOU AND DAD.
IT'LL BE... LIKE A VACATION. YOU'RE VISITING YOUR COUSINS IN ENGLAND. REMEMBER? JIMMY AND JANE?
WHO?
WE DON'T HAVE TIME FOR THIS, ELENA.
I'M NOT GOING.
THIS IS OUR HOUSE. I'M NOT GOING ANYWHERE.
I'M AFRAID YOU ARE, KIDS.

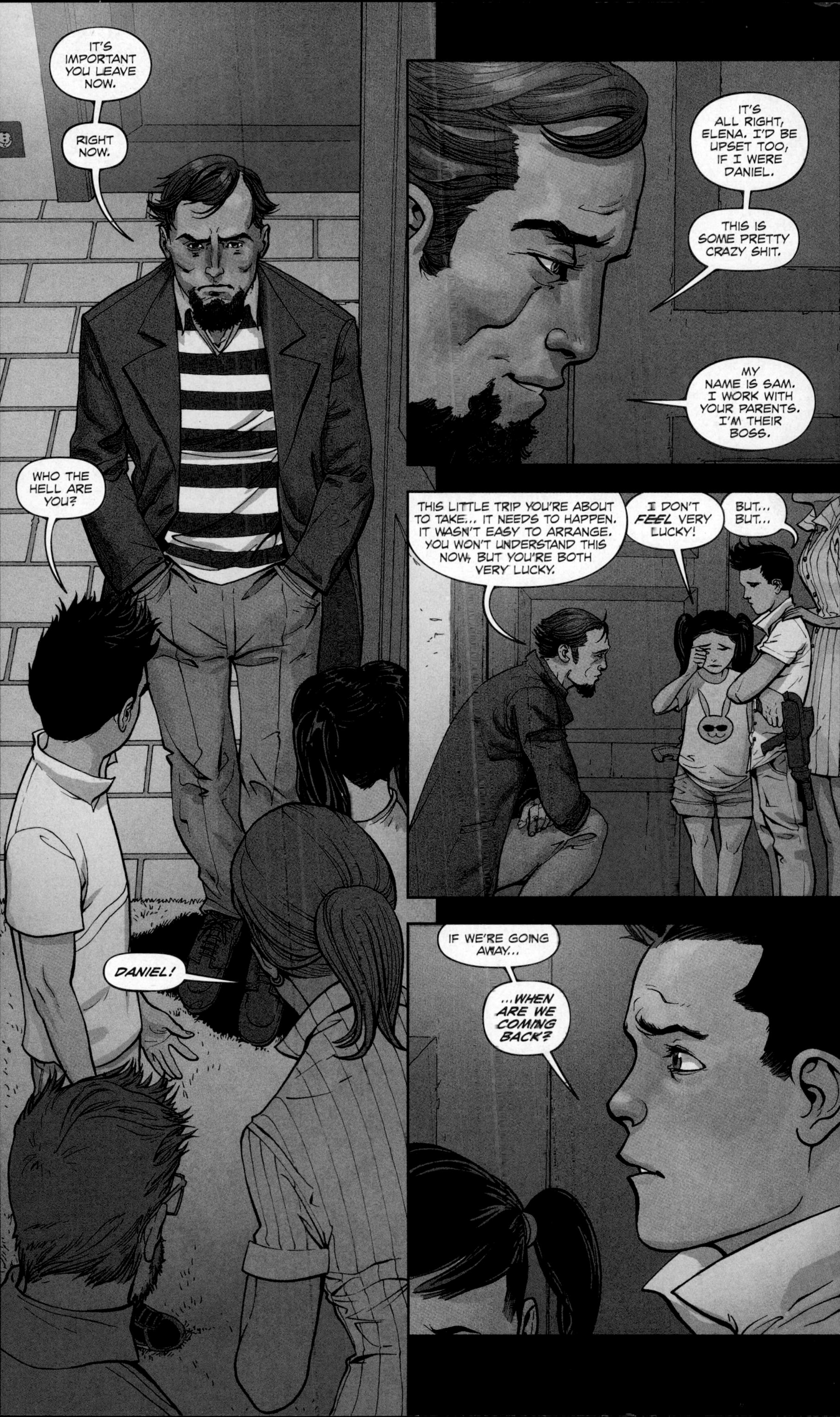

IT'S IMPORTANT YOU LEAVE NOW.
RIGHT NOW.
IT'S ALL RIGHT, ELENA. I'D BE UPSET TOO, IF I WERE DANIEL.
THIS IS SOME PRETTY CRAZY SHIT.
MY NAME IS SAM. I WORK WITH YOUR PARENTS. I'M THEIR BOSS.
WHO THE HELL ARE YOU?
DANIEL!
THIS LITTLE TRIP YOU'RE ABOUT TO TAKE... IT NEEDS TO HAPPEN. IT WASN'T EASY TO ARRANGE. YOU WON'T UNDERSTAND THIS NOW, BUT YOU'RE BOTH VERY LUCKY.
I DON'T FEEL VERY LUCKY!
BUT... BUT...
IF WE'RE GOING AWAY...
...WHEN ARE WE COMING BACK?

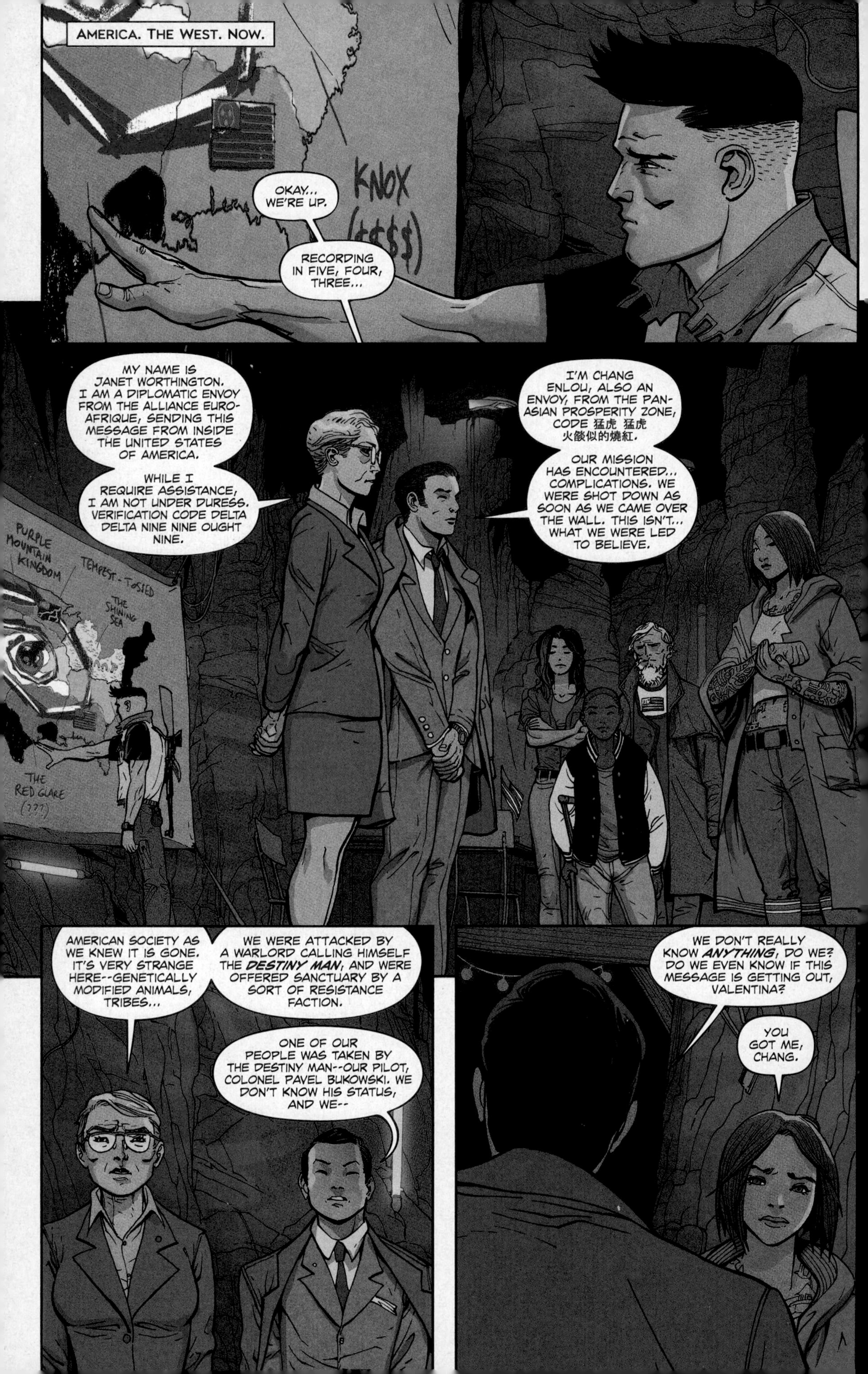
AMERICA. THE WEST. NOW.
KNOX ($$$)
OKAY... WE'RE UP.
RECORDING IN FIVE, FOUR, THREE...
MY NAME IS JANET WORTHINGTON. I AM A DIPLOMATIC ENVOY FROM THE ALLIANCE EURO-AFRIQUE, SENDING THIS MESSAGE FROM INSIDE THE UNITED STATES OF AMERICA.
WHILE I REQUIRE ASSISTANCE, I AM NOT UNDER DURESS. VERIFICATION CODE DELTA DELTA NINE NINE OUGHT NINE.
I'M CHANG ENLOU, ALSO AN ENVOY, FROM THE PAN-ASIAN PROSPERITY ZONE, CODE 猛虎 猛虎 火燄似的燒紅.
OUR MISSION HAS ENCOUNTERED... COMPLICATIONS. WE WERE SHOT DOWN AS SOON AS WE CAME OVER THE WALL. THIS ISN'T... WHAT WE WERE LED TO BELIEVE.
PURPLE MOUNTAIN KINGDOM
TEMPEST-TOSSED
THE SHINING SEA
THE RED GLARE (???)
AMERICAN SOCIETY AS WE KNEW IT IS GONE. IT'S VERY STRANGE HERE--GENETICALLY MODIFIED ANIMALS, TRIBES...
WE WERE ATTACKED BY A WARLORD CALLING HIMSELF THE *DESTINY MAN*, AND WERE OFFERED SANCTUARY BY A SORT OF RESISTANCE FACTION.
ONE OF OUR PEOPLE WAS TAKEN BY THE DESTINY MAN--OUR PILOT, COLONEL PAVEL BUKOWSKI. WE DON'T KNOW HIS STATUS, AND WE--
WE DON'T REALLY KNOW *ANYTHING*, DO WE? DO WE EVEN KNOW IF THIS MESSAGE IS GETTING OUT, VALENTINA?
YOU GOT ME, CHANG.

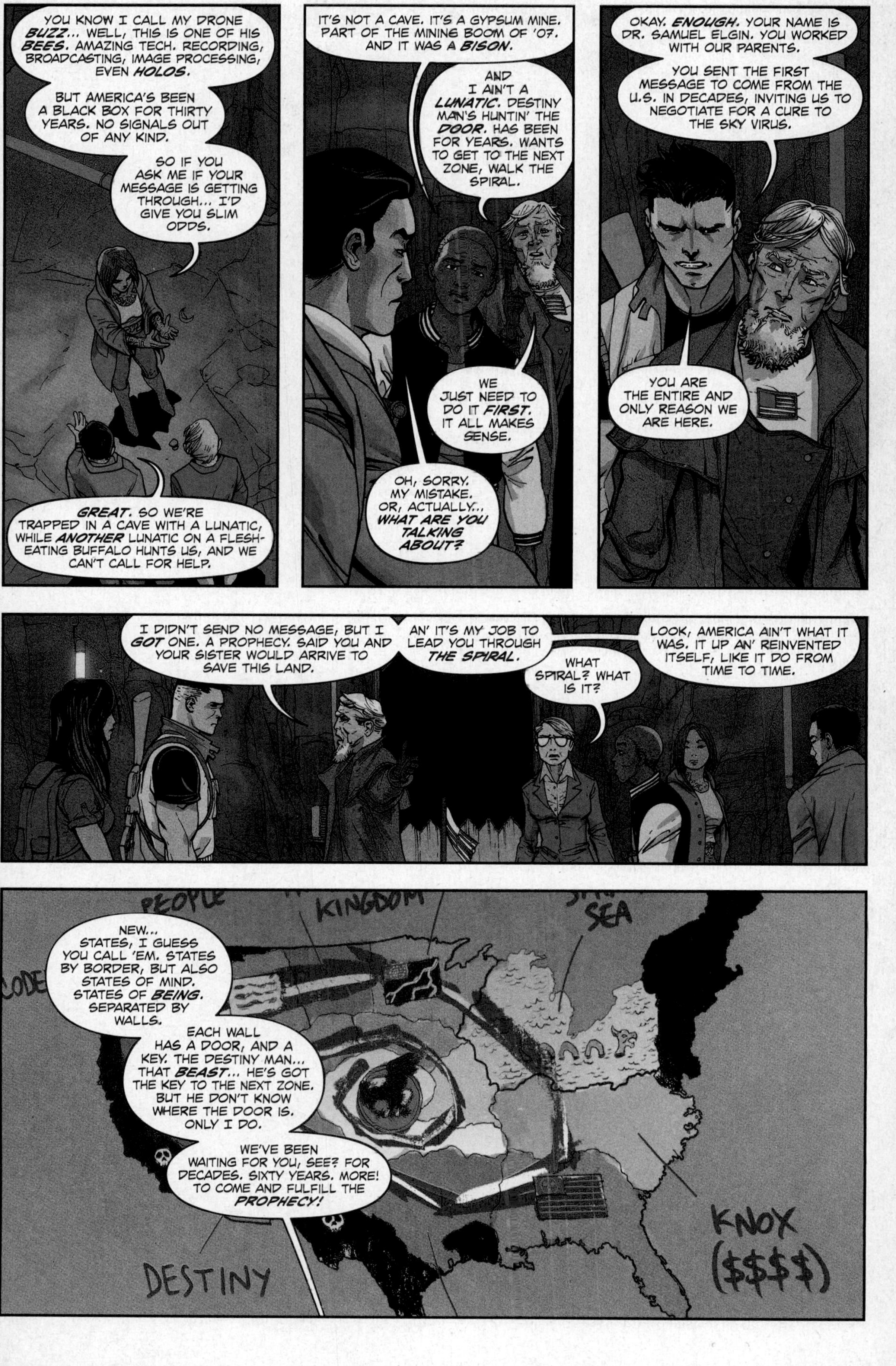

YOU KNOW I CALL MY DRONE **BUZZ**... WELL, THIS IS ONE OF HIS **BEES**. AMAZING TECH. RECORDING, BROADCASTING, IMAGE PROCESSING, EVEN **HOLOS**.
BUT AMERICA'S BEEN A BLACK BOX FOR THIRTY YEARS. NO SIGNALS OUT OF ANY KIND.
SO IF YOU ASK ME IF YOUR MESSAGE IS GETTING THROUGH... I'D GIVE YOU SLIM ODDS.
GREAT. SO WE'RE TRAPPED IN A CAVE WITH A LUNATIC, WHILE **ANOTHER** LUNATIC ON A FLESH-EATING BUFFALO HUNTS US, AND WE CAN'T CALL FOR HELP.
IT'S NOT A CAVE. IT'S A GYPSUM MINE. PART OF THE MINING BOOM OF '07. AND IT WAS A **BISON**.
AND I AIN'T A **LUNATIC**. DESTINY MAN'S HUNTIN' THE **DOOR**. HAS BEEN FOR YEARS. WANTS TO GET TO THE NEXT ZONE, WALK THE SPIRAL.
WE JUST NEED TO DO IT **FIRST**. IT ALL MAKES SENSE.
OH, SORRY. MY MISTAKE. OR, ACTUALLY... **WHAT ARE YOU TALKING ABOUT?**
OKAY. **ENOUGH**. YOUR NAME IS DR. SAMUEL ELGIN. YOU WORKED WITH OUR PARENTS.
YOU SENT THE FIRST MESSAGE TO COME FROM THE U.S. IN DECADES, INVITING US TO NEGOTIATE FOR A CURE TO THE SKY VIRUS.
YOU ARE THE ENTIRE AND ONLY REASON WE ARE HERE.
I DIDN'T SEND NO MESSAGE, BUT I **GOT** ONE. A PROPHECY. SAID YOU AND YOUR SISTER WOULD ARRIVE TO SAVE THIS LAND.
AN' IT'S MY JOB TO LEAD YOU THROUGH **THE SPIRAL**.
WHAT SPIRAL? WHAT IS IT?
LOOK, AMERICA AIN'T WHAT IT WAS. IT UP AN' REINVENTED ITSELF, LIKE IT DO FROM TIME TO TIME.
PEOPLE
KINGDOM
SEA
CODE
NEW... STATES, I GUESS YOU CALL 'EM. STATES BY BORDER, BUT ALSO STATES OF MIND. STATES OF **BEING**. SEPARATED BY WALLS.
EACH WALL HAS A DOOR, AND A KEY. THE DESTINY MAN... THAT **BEAST**... HE'S GOT THE KEY TO THE NEXT ZONE. BUT HE DON'T KNOW WHERE THE DOOR IS. ONLY I DO.
WE'VE BEEN WAITING FOR YOU, SEE? FOR DECADES. SIXTY YEARS. MORE! TO COME AND FULFILL THE **PROPHECY!**
DESTINY
KNOX ($$$)

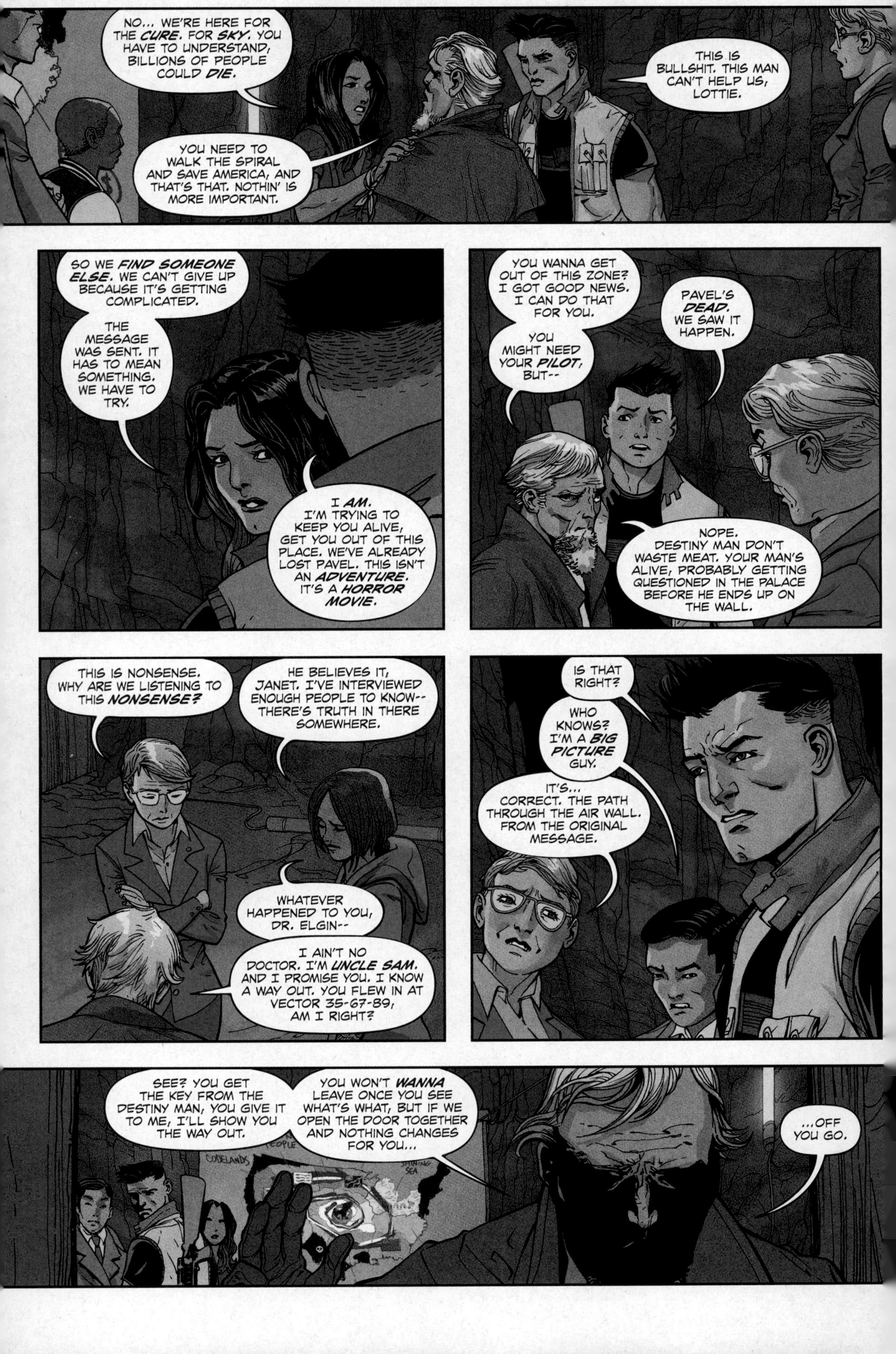
NO... WE'RE HERE FOR THE *CURE*. FOR *SKY*. YOU HAVE TO UNDERSTAND, BILLIONS OF PEOPLE COULD *DIE*.
YOU NEED TO WALK THE SPIRAL AND SAVE AMERICA, AND THAT'S THAT. NOTHIN' IS MORE IMPORTANT.
THIS IS BULLSHIT. THIS MAN CAN'T HELP US, LOTTIE.
SO WE *FIND SOMEONE ELSE*. WE CAN'T GIVE UP BECAUSE IT'S GETTING COMPLICATED.
THE MESSAGE WAS SENT. IT HAS TO MEAN SOMETHING. WE HAVE TO TRY.
I *AM*. I'M TRYING TO KEEP YOU ALIVE, GET YOU OUT OF THIS PLACE. WE'VE ALREADY LOST PAVEL. THIS ISN'T AN *ADVENTURE*. IT'S A *HORROR MOVIE*.
YOU WANNA GET OUT OF THIS ZONE? I GOT GOOD NEWS. I CAN DO THAT FOR YOU.
YOU MIGHT NEED YOUR *PILOT*, BUT--
PAVEL'S *DEAD*. WE SAW IT HAPPEN.
NOPE. DESTINY MAN DON'T WASTE MEAT. YOUR MAN'S ALIVE, PROBABLY GETTING QUESTIONED IN THE PALACE BEFORE HE ENDS UP ON THE WALL.
THIS IS NONSENSE. WHY ARE WE LISTENING TO THIS *NONSENSE?*
HE BELIEVES IT, JANET. I'VE INTERVIEWED ENOUGH PEOPLE TO KNOW-- THERE'S TRUTH IN THERE SOMEWHERE.
WHATEVER HAPPENED TO YOU, DR. ELGIN--
I AIN'T NO DOCTOR. I'M *UNCLE SAM*. AND I PROMISE YOU. I KNOW A WAY OUT. YOU FLEW IN AT VECTOR 35-67-89, AM I RIGHT?
IS THAT RIGHT?
WHO KNOWS? I'M A *BIG PICTURE* GUY.
IT'S... CORRECT. THE PATH THROUGH THE AIR WALL. FROM THE ORIGINAL MESSAGE.
SEE? YOU GET THE KEY FROM THE DESTINY MAN, YOU GIVE IT TO ME, I'LL SHOW YOU THE WAY OUT.
YOU WON'T *WANNA* LEAVE ONCE YOU SEE WHAT'S WHAT, BUT IF WE OPEN THE DOOR TOGETHER AND NOTHING CHANGES FOR YOU...
...OFF YOU GO.

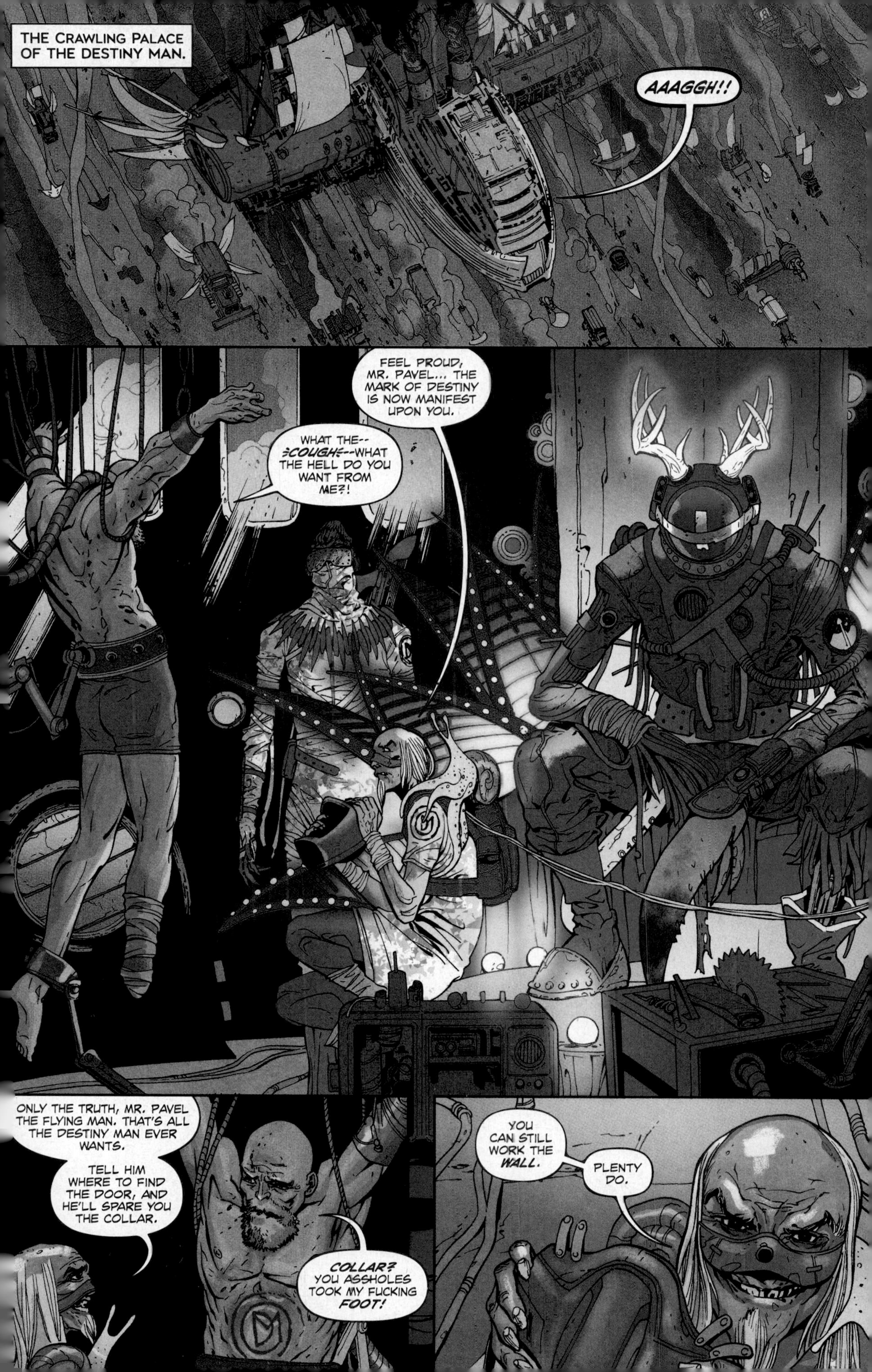
THE CRAWLING PALACE OF THE DESTINY MAN.
AAAGGH!!
FEEL PROUD, MR. PAVEL... THE MARK OF DESTINY IS NOW MANIFEST UPON YOU.
WHAT THE-- COUGH--WHAT THE HELL DO YOU WANT FROM ME?!
ONLY THE TRUTH, MR. PAVEL THE FLYING MAN. THAT'S ALL THE DESTINY MAN EVER WANTS.
TELL HIM WHERE TO FIND THE DOOR, AND HE'LL SPARE YOU THE COLLAR.
COLLAR? YOU ASSHOLES TOOK MY FUCKING FOOT!
YOU CAN STILL WORK THE WALL.
PLENTY DO.

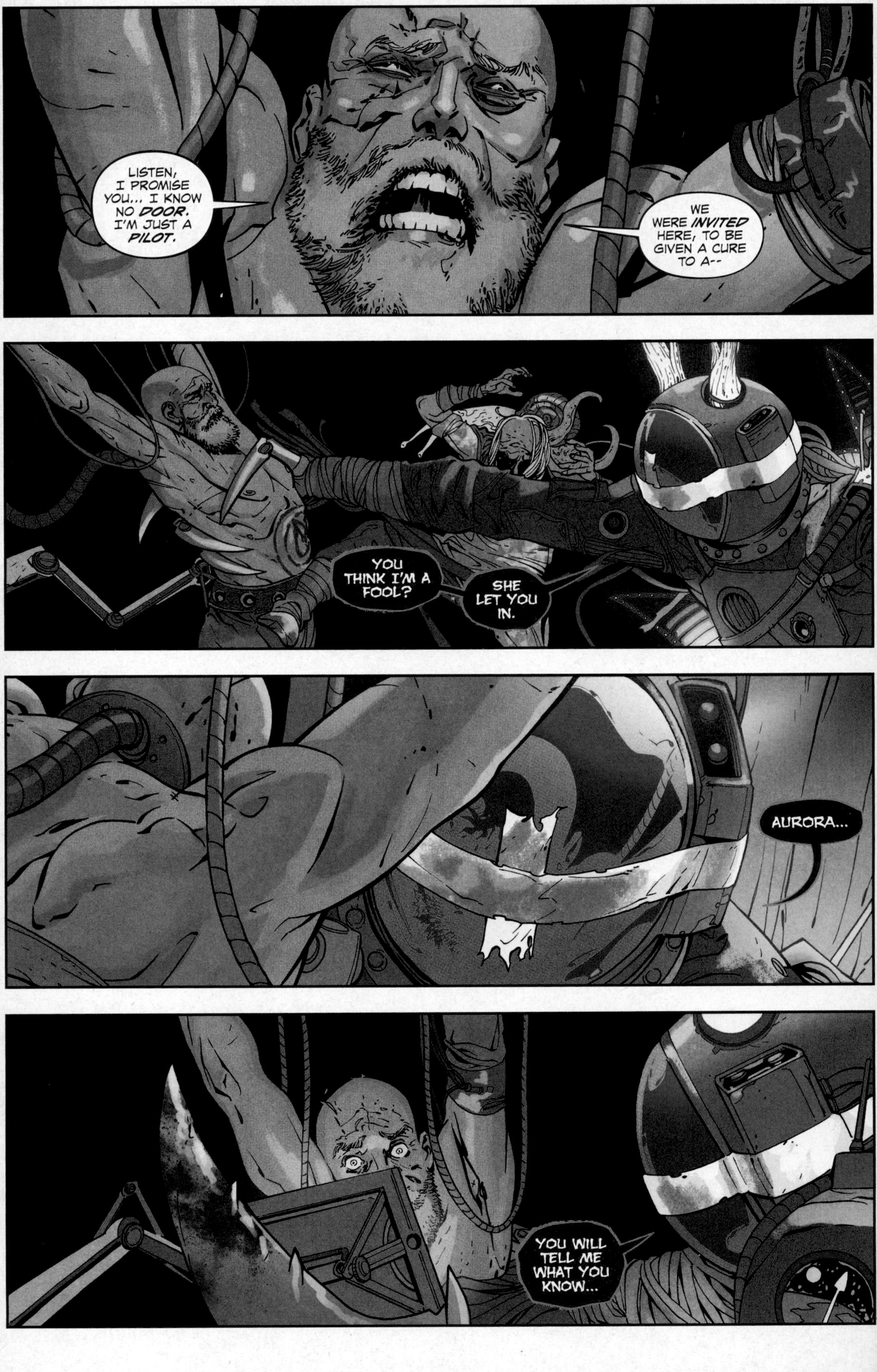
LISTEN, I PROMISE YOU... I KNOW NO DOOR. I'M JUST A PILOT.
WE WERE INVITED HERE, TO BE GIVEN A CURE TO A--
YOU THINK I'M A FOOL?
SHE LET YOU IN.
AURORA...
YOU WILL TELL ME WHAT YOU KNOW...

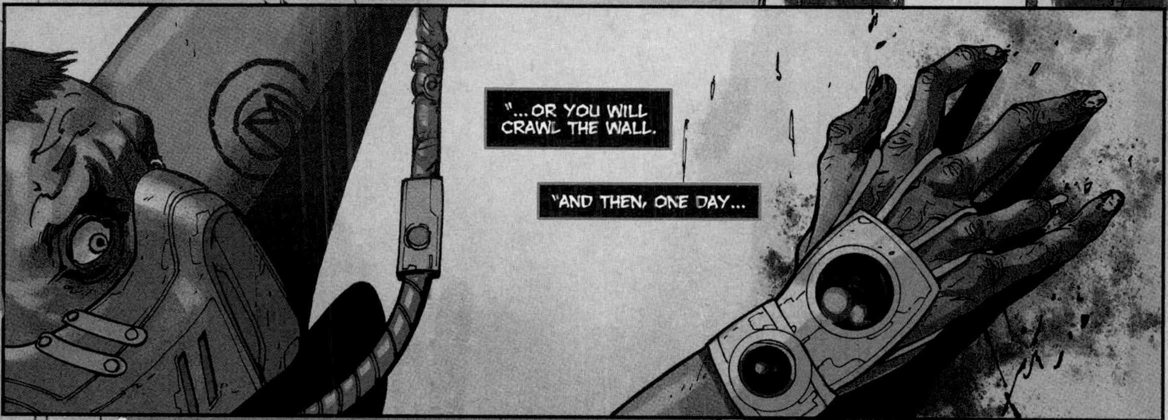
"...OR YOU WILL CRAWL THE WALL.
"AND THEN, ONE DAY...

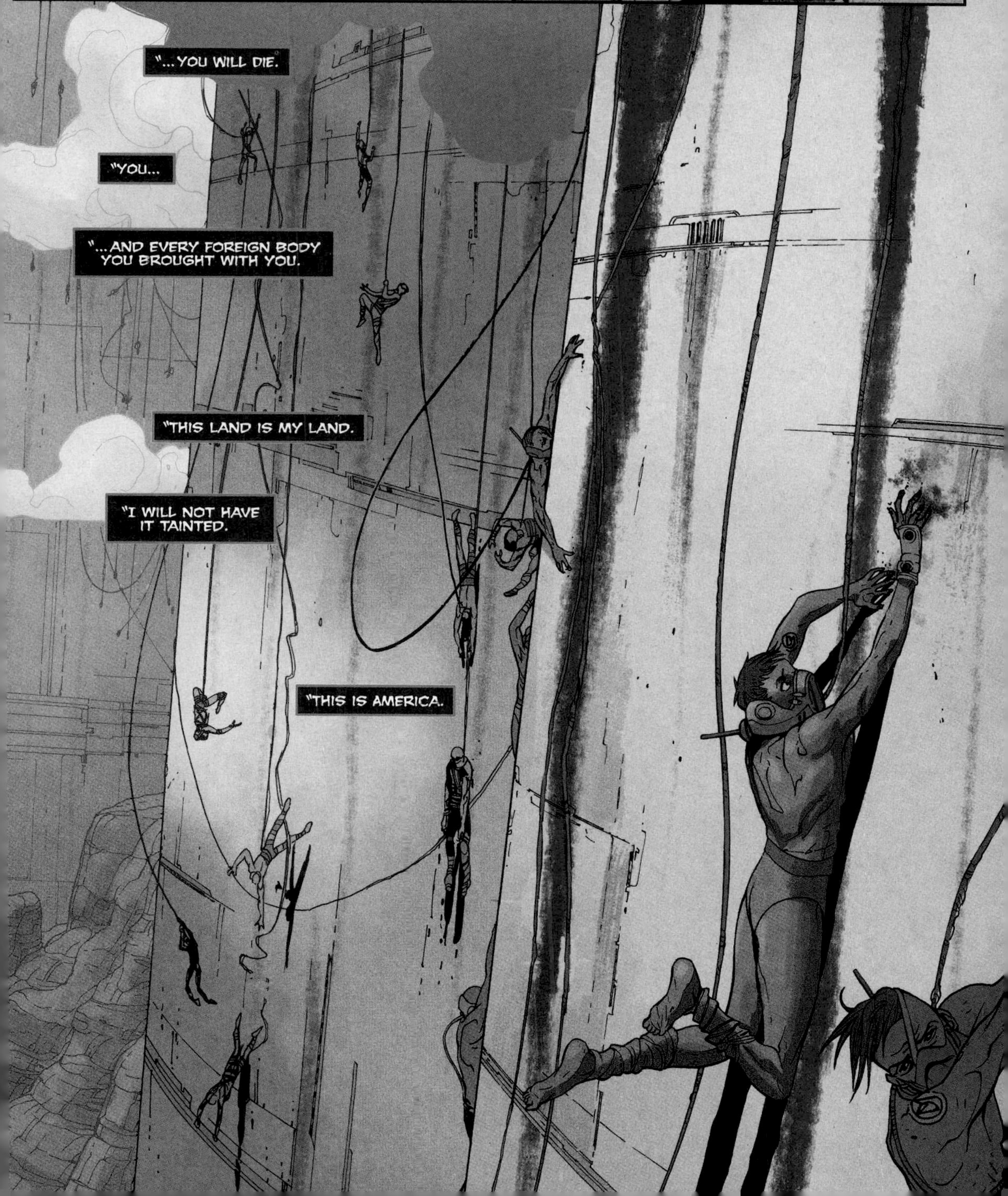
"...YOU WILL DIE.
"YOU...
"...AND EVERY FOREIGN BODY YOU BROUGHT WITH YOU.
"THIS LAND IS MY LAND.
"I WILL NOT HAVE IT TAINTED.
"THIS IS AMERICA.

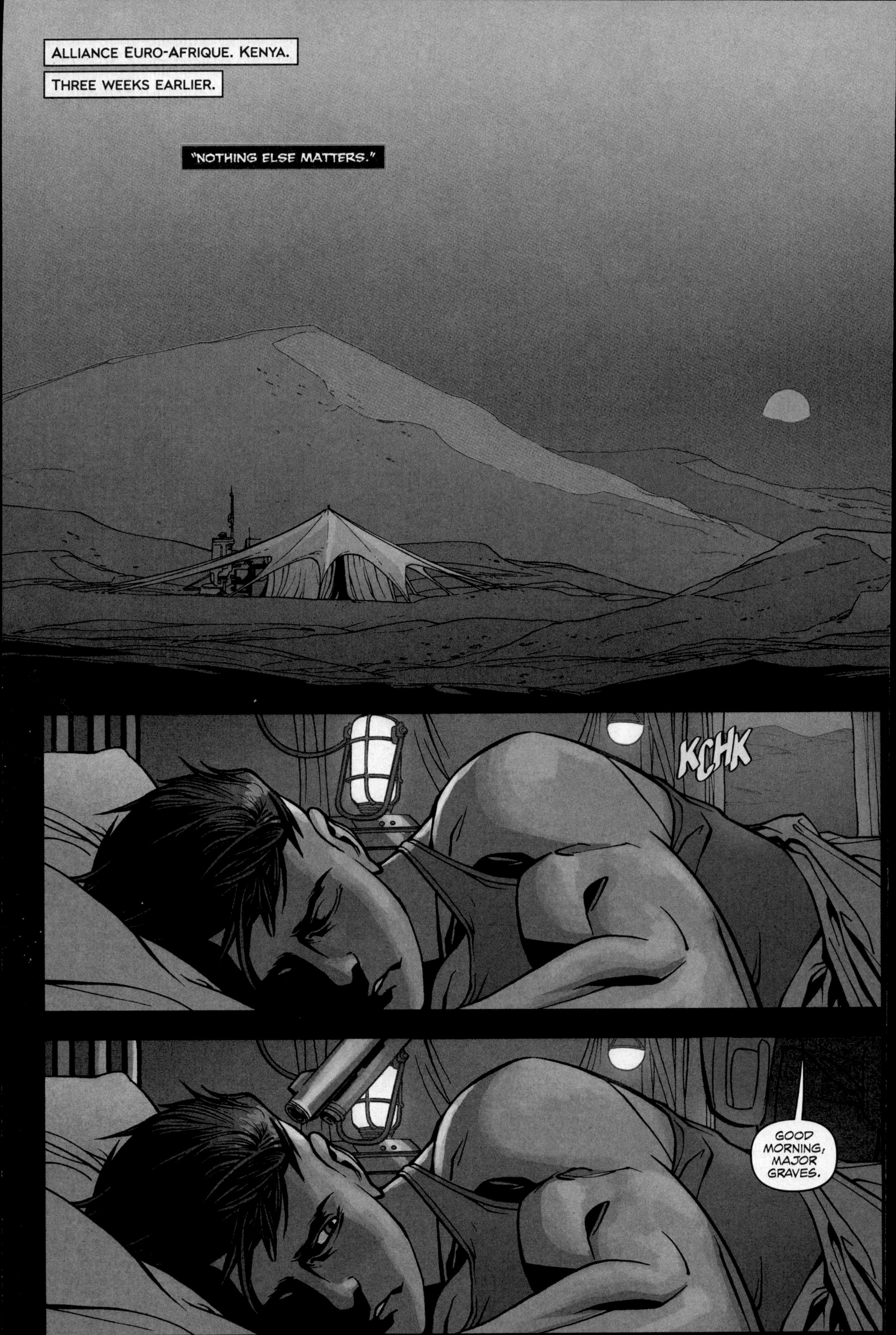
ALLIANCE EURO-AFRIQUE. KENYA.
THREE WEEKS EARLIER.
"NOTHING ELSE MATTERS."
KCHK
GOOD MORNING, MAJOR GRAVES.

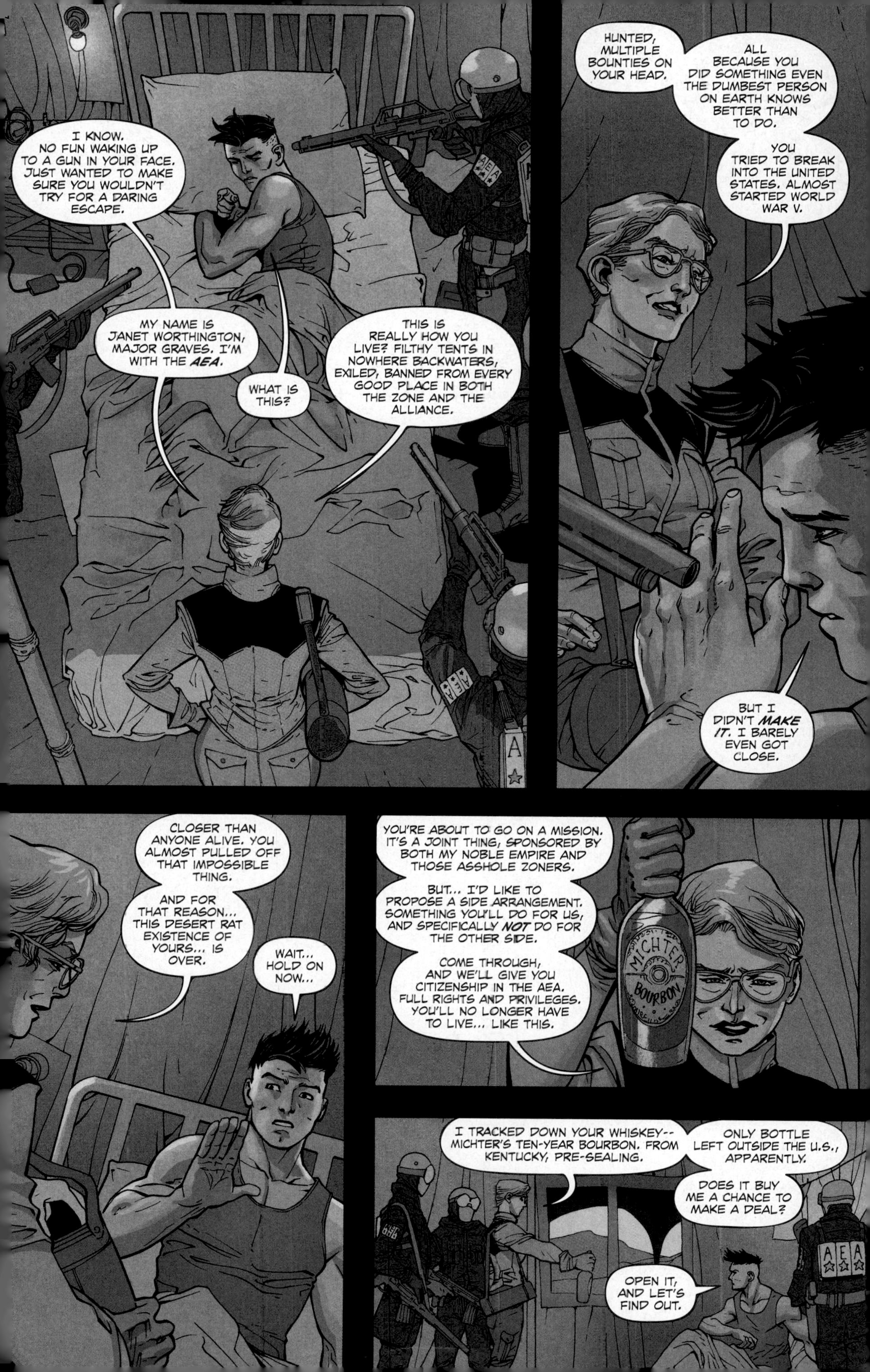

I KNOW. NO FUN WAKING UP TO A GUN IN YOUR FACE. JUST WANTED TO MAKE SURE YOU WOULDN'T TRY FOR A DARING ESCAPE.
MY NAME IS JANET WORTHINGTON, MAJOR GRAVES. I'M WITH THE *AEA*.
WHAT IS THIS?
THIS IS REALLY HOW YOU LIVE? FILTHY TENTS IN NOWHERE BACKWATERS, EXILED, BANNED FROM EVERY GOOD PLACE IN BOTH THE ZONE AND THE ALLIANCE.
HUNTED, MULTIPLE BOUNTIES ON YOUR HEAD.
ALL BECAUSE YOU DID SOMETHING EVEN THE DUMBEST PERSON ON EARTH KNOWS BETTER THAN TO DO.
YOU TRIED TO BREAK INTO THE UNITED STATES. ALMOST STARTED WORLD WAR V.
BUT I DIDN'T *MAKE IT*. I BARELY EVEN GOT CLOSE.
CLOSER THAN ANYONE ALIVE. YOU ALMOST PULLED OFF THAT IMPOSSIBLE THING.
AND FOR THAT REASON... THIS DESERT RAT EXISTENCE OF YOURS... IS OVER.
WAIT... HOLD ON NOW...
YOU'RE ABOUT TO GO ON A MISSION. IT'S A JOINT THING, SPONSORED BY BOTH MY NOBLE EMPIRE AND THOSE ASSHOLE ZONERS.
BUT... I'D LIKE TO PROPOSE A SIDE ARRANGEMENT. SOMETHING YOU'LL DO FOR US, AND SPECIFICALLY *NOT* DO FOR THE OTHER SIDE.
COME THROUGH, AND WE'LL GIVE YOU CITIZENSHIP IN THE AEA. FULL RIGHTS AND PRIVILEGES. YOU'LL NO LONGER HAVE TO LIVE... LIKE THIS.
MICHTER
BOURBON
I TRACKED DOWN YOUR WHISKEY-- MICHTER'S TEN-YEAR BOURBON. FROM KENTUCKY, PRE-SEALING.
ONLY BOTTLE LEFT OUTSIDE THE U.S., APPARENTLY.
DOES IT BUY ME A CHANCE TO MAKE A DEAL?
OPEN IT, AND LET'S FIND OUT.

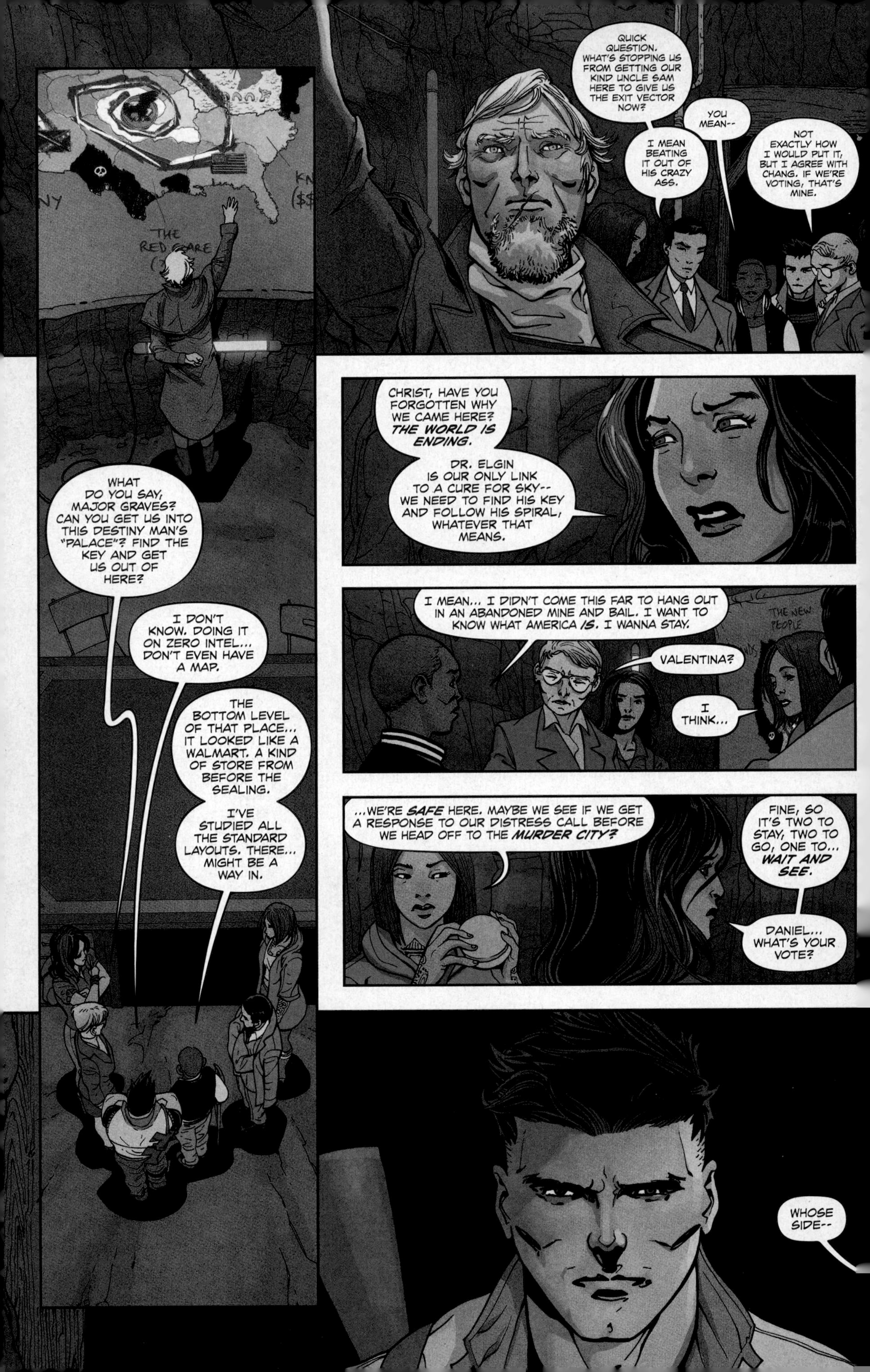
THE RED SCARE
QUICK QUESTION. WHAT'S STOPPING US FROM GETTING OUR KIND UNCLE SAM HERE TO GIVE US THE EXIT VECTOR NOW?
YOU MEAN--
I MEAN BEATING IT OUT OF HIS CRAZY ASS.
NOT EXACTLY HOW I WOULD PUT IT, BUT I AGREE WITH CHANG. IF WE'RE VOTING, THAT'S MINE.
CHRIST, HAVE YOU FORGOTTEN WHY WE CAME HERE? THE WORLD IS ENDING.
DR. ELGIN IS OUR ONLY LINK TO A CURE FOR SKY-- WE NEED TO FIND HIS KEY AND FOLLOW HIS SPIRAL, WHATEVER THAT MEANS.
WHAT DO YOU SAY, MAJOR GRAVES? CAN YOU GET US INTO THIS DESTINY MAN'S "PALACE"? FIND THE KEY AND GET US OUT OF HERE?
I DON'T KNOW. DOING IT ON ZERO INTEL... DON'T EVEN HAVE A MAP.
THE BOTTOM LEVEL OF THAT PLACE... IT LOOKED LIKE A WALMART. A KIND OF STORE FROM BEFORE THE SEALING.
I'VE STUDIED ALL THE STANDARD LAYOUTS. THERE... MIGHT BE A WAY IN.
I MEAN... I DIDN'T COME THIS FAR TO HANG OUT IN AN ABANDONED MINE AND BAIL. I WANT TO KNOW WHAT AMERICA IS. I WANNA STAY.
THE NEW PEOPLE
VALENTINA?
I THINK...
...WE'RE SAFE HERE. MAYBE WE SEE IF WE GET A RESPONSE TO OUR DISTRESS CALL BEFORE WE HEAD OFF TO THE MURDER CITY?
FINE, SO IT'S TWO TO STAY, TWO TO GO, ONE TO... WAIT AND SEE.
DANIEL... WHAT'S YOUR VOTE?
WHOSE SIDE--

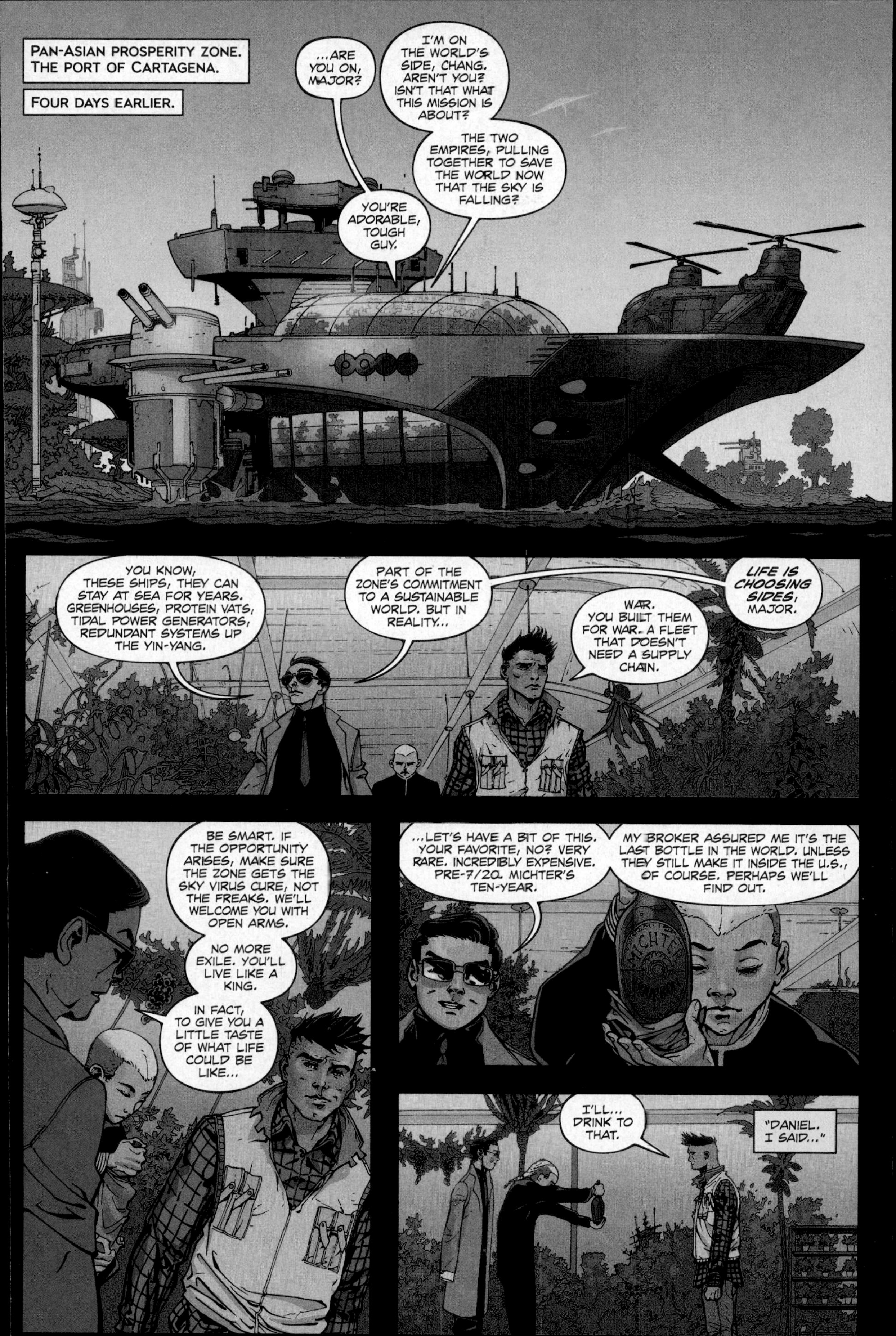

PAN-ASIAN PROSPERITY ZONE. THE PORT OF CARTAGENA.
FOUR DAYS EARLIER.
I'M ON THE WORLD'S SIDE, CHANG. AREN'T YOU? ISN'T THAT WHAT THIS MISSION IS ABOUT?
THE TWO EMPIRES, PULLING TOGETHER TO SAVE THE WORLD NOW THAT THE SKY IS FALLING?
...ARE YOU ON, MAJOR?
YOU'RE ADORABLE, TOUGH GUY.
YOU KNOW, THESE SHIPS, THEY CAN STAY AT SEA FOR YEARS. GREENHOUSES, PROTEIN VATS, TIDAL POWER GENERATORS, REDUNDANT SYSTEMS UP THE YIN-YANG.
PART OF THE ZONE'S COMMITMENT TO A SUSTAINABLE WORLD. BUT IN REALITY...
WAR. YOU BUILT THEM FOR WAR. A FLEET THAT DOESN'T NEED A SUPPLY CHAIN.
LIFE IS CHOOSING SIDES, MAJOR.
BE SMART. IF THE OPPORTUNITY ARISES, MAKE SURE THE ZONE GETS THE SKY VIRUS CURE, NOT THE FREAKS. WE'LL WELCOME YOU WITH OPEN ARMS.
NO MORE EXILE. YOU'LL LIVE LIKE A KING.
IN FACT, TO GIVE YOU A LITTLE TASTE OF WHAT LIFE COULD BE LIKE...
...LET'S HAVE A BIT OF THIS. YOUR FAVORITE, NO? VERY RARE. INCREDIBLY EXPENSIVE. PRE-7/20. MICHTER'S TEN-YEAR.
MY BROKER ASSURED ME IT'S THE LAST BOTTLE IN THE WORLD. UNLESS THEY STILL MAKE IT INSIDE THE U.S., OF COURSE. PERHAPS WE'LL FIND OUT.
MICHTER
I'LL... DRINK TO THAT.
"DANIEL. I SAID..."

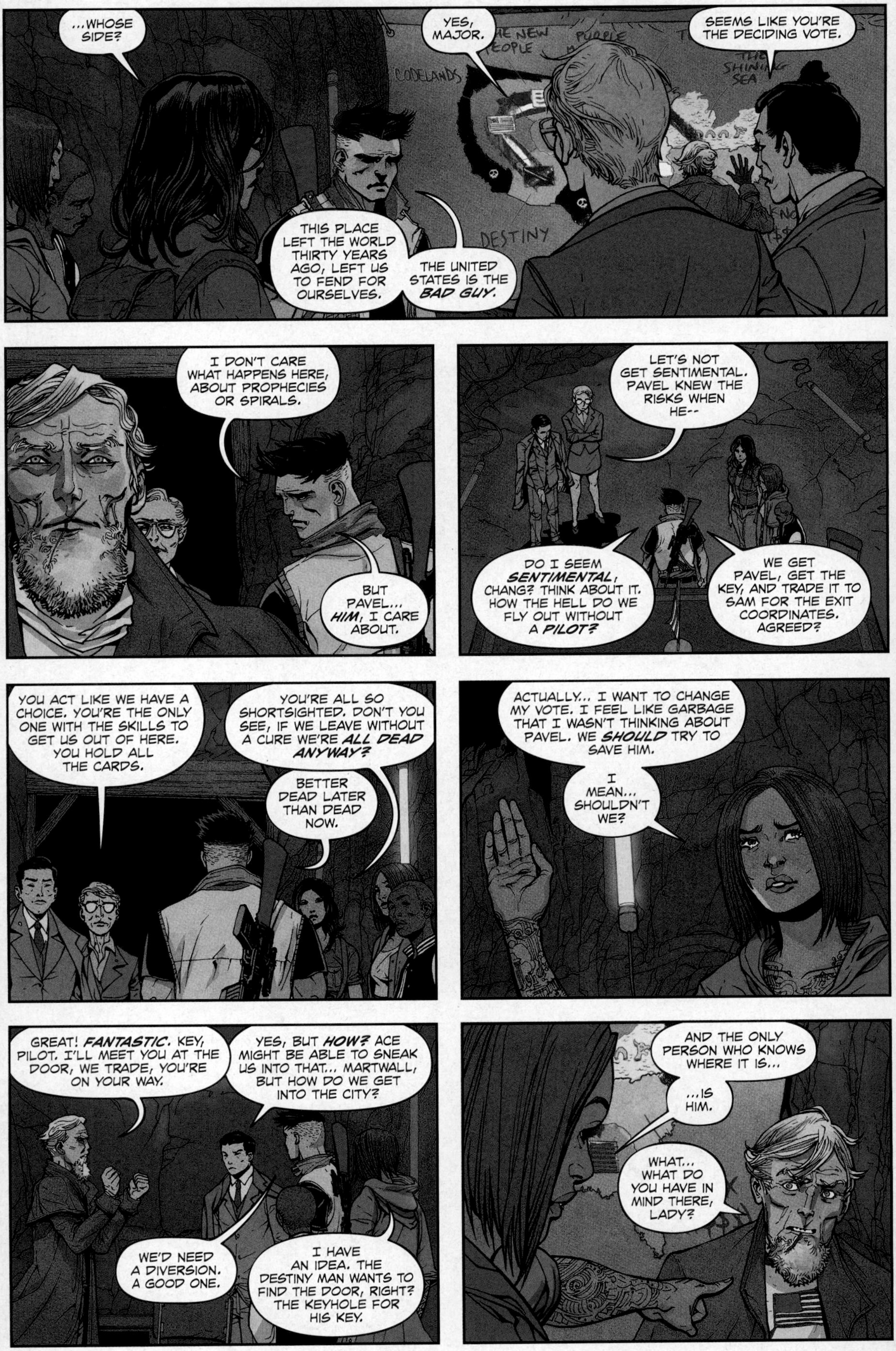

...WHOSE SIDE?
YES, MAJOR.
SEEMS LIKE YOU'RE THE DECIDING VOTE.
CODELANDS
PURPLE
THE SHINING SEA
DESTINY
THIS PLACE LEFT THE WORLD THIRTY YEARS AGO, LEFT US TO FEND FOR OURSELVES.
THE UNITED STATES IS THE BAD GUY.
I DON'T CARE WHAT HAPPENS HERE, ABOUT PROPHECIES OR SPIRALS.
BUT PAVEL... HIM, I CARE ABOUT.
LET'S NOT GET SENTIMENTAL. PAVEL KNEW THE RISKS WHEN HE--
DO I SEEM SENTIMENTAL, CHANG? THINK ABOUT IT. HOW THE HELL DO WE FLY OUT WITHOUT A PILOT?
WE GET PAVEL, GET THE KEY, AND TRADE IT TO SAM FOR THE EXIT COORDINATES. AGREED?
YOU ACT LIKE WE HAVE A CHOICE. YOU'RE THE ONLY ONE WITH THE SKILLS TO GET US OUT OF HERE. YOU HOLD ALL THE CARDS.
YOU'RE ALL SO SHORTSIGHTED. DON'T YOU SEE, IF WE LEAVE WITHOUT A CURE WE'RE ALL DEAD ANYWAY?
BETTER DEAD LATER THAN DEAD NOW.
ACTUALLY... I WANT TO CHANGE MY VOTE. I FEEL LIKE GARBAGE THAT I WASN'T THINKING ABOUT PAVEL. WE SHOULD TRY TO SAVE HIM.
I MEAN... SHOULDN'T WE?
GREAT! FANTASTIC. KEY, PILOT. I'LL MEET YOU AT THE DOOR, WE TRADE, YOU'RE ON YOUR WAY.
YES, BUT HOW? ACE MIGHT BE ABLE TO SNEAK US INTO THAT... MARTWALL, BUT HOW DO WE GET INTO THE CITY?
WE'D NEED A DIVERSION. A GOOD ONE.
I HAVE AN IDEA. THE DESTINY MAN WANTS TO FIND THE DOOR, RIGHT? THE KEYHOLE FOR HIS KEY.
AND THE ONLY PERSON WHO KNOWS WHERE IT IS...
...IS HIM.
WHAT... WHAT DO YOU HAVE IN MIND THERE, LADY?

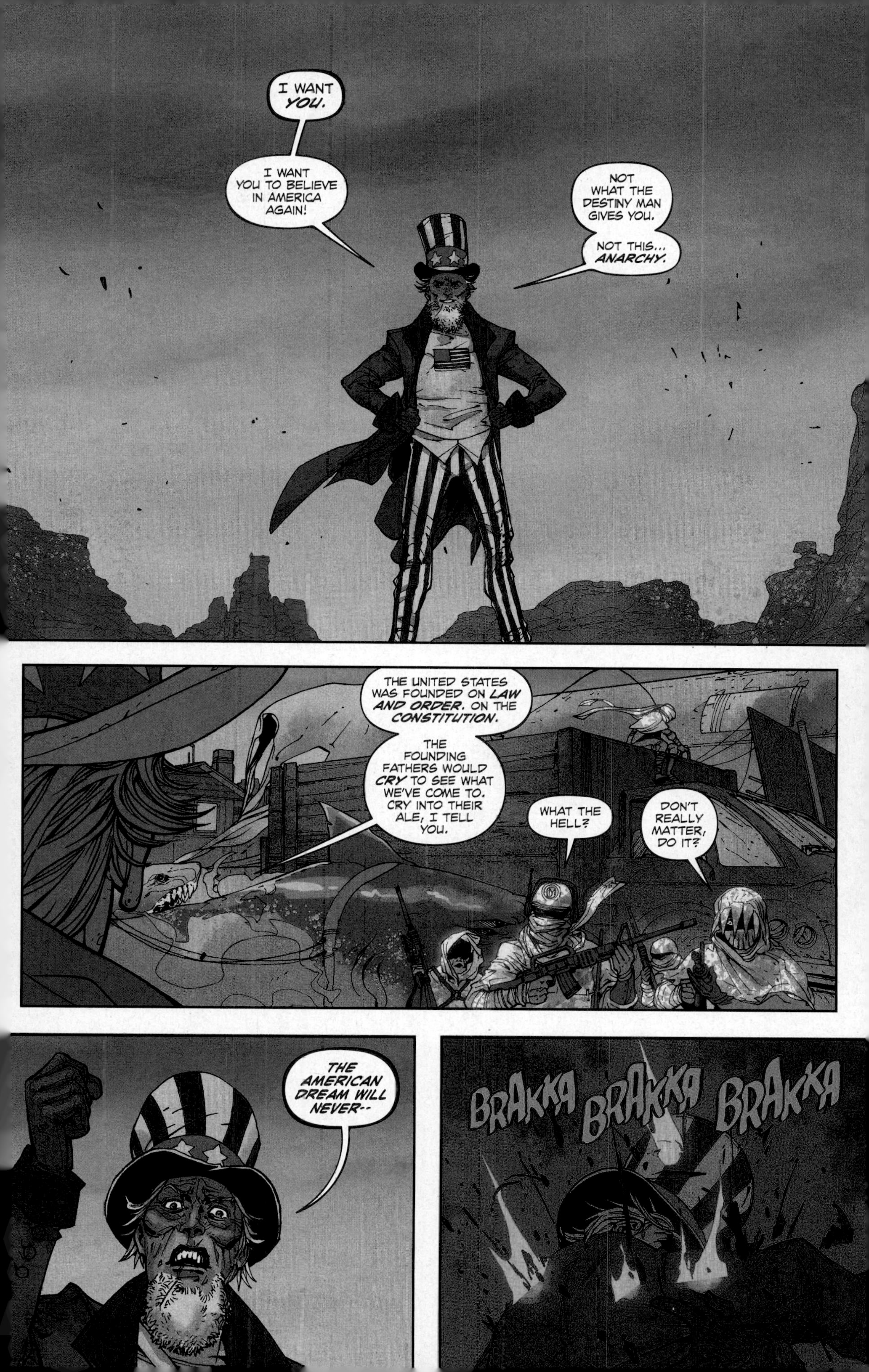

I WANT *YOU.*
I WANT YOU TO BELIEVE IN AMERICA AGAIN!
NOT WHAT THE DESTINY MAN GIVES YOU.
NOT THIS... *ANARCHY.*
THE UNITED STATES WAS FOUNDED ON *LAW AND ORDER.* ON THE *CONSTITUTION.*
THE FOUNDING FATHERS WOULD *CRY* TO SEE WHAT WE'VE COME TO. CRY INTO THEIR ALE, I TELL YOU.
WHAT THE HELL?
DON'T REALLY MATTER, DO IT?
THE AMERICAN DREAM WILL NEVER--
BRAKKA BRAKKA BRAKKA

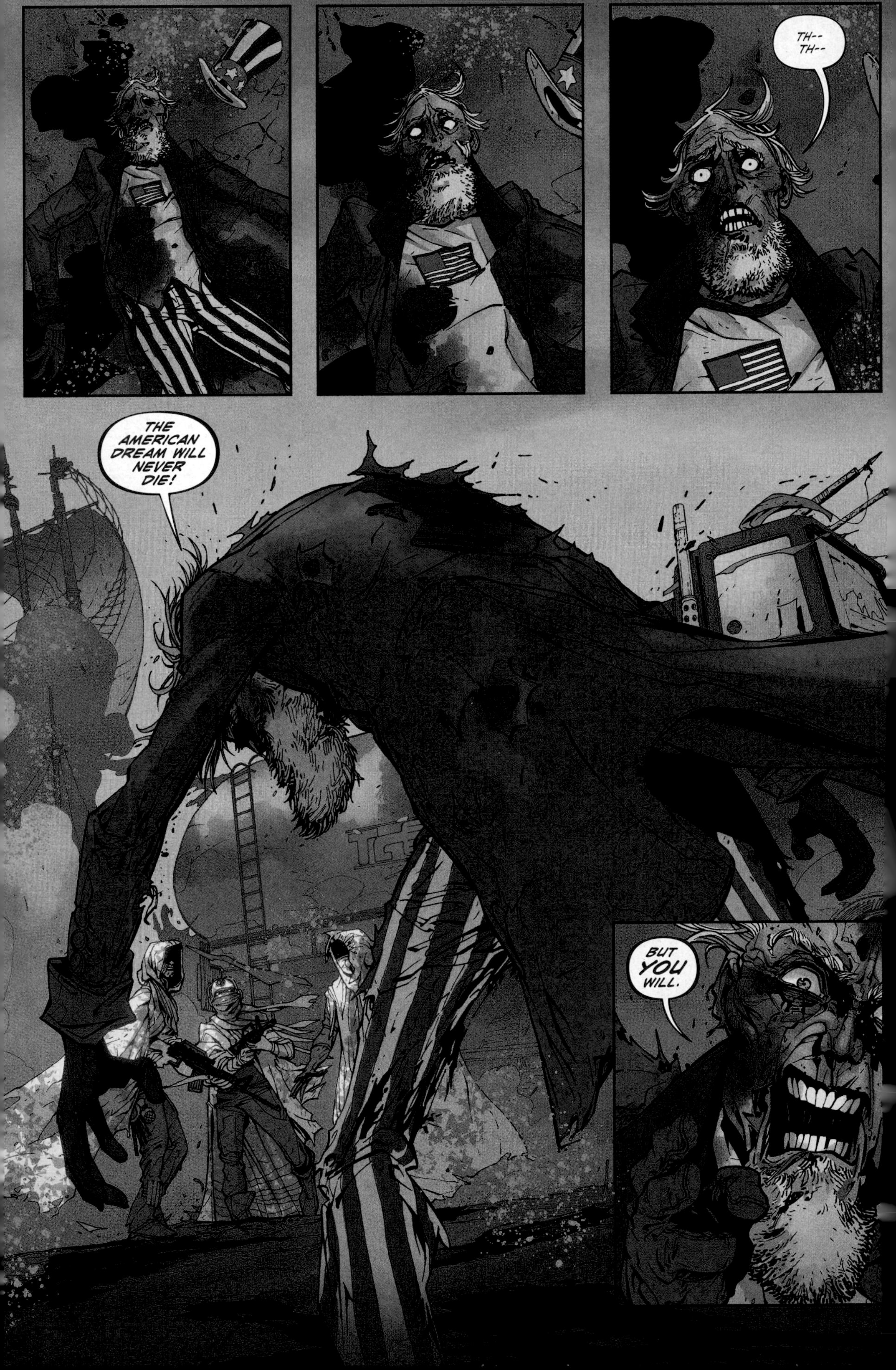
TH--
TH--
THE AMERICAN DREAM WILL NEVER DIE!
BUT YOU WILL.

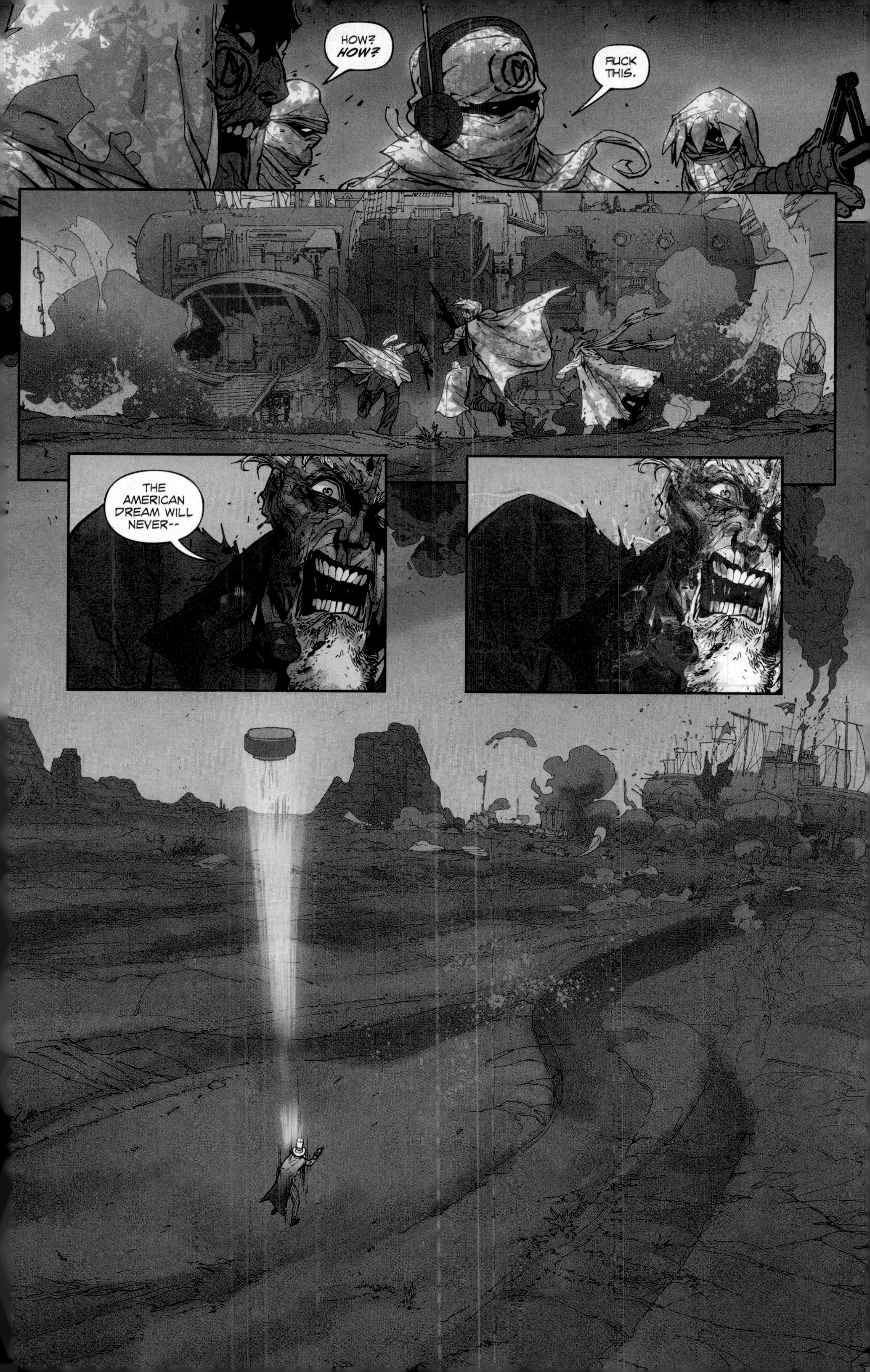
HOW? HOW?
FUCK THIS.
THE AMERICAN DREAM WILL NEVER--

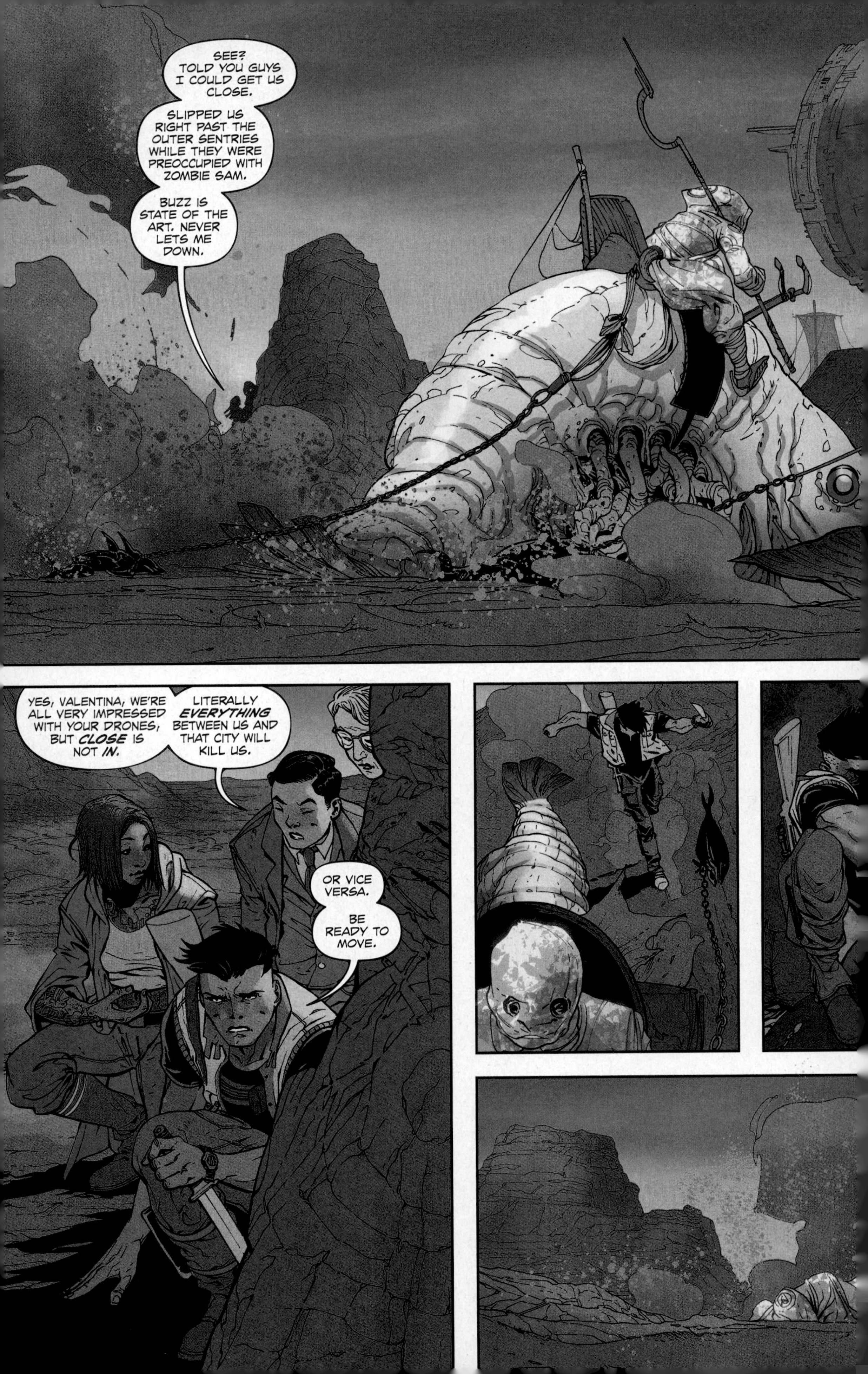
SEE? TOLD YOU GUYS I COULD GET US CLOSE.
SLIPPED US RIGHT PAST THE OUTER SENTRIES WHILE THEY WERE PREOCCUPIED WITH ZOMBIE SAM.
BUZZ IS STATE OF THE ART. NEVER LETS ME DOWN.
YES, VALENTINA, WE'RE ALL VERY IMPRESSED WITH YOUR DRONES, BUT *CLOSE* IS NOT *IN*.
LITERALLY *EVERYTHING* BETWEEN US AND THAT CITY WILL KILL US.
OR VICE VERSA.
BE READY TO MOVE.

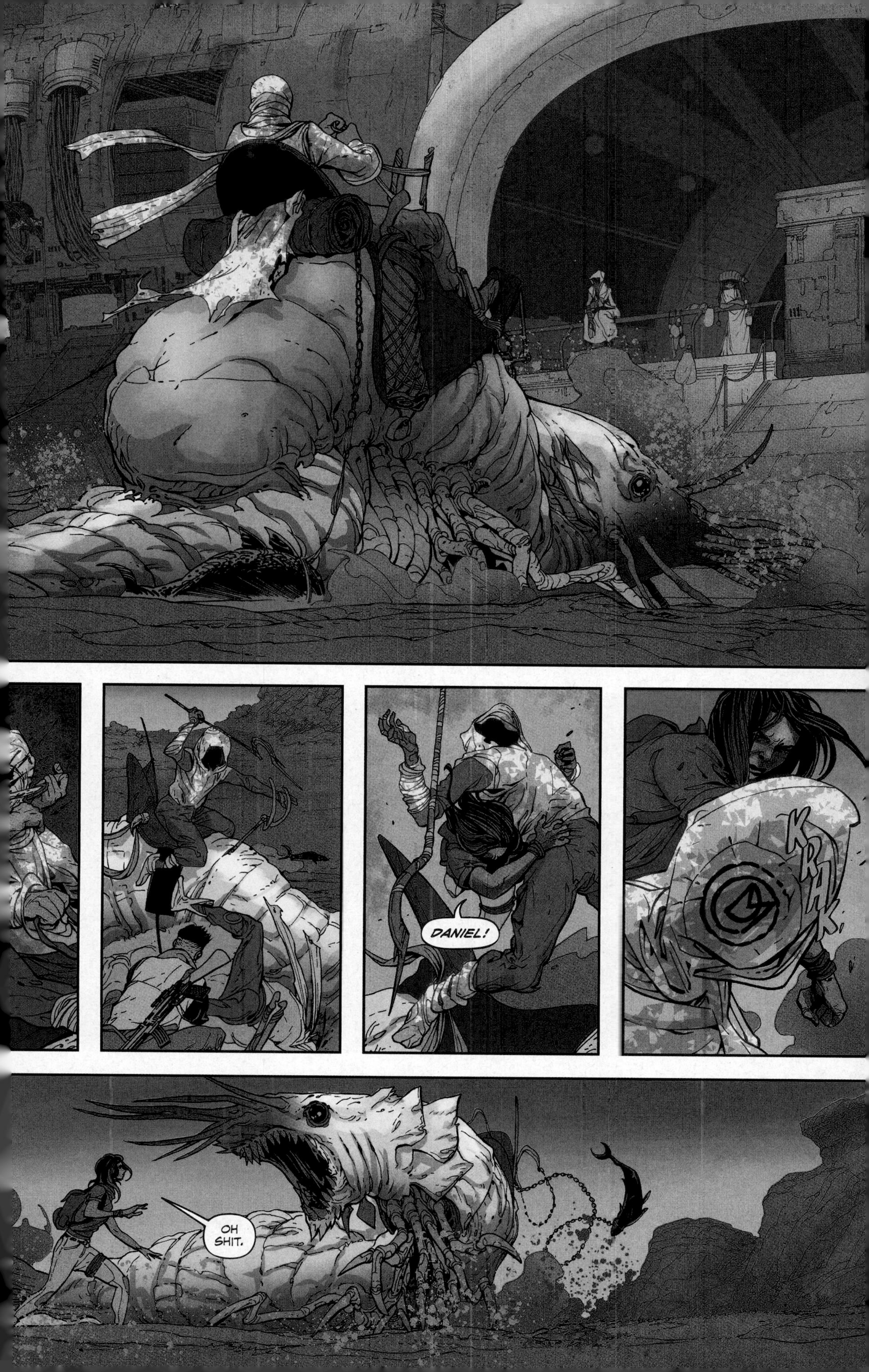
DANIEL!
KRAK
OH SHIT.

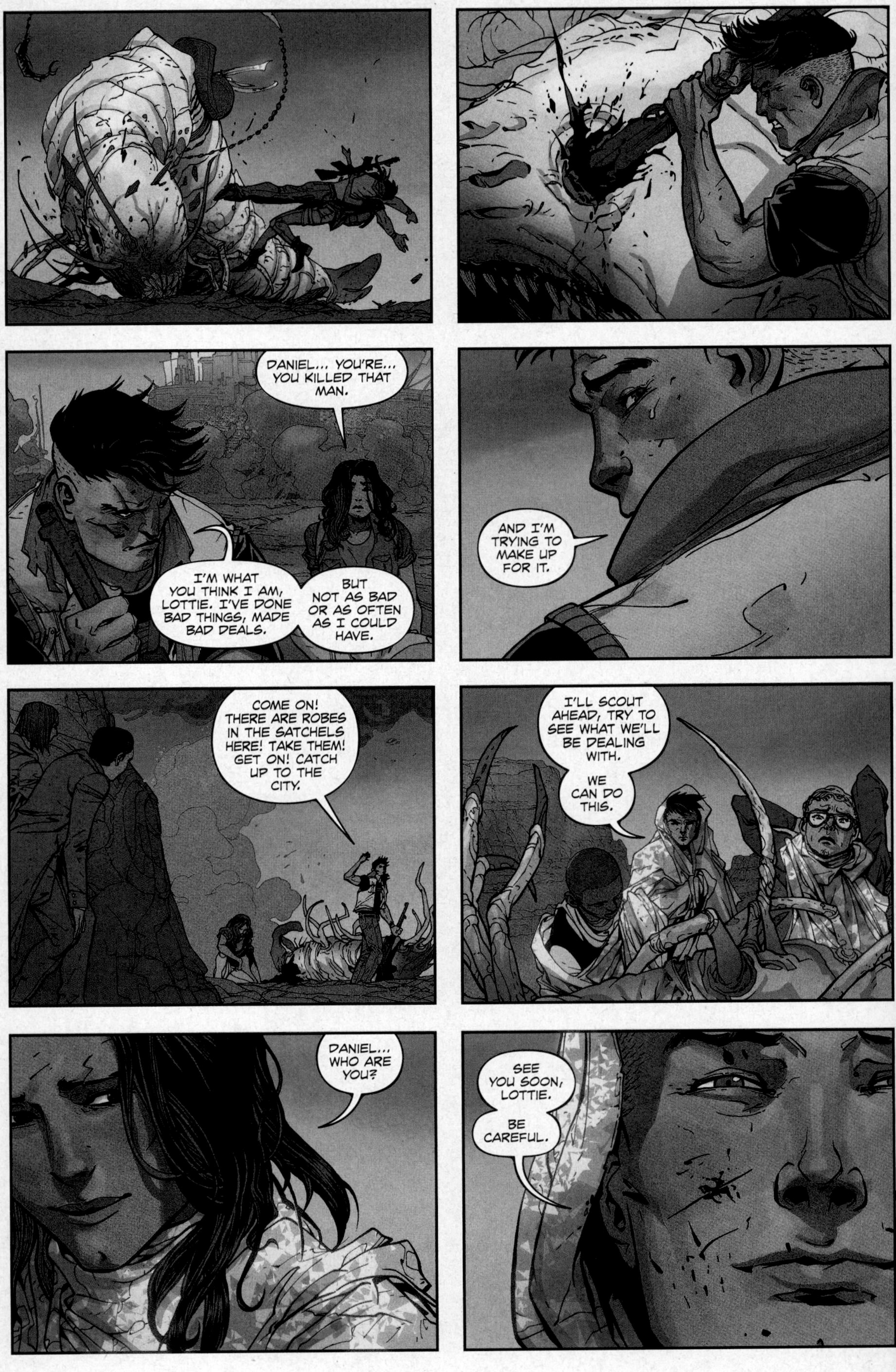
DANIEL... YOU'RE... YOU KILLED THAT MAN.
I'M WHAT YOU THINK I AM, LOTTIE. I'VE DONE BAD THINGS, MADE BAD DEALS.
BUT NOT AS BAD OR AS OFTEN AS I COULD HAVE.
AND I'M TRYING TO MAKE UP FOR IT.
COME ON! THERE ARE ROBES IN THE SATCHELS HERE! TAKE THEM! GET ON! CATCH UP TO THE CITY.
I'LL SCOUT AHEAD, TRY TO SEE WHAT WE'LL BE DEALING WITH.
WE CAN DO THIS.
DANIEL... WHO ARE YOU?
SEE YOU SOON, LOTTIE.
BE CAREFUL.

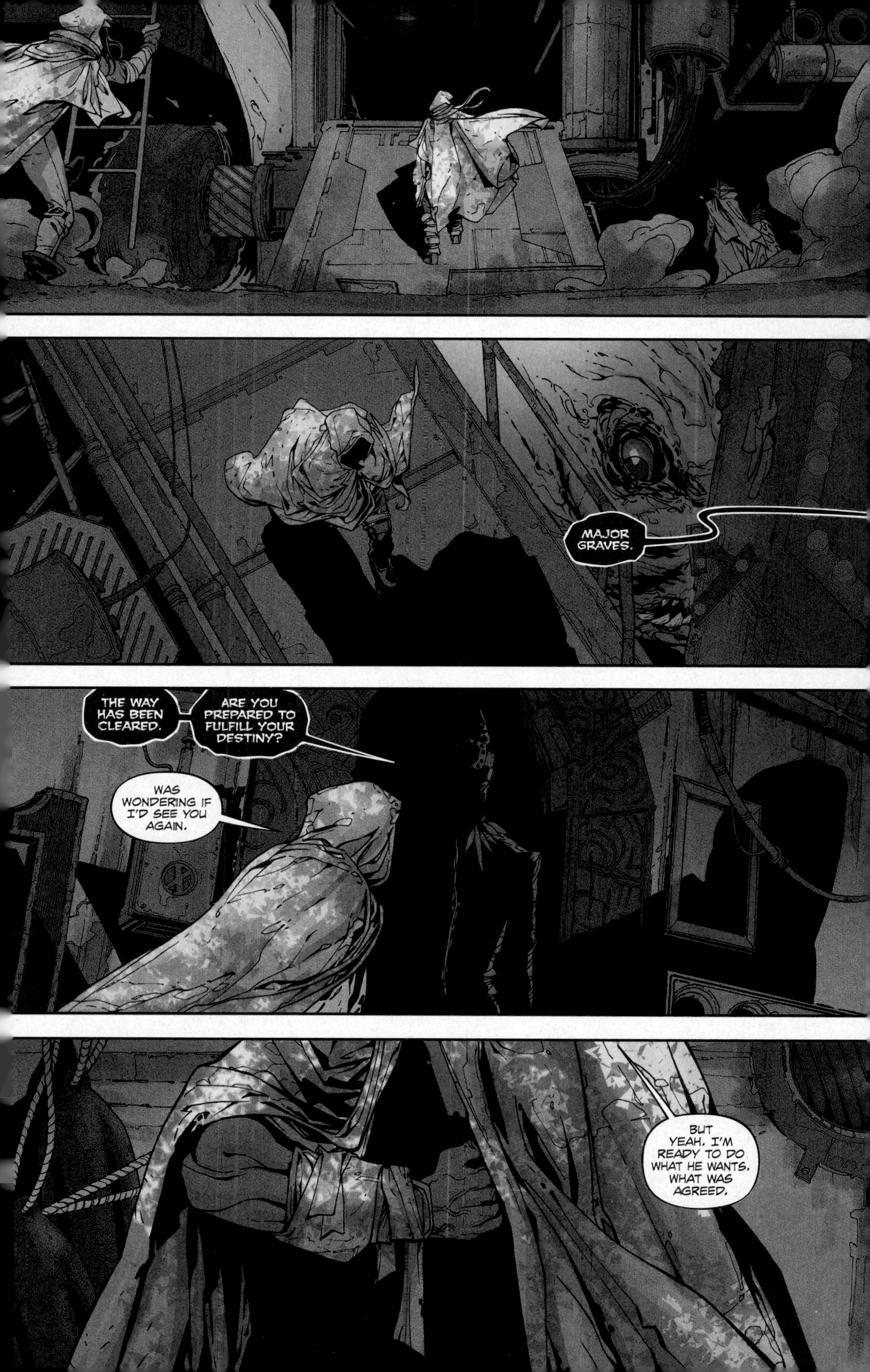
MAJOR GRAVES.
THE WAY HAS BEEN CLEARED.
ARE YOU PREPARED TO FULFILL YOUR DESTINY?
WAS WONDERING IF I'D SEE YOU AGAIN.
BUT YEAH. I'M READY TO DO WHAT HE WANTS. WHAT WAS AGREED.

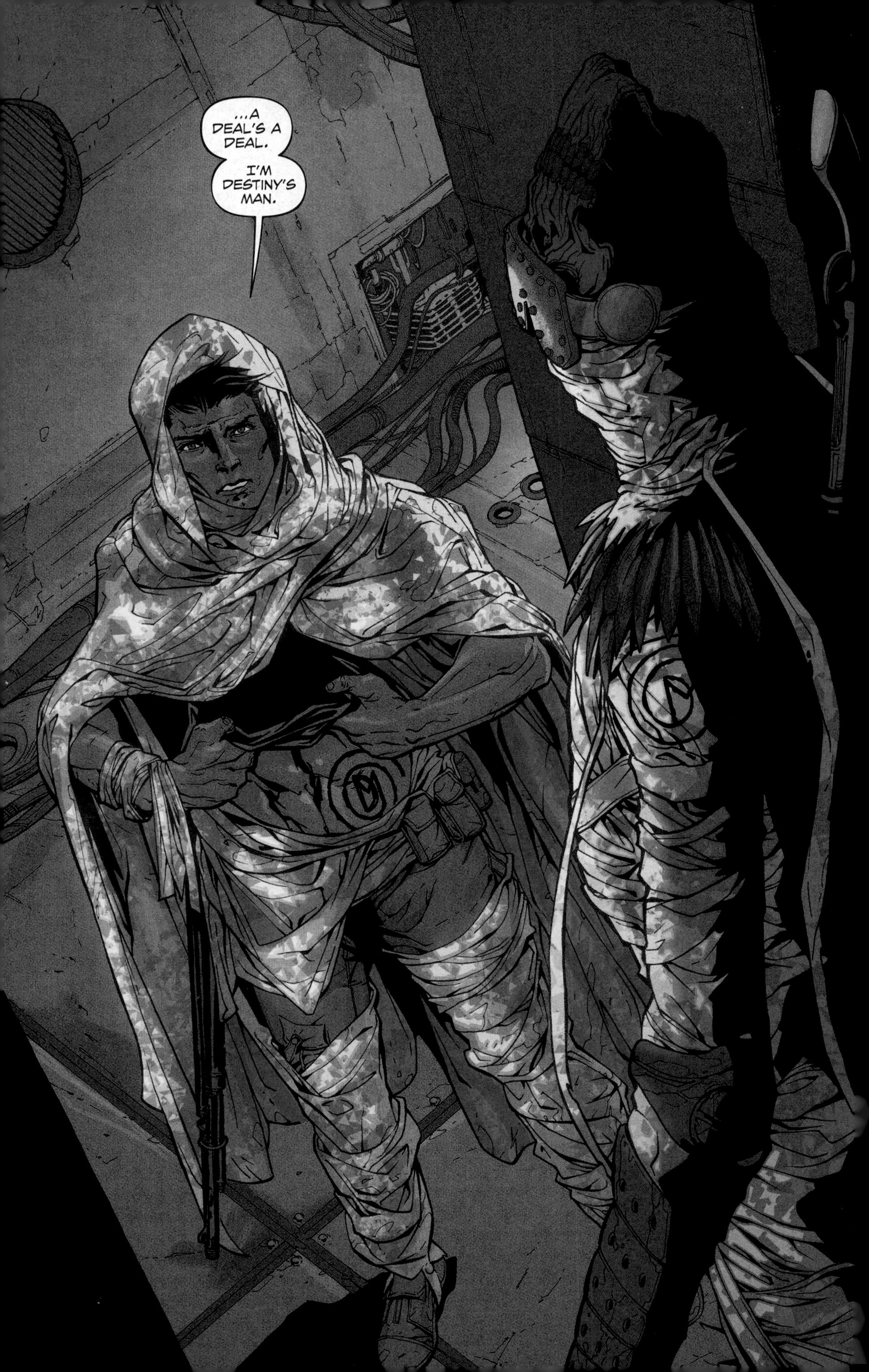
...A DEAL'S A DEAL.
I'M DESTINY'S MAN.

"I miss the music. Do you think American bands kept recording albums after the Sealing? I wonder if we'll ever hear them."

—Siobhan Shalvey, 42, architect, Dublin, Alliance Euro-Afrique

"They made Episode XII but I didn't like it as much. It was after the Sealing so half of the actors were digital, and back then, they still looked pretty fake."

—Mani Acharya, 21, student, Mumbai, Pan-Asian Prosperity Zone

"My husband and I were on our honeymoon when the Sealing happened. We thought we'd spend a nice few weeks in Italy, then head back home to Pittsburgh to our apartment and begin our lives together. Didn't work out that way, obviously. We've been in Milan ever since. It could be worse, though. I was originally supposed to meet him a few days later, and decided to fly over early as a surprise. If I'd waited... we'd never have seen each other again."

—Jerry Nolan, 65, Milan, Alliance Euro-Afrique

Quotes from *The New World: An Oral History of the Sealing* by Valentina Sandoval.

CHAPTER THREE

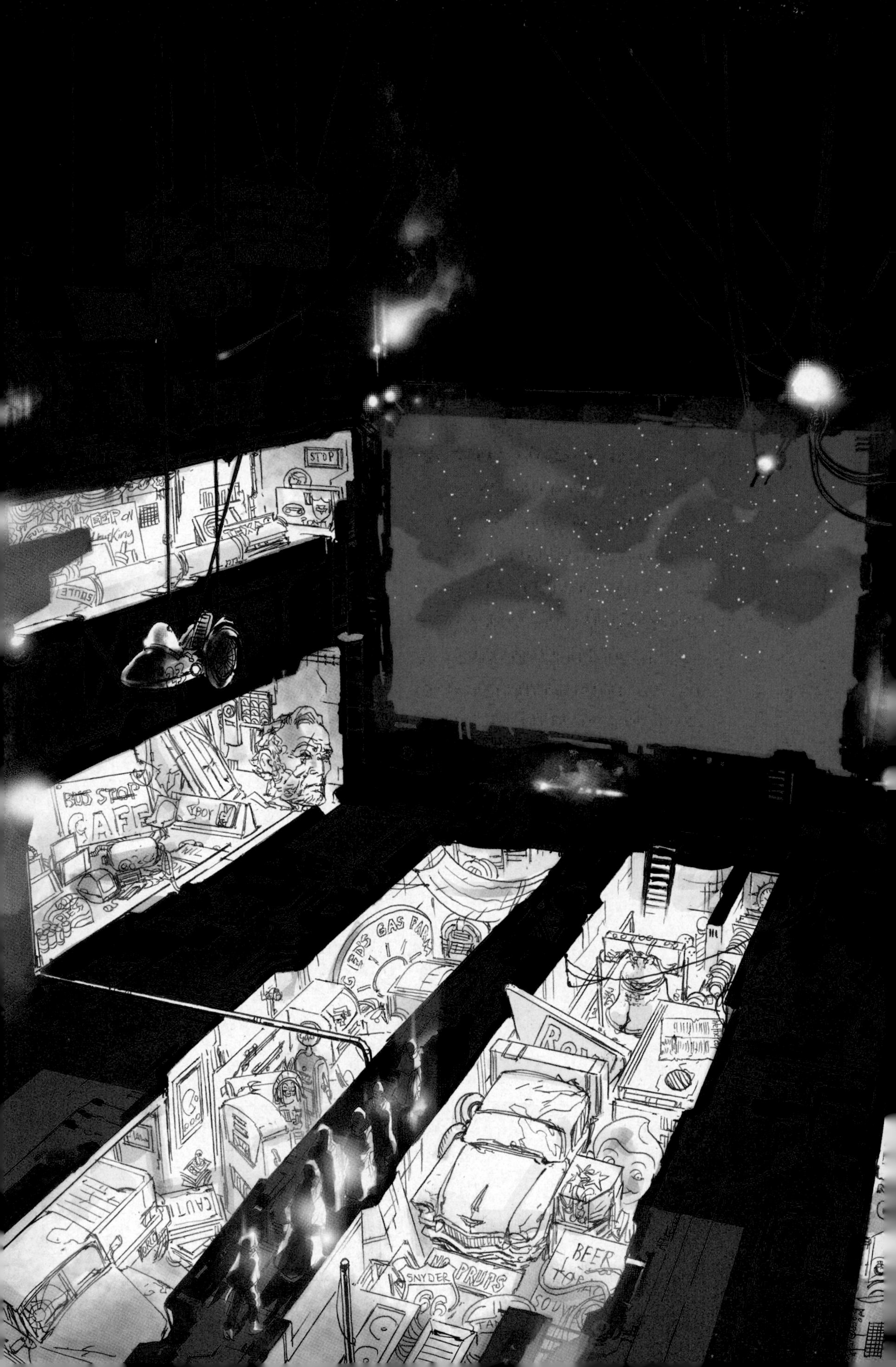
STOP
BUS STOP
CAFE
BEER
SNYDER

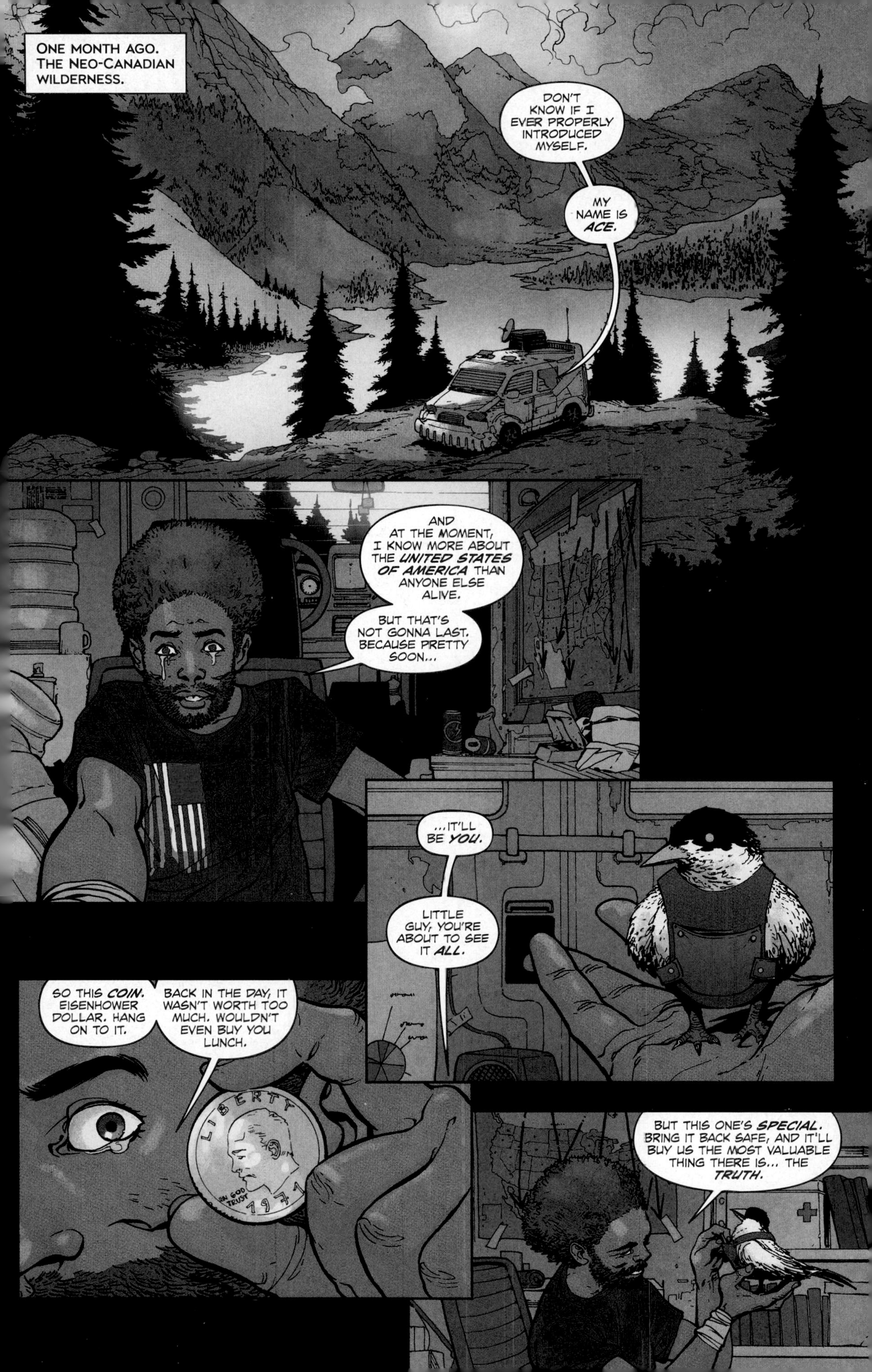

ONE MONTH AGO. THE NEO-CANADIAN WILDERNESS.
DON'T KNOW IF I EVER PROPERLY INTRODUCED MYSELF.
MY NAME IS ACE.
AND AT THE MOMENT, I KNOW MORE ABOUT THE UNITED STATES OF AMERICA THAN ANYONE ELSE ALIVE.
BUT THAT'S NOT GONNA LAST. BECAUSE PRETTY SOON...
...IT'LL BE YOU.
LITTLE GUY, YOU'RE ABOUT TO SEE IT ALL.
SO THIS COIN. EISENHOWER DOLLAR. HANG ON TO IT.
BACK IN THE DAY, IT WASN'T WORTH TOO MUCH. WOULDN'T EVEN BUY YOU LUNCH.
LIBERTY
1971
BUT THIS ONE'S SPECIAL. BRING IT BACK SAFE, AND IT'LL BUY US THE MOST VALUABLE THING THERE IS... THE TRUTH.

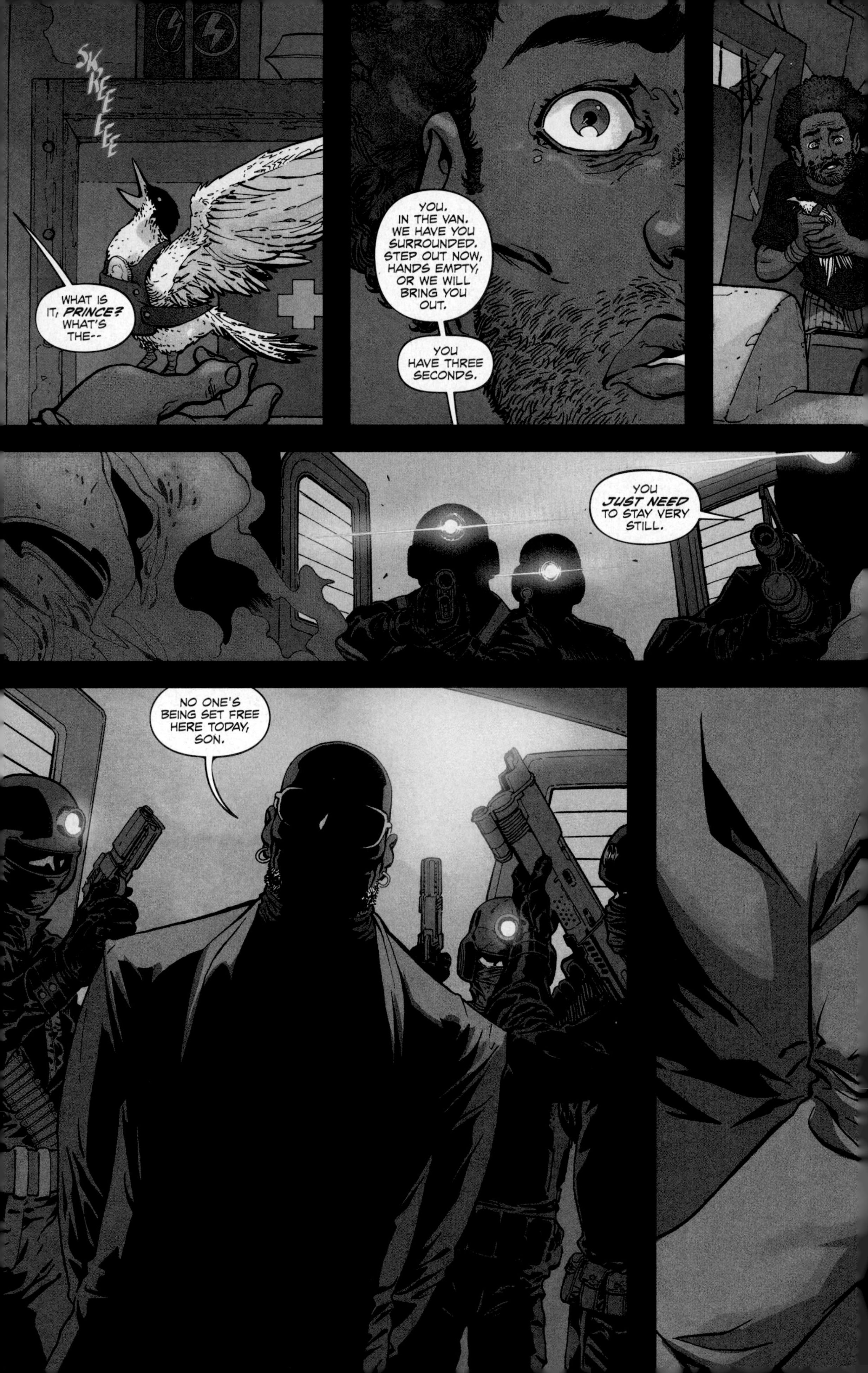

SKREEEEEE
WHAT IS IT, *PRINCE?* WHAT'S THE--
YOU. IN THE VAN. WE HAVE YOU SURROUNDED. STEP OUT NOW, HANDS EMPTY, OR WE WILL BRING YOU OUT.
YOU HAVE THREE SECONDS.
YOU *JUST NEED* TO STAY VERY STILL.
NO ONE'S BEING SET FREE HERE TODAY, SON.

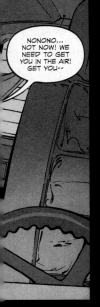

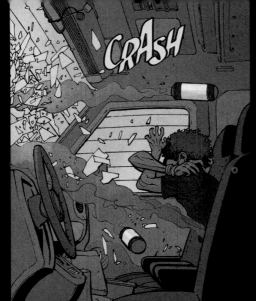

NONONO... NOT NOW! WE NEED TO GET YOU IN THE AIR! GET YOU--
CRASH
GAK! PLEASE... I JUST NEED--
TSSSSSSSSSSSS
I'LL--COUGH COUGH I'LL GIVE YOU EVERYTHING I HAVE! JUST... THE BIRD! JUST LET ME SET HIM FREE!
WARREN? WHAT THE HELL? WHY?
WHY ARE YOU DOING THIS?!
YOU KNOW WHY.
YOU'RE THE GREAT ACE KENYATTA.
TO HEAR YOU TELL IT, YOU KNOW MORE ABOUT THE UNITED STATES OF AMERICA THAN ANYONE ELSE ALIVE.
LET'S HOPE YOU'RE RIGHT.
LIBERTY

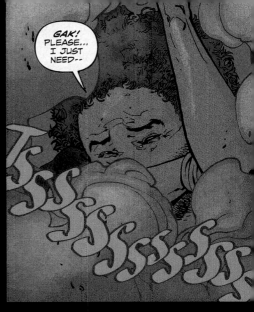

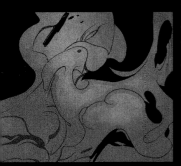

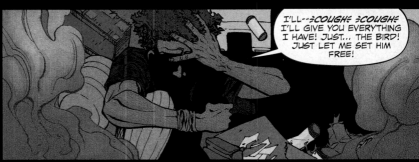

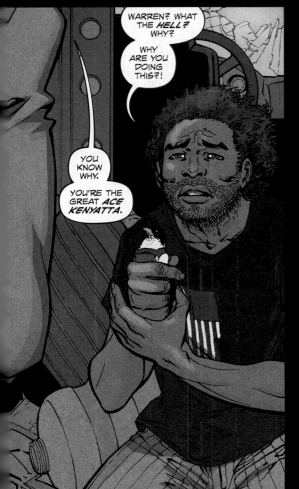

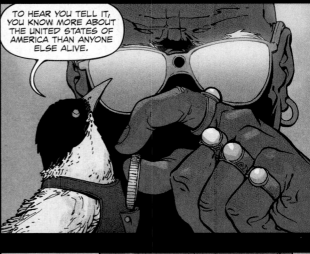

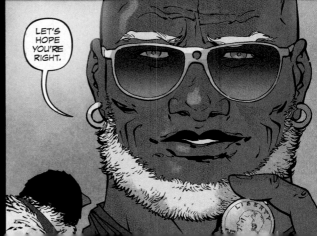

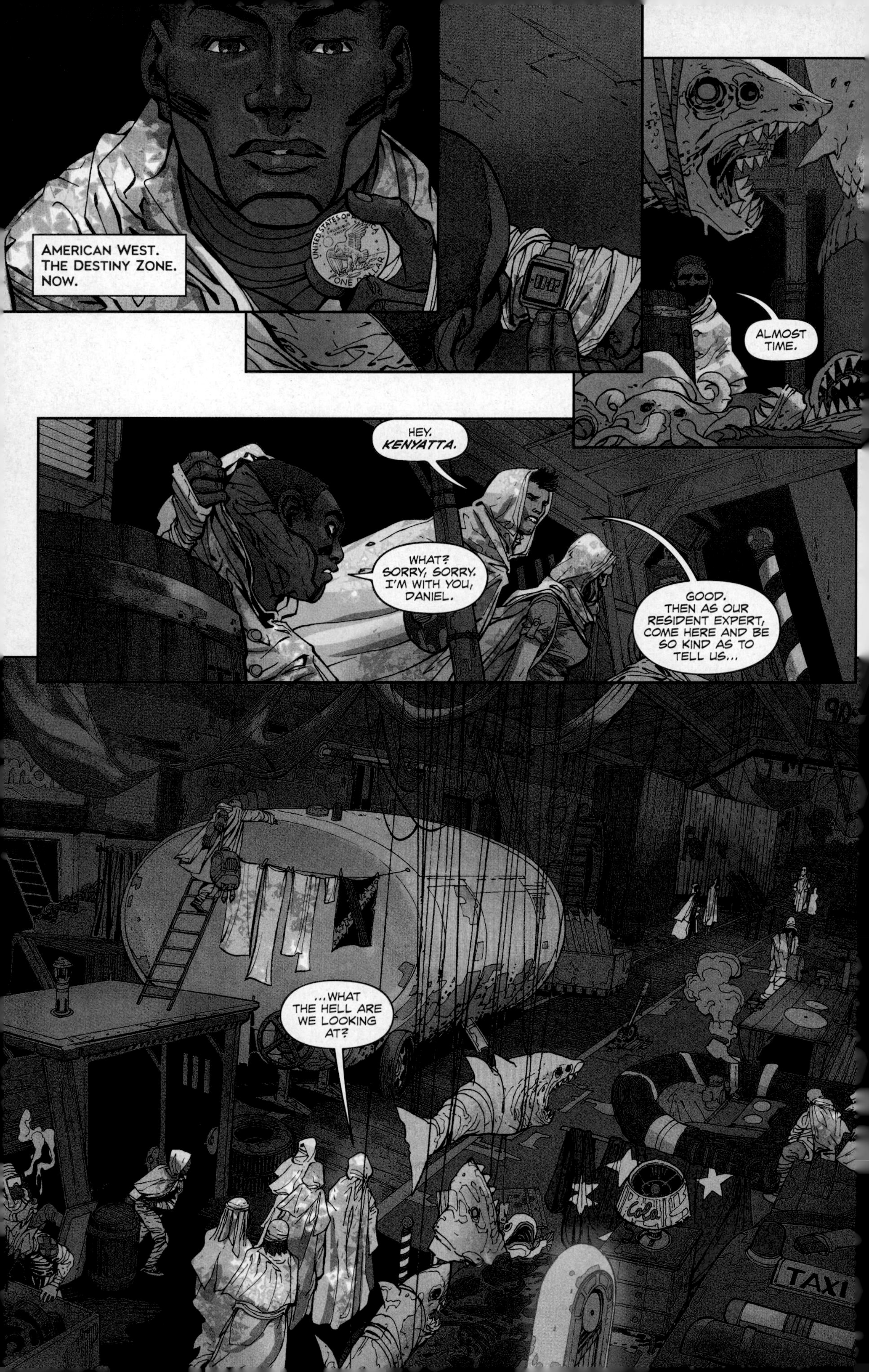
AMERICAN WEST.
THE DESTINY ZONE.
NOW.
ALMOST TIME.
HEY. *KENYATTA.*
WHAT? SORRY, SORRY. I'M WITH YOU, DANIEL.
GOOD. THEN AS OUR RESIDENT EXPERT, COME HERE AND BE SO KIND AS TO TELL US...
...WHAT THE HELL ARE WE LOOKING AT?
TAXI

IT'S... A MARKET. BUILT FROM AN OLD BOX STORE. I THINK IT'S A **WALMART**, PROBABLY CONVERTED TO AN **AMAZON BROWSE** AFTER THE GREAT ABSORPTION IN 2024. THAT'S WHEN--

WE DON'T NEED A HISTORY LESSON. WE NEED A WAY THROUGH.

DR. ELGIN... COME IN!

WE SHOULD MOVE. FOLKS ARE STARTING TO NOTICE US...

DR. ELGIN! "UNCLE **SAM**." ARE YOU THERE?

HERE AND LISTENING.

WE'RE INSIDE THE DESTINY MAN'S CITY. WHERE'S THIS **KEY** WE NEED?

THE DESTINY CARAVAN HAS THREE LEVELS. THE MARKET, THE PARKING LOT, AND--**ZZZT**-- UP TOP IS THE **NEON THRONE ROOM.**

THAT'S WHERE THE DESTINY MAN LIVES, AND IF YOU CAN GET UP THERE, THAT'S WHERE YOU'LL FIND HIS **KEY.**

WHICH I'M SURE HE'LL JUST **GLADLY** HAND OVER.

ONE PROBLEM AT A TIME, CHANG.

I... I CAN GET US UP TOP, I THINK. THAT'S SOMETHING, AT LEAST.

JUST GIVE ME A SECOND TO--I WANT TO JUST CHECK ONE THING...

HMM... YEAH, I THINK--

ACE! **FOCUS!**

VALENTINA WAS RIGHT. PEOPLE **WILL** NOTICE US IF WE STAND AROUND TOO LONG, AND THAT'S HOW WE GET EATEN BY THE WALKING SHARKS.

IF YOU'VE GOT AN IDEA, STOP CHECKING YOUR DAMN WATCH AND LET'S HEAR IT.

I **DO** HAVE AN IDEA, DANIEL, BUT THE TIME IS--

THE TIME IS **NOW**, ASSHOLE. EITHER HELP OR **I'LL** FEED YOU TO THE SHARKS MYSELF!

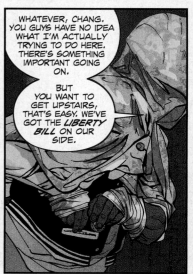

WHATEVER, CHANG. YOU GUYS HAVE NO IDEA WHAT I'M ACTUALLY TRYING TO DO HERE. THERE'S SOMETHING IMPORTANT GOING ON.

BUT YOU WANT TO GET UPSTAIRS, THAT'S EASY. WE'VE GOT THE **LIBERTY BILL** ON OUR SIDE.

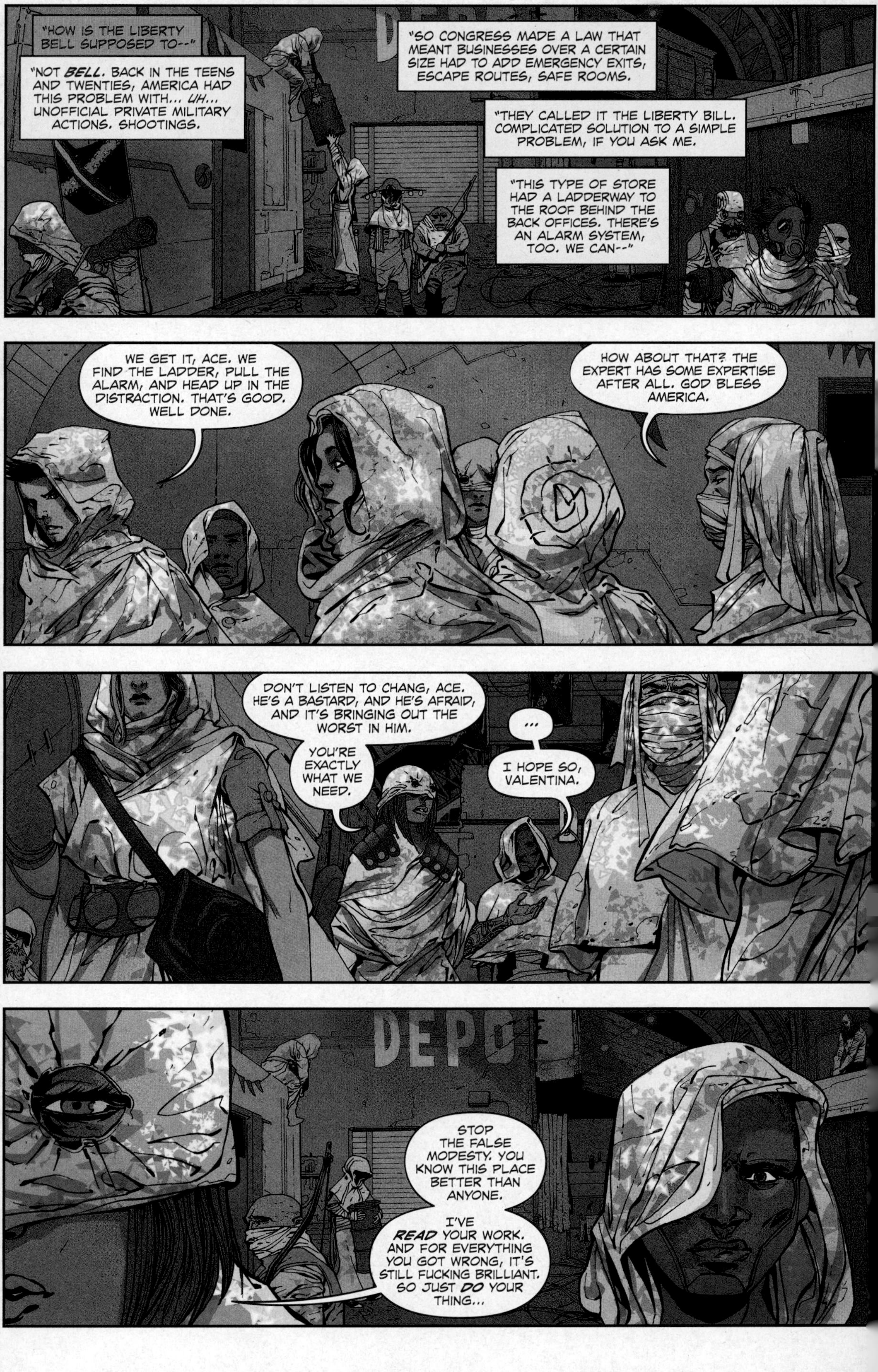

"HOW IS THE LIBERTY BELL SUPPOSED TO--"
"NOT *BELL*. BACK IN THE TEENS AND TWENTIES, AMERICA HAD THIS PROBLEM WITH... *UH*... UNOFFICIAL PRIVATE MILITARY ACTIONS. SHOOTINGS.
"SO CONGRESS MADE A LAW THAT MEANT BUSINESSES OVER A CERTAIN SIZE HAD TO ADD EMERGENCY EXITS, ESCAPE ROUTES, SAFE ROOMS.
"THEY CALLED IT THE LIBERTY BILL. COMPLICATED SOLUTION TO A SIMPLE PROBLEM, IF YOU ASK ME.
"THIS TYPE OF STORE HAD A LADDERWAY TO THE ROOF BEHIND THE BACK OFFICES. THERE'S AN ALARM SYSTEM, TOO. WE CAN--"
WE GET IT, ACE. WE FIND THE LADDER, PULL THE ALARM, AND HEAD UP IN THE DISTRACTION. THAT'S GOOD. WELL DONE.
HOW ABOUT THAT? THE EXPERT HAS SOME EXPERTISE AFTER ALL. GOD BLESS AMERICA.
DON'T LISTEN TO CHANG, ACE. HE'S A BASTARD, AND HE'S AFRAID, AND IT'S BRINGING OUT THE WORST IN HIM.
YOU'RE EXACTLY WHAT WE NEED.
...
I HOPE SO, VALENTINA.
DEPO
STOP THE FALSE MODESTY. YOU KNOW THIS PLACE BETTER THAN ANYONE.
I'VE *READ* YOUR WORK. AND FOR EVERYTHING YOU GOT WRONG, IT'S STILL FUCKING BRILLIANT. SO JUST *DO* YOUR THING...

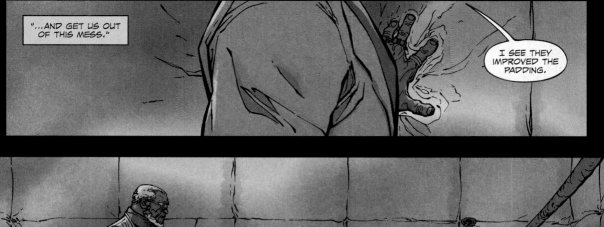

"...AND GET US OUT OF THIS MESS."

I SEE THEY IMPROVED THE PADDING.

LOOK AT THAT. CHANGES COLOR, TOO. I HEAR IT'S SUPPOSED TO BE GOOD FOR THE SPIRIT.

HOW'S YOUR SPIRIT THESE DAYS, DR. KENYATTA?

WHAT DO YOU WANT, WARREN?

IT PAINS ME SEEING YOU LIKE THIS. ALL YOUR WRITINGS... THE INSIGHTS INTO THE SEALED AMERICA. SUCH FURY, SUCH HOPE.

"FINAL FORM CAPITALISM: A HIGHER STANDARD." "THE WALLED GARDEN: AN AMERICAN DIGRESSION." AND THEN... =SIGH=

THEN I WENT WHERE THE RESEARCH LED!

MM. YOUR RESEARCH. THE IDEAS THAT LED YOU TO BE A DANGER TO YOURSELF AND OTHERS, AND WHICH, ULTIMATELY, BROUGHT YOU HERE.

YES, LET'S TALK ABOUT YOUR RESEARCH.

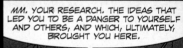

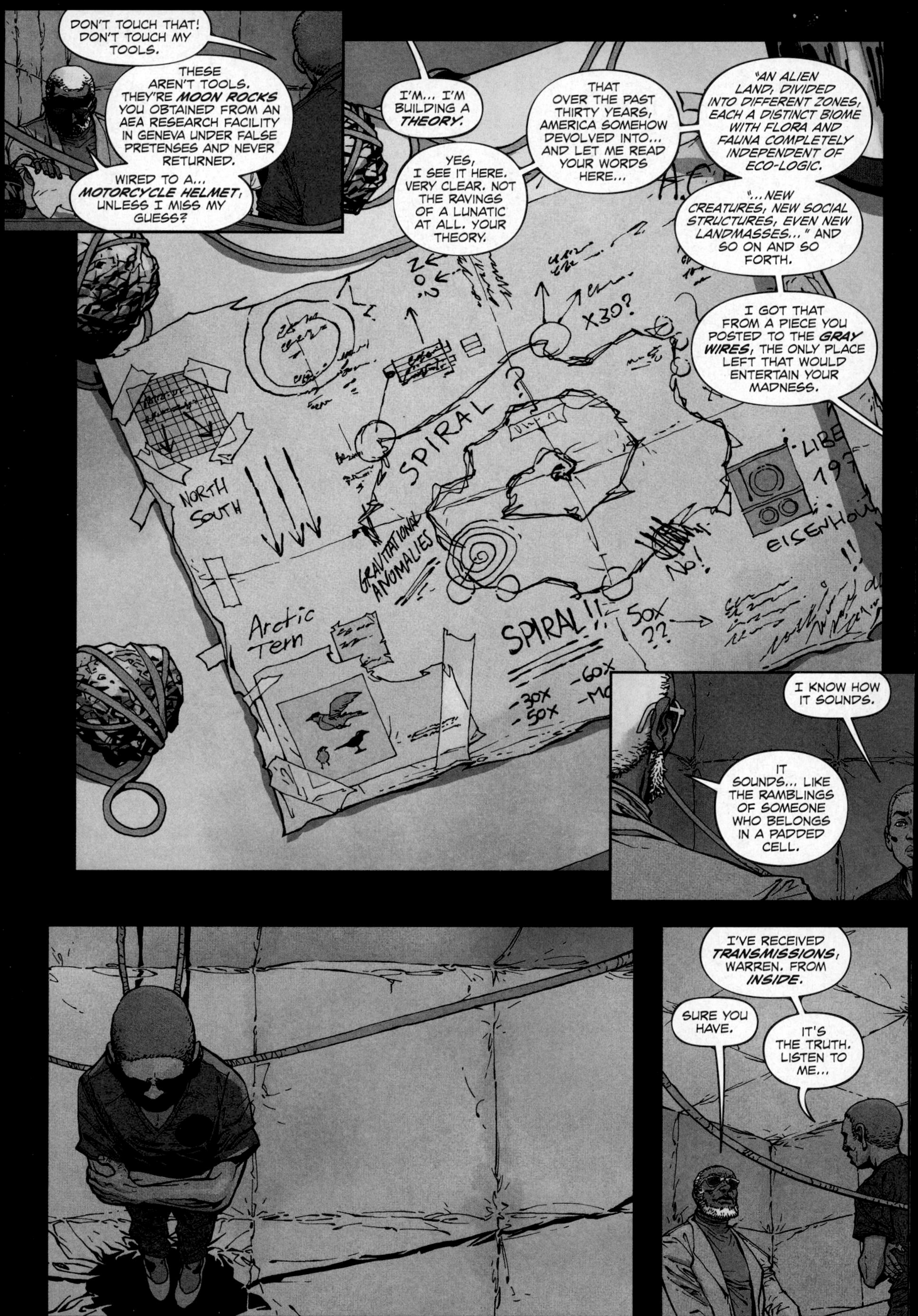
DON'T TOUCH THAT! DON'T TOUCH MY TOOLS.
THESE AREN'T TOOLS. THEY'RE MOON ROCKS YOU OBTAINED FROM AN AEA RESEARCH FACILITY IN GENEVA UNDER FALSE PRETENSES AND NEVER RETURNED.
WIRED TO A... MOTORCYCLE HELMET, UNLESS I MISS MY GUESS?
I'M... I'M BUILDING A THEORY.
YES, I SEE IT HERE. VERY CLEAR. NOT THE RAVINGS OF A LUNATIC AT ALL. YOUR THEORY.
THAT OVER THE PAST THIRTY YEARS, AMERICA SOMEHOW DEVOLVED INTO... AND LET ME READ YOUR WORDS HERE...
"AN ALIEN LAND, DIVIDED INTO DIFFERENT ZONES, EACH A DISTINCT BIOME WITH FLORA AND FAUNA COMPLETELY INDEPENDENT OF ECO-LOGIC.
"...NEW CREATURES, NEW SOCIAL STRUCTURES, EVEN NEW LANDMASSES..." AND SO ON AND SO FORTH.
I GOT THAT FROM A PIECE YOU POSTED TO THE GRAY WIRES, THE ONLY PLACE LEFT THAT WOULD ENTERTAIN YOUR MADNESS.
X30?
SPIRAL ?
NORTH
SOUTH
SPIRAL
GRAVITATIONAL ANOMALIES
NO!
EISENHOU
Arctic Tern
SPIRAL!!
50x ??
-30x
-50x
-60x
I KNOW HOW IT SOUNDS.
IT SOUNDS... LIKE THE RAMBLINGS OF SOMEONE WHO BELONGS IN A PADDED CELL.
I'VE RECEIVED TRANSMISSIONS, WARREN. FROM INSIDE.
SURE YOU HAVE.
IT'S THE TRUTH. LISTEN TO ME...

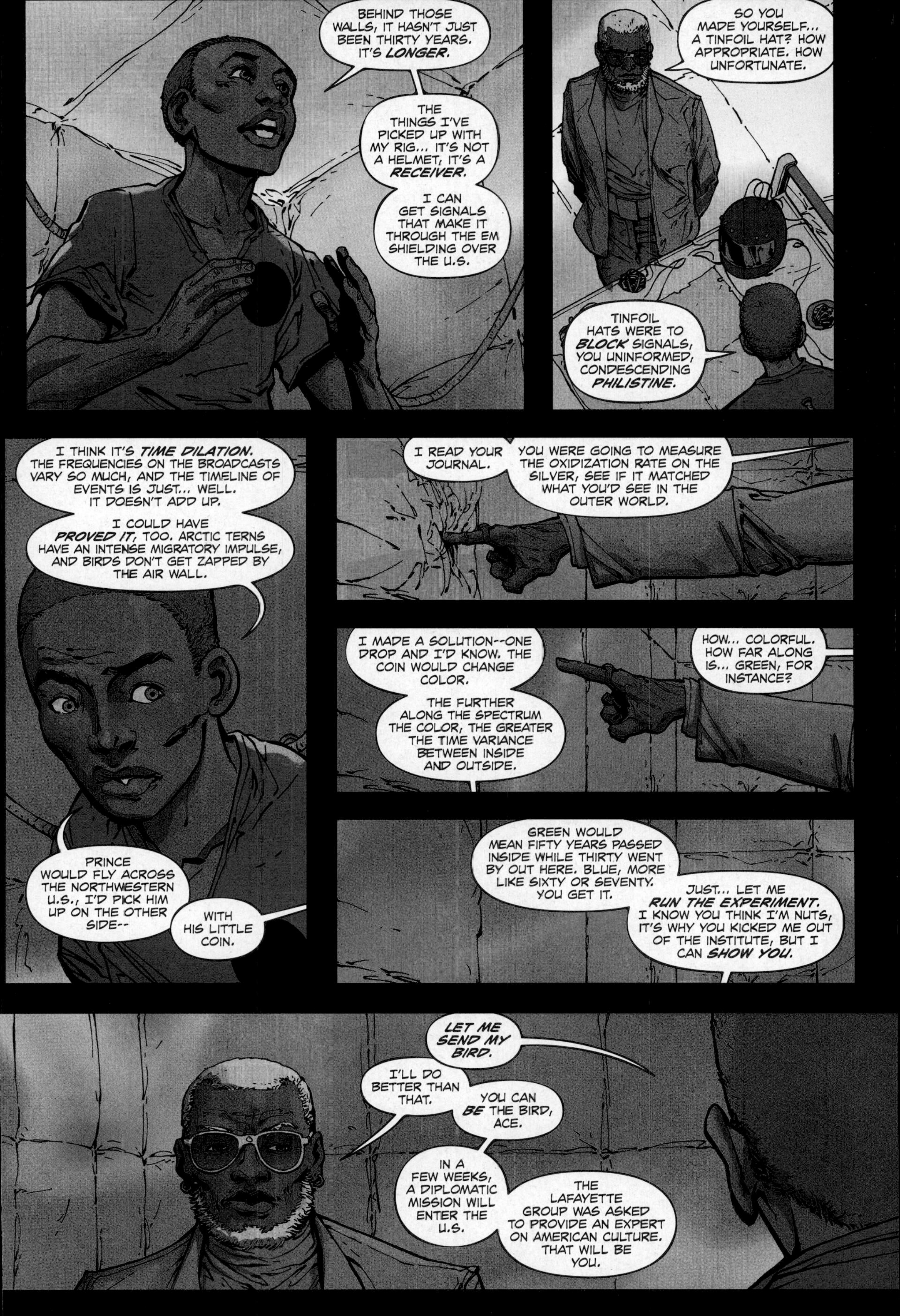
BEHIND THOSE WALLS, IT HASN'T JUST BEEN THIRTY YEARS. IT'S *LONGER*.
THE THINGS I'VE PICKED UP WITH MY RIG... IT'S NOT A HELMET, IT'S A *RECEIVER*.
I CAN GET SIGNALS THAT MAKE IT THROUGH THE EM SHIELDING OVER THE U.S.
SO YOU MADE YOURSELF... A TINFOIL HAT? HOW APPROPRIATE. HOW UNFORTUNATE.
TINFOIL HATS WERE TO *BLOCK* SIGNALS, YOU UNINFORMED, CONDESCENDING *PHILISTINE*.
I THINK IT'S *TIME DILATION*. THE FREQUENCIES ON THE BROADCASTS VARY SO MUCH, AND THE TIMELINE OF EVENTS IS JUST... WELL. IT DOESN'T ADD UP.
I COULD HAVE *PROVED IT*, TOO. ARCTIC TERNS HAVE AN INTENSE MIGRATORY IMPULSE, AND BIRDS DON'T GET ZAPPED BY THE AIR WALL.
PRINCE WOULD FLY ACROSS THE NORTHWESTERN U.S., I'D PICK HIM UP ON THE OTHER SIDE--
WITH HIS LITTLE COIN.
I READ YOUR JOURNAL.
YOU WERE GOING TO MEASURE THE OXIDIZATION RATE ON THE SILVER, SEE IF IT MATCHED WHAT YOU'D SEE IN THE OUTER WORLD.
I MADE A SOLUTION--ONE DROP AND I'D KNOW. THE COIN WOULD CHANGE COLOR.
THE FURTHER ALONG THE SPECTRUM THE COLOR, THE GREATER THE TIME VARIANCE BETWEEN INSIDE AND OUTSIDE.
HOW... COLORFUL. HOW FAR ALONG IS... GREEN, FOR INSTANCE?
GREEN WOULD MEAN FIFTY YEARS PASSED INSIDE WHILE THIRTY WENT BY OUT HERE. BLUE, MORE LIKE SIXTY OR SEVENTY. YOU GET IT.
JUST... LET ME *RUN THE EXPERIMENT*. I KNOW YOU THINK I'M NUTS, IT'S WHY YOU KICKED ME OUT OF THE INSTITUTE, BUT I CAN *SHOW YOU*.
LET ME SEND MY BIRD.
I'LL DO BETTER THAN THAT.
YOU CAN *BE* THE BIRD, ACE.
IN A FEW WEEKS, A DIPLOMATIC MISSION WILL ENTER THE U.S.
THE LAFAYETTE GROUP WAS ASKED TO PROVIDE AN EXPERT ON AMERICAN CULTURE. THAT WILL BE YOU.

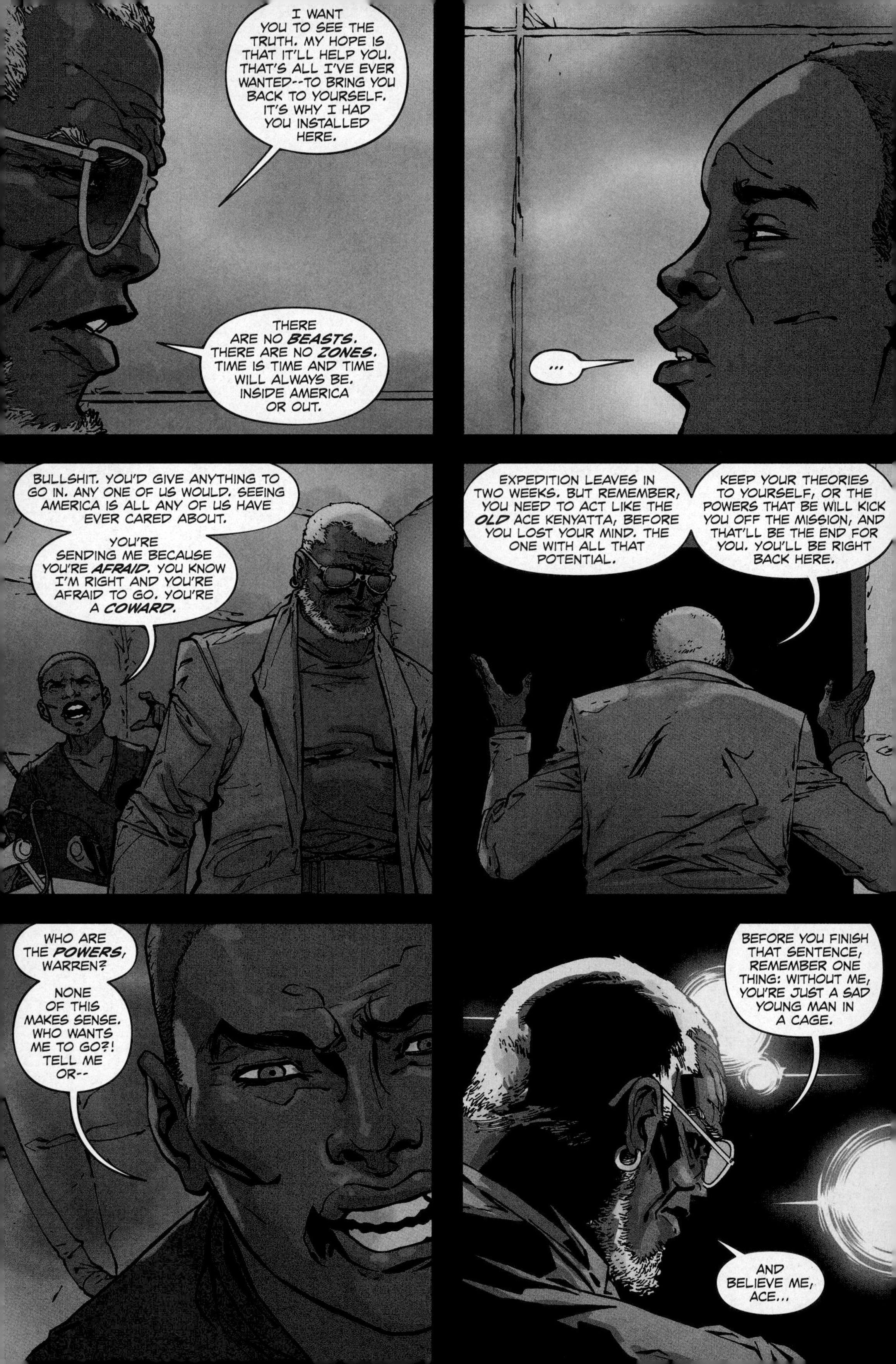
I WANT YOU TO SEE THE TRUTH. MY HOPE IS THAT IT'LL HELP YOU. THAT'S ALL I'VE EVER WANTED--TO BRING YOU BACK TO YOURSELF. IT'S WHY I HAD YOU INSTALLED HERE.
THERE ARE NO *BEASTS*. THERE ARE NO *ZONES*. TIME IS TIME AND TIME WILL ALWAYS BE. INSIDE AMERICA OR OUT.
...
BULLSHIT. YOU'D GIVE ANYTHING TO GO IN. ANY ONE OF US WOULD. SEEING AMERICA IS ALL ANY OF US HAVE EVER CARED ABOUT.
YOU'RE SENDING ME BECAUSE YOU'RE *AFRAID*. YOU KNOW I'M RIGHT AND YOU'RE AFRAID TO GO. YOU'RE A *COWARD*.
EXPEDITION LEAVES IN TWO WEEKS. BUT REMEMBER, YOU NEED TO ACT LIKE THE *OLD* ACE KENYATTA, BEFORE YOU LOST YOUR MIND. THE ONE WITH ALL THAT POTENTIAL.
KEEP YOUR THEORIES TO YOURSELF, OR THE POWERS THAT BE WILL KICK YOU OFF THE MISSION, AND THAT'LL BE THE END FOR YOU. YOU'LL BE RIGHT BACK HERE.
WHO ARE THE *POWERS*, WARREN?
NONE OF THIS MAKES SENSE. WHO WANTS ME TO GO?! TELL ME OR--
BEFORE YOU FINISH THAT SENTENCE, REMEMBER ONE THING: WITHOUT ME, YOU'RE JUST A SAD YOUNG MAN IN A CAGE.
AND BELIEVE ME, ACE...

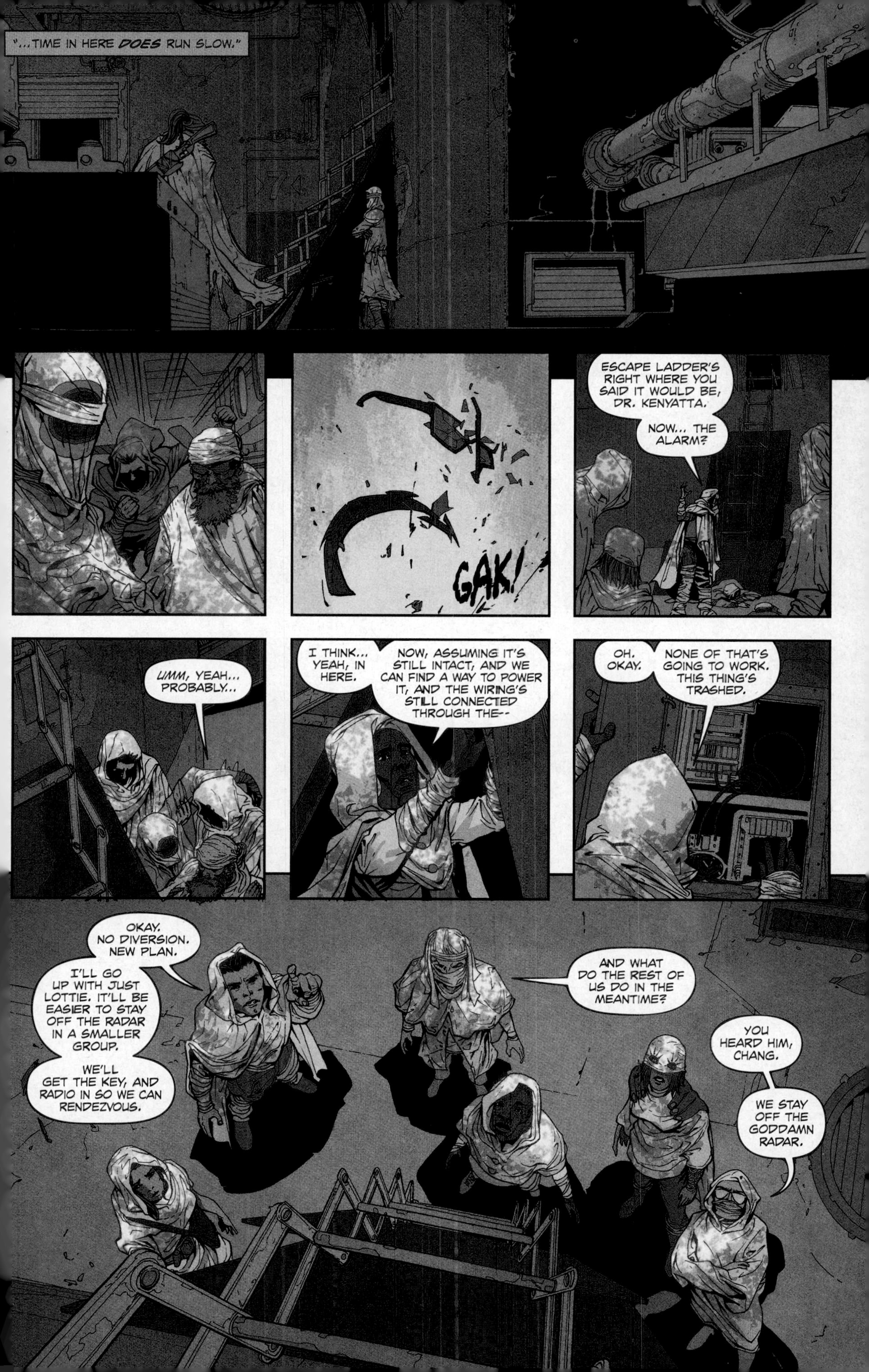
"...TIME IN HERE DOES RUN SLOW."
GAK!
ESCAPE LADDER'S RIGHT WHERE YOU SAID IT WOULD BE, DR. KENYATTA.
NOW... THE ALARM?
UMM, YEAH... PROBABLY...
I THINK... YEAH, IN HERE.
NOW, ASSUMING IT'S STILL INTACT, AND WE CAN FIND A WAY TO POWER IT, AND THE WIRING'S STILL CONNECTED THROUGH THE--
OH. OKAY.
NONE OF THAT'S GOING TO WORK. THIS THING'S TRASHED.
OKAY. NO DIVERSION. NEW PLAN.
I'LL GO UP WITH JUST LOTTIE. IT'LL BE EASIER TO STAY OFF THE RADAR IN A SMALLER GROUP.
WE'LL GET THE KEY, AND RADIO IN SO WE CAN RENDEZVOUS.
AND WHAT DO THE REST OF US DO IN THE MEANTIME?
YOU HEARD HIM, CHANG.
WE STAY OFF THE GODDAMN RADAR.

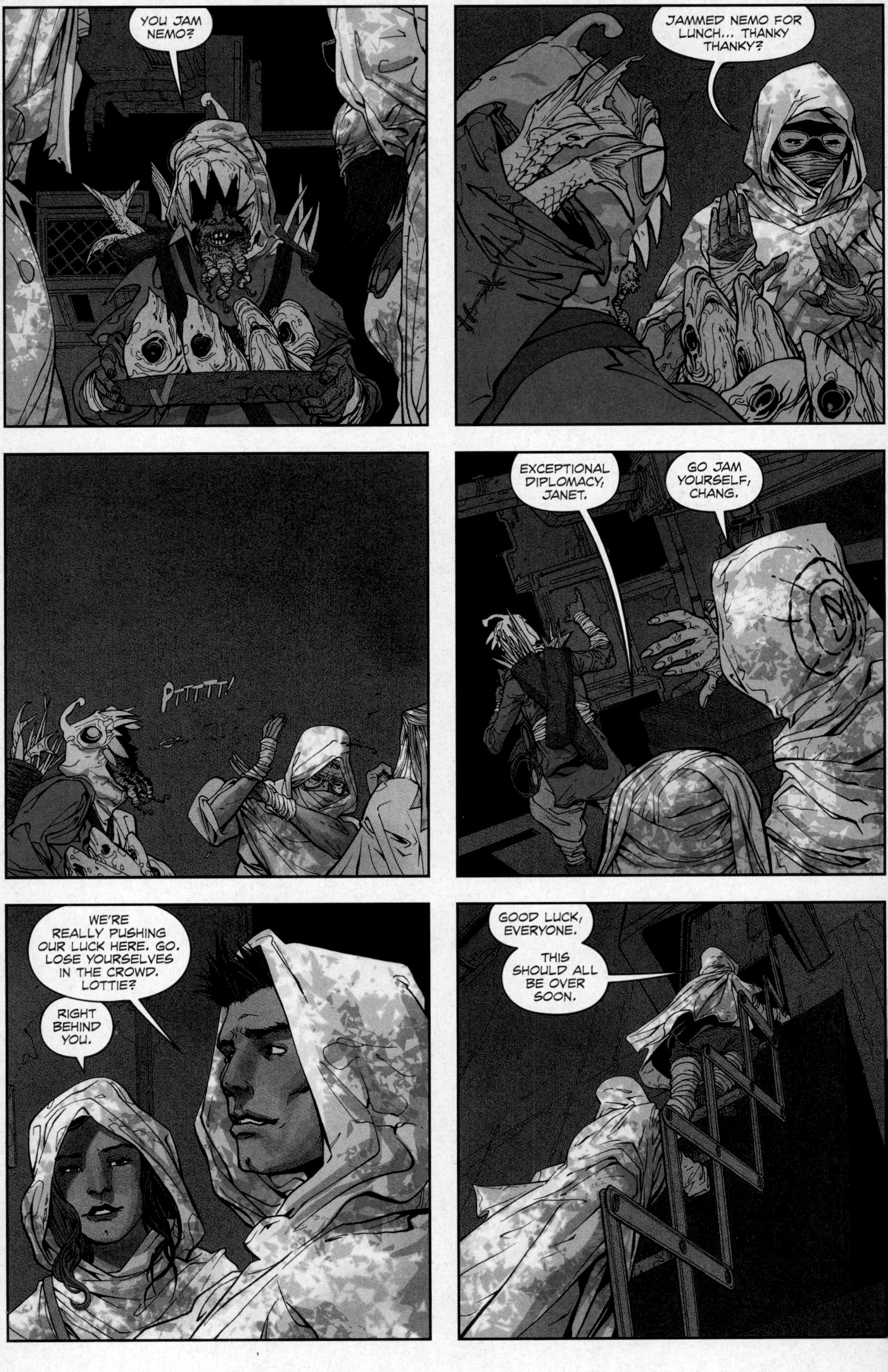

YOU JAM NEMO?
JAMMED NEMO FOR LUNCH... THANKY THANKY?
PTTTTT!
EXCEPTIONAL DIPLOMACY, JANET.
GO JAM YOURSELF, CHANG.
WE'RE REALLY PUSHING OUR LUCK HERE. GO. LOSE YOURSELVES IN THE CROWD. LOTTIE?
RIGHT BEHIND YOU.
GOOD LUCK, EVERYONE.
THIS SHOULD ALL BE OVER SOON.

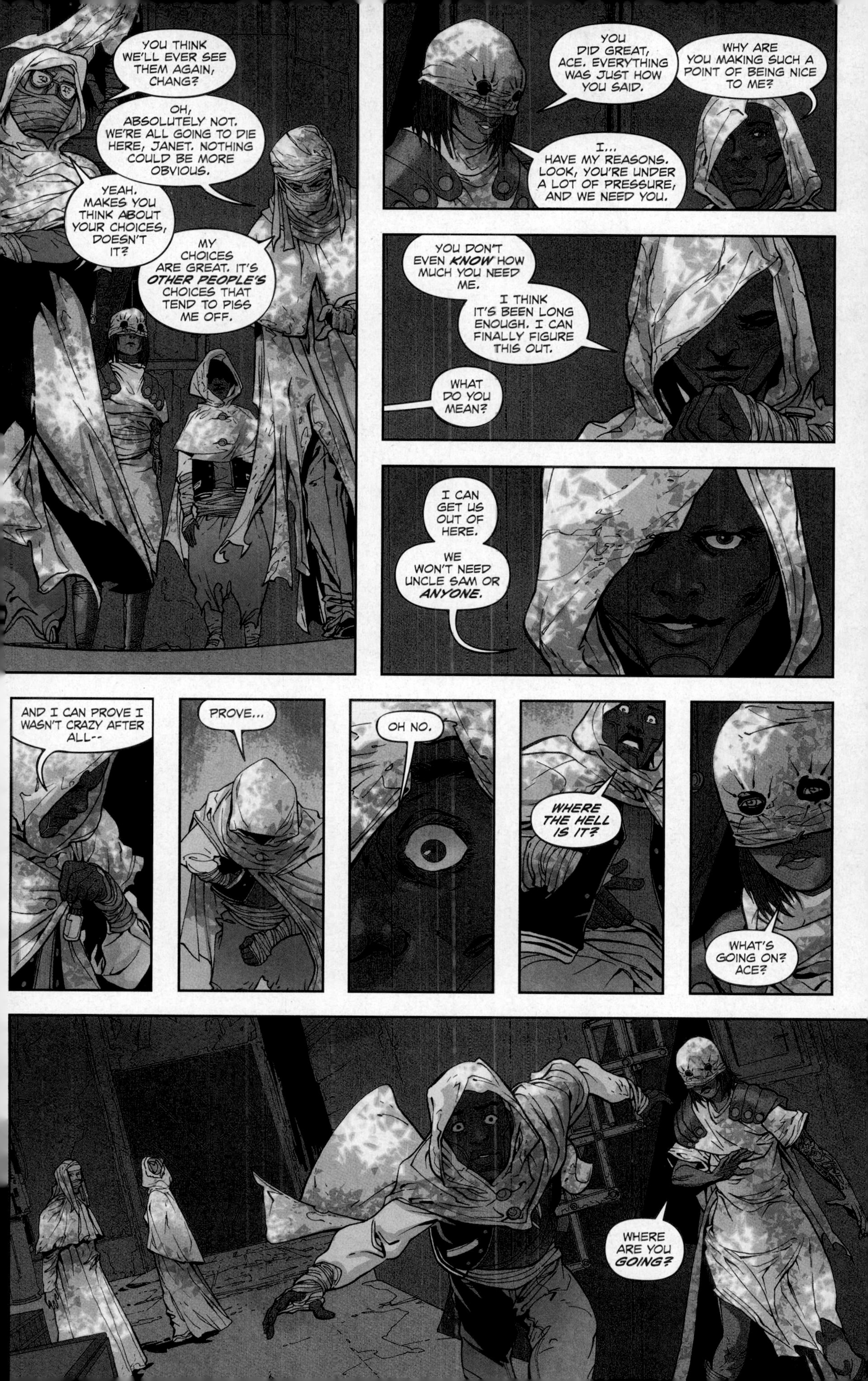
YOU THINK WE'LL EVER SEE THEM AGAIN, CHANG?
OH, ABSOLUTELY NOT. WE'RE ALL GOING TO DIE HERE, JANET. NOTHING COULD BE MORE OBVIOUS.
YEAH. MAKES YOU THINK ABOUT YOUR CHOICES, DOESN'T IT?
MY CHOICES ARE GREAT. IT'S OTHER PEOPLE'S CHOICES THAT TEND TO PISS ME OFF.
YOU DID GREAT, ACE. EVERYTHING WAS JUST HOW YOU SAID.
WHY ARE YOU MAKING SUCH A POINT OF BEING NICE TO ME?
I... HAVE MY REASONS. LOOK, YOU'RE UNDER A LOT OF PRESSURE, AND WE NEED YOU.
YOU DON'T EVEN KNOW HOW MUCH YOU NEED ME.
I THINK IT'S BEEN LONG ENOUGH. I CAN FINALLY FIGURE THIS OUT.
WHAT DO YOU MEAN?
I CAN GET US OUT OF HERE.
WE WON'T NEED UNCLE SAM OR ANYONE.
AND I CAN PROVE I WASN'T CRAZY AFTER ALL--
PROVE...
OH NO.
WHERE THE HELL IS IT?
WHAT'S GOING ON? ACE?
WHERE ARE YOU GOING?

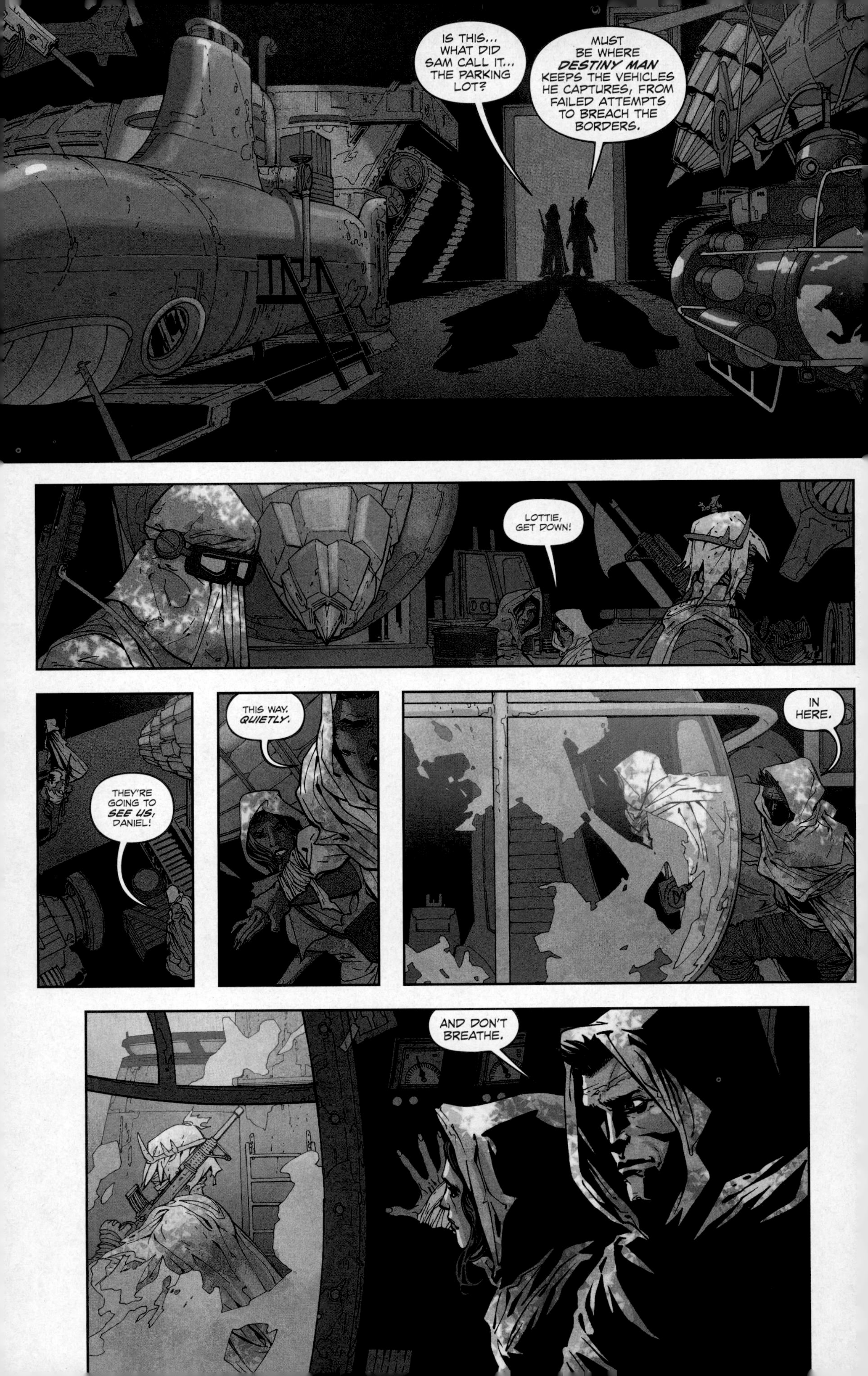
IS THIS... WHAT DID SAM CALL IT... THE PARKING LOT?
MUST BE WHERE DESTINY MAN KEEPS THE VEHICLES HE CAPTURES, FROM FAILED ATTEMPTS TO BREACH THE BORDERS.
LOTTIE, GET DOWN!
THEY'RE GOING TO SEE US, DANIEL!
THIS WAY. QUIETLY.
IN HERE.
AND DON'T BREATHE.

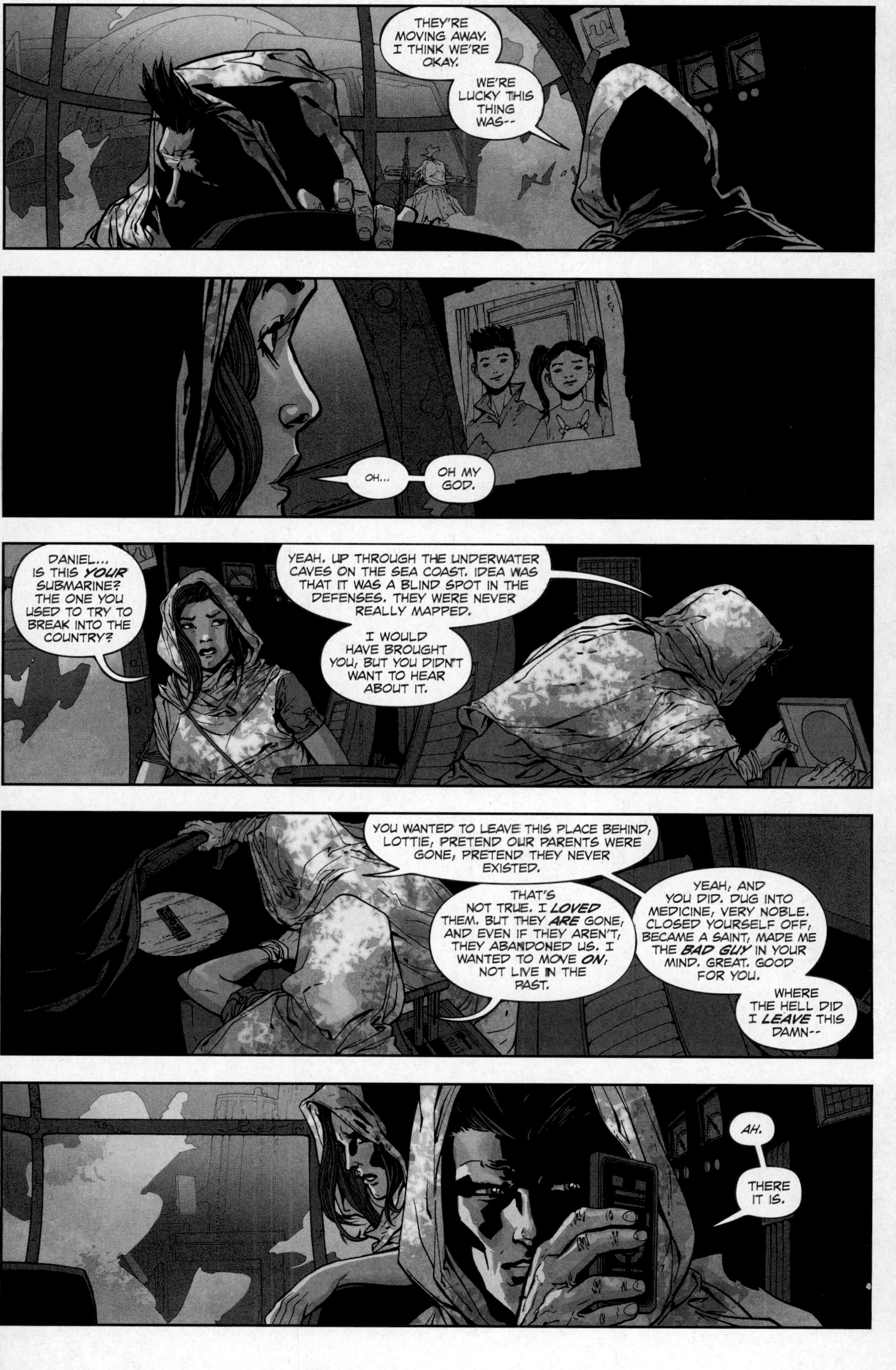
THEY'RE MOVING AWAY. I THINK WE'RE OKAY.
WE'RE LUCKY THIS THING WAS--
OH...
OH MY GOD.
DANIEL... IS THIS YOUR SUBMARINE? THE ONE YOU USED TO TRY TO BREAK INTO THE COUNTRY?
YEAH. UP THROUGH THE UNDERWATER CAVES ON THE SEA COAST. IDEA WAS THAT IT WAS A BLIND SPOT IN THE DEFENSES. THEY WERE NEVER REALLY MAPPED.
I WOULD HAVE BROUGHT YOU, BUT YOU DIDN'T WANT TO HEAR ABOUT IT.
YOU WANTED TO LEAVE THIS PLACE BEHIND, LOTTIE, PRETEND OUR PARENTS WERE GONE, PRETEND THEY NEVER EXISTED.
THAT'S NOT TRUE. I LOVED THEM. BUT THEY ARE GONE, AND EVEN IF THEY AREN'T, THEY ABANDONED US. I WANTED TO MOVE ON, NOT LIVE IN THE PAST.
YEAH, AND YOU DID. DUG INTO MEDICINE, VERY NOBLE. CLOSED YOURSELF OFF, BECAME A SAINT, MADE ME THE BAD GUY IN YOUR MIND. GREAT. GOOD FOR YOU.
WHERE THE HELL DID I LEAVE THIS DAMN--
AH.
THERE IT IS.

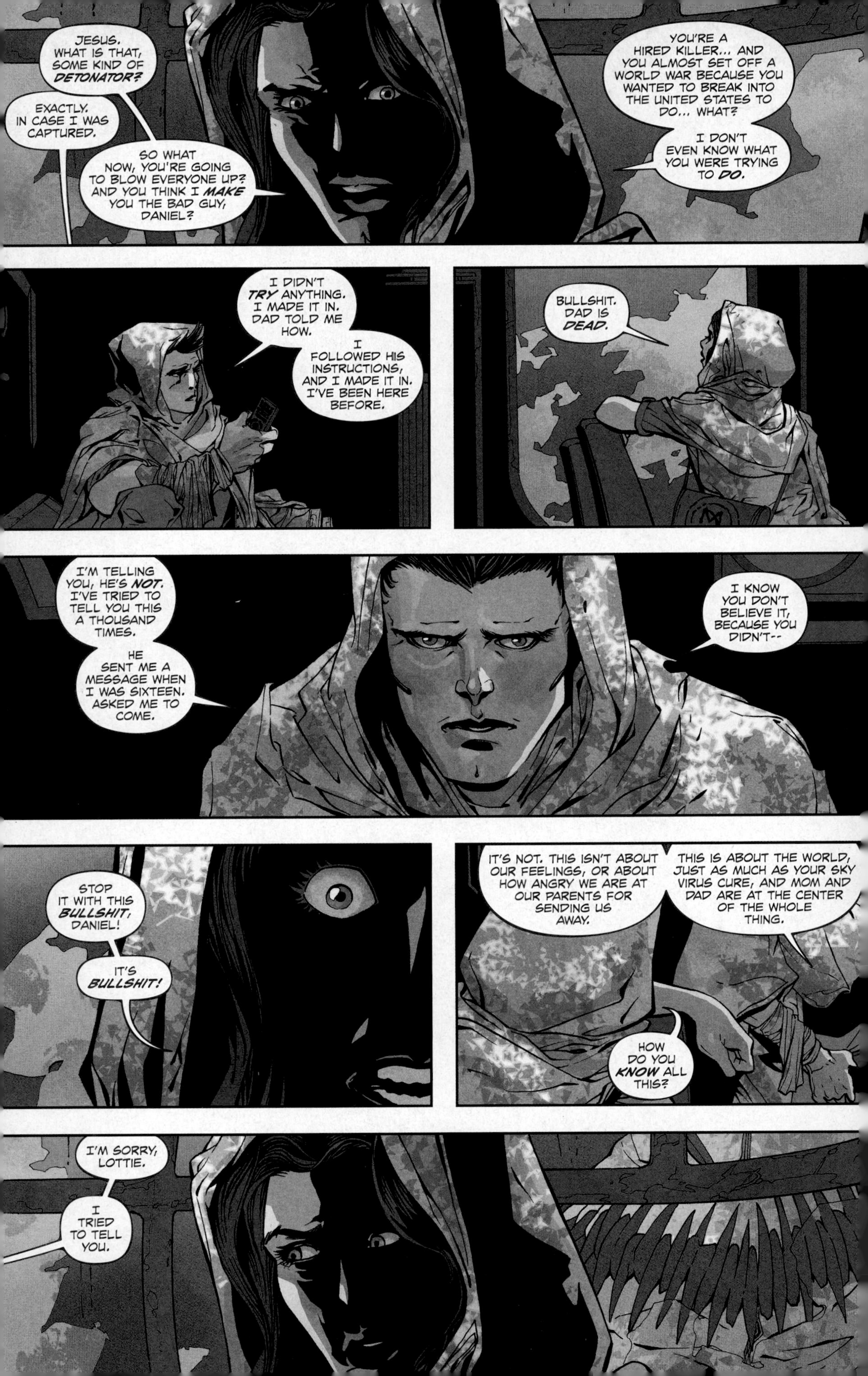

JESUS. WHAT IS THAT, SOME KIND OF DETONATOR?
EXACTLY. IN CASE I WAS CAPTURED.
SO WHAT NOW, YOU'RE GOING TO BLOW EVERYONE UP? AND YOU THINK I MAKE YOU THE BAD GUY, DANIEL?
YOU'RE A HIRED KILLER... AND YOU ALMOST SET OFF A WORLD WAR BECAUSE YOU WANTED TO BREAK INTO THE UNITED STATES TO DO... WHAT?
I DON'T EVEN KNOW WHAT YOU WERE TRYING TO DO.
I DIDN'T TRY ANYTHING. I MADE IT IN. DAD TOLD ME HOW.
I FOLLOWED HIS INSTRUCTIONS, AND I MADE IT IN. I'VE BEEN HERE BEFORE.
BULLSHIT. DAD IS DEAD.
I'M TELLING YOU, HE'S NOT. I'VE TRIED TO TELL YOU THIS A THOUSAND TIMES.
HE SENT ME A MESSAGE WHEN I WAS SIXTEEN. ASKED ME TO COME.
I KNOW YOU DON'T BELIEVE IT, BECAUSE YOU DIDN'T--
STOP IT WITH THIS BULLSHIT, DANIEL!
IT'S BULLSHIT!
IT'S NOT. THIS ISN'T ABOUT OUR FEELINGS, OR ABOUT HOW ANGRY WE ARE AT OUR PARENTS FOR SENDING US AWAY.
THIS IS ABOUT THE WORLD, JUST AS MUCH AS YOUR SKY VIRUS CURE, AND MOM AND DAD ARE AT THE CENTER OF THE WHOLE THING.
HOW DO YOU KNOW ALL THIS?
I'M SORRY, LOTTIE.
I TRIED TO TELL YOU.

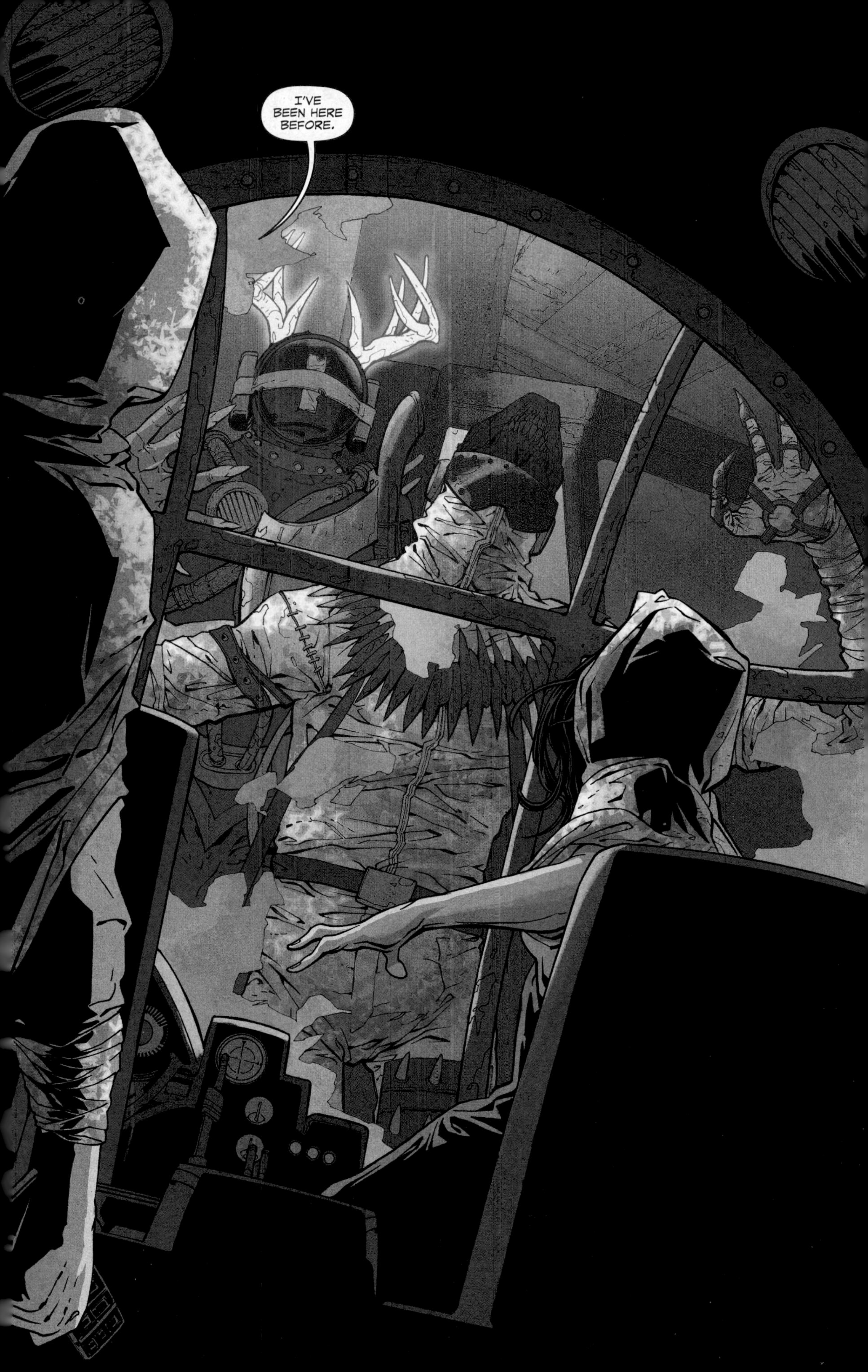
I'VE BEEN HERE BEFORE.

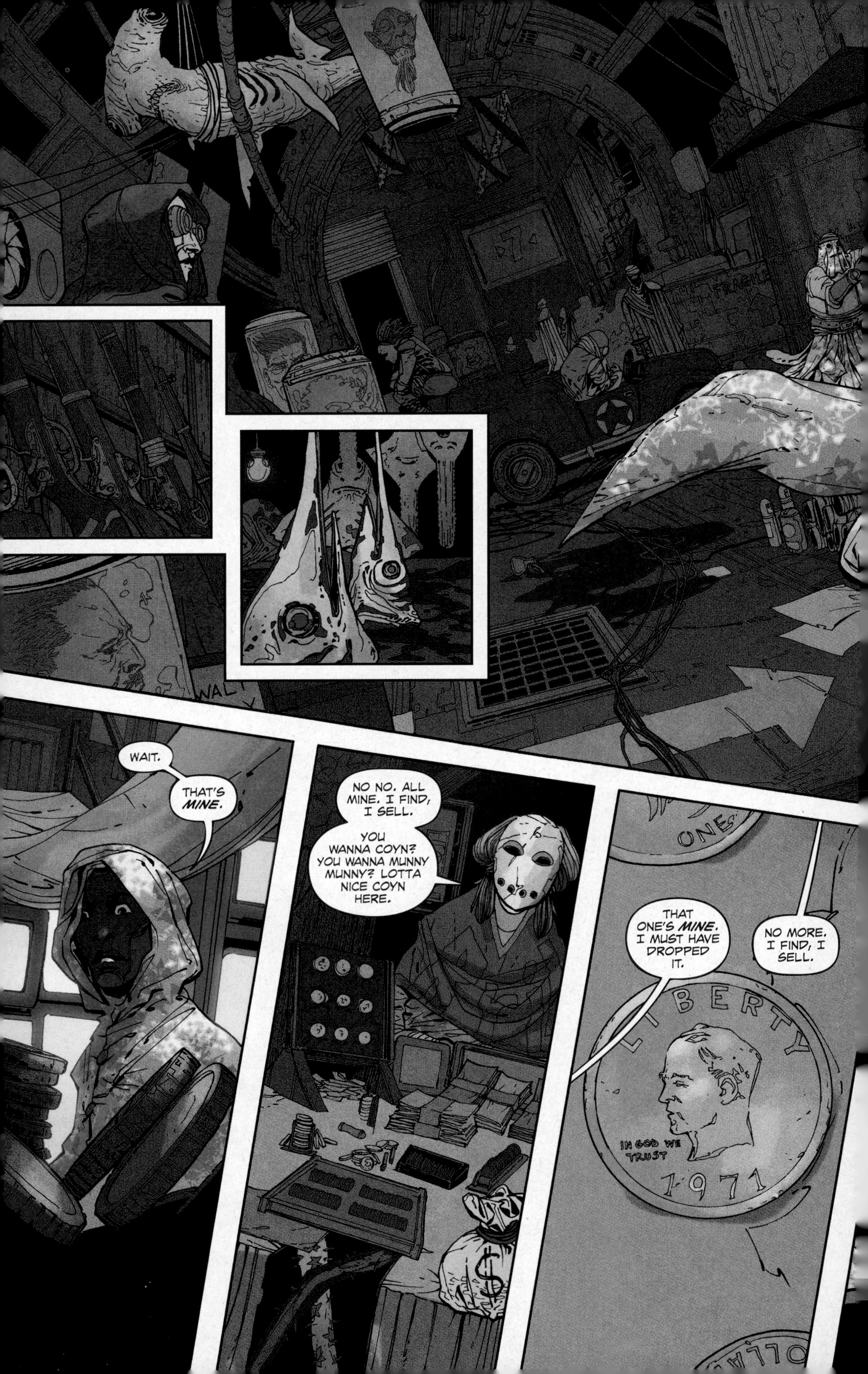
FRAGILE
WAIT.
THAT'S *MINE*.
NO NO. ALL MINE. I FIND, I SELL.
YOU WANNA COYN? YOU WANNA MUNNY MUNNY? LOTTA NICE COYN HERE.
ONE
THAT ONE'S *MINE*. I MUST HAVE DROPPED IT.
NO MORE. I FIND, I SELL.
LIBERTY
IN GOD WE TRUST
1971

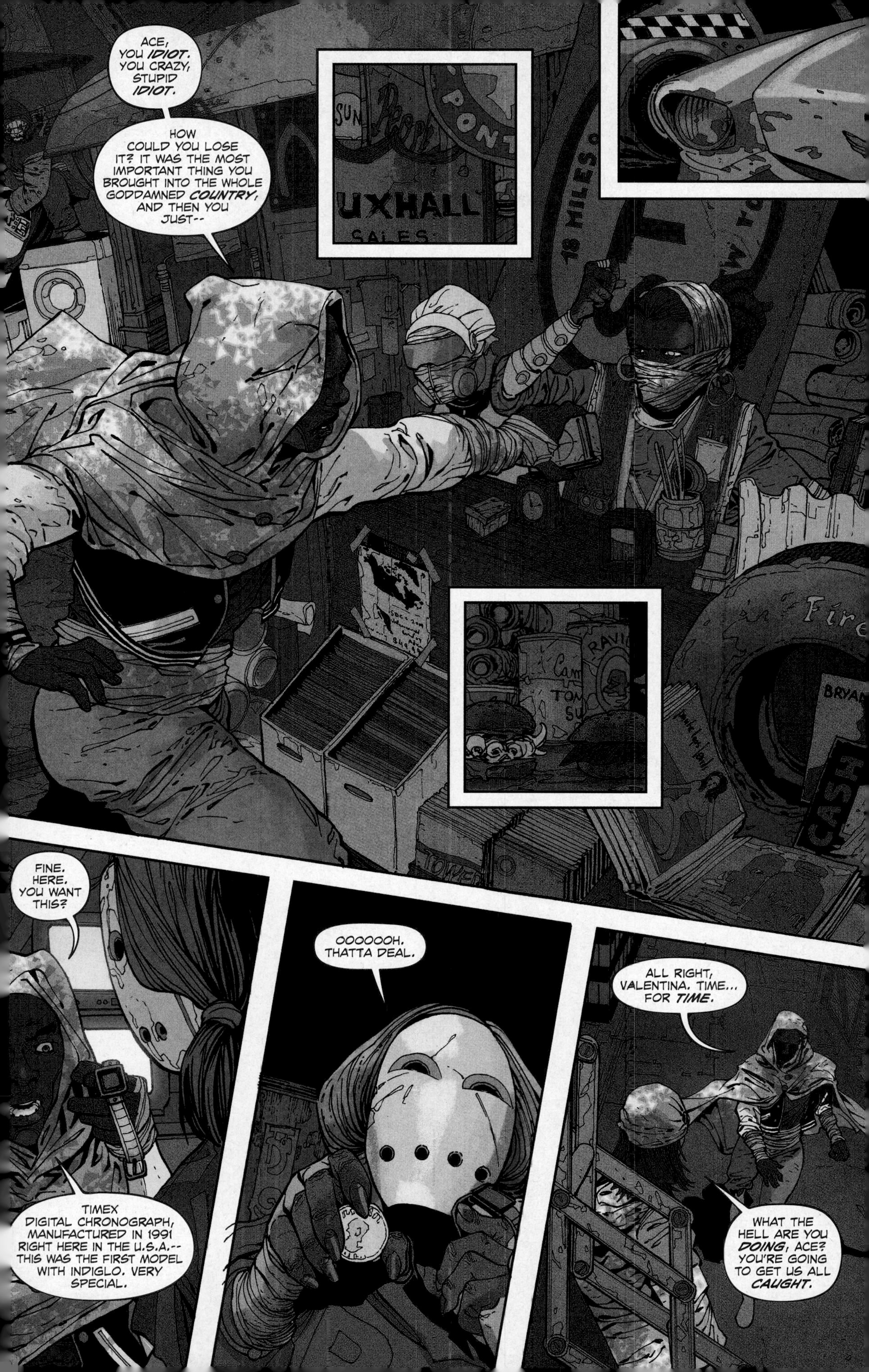
ACE, YOU *IDIOT*. YOU CRAZY, STUPID *IDIOT*.
HOW COULD YOU LOSE IT? IT WAS THE MOST IMPORTANT THING YOU BROUGHT INTO THE WHOLE GODDAMNED *COUNTRY*, AND THEN YOU JUST--
UXHALL
SALES
18 MILES
FINE. HERE. YOU WANT THIS?
TIMEX DIGITAL CHRONOGRAPH, MANUFACTURED IN 1991 RIGHT HERE IN THE U.S.A.-- THIS WAS THE FIRST MODEL WITH INDIGLO. VERY SPECIAL.
OOOOOOH. THATTA DEAL.
ALL RIGHT, VALENTINA. TIME... FOR *TIME*.
WHAT THE HELL ARE YOU *DOING*, ACE? YOU'RE GOING TO GET US ALL *CAUGHT*.

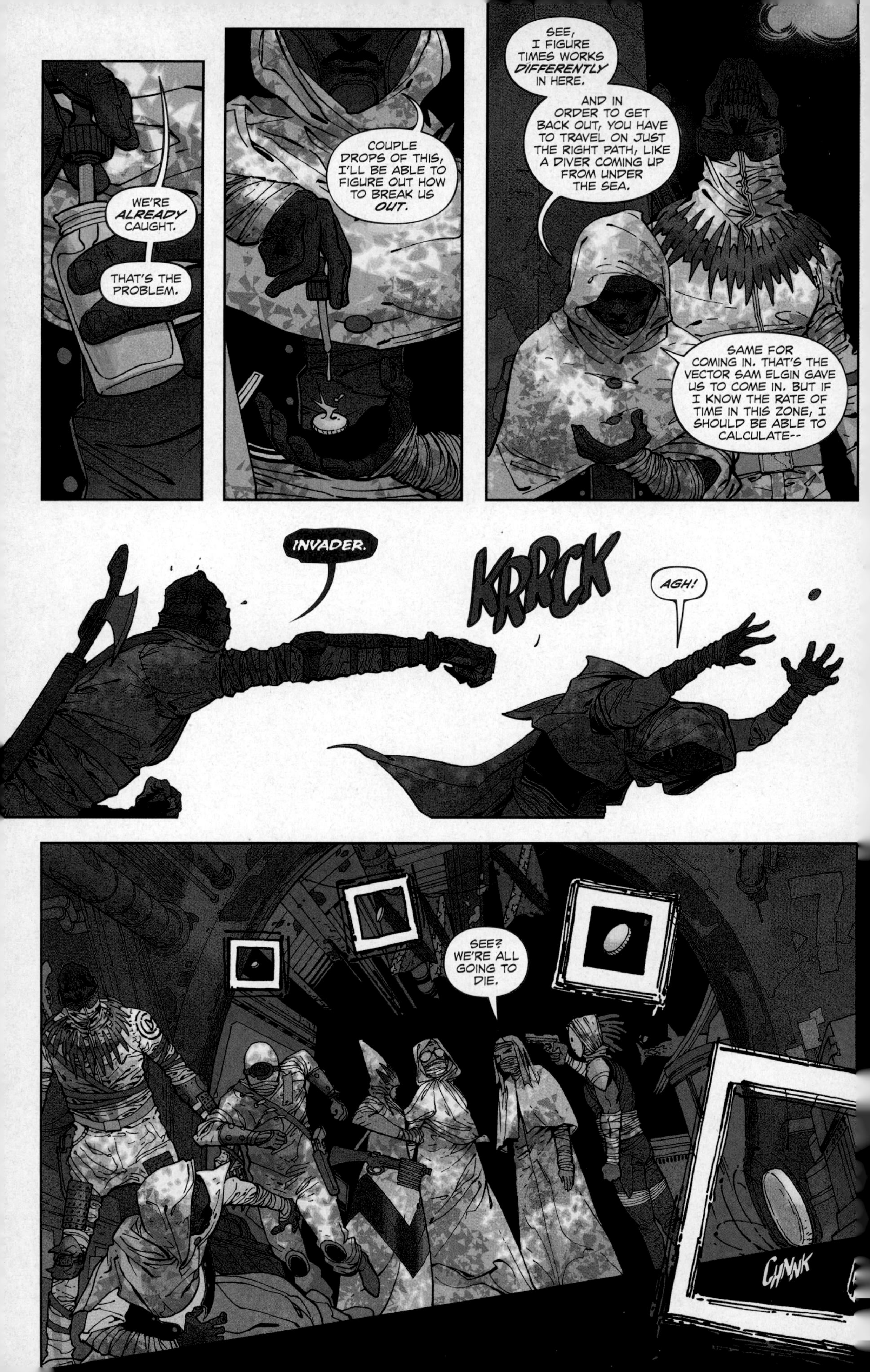
WE'RE ALREADY CAUGHT.
THAT'S THE PROBLEM.
COUPLE DROPS OF THIS, I'LL BE ABLE TO FIGURE OUT HOW TO BREAK US OUT.
SEE, I FIGURE TIMES WORKS DIFFERENTLY IN HERE.
AND IN ORDER TO GET BACK OUT, YOU HAVE TO TRAVEL ON JUST THE RIGHT PATH, LIKE A DIVER COMING UP FROM UNDER THE SEA.
SAME FOR COMING IN. THAT'S THE VECTOR SAM ELGIN GAVE US TO COME IN. BUT IF I KNOW THE RATE OF TIME IN THIS ZONE, I SHOULD BE ABLE TO CALCULATE--
INVADER.
KRRCK
AGH!
SEE? WE'RE ALL GOING TO DIE.
CHNNK

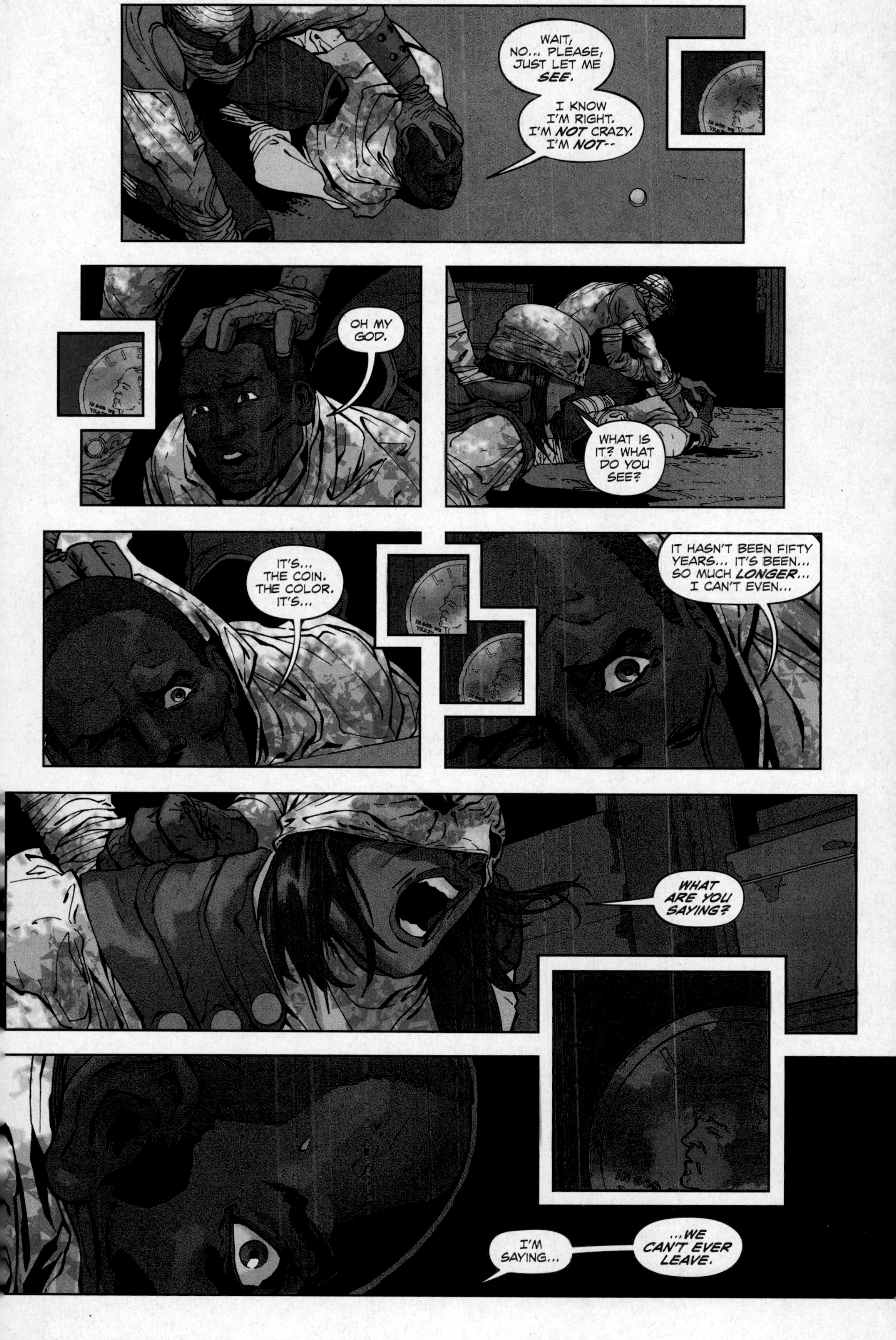
WAIT, NO... PLEASE, JUST LET ME *SEE*.
I KNOW I'M RIGHT. I'M *NOT* CRAZY. I'M *NOT*--
OH MY GOD.
WHAT IS IT? WHAT DO YOU SEE?
IT'S... THE COIN. THE COLOR. IT'S...
IT HASN'T BEEN FIFTY YEARS... IT'S BEEN... SO MUCH *LONGER*... I CAN'T EVEN...
WHAT ARE YOU SAYING?
I'M SAYING...
...WE CAN'T EVER LEAVE.

CHAPTER FOUR

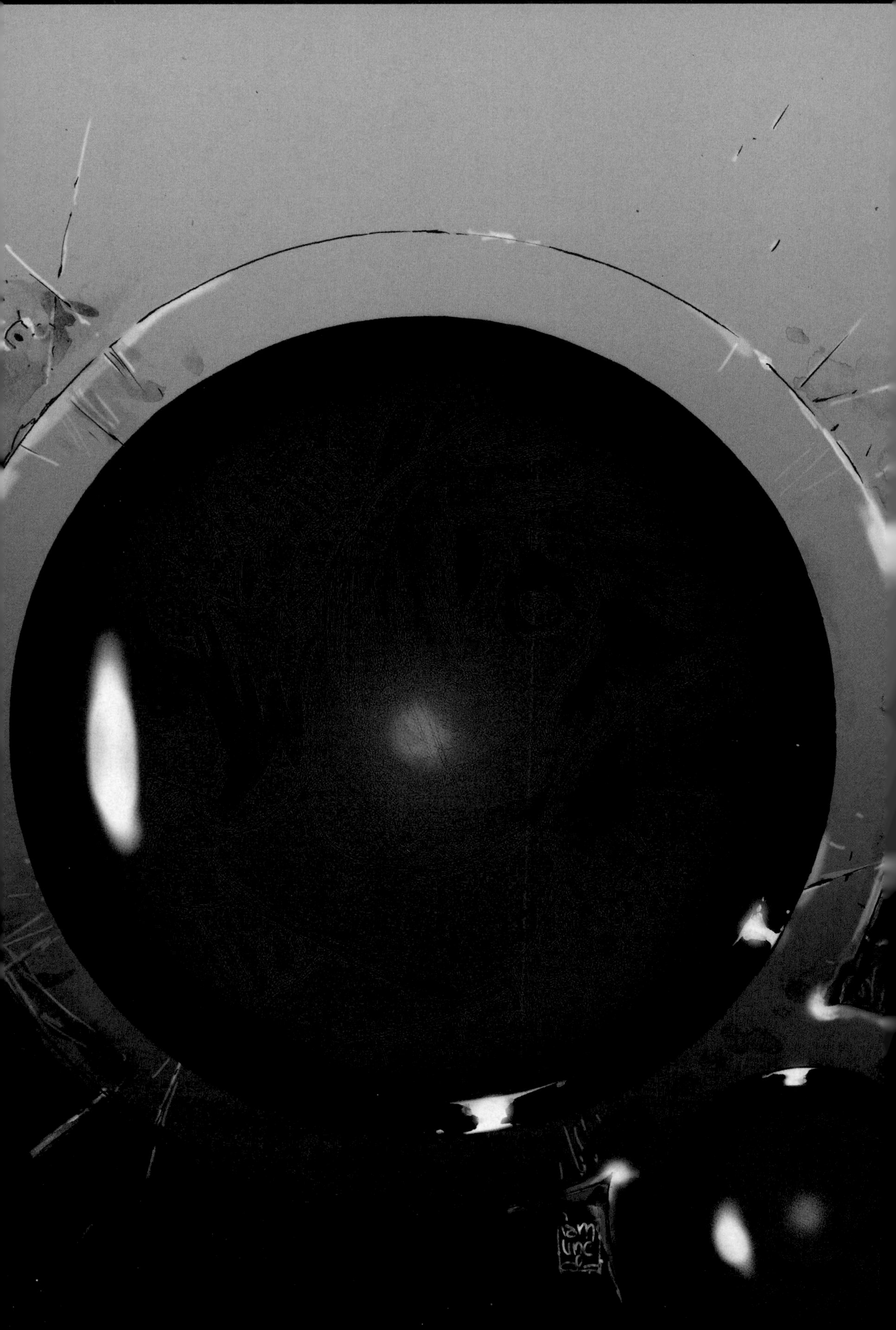

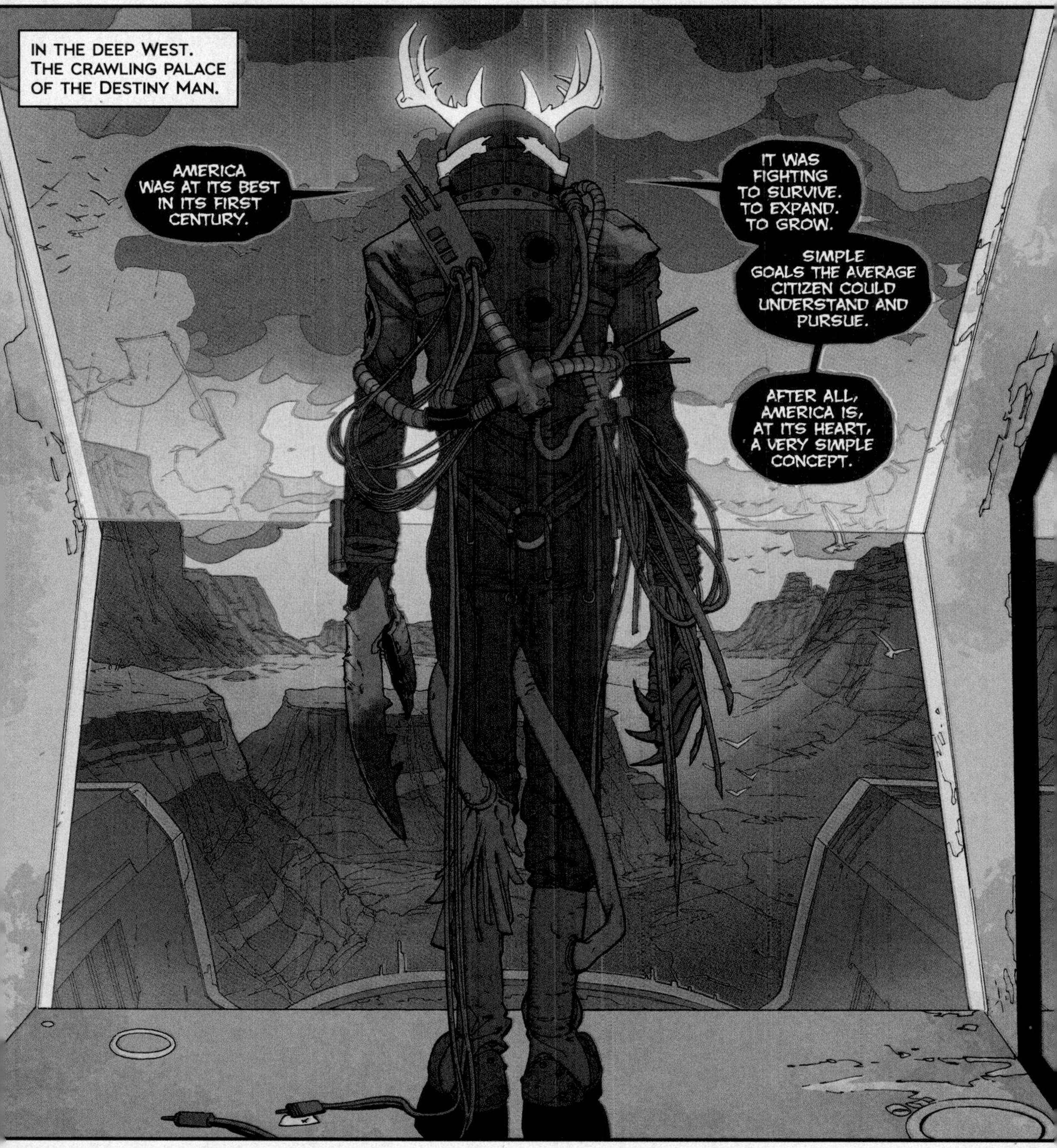
IN THE DEEP WEST. THE CRAWLING PALACE OF THE DESTINY MAN.
AMERICA WAS AT ITS BEST IN ITS FIRST CENTURY.
IT WAS FIGHTING TO SURVIVE. TO EXPAND. TO GROW.
SIMPLE GOALS THE AVERAGE CITIZEN COULD UNDERSTAND AND PURSUE.
AFTER ALL, AMERICA IS, AT ITS HEART, A VERY SIMPLE CONCEPT.

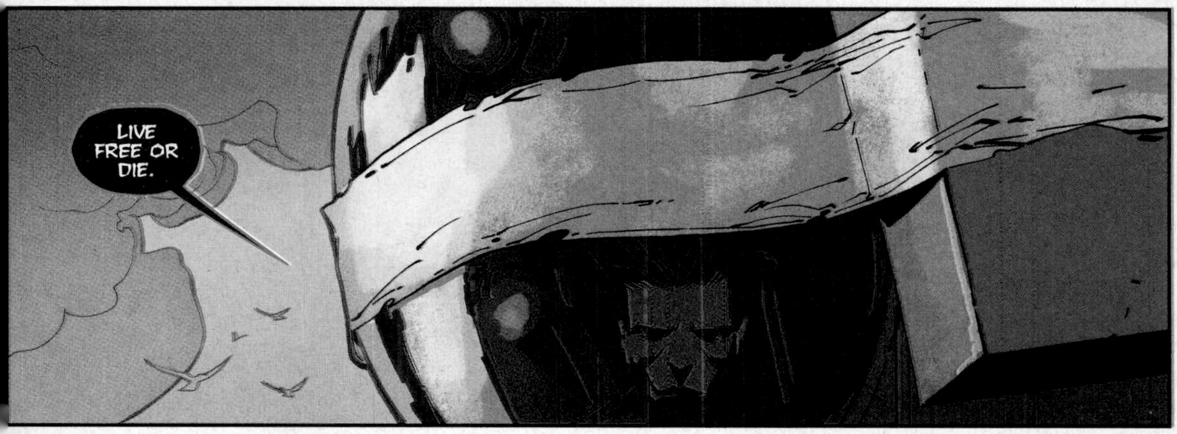
LIVE FREE OR DIE.

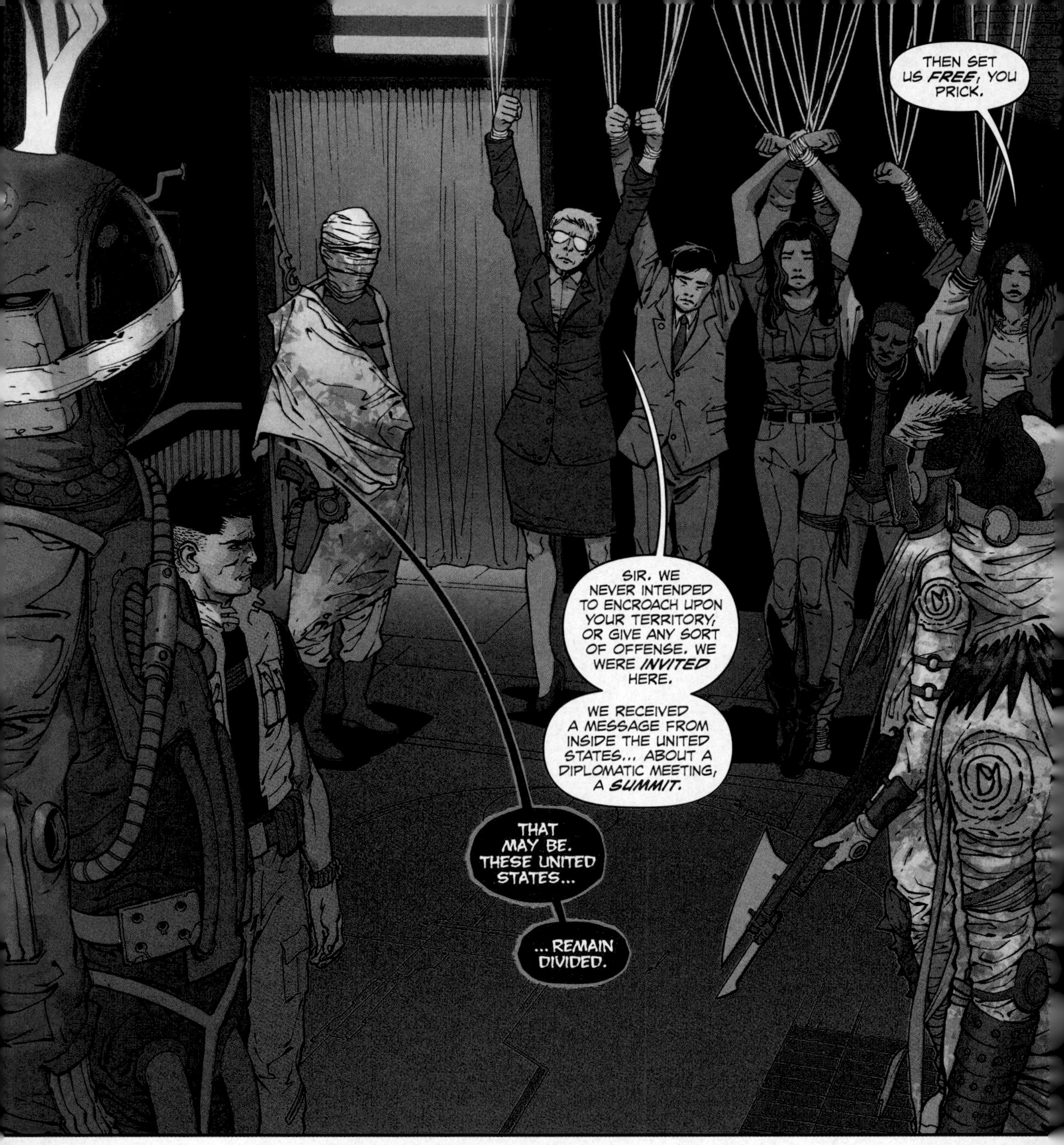
THEN SET US FREE, YOU PRICK.
SIR. WE NEVER INTENDED TO ENCROACH UPON YOUR TERRITORY, OR GIVE ANY SORT OF OFFENSE. WE WERE INVITED HERE.
WE RECEIVED A MESSAGE FROM INSIDE THE UNITED STATES... ABOUT A DIPLOMATIC MEETING, A SUMMIT.
THAT MAY BE. THESE UNITED STATES...
...REMAIN DIVIDED.

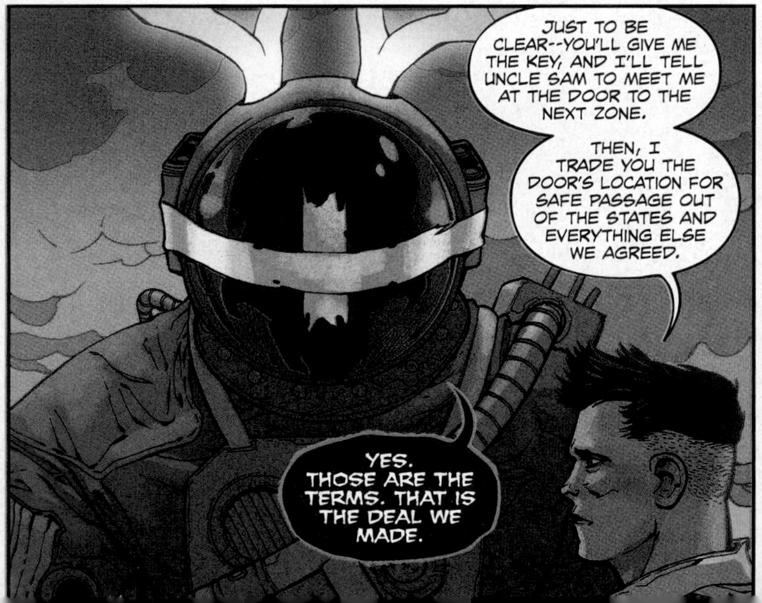
JUST TO BE CLEAR--YOU'LL GIVE ME THE KEY, AND I'LL TELL UNCLE SAM TO MEET ME AT THE DOOR TO THE NEXT ZONE.
THEN, I TRADE YOU THE DOOR'S LOCATION FOR SAFE PASSAGE OUT OF THE STATES AND EVERYTHING ELSE WE AGREED.
YES. THOSE ARE THE TERMS. THAT IS THE DEAL WE MADE.

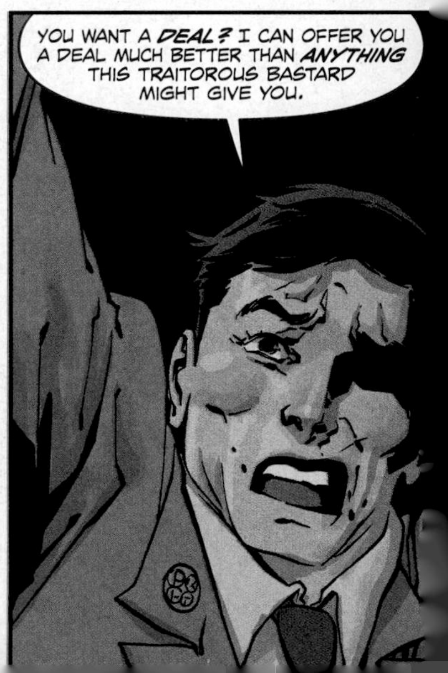
YOU WANT A DEAL? I CAN OFFER YOU A DEAL MUCH BETTER THAN ANYTHING THIS TRAITOROUS BASTARD MIGHT GIVE YOU.

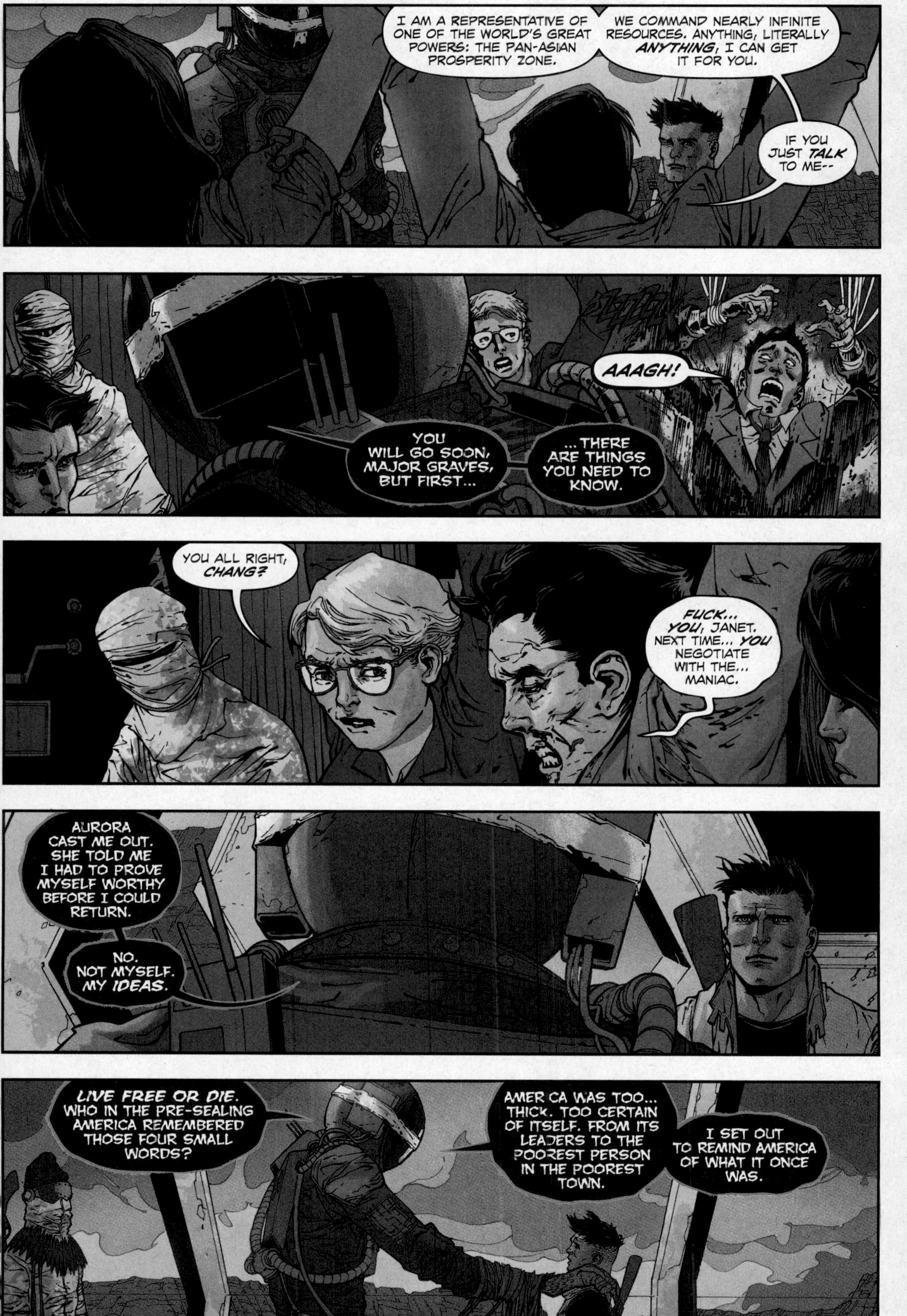

I AM A REPRESENTATIVE OF ONE OF THE WORLD'S GREAT POWERS: THE PAN-ASIAN PROSPERITY ZONE.
WE COMMAND NEARLY INFINITE RESOURCES. ANYTHING, LITERALLY *ANYTHING*, I CAN GET IT FOR YOU.
IF YOU JUST *TALK* TO ME--
AAAGH!
YOU WILL GO SOON, MAJOR GRAVES, BUT FIRST...
...THERE ARE THINGS YOU NEED TO KNOW.
YOU ALL RIGHT, *CHANG?*
FUCK... YOU, JANET. NEXT TIME... *YOU* NEGOTIATE WITH THE... MANIAC.
AURORA CAST ME OUT. SHE TOLD ME I HAD TO PROVE MYSELF WORTHY BEFORE I COULD RETURN.
NO. NOT MYSELF. MY *IDEAS*.
LIVE FREE OR DIE. WHO IN THE PRE-SEALING AMERICA REMEMBERED THOSE FOUR SMALL WORDS?
AMER CA WAS TOO... THICK. TOO CERTAIN OF ITSELF. FROM ITS LEADERS TO THE POOREST PERSON IN THE POOREST TOWN.
I SET OUT TO REMIND AMERICA OF WHAT IT ONCE WAS.

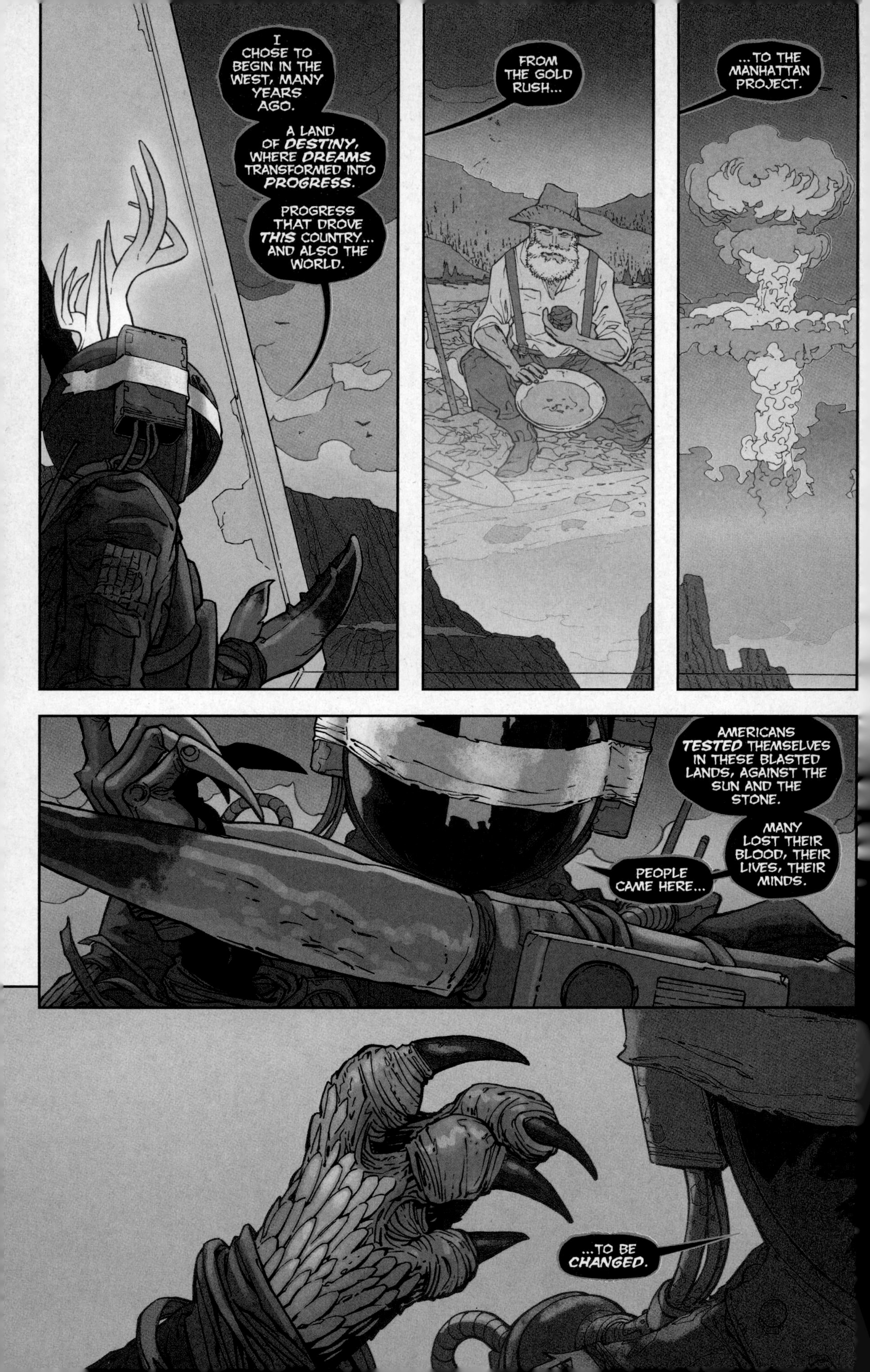
I CHOSE TO BEGIN IN THE WEST, MANY YEARS AGO.
A LAND OF DESTINY, WHERE DREAMS TRANSFORMED INTO PROGRESS.
PROGRESS THAT DROVE THIS COUNTRY... AND ALSO THE WORLD.
FROM THE GOLD RUSH...
...TO THE MANHATTAN PROJECT.
AMERICANS TESTED THEMSELVES IN THESE BLASTED LANDS, AGAINST THE SUN AND THE STONE.
MANY LOST THEIR BLOOD, THEIR LIVES, THEIR MINDS.
PEOPLE CAME HERE...
...TO BE CHANGED.

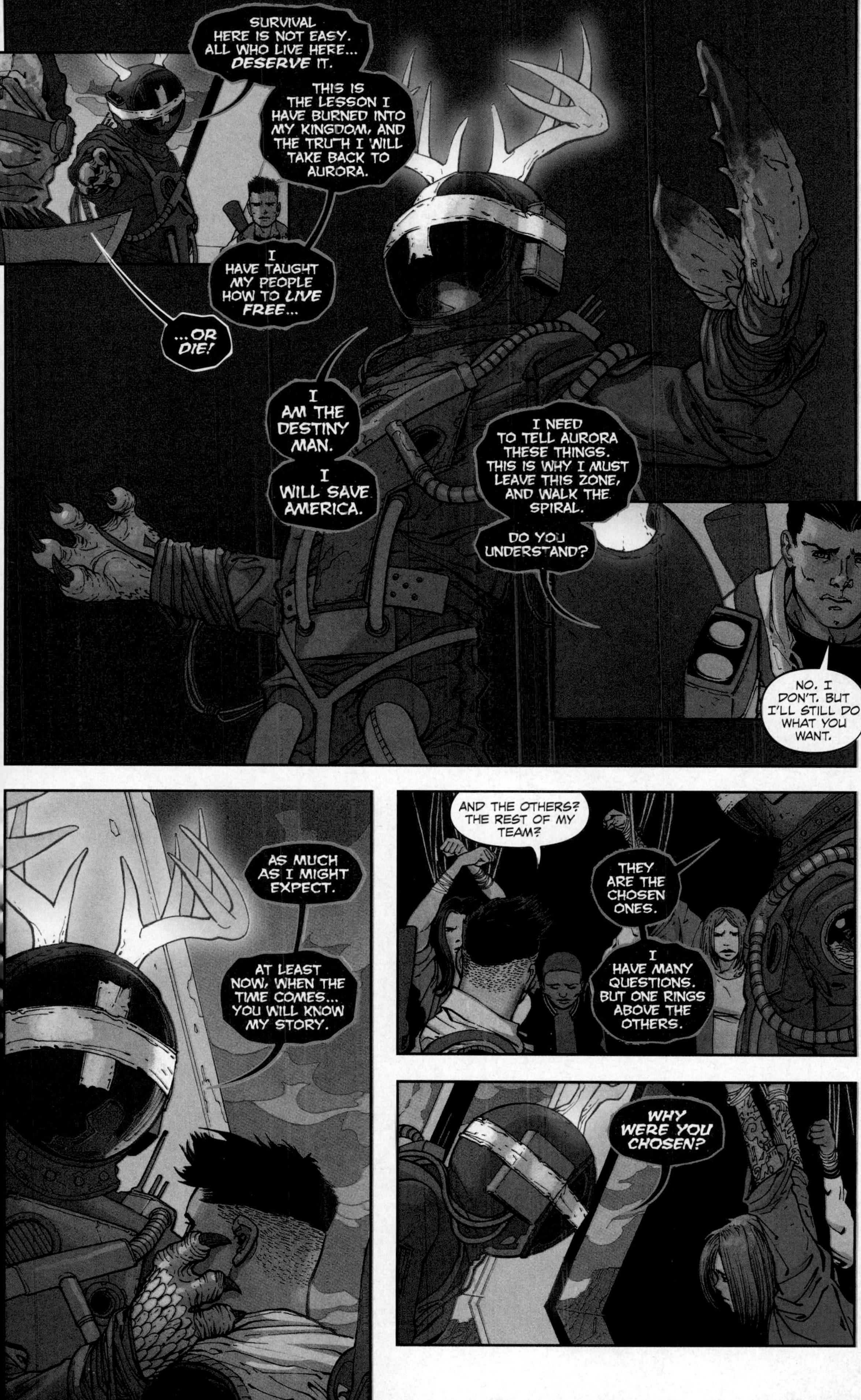
SURVIVAL HERE IS NOT EASY. ALL WHO LIVE HERE... *DESERVE* IT.
THIS IS THE LESSON I HAVE BURNED INTO MY KINGDOM, AND THE TRUTH I WILL TAKE BACK TO AURORA.
I HAVE TAUGHT MY PEOPLE HOW TO *LIVE FREE*...
...OR DIE!
I AM THE DESTINY MAN.
I WILL SAVE AMERICA.
I NEED TO TELL AURORA THESE THINGS. THIS IS WHY I MUST LEAVE THIS ZONE, AND WALK THE SPIRAL.
DO YOU UNDERSTAND?
NO. I DON'T. BUT I'LL STILL DO WHAT YOU WANT.
AS MUCH AS I MIGHT EXPECT.
AT LEAST NOW, WHEN THE TIME COMES... YOU WILL KNOW MY STORY.
AND THE OTHERS? THE REST OF MY TEAM?
THEY ARE THE CHOSEN ONES.
I HAVE MANY QUESTIONS. BUT ONE RINGS ABOVE THE OTHERS.
WHY WERE YOU CHOSEN?

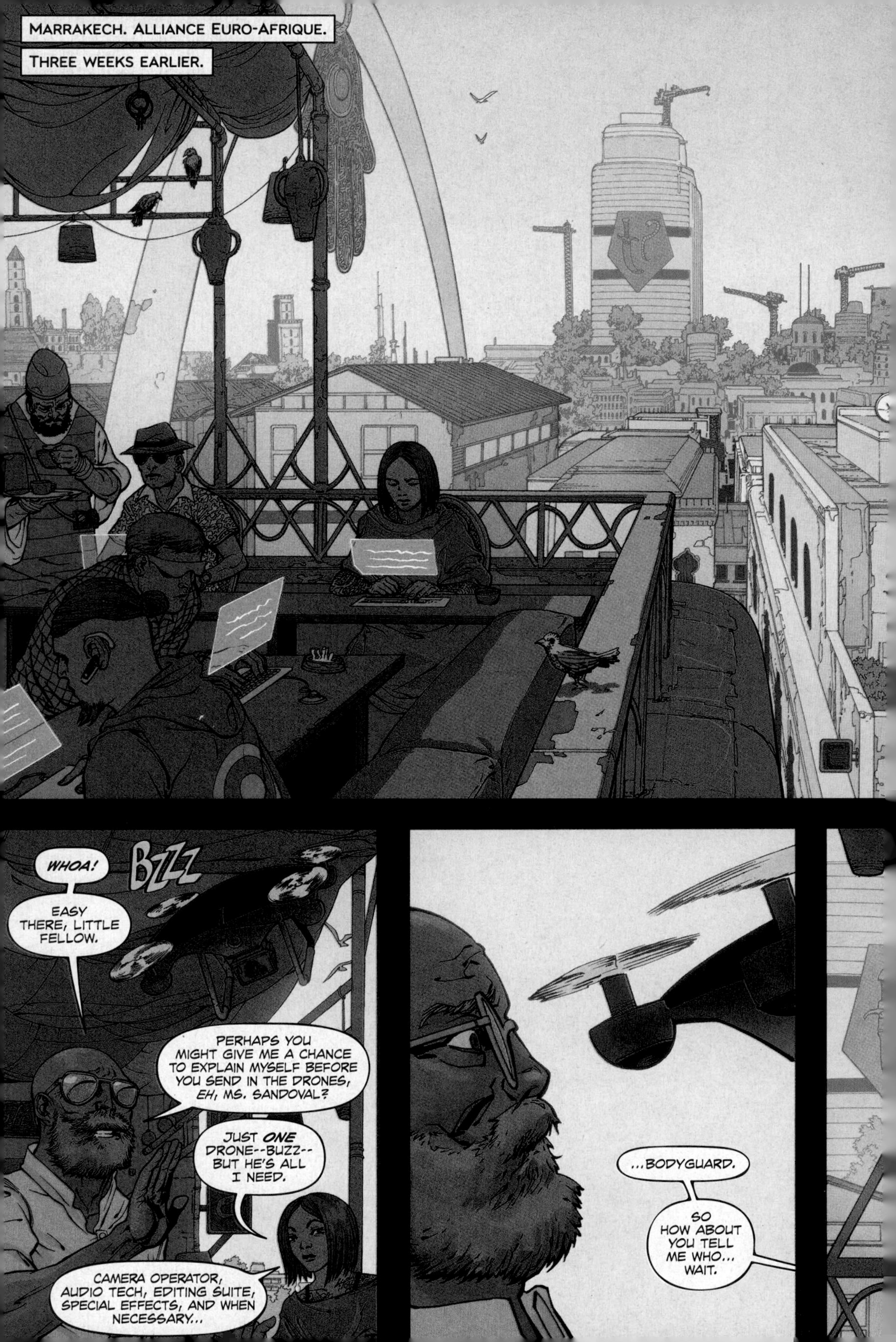
MARRAKECH. ALLIANCE EURO-AFRIQUE.
THREE WEEKS EARLIER.
WHOA!
BZZZ
EASY THERE, LITTLE FELLOW.
PERHAPS YOU MIGHT GIVE ME A CHANCE TO EXPLAIN MYSELF BEFORE YOU SEND IN THE DRONES, EH, MS. SANDOVAL?
JUST ONE DRONE--BUZZ--BUT HE'S ALL I NEED.
CAMERA OPERATOR, AUDIO TECH, EDITING SUITE, SPECIAL EFFECTS, AND WHEN NECESSARY...
...BODYGUARD.
SO HOW ABOUT YOU TELL ME WHO... WAIT.

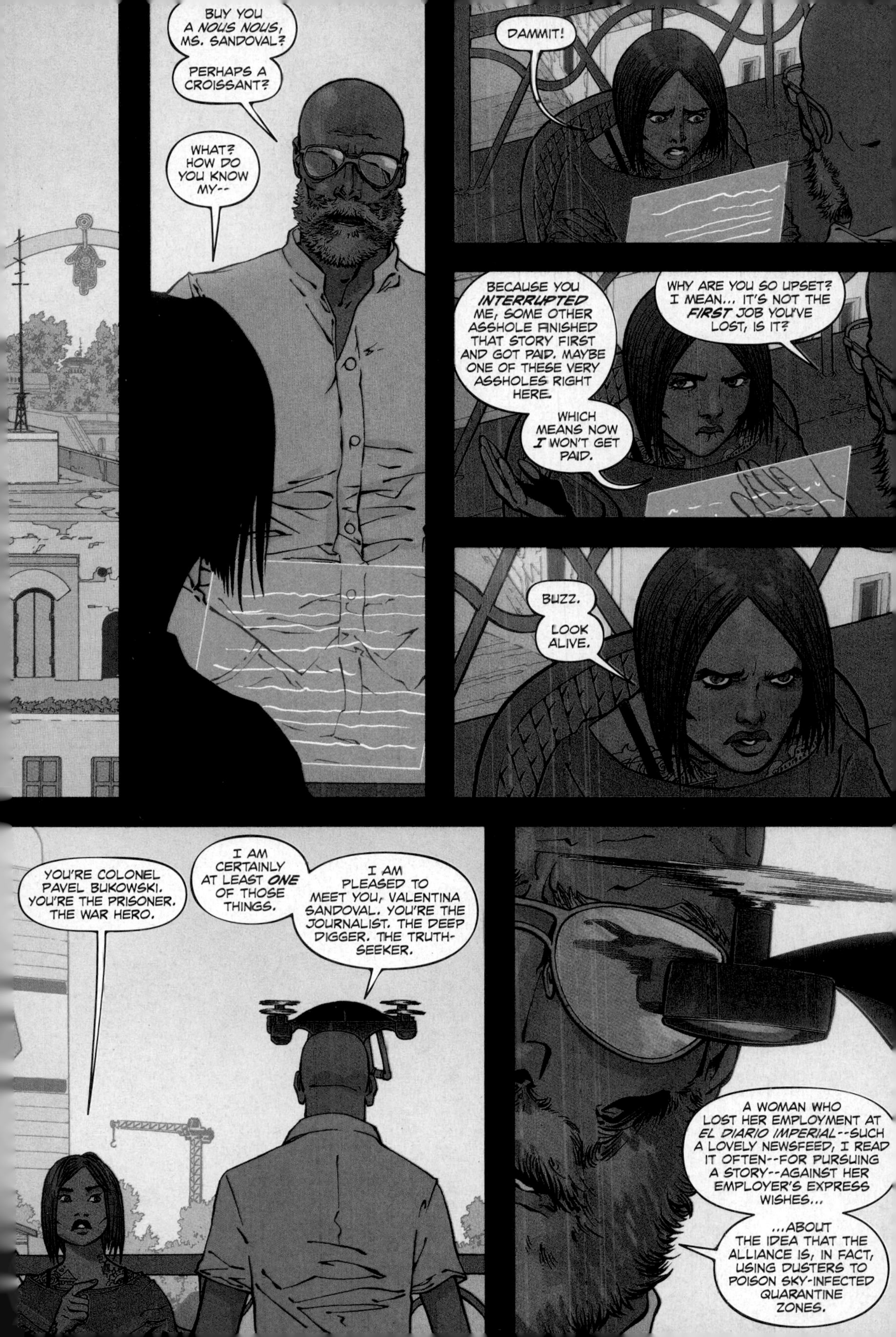
BUY YOU A *NOUS NOUS*, MS. SANDOVAL?
PERHAPS A CROISSANT?
WHAT? HOW DO YOU KNOW MY--
DAMMIT!
BECAUSE YOU ***INTERRUPTED*** ME, SOME OTHER ASSHOLE FINISHED THAT STORY FIRST AND GOT PAID. MAYBE ONE OF THESE VERY ASSHOLES RIGHT HERE.
WHICH MEANS NOW ***I*** WON'T GET PAID.
WHY ARE YOU SO UPSET? I MEAN... IT'S NOT THE ***FIRST*** JOB YOU'VE LOST, IS IT?
BUZZ.
LOOK ALIVE.
YOU'RE COLONEL PAVEL BUKOWSKI. YOU'RE THE PRISONER. THE WAR HERO.
I AM CERTAINLY AT LEAST ***ONE*** OF THOSE THINGS.
I AM PLEASED TO MEET YOU, VALENTINA SANDOVAL. YOU'RE THE JOURNALIST. THE DEEP DIGGER. THE TRUTH-SEEKER.
A WOMAN WHO LOST HER EMPLOYMENT AT *EL DIARIO IMPERIAL*--SUCH A LOVELY NEWSFEED, I READ IT OFTEN--FOR PURSUING A STORY--AGAINST HER EMPLOYER'S EXPRESS WISHES...
...ABOUT THE IDEA THAT THE ALLIANCE IS, IN FACT, USING DUSTERS TO POISON SKY-INFECTED QUARANTINE ZONES.

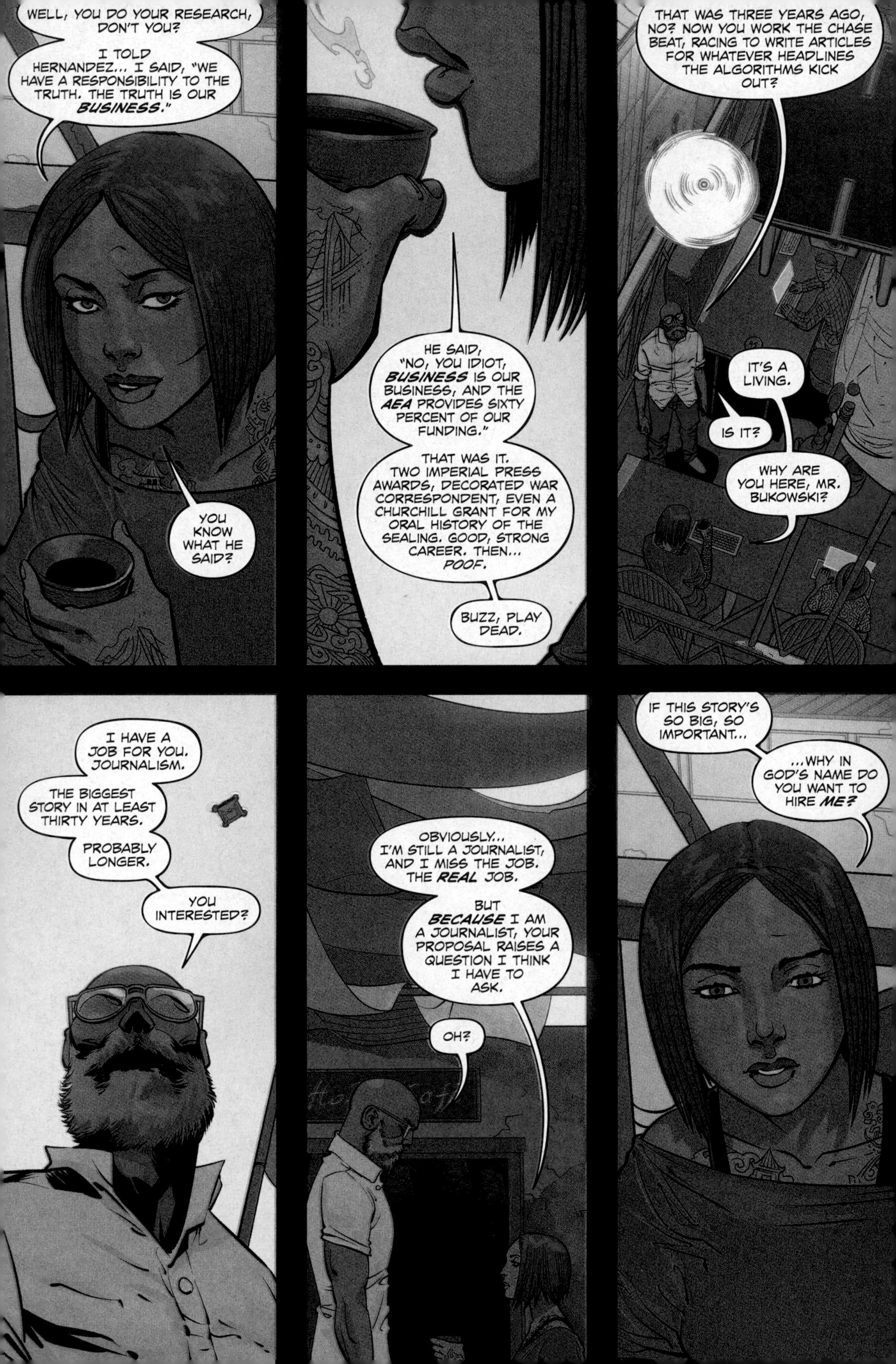
WELL, YOU DO YOUR RESEARCH, DON'T YOU?
I TOLD HERNANDEZ... I SAID, "WE HAVE A RESPONSIBILITY TO THE TRUTH. THE TRUTH IS OUR ***BUSINESS***."
YOU KNOW WHAT HE SAID?
HE SAID, "NO, YOU IDIOT, ***BUSINESS*** IS OUR BUSINESS, AND THE ***AEA*** PROVIDES SIXTY PERCENT OF OUR FUNDING."
THAT WAS IT. TWO IMPERIAL PRESS AWARDS, DECORATED WAR CORRESPONDENT, EVEN A CHURCHILL GRANT FOR MY ORAL HISTORY OF THE SEALING. GOOD, STRONG CAREER. THEN... *POOF*.
BUZZ, PLAY DEAD.
THAT WAS THREE YEARS AGO, NO? NOW YOU WORK THE CHASE BEAT, RACING TO WRITE ARTICLES FOR WHATEVER HEADLINES THE ALGORITHMS KICK OUT?
IT'S A LIVING.
IS IT?
WHY ARE YOU HERE, MR. BUKOWSKI?
I HAVE A JOB FOR YOU. JOURNALISM.
THE BIGGEST STORY IN AT LEAST THIRTY YEARS.
PROBABLY LONGER.
YOU INTERESTED?
OBVIOUSLY... I'M STILL A JOURNALIST, AND I MISS THE JOB. THE ***REAL*** JOB.
BUT ***BECAUSE*** I AM A JOURNALIST, YOUR PROPOSAL RAISES A QUESTION I THINK I HAVE TO ASK.
OH?
IF THIS STORY'S SO BIG, SO IMPORTANT...
...WHY IN GOD'S NAME DO YOU WANT TO HIRE ***ME***?

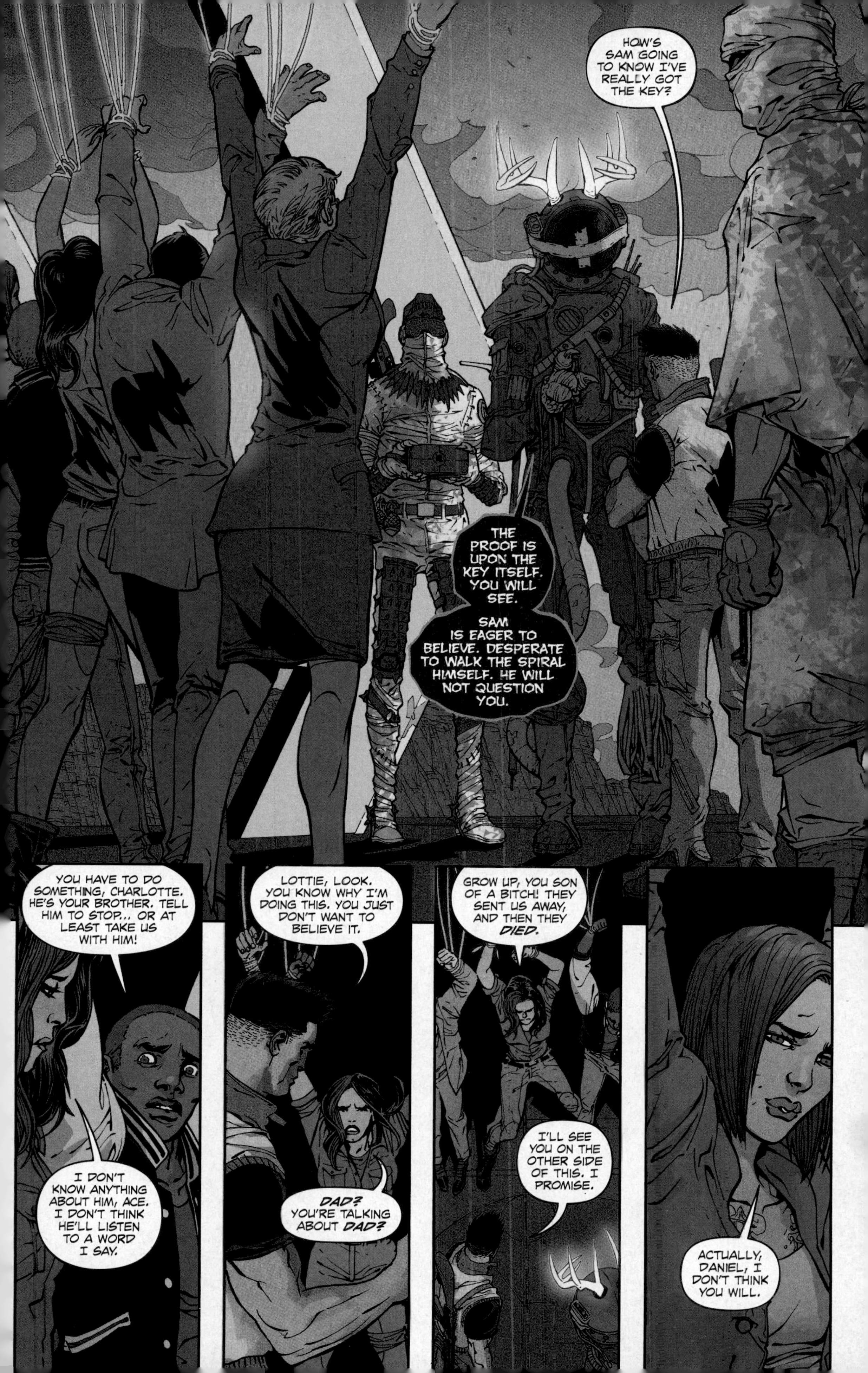
HOW'S SAM GOING TO KNOW I'VE REALLY GOT THE KEY?
THE PROOF IS UPON THE KEY ITSELF. YOU WILL SEE.
SAM IS EAGER TO BELIEVE. DESPERATE TO WALK THE SPIRAL HIMSELF. HE WILL NOT QUESTION YOU.
YOU HAVE TO DO SOMETHING, CHARLOTTE. HE'S YOUR BROTHER. TELL HIM TO STOP... OR AT LEAST TAKE US WITH HIM!
I DON'T KNOW ANYTHING ABOUT HIM, ACE. I DON'T THINK HE'LL LISTEN TO A WORD I SAY.
LOTTIE, LOOK. YOU KNOW WHY I'M DOING THIS. YOU JUST DON'T WANT TO BELIEVE IT.
DAD? YOU'RE TALKING ABOUT DAD?
GROW UP, YOU SON OF A BITCH! THEY SENT US AWAY, AND THEN THEY DIED.
I'LL SEE YOU ON THE OTHER SIDE OF THIS. I PROMISE.
ACTUALLY, DANIEL, I DON'T THINK YOU WILL.

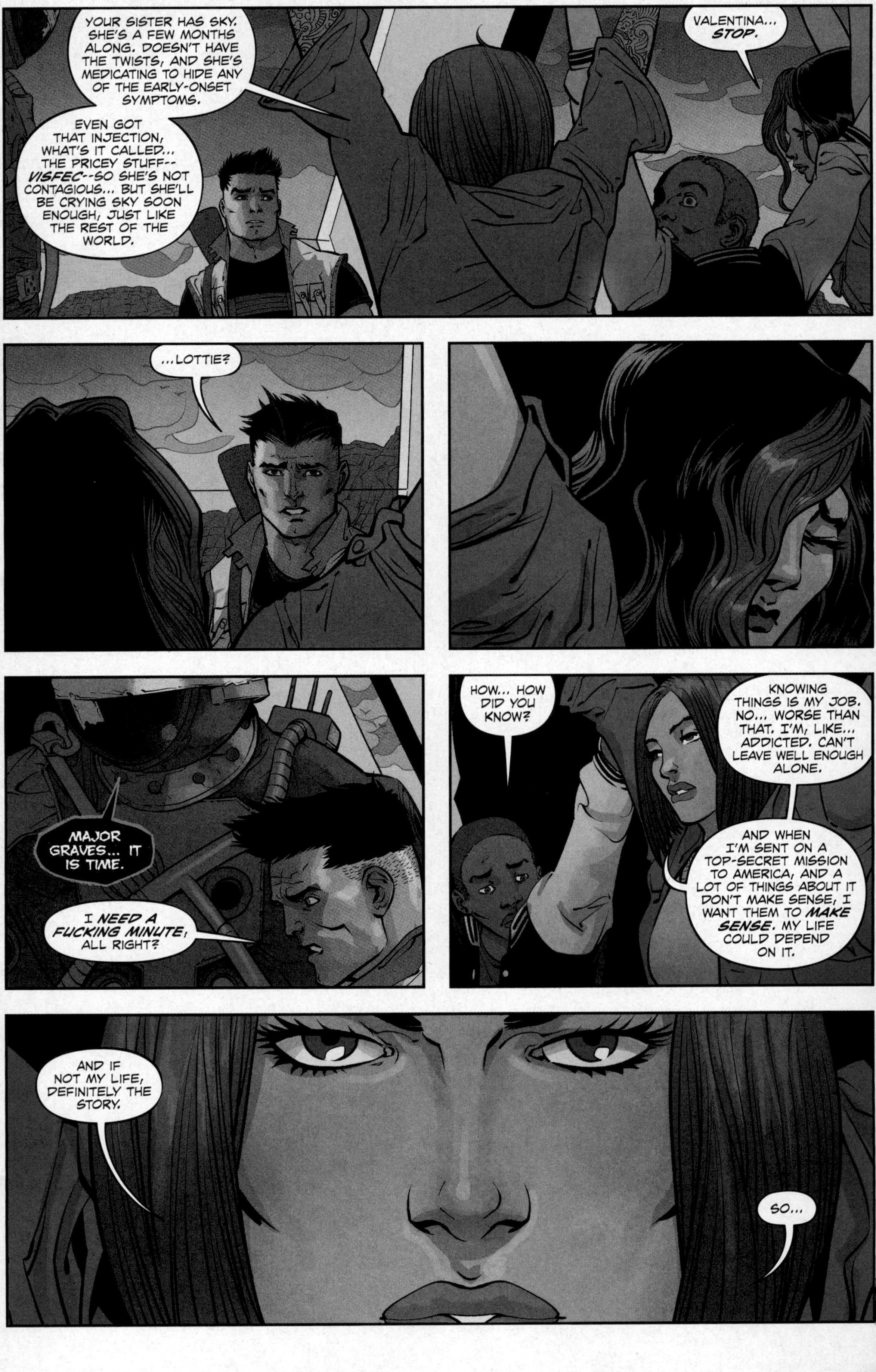
YOUR SISTER HAS SKY. SHE'S A FEW MONTHS ALONG. DOESN'T HAVE THE TWISTS, AND SHE'S MEDICATING TO HIDE ANY OF THE EARLY-ONSET SYMPTOMS.
EVEN GOT THAT INJECTION, WHAT'S IT CALLED... THE PRICEY STUFF-- *VISFEC*--SO SHE'S NOT CONTAGIOUS... BUT SHE'LL BE CRYING SKY SOON ENOUGH, JUST LIKE THE REST OF THE WORLD.
VALENTINA... *STOP.*
...LOTTIE?
MAJOR GRAVES... IT IS TIME.
I *NEED A FUCKING MINUTE*, ALL RIGHT?
HOW... HOW DID YOU KNOW?
KNOWING THINGS IS MY JOB. NO... WORSE THAN THAT. I'M, LIKE... ADDICTED. CAN'T LEAVE WELL ENOUGH ALONE.
AND WHEN I'M SENT ON A TOP-SECRET MISSION TO AMERICA, AND A LOT OF THINGS ABOUT IT DON'T MAKE SENSE, I WANT THEM TO *MAKE SENSE*. MY LIFE COULD DEPEND ON IT.
AND IF NOT MY LIFE, DEFINITELY THE STORY.
SO...

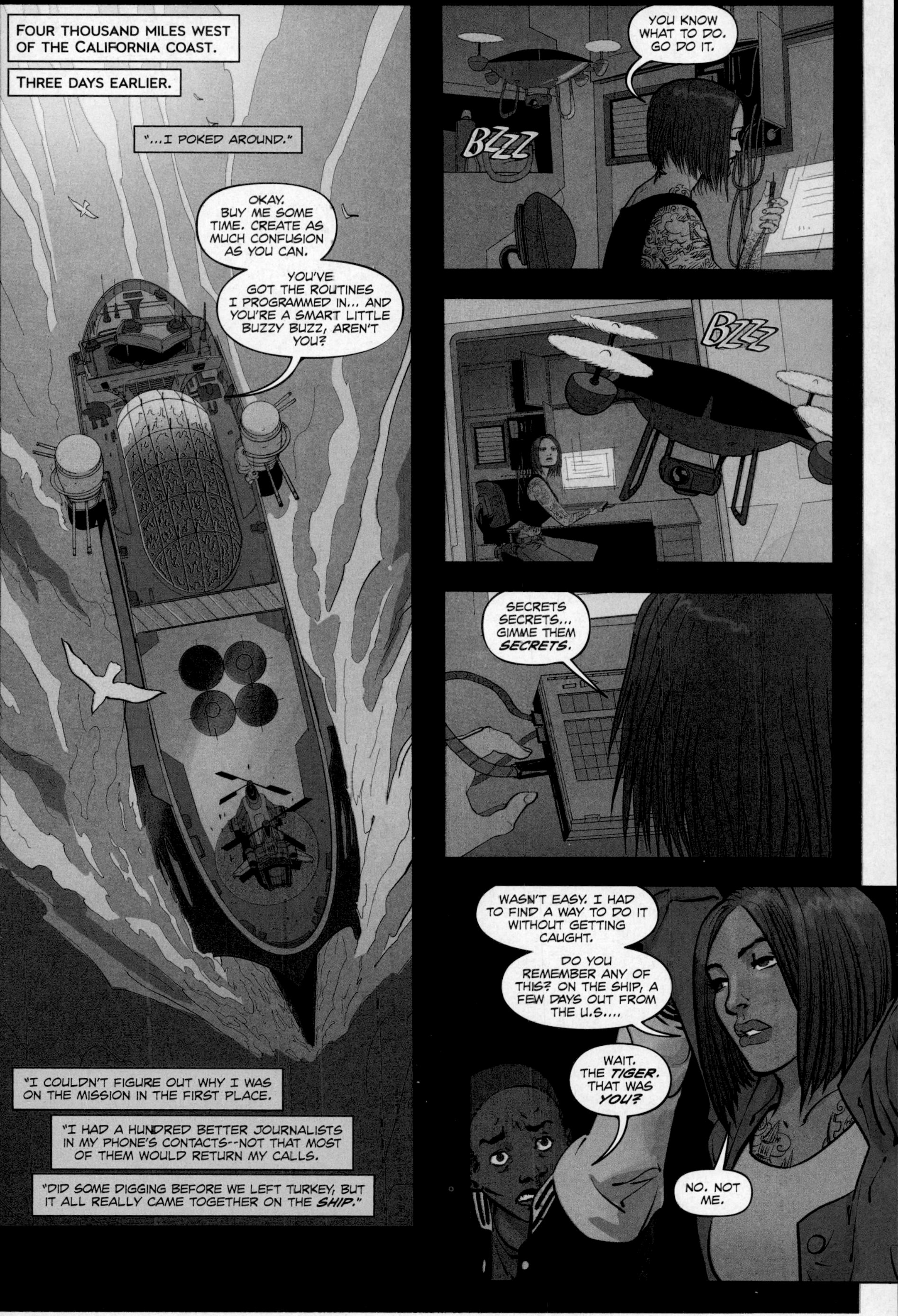
FOUR THOUSAND MILES WEST OF THE CALIFORNIA COAST.
THREE DAYS EARLIER.
"...I POKED AROUND."
OKAY. BUY ME SOME TIME. CREATE AS MUCH CONFUSION AS YOU CAN.
YOU'VE GOT THE ROUTINES I PROGRAMMED IN... AND YOU'RE A SMART LITTLE BUZZY BUZZ, AREN'T YOU?
"I COULDN'T FIGURE OUT WHY I WAS ON THE MISSION IN THE FIRST PLACE.
"I HAD A HUNDRED BETTER JOURNALISTS IN MY PHONE'S CONTACTS--NOT THAT MOST OF THEM WOULD RETURN MY CALLS.
"DID SOME DIGGING BEFORE WE LEFT TURKEY, BUT IT ALL REALLY CAME TOGETHER ON THE *SHIP*."
BZZZ
YOU KNOW WHAT TO DO. GO DO IT.
BZZZ
SECRETS SECRETS... GIMME THEM *SECRETS*.
WASN'T EASY. I HAD TO FIND A WAY TO DO IT WITHOUT GETTING CAUGHT.
DO YOU REMEMBER ANY OF THIS? ON THE SHIP, A FEW DAYS OUT FROM THE U.S....
WAIT. THE *TIGER*. THAT WAS *YOU?*
NO. NOT ME.

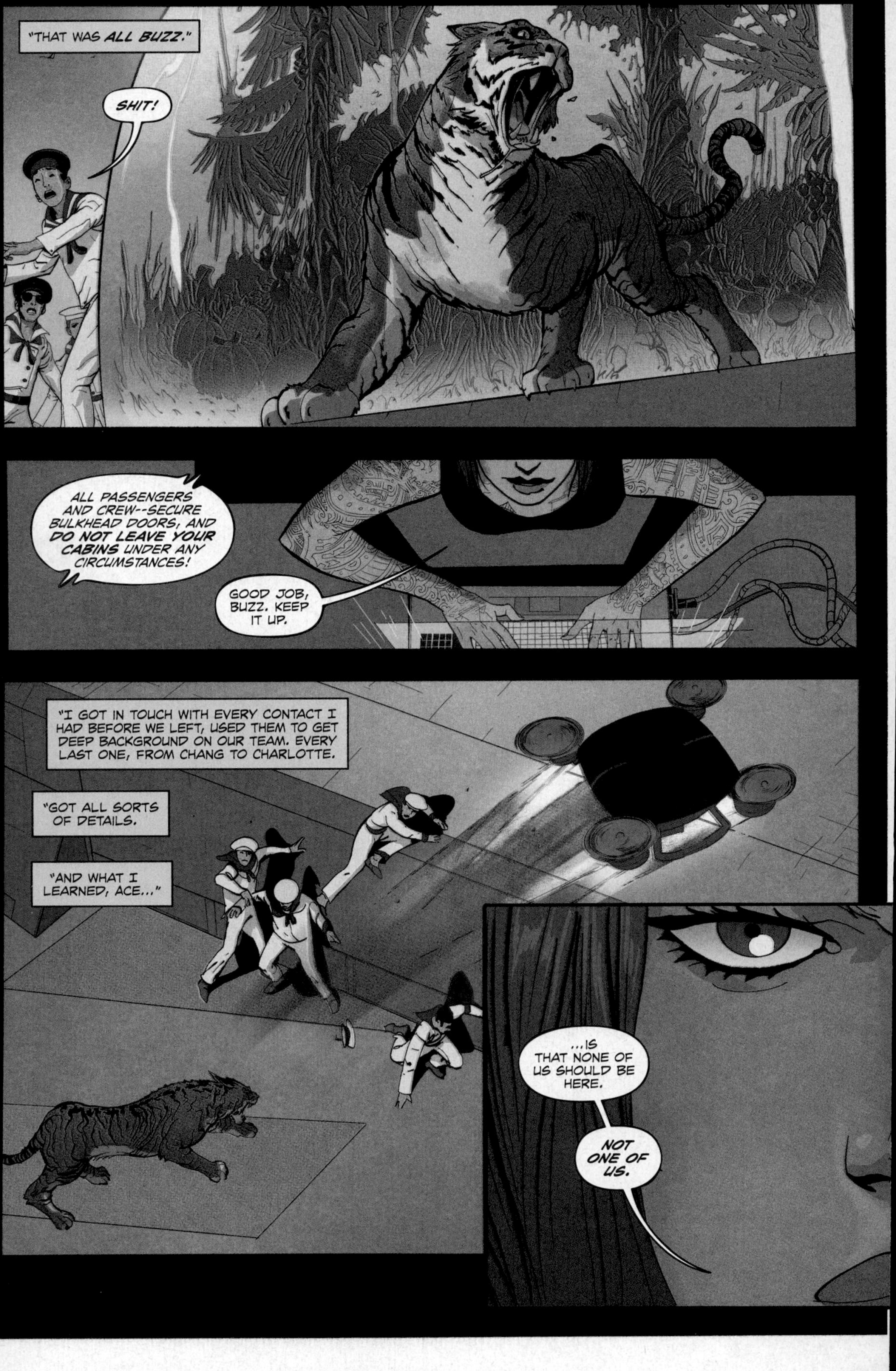
"THAT WAS ALL BUZZ."
SHIT!
ALL PASSENGERS AND CREW--SECURE BULKHEAD DOORS, AND DO NOT LEAVE YOUR CABINS UNDER ANY CIRCUMSTANCES!
GOOD JOB, BUZZ. KEEP IT UP.
"I GOT IN TOUCH WITH EVERY CONTACT I HAD BEFORE WE LEFT, USED THEM TO GET DEEP BACKGROUND ON OUR TEAM. EVERY LAST ONE, FROM CHANG TO CHARLOTTE.
"GOT ALL SORTS OF DETAILS.
"AND WHAT I LEARNED, ACE..."
...IS THAT NONE OF US SHOULD BE HERE.
NOT ONE OF US.

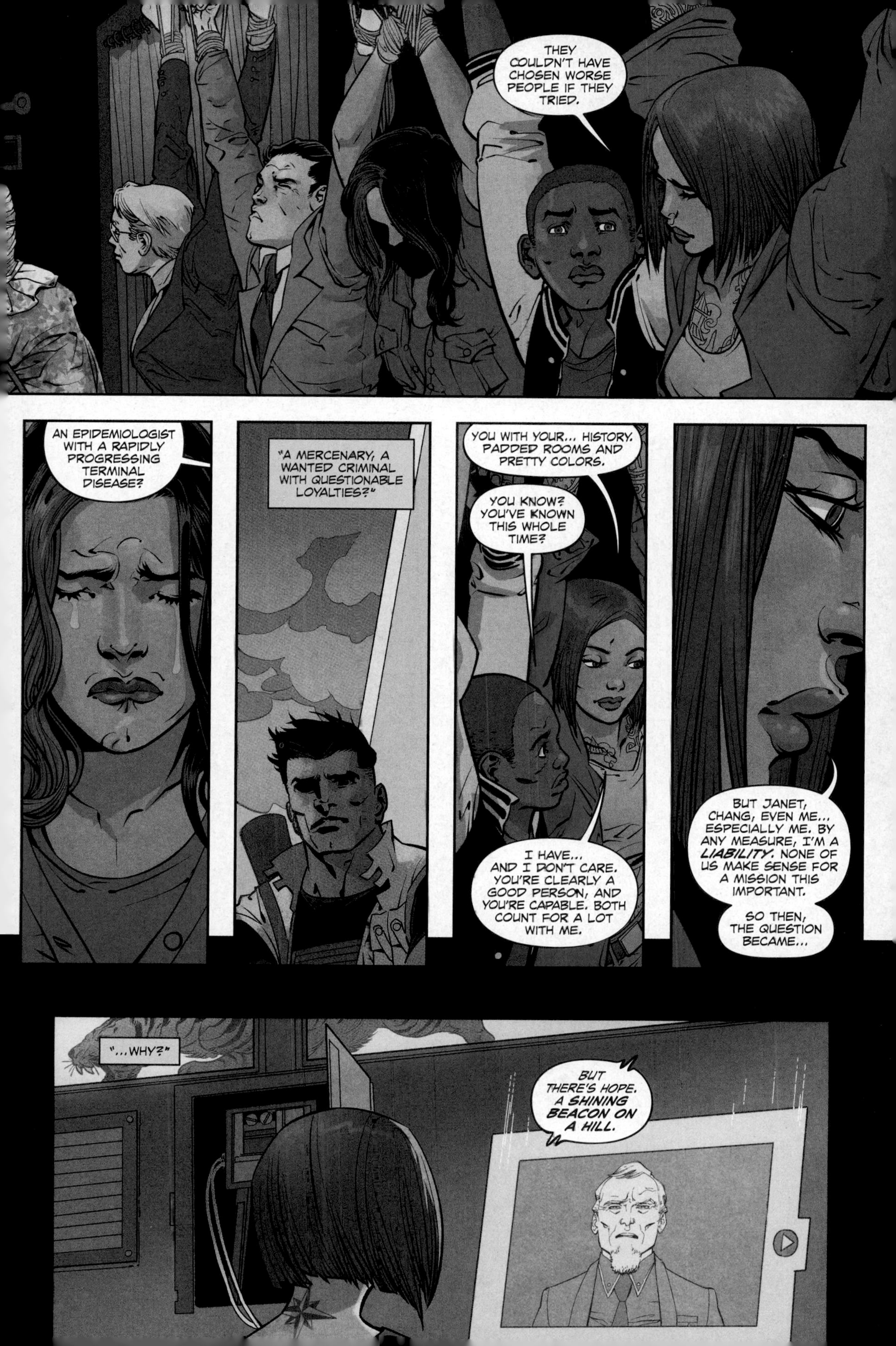
THEY COULDN'T HAVE CHOSEN WORSE PEOPLE IF THEY TRIED.
AN EPIDEMIOLOGIST WITH A RAPIDLY PROGRESSING TERMINAL DISEASE?
"A MERCENARY, A WANTED CRIMINAL WITH QUESTIONABLE LOYALTIES?"
YOU WITH YOUR... HISTORY. PADDED ROOMS AND PRETTY COLORS.
YOU KNOW? YOU'VE KNOWN THIS WHOLE TIME?
I HAVE... AND I DON'T CARE. YOU'RE CLEARLY A GOOD PERSON, AND YOU'RE CAPABLE. BOTH COUNT FOR A LOT WITH ME.
BUT JANET, CHANG, EVEN ME... ESPECIALLY ME. BY ANY MEASURE, I'M A *LIABILITY*. NONE OF US MAKE SENSE FOR A MISSION THIS IMPORTANT.
SO THEN, THE QUESTION BECAME...
"...WHY?"
*BUT THERE'S HOPE. A **SHINING BEACON** ON A **HILL**.*

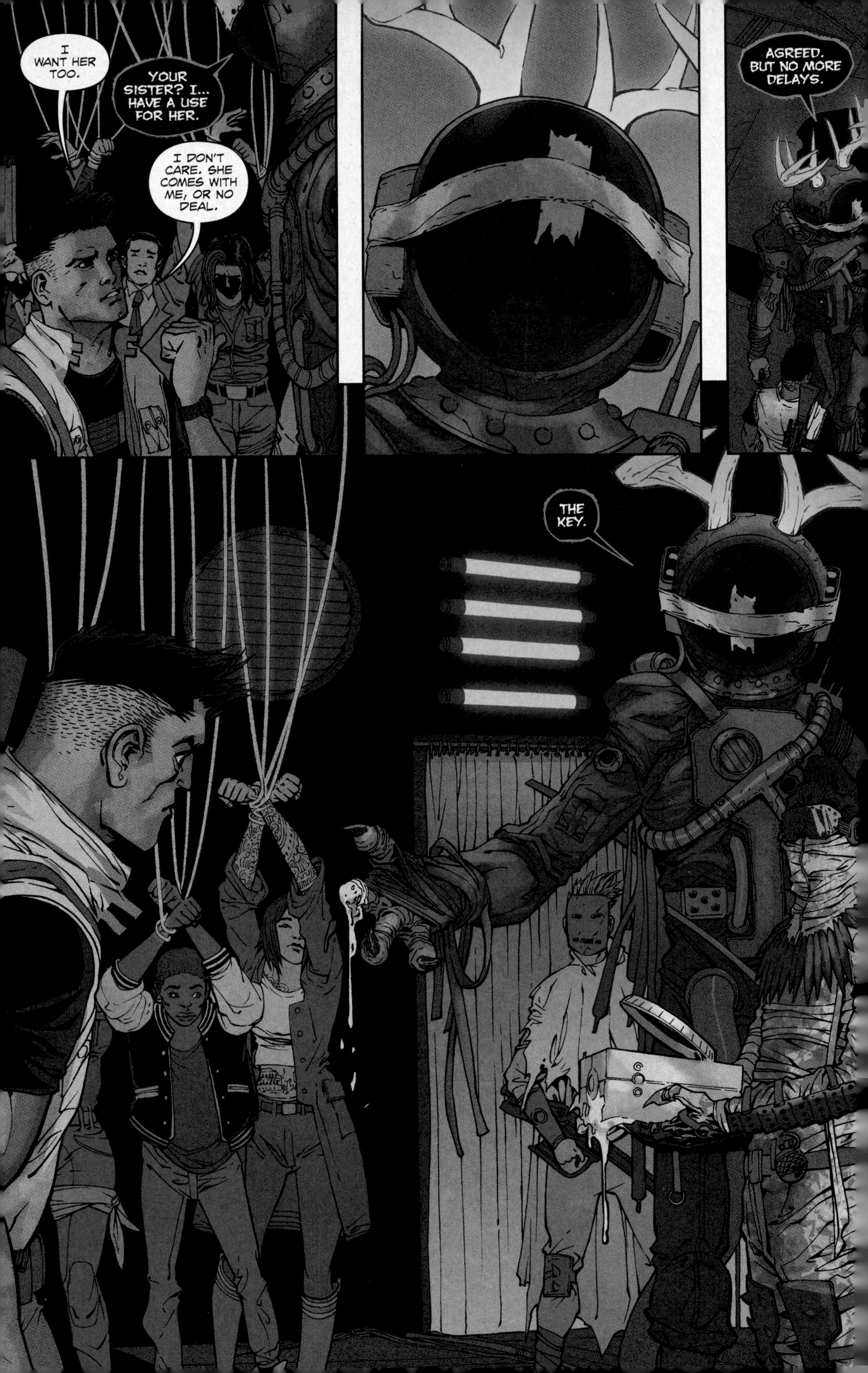
I WANT HER TOO.
YOUR SISTER? I... HAVE A USE FOR HER.
I DON'T CARE. SHE COMES WITH ME, OR NO DEAL.
AGREED. BUT NO MORE DELAYS.
THE KEY.

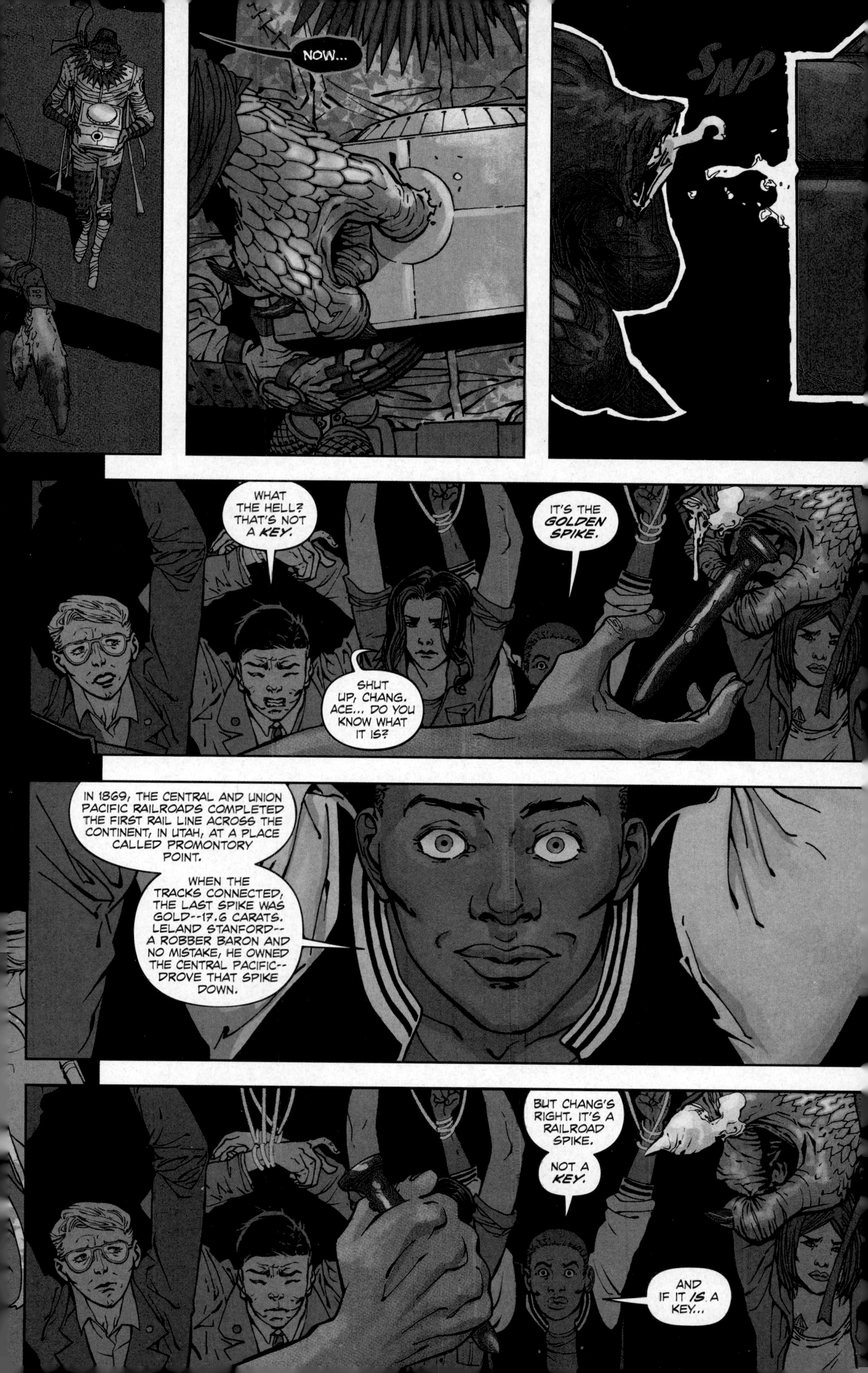
NOW...
SNP
WHAT THE HELL? THAT'S NOT A KEY.
IT'S THE GOLDEN SPIKE.
SHUT UP, CHANG. ACE... DO YOU KNOW WHAT IT IS?
IN 1869, THE CENTRAL AND UNION PACIFIC RAILROADS COMPLETED THE FIRST RAIL LINE ACROSS THE CONTINENT, IN UTAH, AT A PLACE CALLED PROMONTORY POINT.
WHEN THE TRACKS CONNECTED, THE LAST SPIKE WAS GOLD--17.6 CARATS. LELAND STANFORD-- A ROBBER BARON AND NO MISTAKE, HE OWNED THE CENTRAL PACIFIC-- DROVE THAT SPIKE DOWN.
BUT CHANG'S RIGHT. IT'S A RAILROAD SPIKE.
NOT A KEY.
AND IF IT IS A KEY...

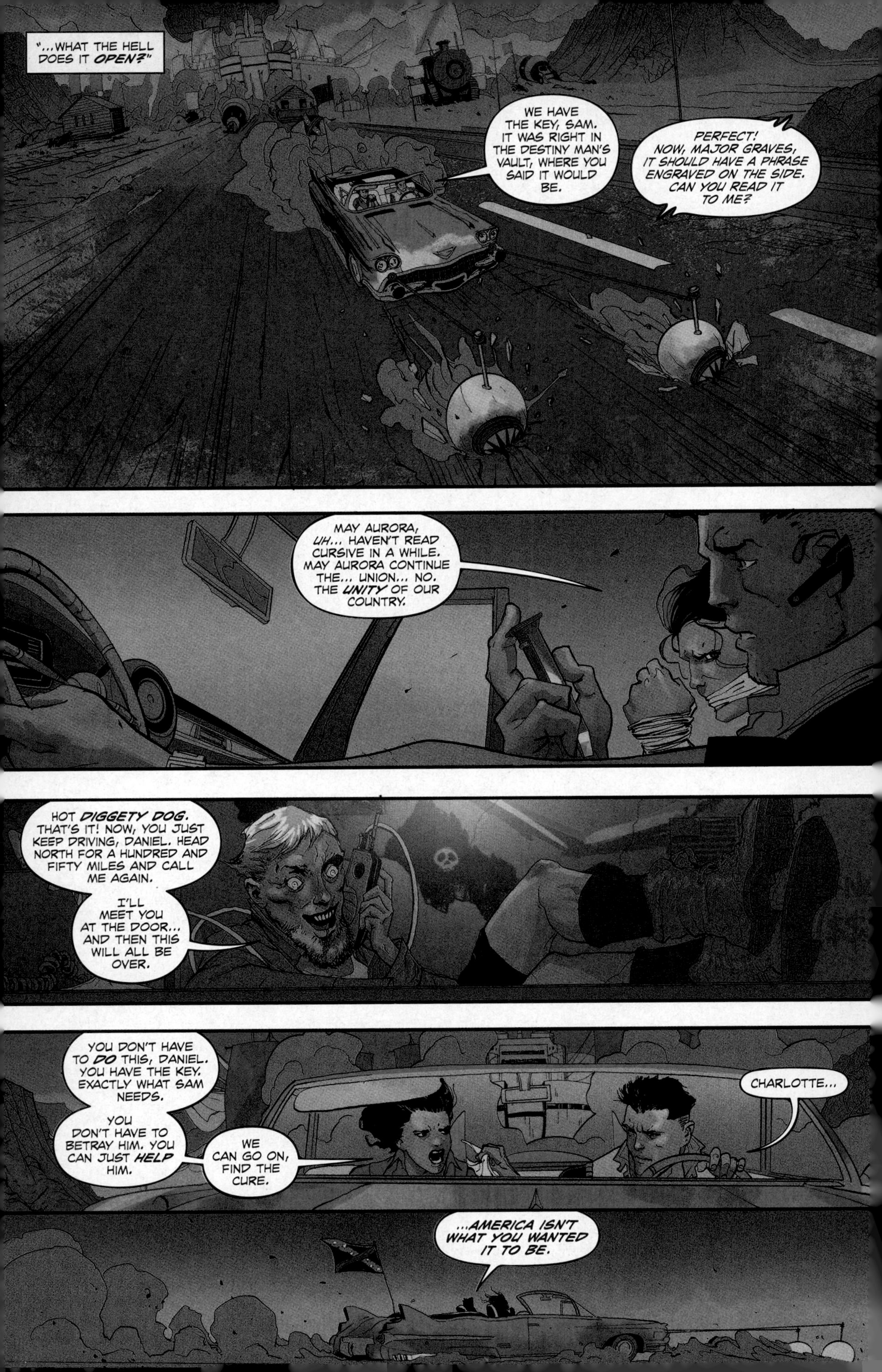
"...WHAT THE HELL DOES IT OPEN?"
WE HAVE THE KEY, SAM. IT WAS RIGHT IN THE DESTINY MAN'S VAULT, WHERE YOU SAID IT WOULD BE.
PERFECT! NOW, MAJOR GRAVES, IT SHOULD HAVE A PHRASE ENGRAVED ON THE SIDE. CAN YOU READ IT TO ME?
MAY AURORA, UH... HAVEN'T READ CURSIVE IN A WHILE. MAY AURORA CONTINUE THE... UNION... NO. THE UNITY OF OUR COUNTRY.
HOT DIGGETY DOG. THAT'S IT! NOW, YOU JUST KEEP DRIVING, DANIEL. HEAD NORTH FOR A HUNDRED AND FIFTY MILES AND CALL ME AGAIN.
I'LL MEET YOU AT THE DOOR... AND THEN THIS WILL ALL BE OVER.
YOU DON'T HAVE TO DO THIS, DANIEL. YOU HAVE THE KEY. EXACTLY WHAT SAM NEEDS.
YOU DON'T HAVE TO BETRAY HIM. YOU CAN JUST HELP HIM.
WE CAN GO ON, FIND THE CURE.
CHARLOTTE...
...AMERICA ISN'T WHAT YOU WANTED IT TO BE.

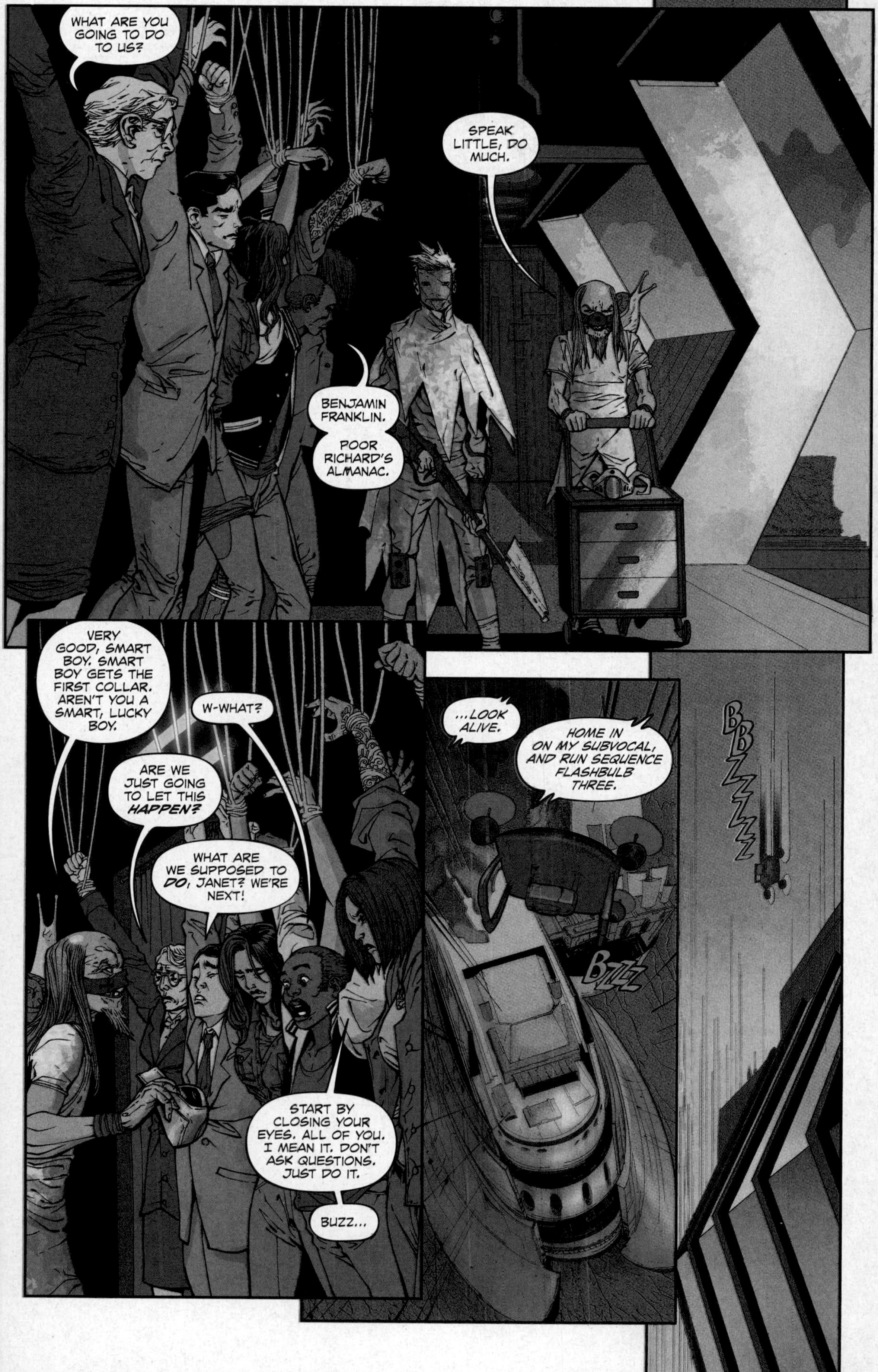
WHAT ARE YOU GOING TO DO TO US?
SPEAK LITTLE, DO MUCH.
BENJAMIN FRANKLIN.
POOR RICHARD'S ALMANAC.
VERY GOOD, SMART BOY. SMART BOY GETS THE FIRST COLLAR. AREN'T YOU A SMART, LUCKY BOY.
W-WHAT?
ARE WE JUST GOING TO LET THIS HAPPEN?
WHAT ARE WE SUPPOSED TO DO, JANET? WE'RE NEXT!
START BY CLOSING YOUR EYES. ALL OF YOU. I MEAN IT. DON'T ASK QUESTIONS. JUST DO IT.
BUZZ...
...LOOK ALIVE.
HOME IN ON MY SUBVOCAL, AND RUN SEQUENCE FLASHBULB THREE.
BZZZ
BBZZZZZ

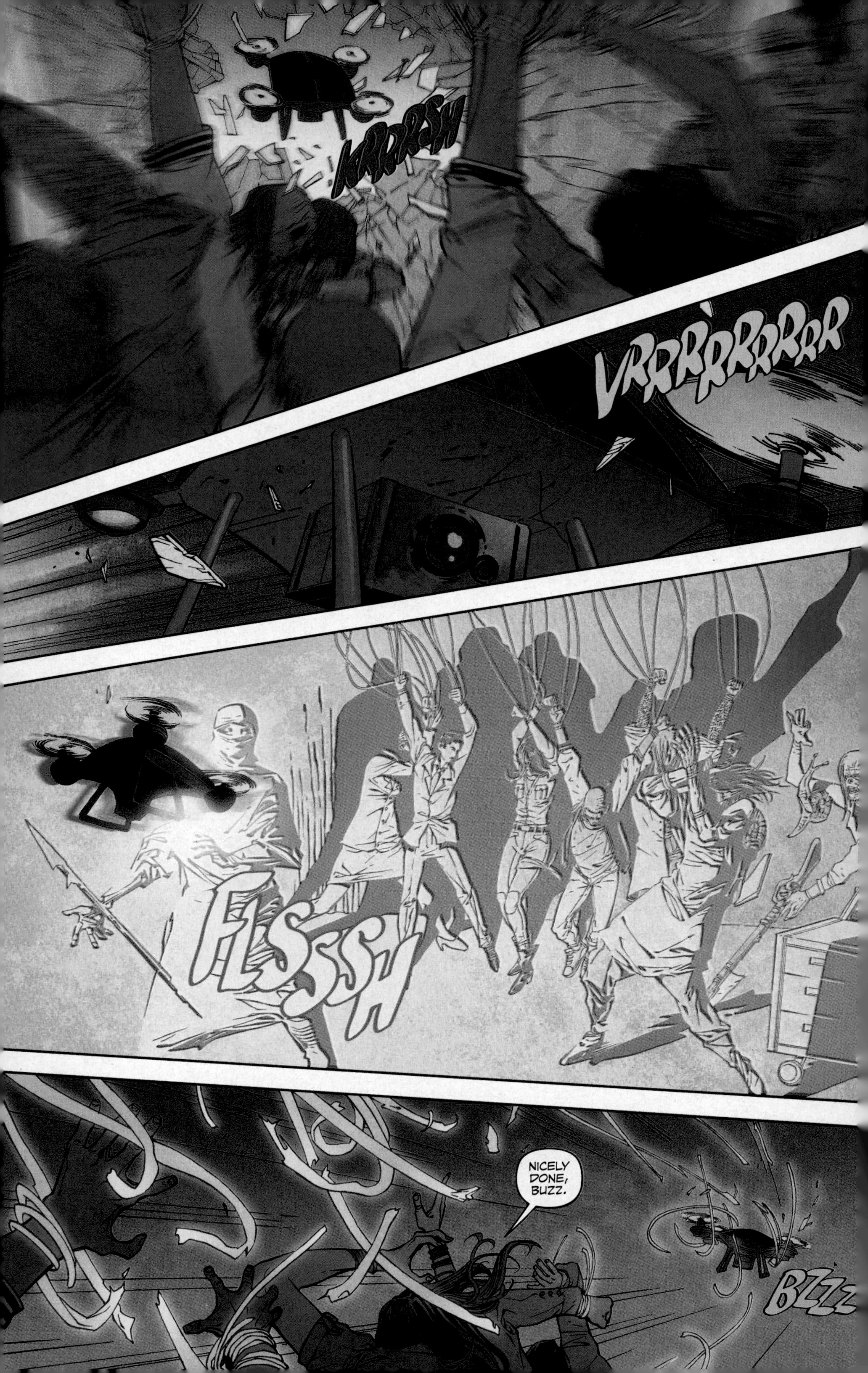
KRRRSH
VRRRRRRRRR
FLSSSH
NICELY DONE, BUZZ.
BZZZ

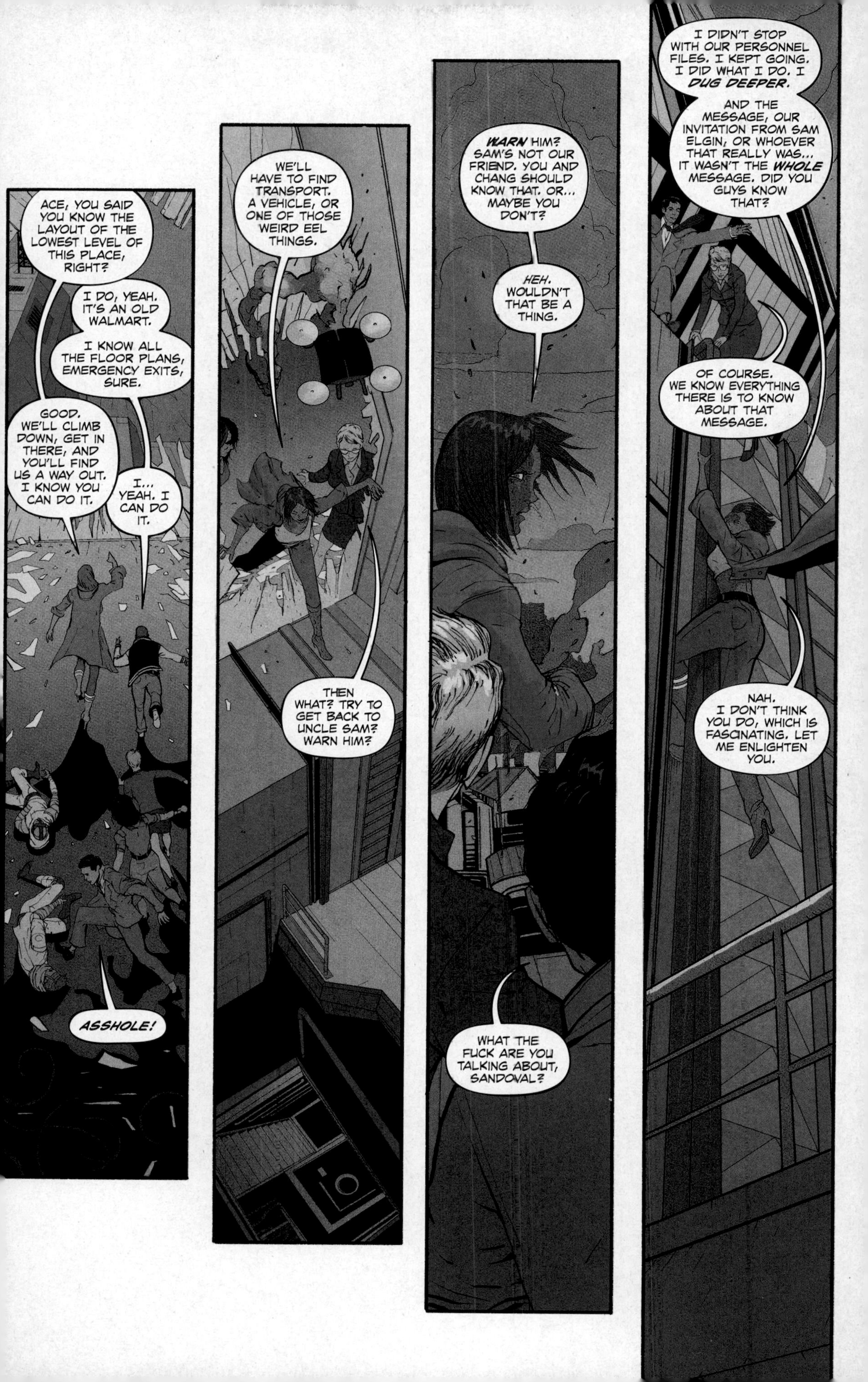
ACE, YOU SAID YOU KNOW THE LAYOUT OF THE LOWEST LEVEL OF THIS PLACE, RIGHT?
I DO, YEAH. IT'S AN OLD WALMART.
I KNOW ALL THE FLOOR PLANS, EMERGENCY EXITS, SURE.
GOOD. WE'LL CLIMB DOWN, GET IN THERE, AND YOU'LL FIND US A WAY OUT. I KNOW YOU CAN DO IT.
I... YEAH. I CAN DO IT.
ASSHOLE!
WE'LL HAVE TO FIND TRANSPORT. A VEHICLE, OR ONE OF THOSE WEIRD EEL THINGS.
THEN WHAT? TRY TO GET BACK TO UNCLE SAM? WARN HIM?
WARN HIM? SAM'S NOT OUR FRIEND. YOU AND CHANG SHOULD KNOW THAT. OR... MAYBE YOU DON'T?
HEH. WOULDN'T THAT BE A THING.
WHAT THE FUCK ARE YOU TALKING ABOUT, SANDOVAL?
I DIDN'T STOP WITH OUR PERSONNEL FILES. I KEPT GOING. I DID WHAT I DO. I DUG DEEPER.
AND THE MESSAGE, OUR INVITATION FROM SAM ELGIN, OR WHOEVER THAT REALLY WAS... IT WASN'T THE WHOLE MESSAGE. DID YOU GUYS KNOW THAT?
OF COURSE. WE KNOW EVERYTHING THERE IS TO KNOW ABOUT THAT MESSAGE.
NAH. I DON'T THINK YOU DO, WHICH IS FASCINATING. LET ME ENLIGHTEN YOU.

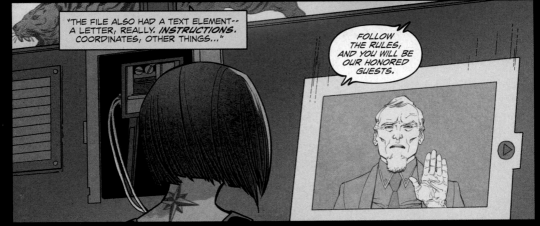

"THE FILE ALSO HAD A TEXT ELEMENT-- A LETTER, REALLY. *INSTRUCTIONS.* COORDINATES, OTHER THINGS..."

FOLLOW THE RULES, AND YOU WILL BE OUR HONORED GUESTS.

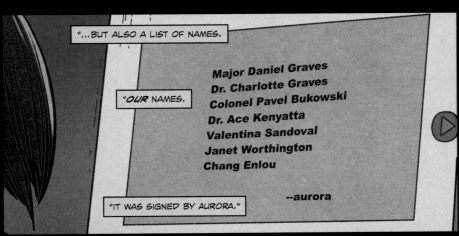

"...BUT ALSO A LIST OF NAMES.

"*OUR* NAMES.

Major Daniel Graves

Dr. Charlotte Graves

Colonel Pavel Bukowski

Dr. Ace Kenyatta

Valentina Sandoval

Janet Worthington

Chang Enlou

--aurora

"IT WAS SIGNED BY AURORA."

WE SEVEN SHOULD *NOT BE HERE,* IF THE GOAL IS TO FIND A CURE TO SAVE HUMANITY FROM SKY. WE ARE *TERRIBLE CHOICES* FOR THAT.

SO I ASKED *WHY...* AND THE ANSWER SEEMS TO BE ONE WORD: *AURORA.*

IT... SHE, OR IT... SPECIFICALLY ASKED FOR US. EVERY LAST ONE OF US.

I'M GOING THAT WAY. COME WITH ME, OR DON'T. I'LL CATCH UP WITH DANIEL, AND BUZZ WILL HELP ME STEAL THAT KEY.

I'LL USE IT TO MAKE UNCLE SAM TELL ME EVERYTHING THAT'S ACTUALLY HAPPENING HERE. THEN... OFF WE GO, BACK OUT TO THE WORLD.

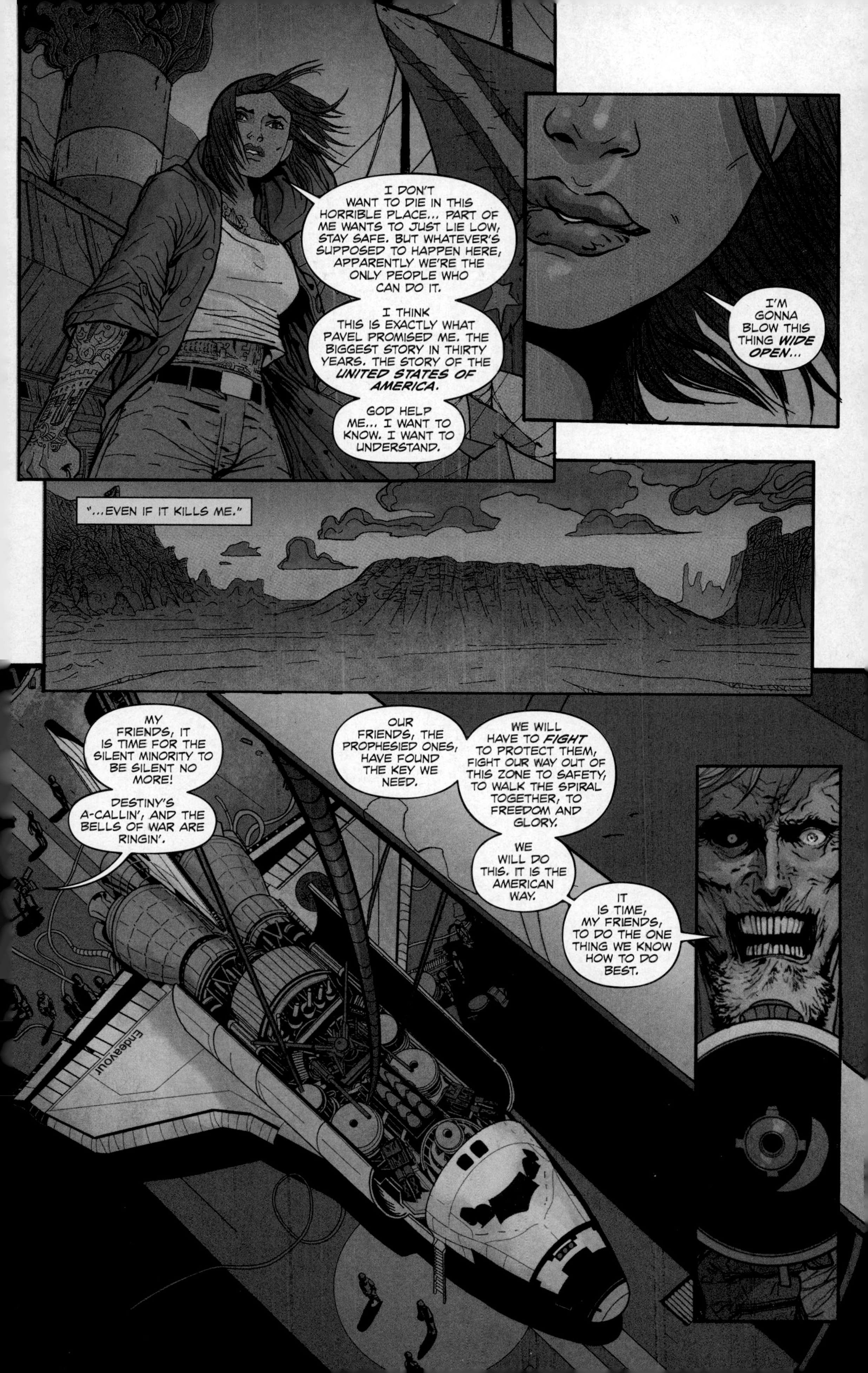
I DON'T WANT TO DIE IN THIS HORRIBLE PLACE... PART OF ME WANTS TO JUST LIE LOW, STAY SAFE. BUT WHATEVER'S SUPPOSED TO HAPPEN HERE, APPARENTLY WE'RE THE ONLY PEOPLE WHO CAN DO IT.
I THINK THIS IS EXACTLY WHAT PAVEL PROMISED ME. THE BIGGEST STORY IN THIRTY YEARS. THE STORY OF THE ***UNITED STATES OF AMERICA.***
GOD HELP ME... I WANT TO KNOW. I WANT TO UNDERSTAND.
I'M GONNA BLOW THIS THING ***WIDE OPEN...***
"...EVEN IF IT KILLS ME."
MY FRIENDS, IT IS TIME FOR THE SILENT MINORITY TO BE SILENT NO MORE!
DESTINY'S A-CALLIN', AND THE BELLS OF WAR ARE RINGIN'.
OUR FRIENDS, THE PROPHESIED ONES, HAVE FOUND THE KEY WE NEED.
WE WILL HAVE TO ***FIGHT*** TO PROTECT THEM, FIGHT OUR WAY OUT OF THIS ZONE TO SAFETY, TO WALK THE SPIRAL TOGETHER, TO FREEDOM AND GLORY.
WE WILL DO THIS. IT IS THE AMERICAN WAY.
IT IS TIME, MY FRIENDS, TO DO THE ONE THING WE KNOW HOW TO DO BEST.
Endeavour

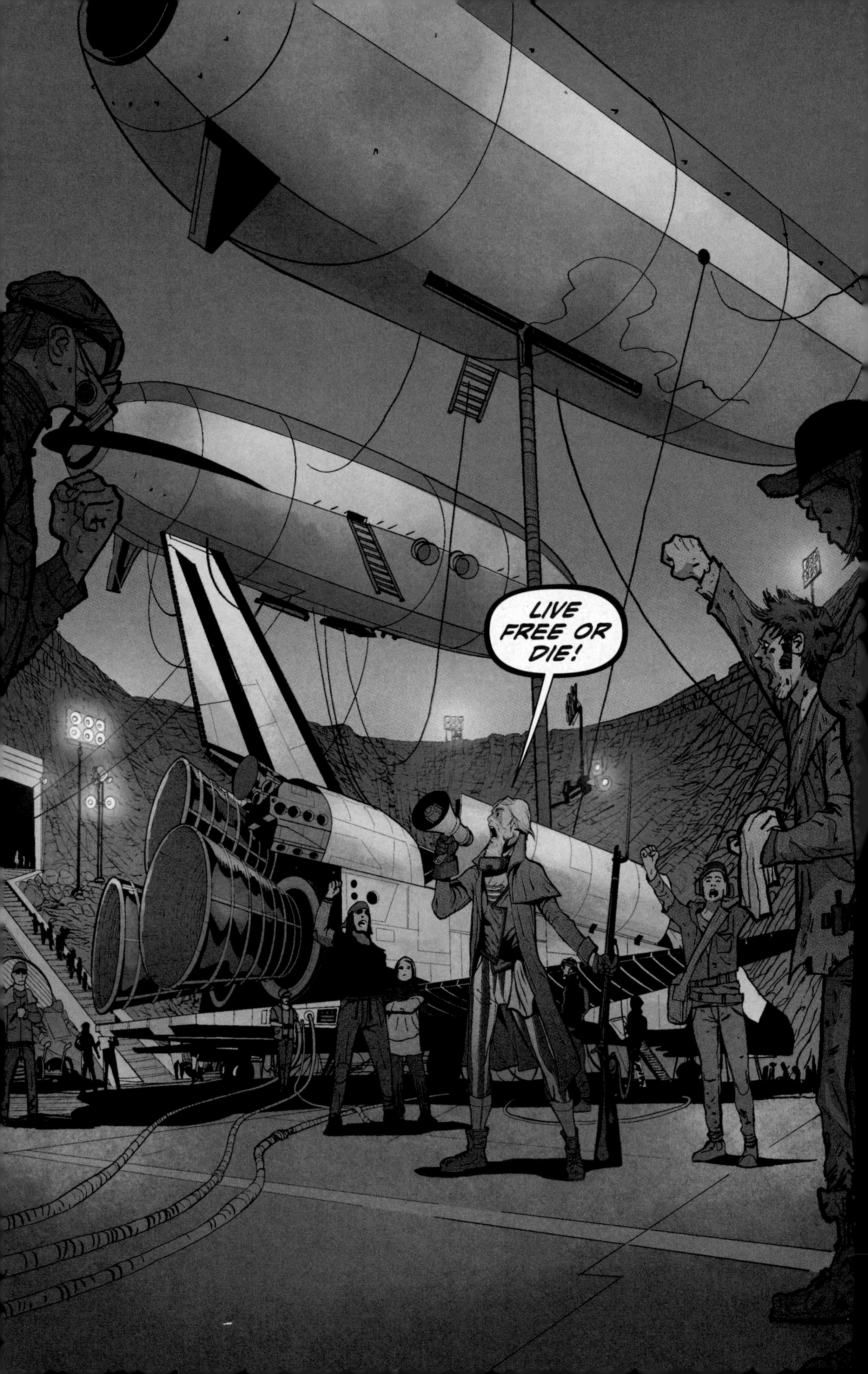
LIVE FREE OR DIE!

"I invested my entire fortune into a construction project in Arizona. My family and I were supposed to get immigrant visas from the process, part of a government plan to encourage foreign money to come to the United States. Two and a half million dollars, which was quite a bit of money then. Then, the Sealing, and there was no way to communicate with anyone. The embassy was closed, empty. No email, no phone. My money, my dream, gone in a day.
A good lesson to learn, I suppose."

–Ling Wang Fang, 73, Hong Kong, Pan-Asian Prosperity Zone

"I was in the Army, a sergeant stationed at Caserma Ederle in Vincenzo, Italy with the 173rd Airborne. No one could really believe it when the US started closing all its military bases outside the borders. The States had a continuous military presence worldwide for more than a century. It was chaos, really. I decided not to go back. I... deserted. I was seeing someone there and couldn't bring them back with me. It was complicated. Kept thinking the MPs would show up one day and grab me—but they never did."

—Edward Jones, 53, Warsaw, Alliance Euro-Afrique

"The United States? Teacher talks about that in school sometimes."

–Melana Lopez, 9, Caracas, Pan-Asian Prosperity Zone

Quotes from *The New World: An Oral History of the Sealing* by Valentina Sandoval.

CHAPTER FIVE

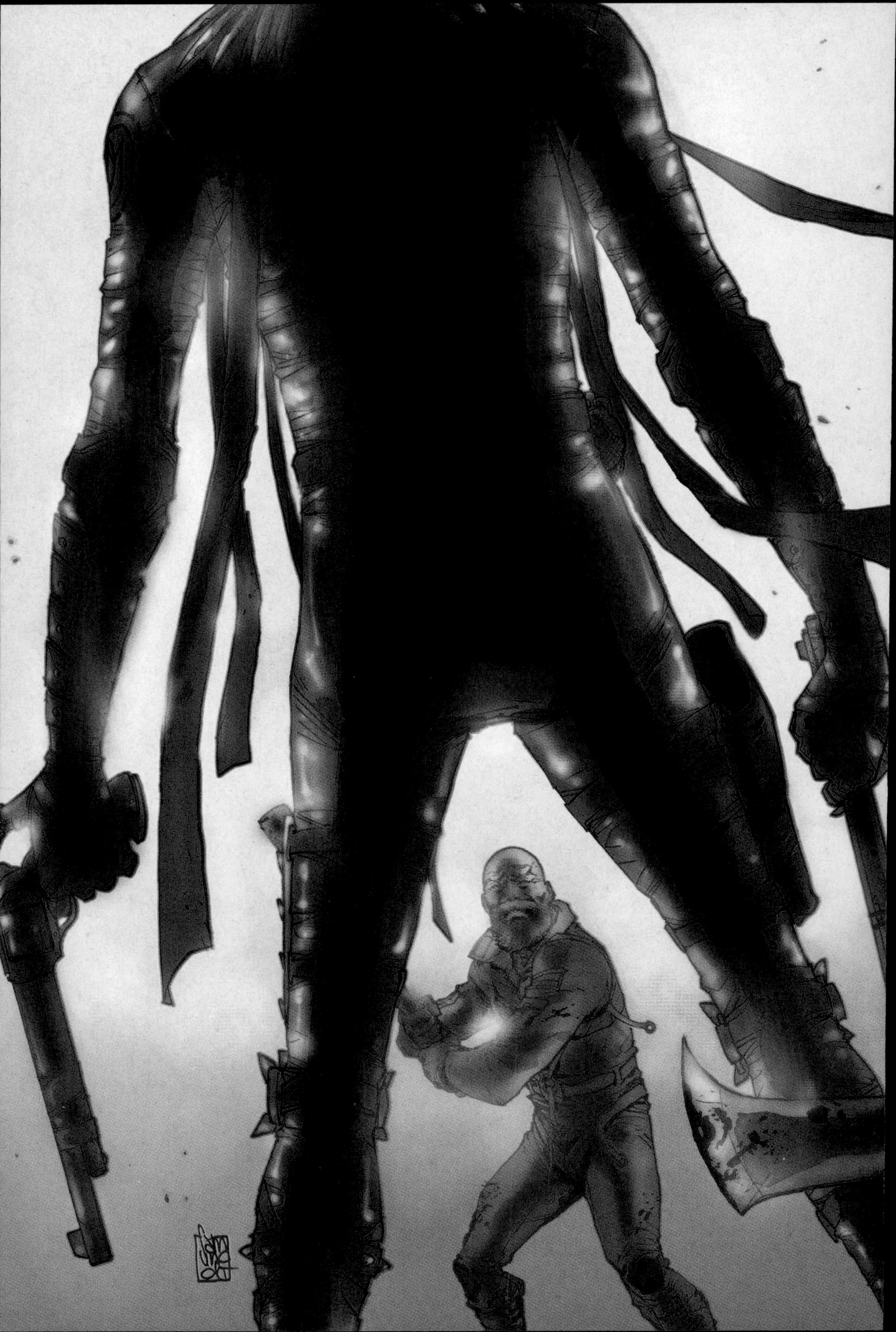

ARNAULD.

ARNAULD! ARE YOU THERE?

I THINK THEY'RE ABANDONING THE CAMP. I THINK IT'S WHY THEY HAVEN'T BEEN BEATING US...

YOU HEAR ME?! ALL WE HAVE TO DO IS HOLD OUT. IF WE CAN HOLD OUT... ALL OF US... MAYBE WE CAN MAKE IT THROUGH.

ARNAULD DAMMIT, ANSWER ME!

WHUMP

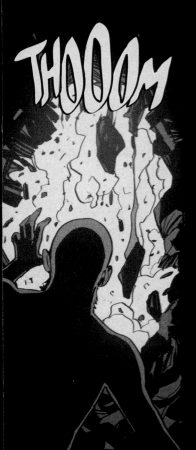

THOOOM

SERGEANT PAVEL?

WE'RE HERE TO RESCUE YOU, SIR.

BUT ARNAULD AND THE OTHERS... WHERE ARE THEY?

TELL ME! WHERE ARE THEY?! I WON'T LEAVE WITHOUT THEM!

I WON'T!

I'M AFRAID THEY'RE ALL DEAD, SIR. BUT YOU...

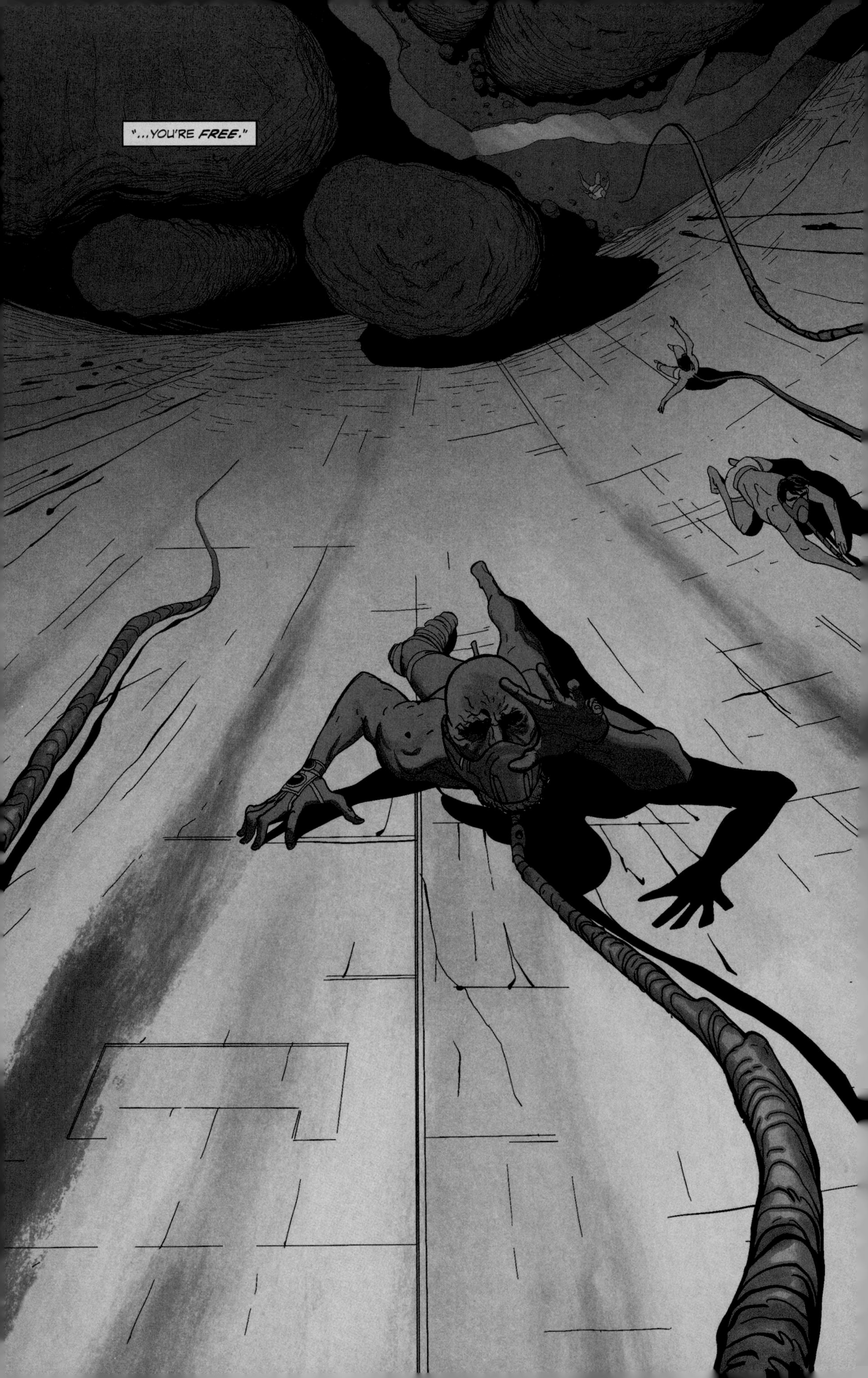
"...YOU'RE FREE."

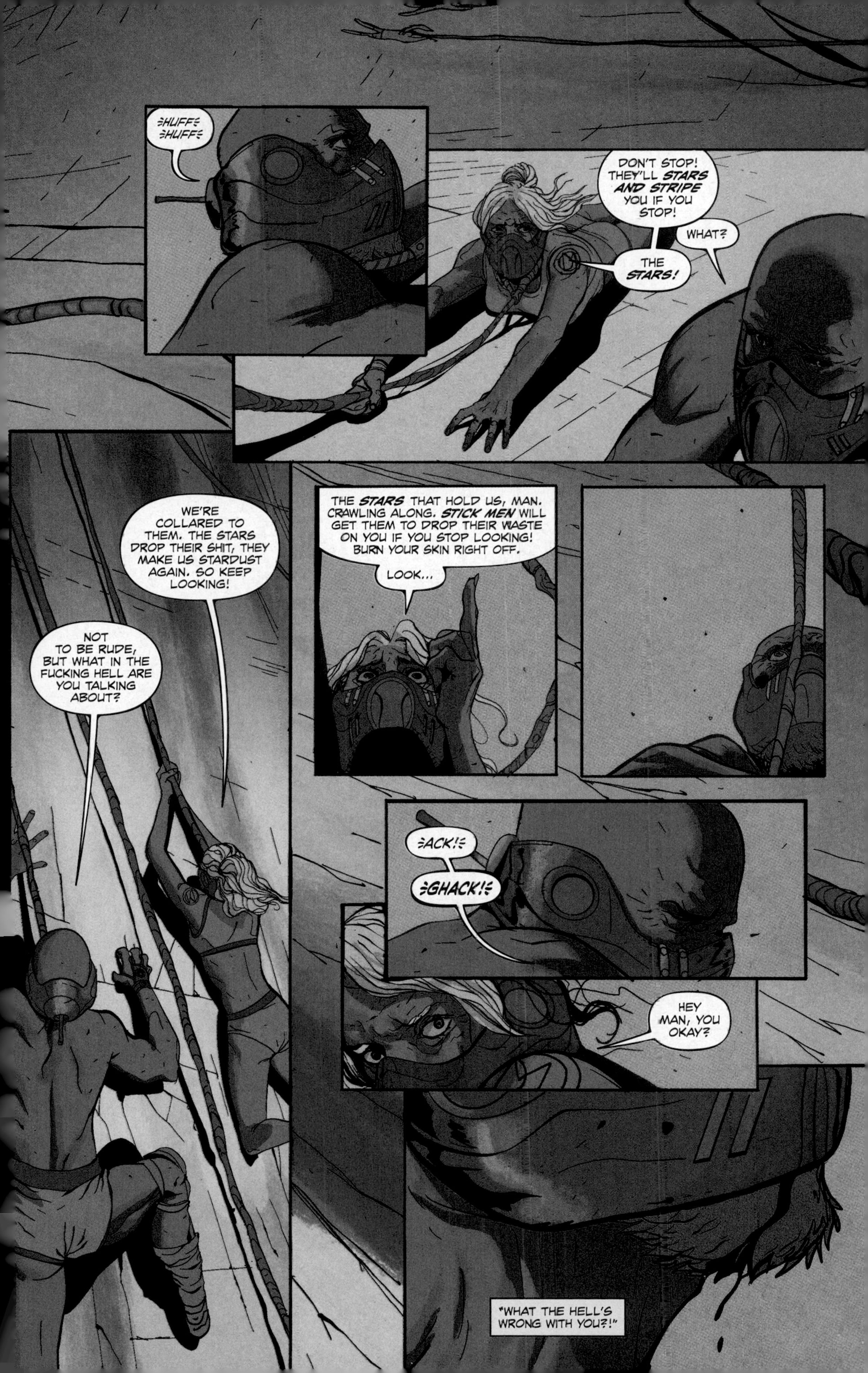

HUFF HUFF
DON'T STOP! THEY'LL STARS AND STRIPE YOU IF YOU STOP!
WHAT?
THE STARS!
WE'RE COLLARED TO THEM. THE STARS DROP THEIR SHIT, THEY MAKE US STARDUST AGAIN. SO KEEP LOOKING!
NOT TO BE RUDE, BUT WHAT IN THE FUCKING HELL ARE YOU TALKING ABOUT?
THE STARS THAT HOLD US, MAN. CRAWLING ALONG. STICK MEN WILL GET THEM TO DROP THEIR WASTE ON YOU IF YOU STOP LOOKING! BURN YOUR SKIN RIGHT OFF.
LOOK...
ACK!
GHACK!
HEY MAN, YOU OKAY?
"WHAT THE HELL'S WRONG WITH YOU?!"

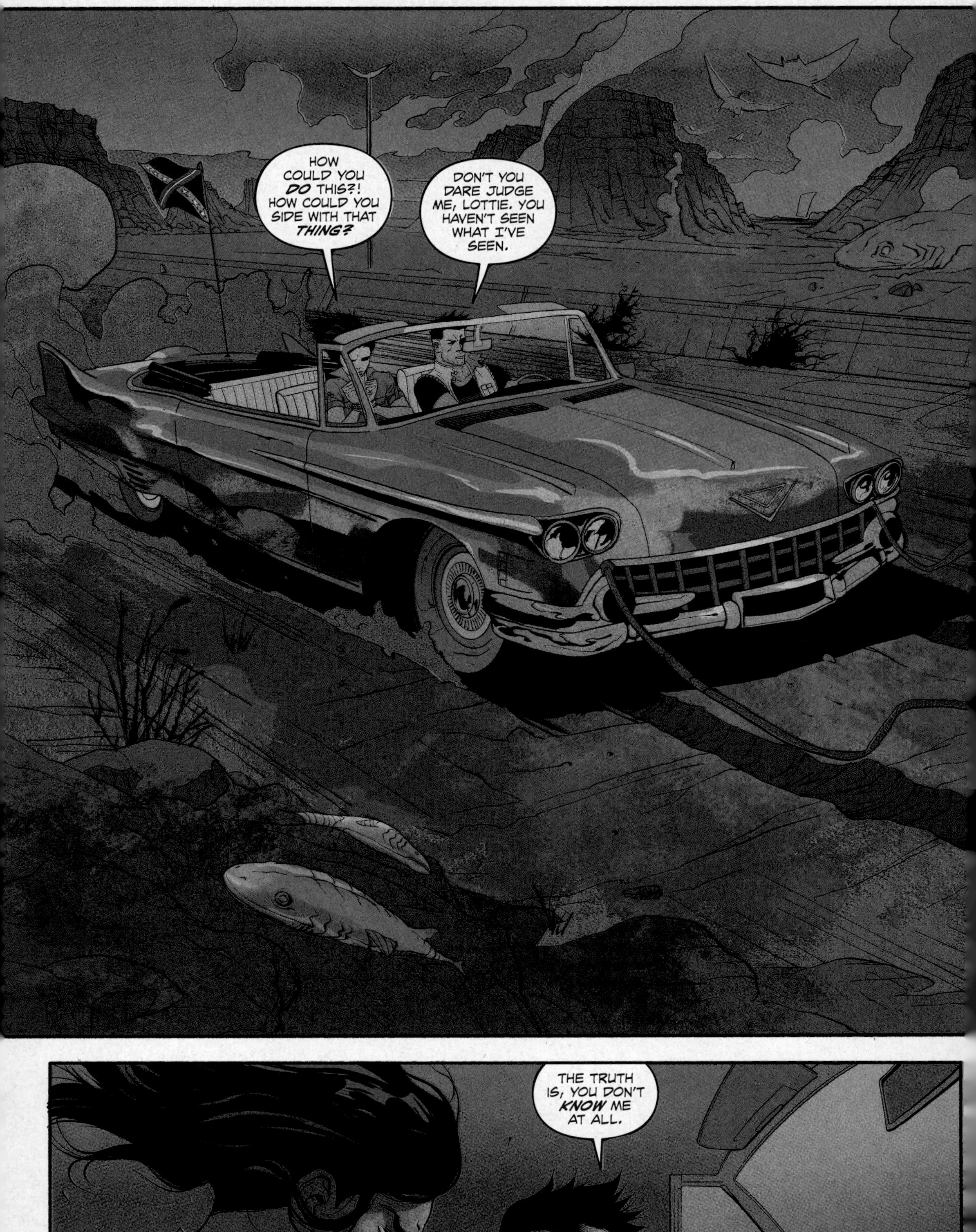
HOW COULD YOU *DO* THIS?! HOW COULD YOU SIDE WITH THAT *THING?*
DON'T YOU DARE JUDGE ME, LOTTIE. YOU HAVEN'T SEEN WHAT I'VE SEEN.

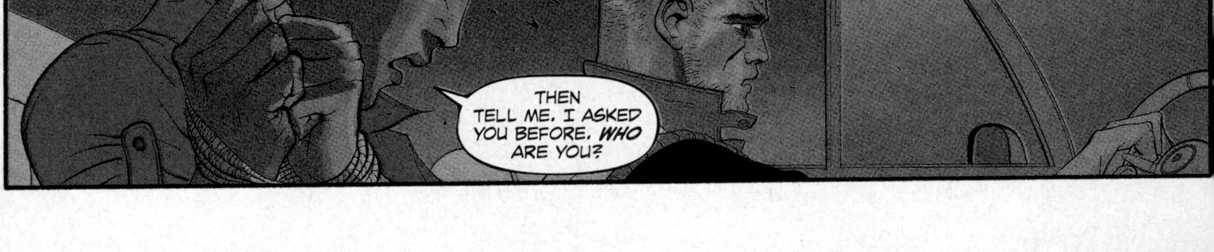
THE TRUTH IS, YOU DON'T *KNOW* ME AT ALL.
THEN TELL ME. I ASKED YOU BEFORE. *WHO* ARE YOU?

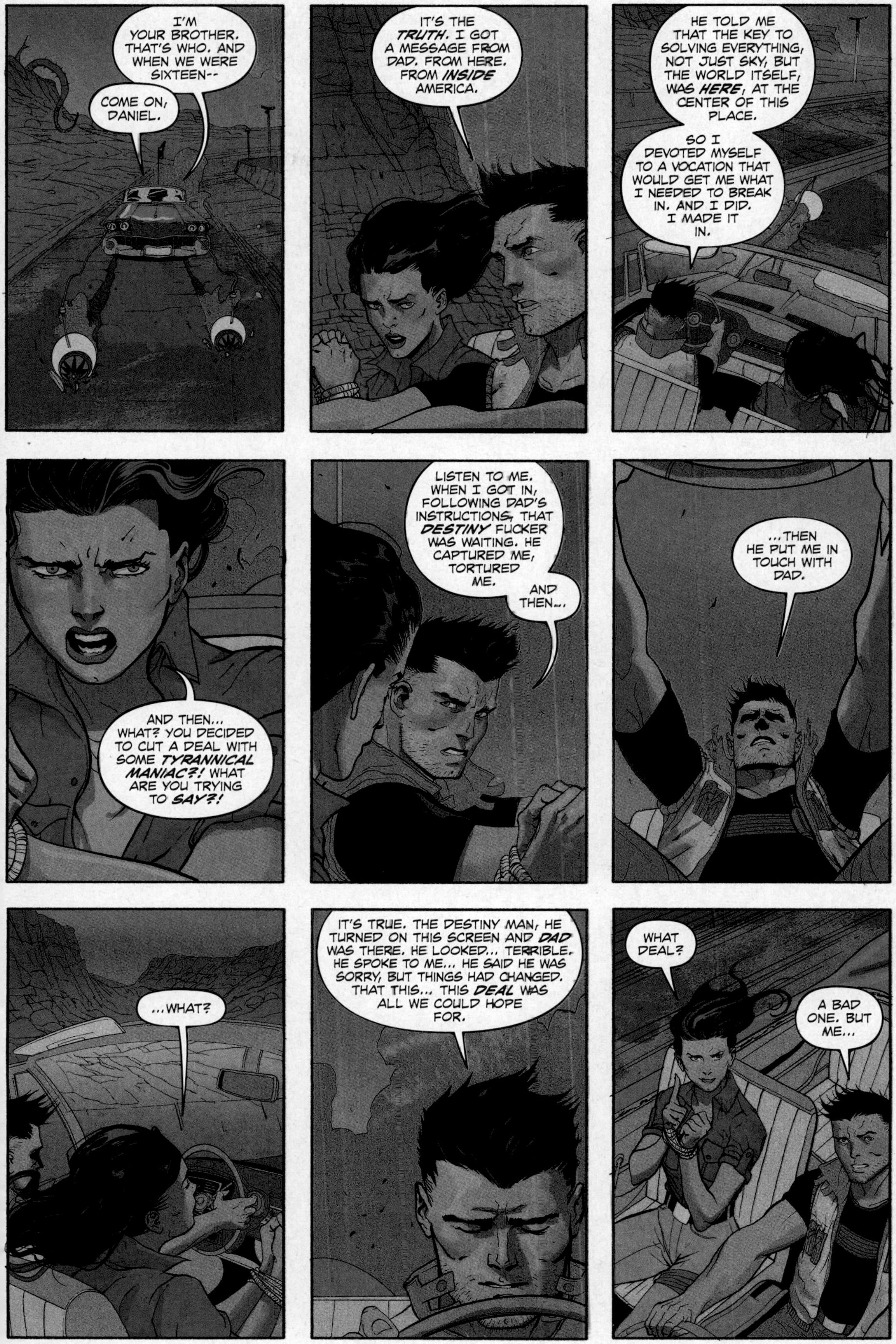
I'M YOUR BROTHER. THAT'S WHO. AND WHEN WE WERE SIXTEEN--
COME ON, DANIEL.
IT'S THE *TRUTH*. I GOT A MESSAGE FROM DAD. FROM HERE. FROM *INSIDE* AMERICA.
HE TOLD ME THAT THE KEY TO SOLVING EVERYTHING, NOT JUST SKY, BUT THE WORLD ITSELF, WAS *HERE*, AT THE CENTER OF THIS PLACE.
SO I DEVOTED MYSELF TO A VOCATION THAT WOULD GET ME WHAT I NEEDED TO BREAK IN. AND I DID. I MADE IT IN.
AND THEN... WHAT? YOU DECIDED TO CUT A DEAL WITH SOME *TYRANNICAL MANIAC?!* WHAT ARE YOU TRYING TO *SAY?!*
LISTEN TO ME. WHEN I GOT IN, FOLLOWING DAD'S INSTRUCTIONS, THAT *DESTINY* FUCKER WAS WAITING. HE CAPTURED ME, TORTURED ME.
AND THEN...
...THEN HE PUT ME IN TOUCH WITH DAD.
...WHAT?
IT'S TRUE. THE DESTINY MAN, HE TURNED ON THIS SCREEN AND *DAD* WAS THERE. HE LOOKED... TERRIBLE. HE SPOKE TO ME... HE SAID HE WAS SORRY, BUT THINGS HAD CHANGED. THAT THIS... THIS *DEAL* WAS ALL WE COULD HOPE FOR.
WHAT DEAL?
A BAD ONE. BUT ME...

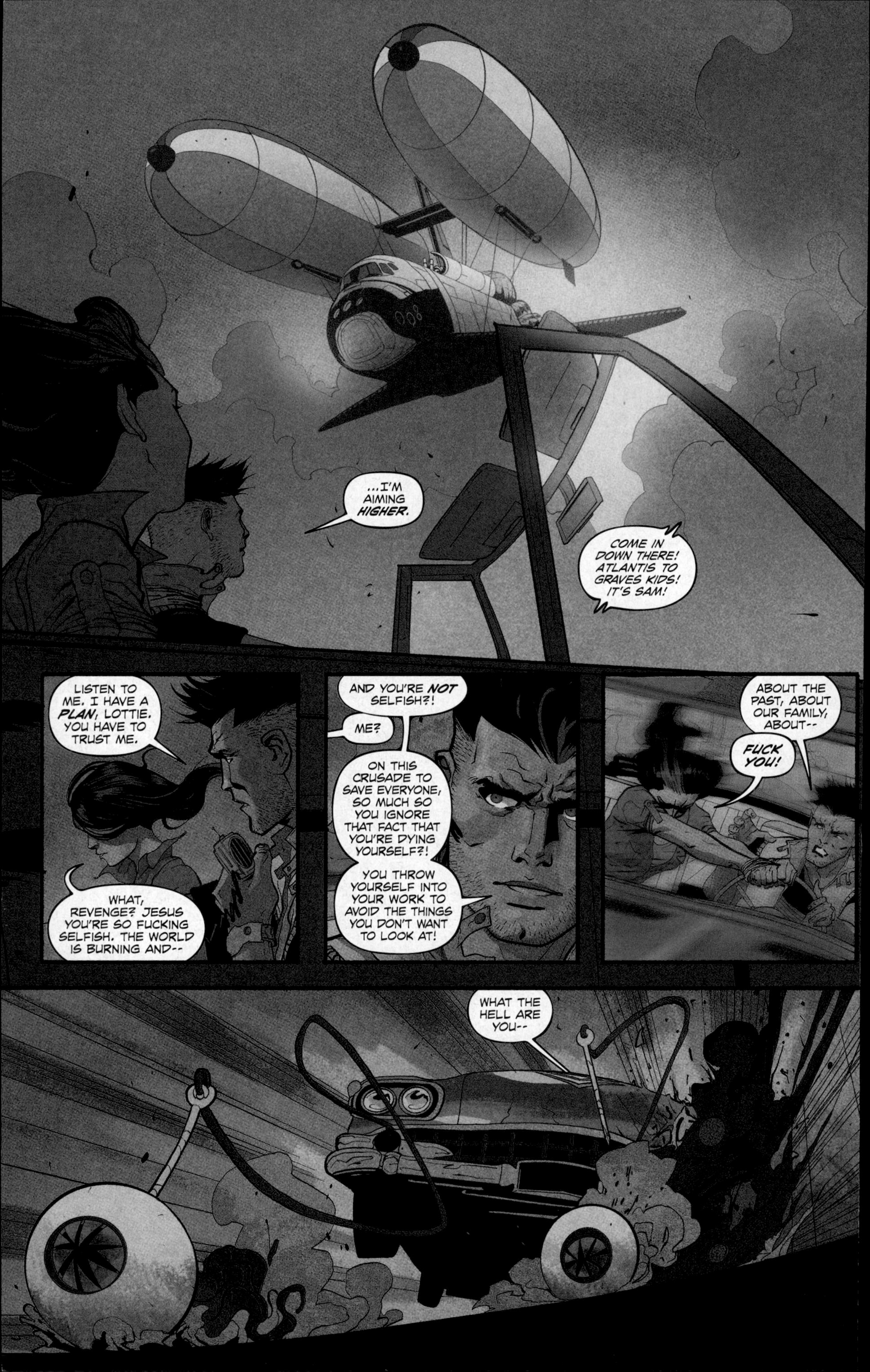
...I'M AIMING HIGHER.
COME IN DOWN THERE! ATLANTIS TO GRAVES KIDS! IT'S SAM!
LISTEN TO ME. I HAVE A PLAN, LOTTIE. YOU HAVE TO TRUST ME.
WHAT, REVENGE? JESUS YOU'RE SO FUCKING SELFISH. THE WORLD IS BURNING AND--
AND YOU'RE NOT SELFISH?!
ME?
ON THIS CRUSADE TO SAVE EVERYONE, SO MUCH SO YOU IGNORE THAT FACT THAT YOU'RE DYING YOURSELF?!
YOU THROW YOURSELF INTO YOUR WORK TO AVOID THE THINGS YOU DON'T WANT TO LOOK AT!
ABOUT THE PAST, ABOUT OUR FAMILY, ABOUT--
FUCK YOU!
WHAT THE HELL ARE YOU--

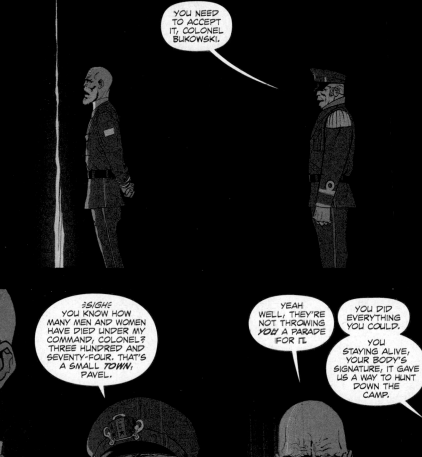

YOU NEED TO ACCEPT IT, COLONEL BUKOWSKI.

≶SIGH≷ YOU KNOW HOW MANY MEN AND WOMEN HAVE DIED UNDER MY COMMAND, COLONEL? THREE HUNDRED AND SEVENTY-FOUR. THAT'S A SMALL *TOWN*, PAVEL.

YEAH WELL, THEY'RE NOT THROWING *YOU* A PARADE FOR IT.

YOU DID EVERYTHING YOU COULD.

YOU STAYING ALIVE, YOUR BODY'S SIGNATURE, IT GAVE US A WAY TO HUNT DOWN THE CAMP.

WE WIPED OUT HALF THE GRAY FUCKING *ZEROES* BECAUSE OF YOU. THAT MAKES YOU A HERO.

PAVEL?

PAVEL, WHAT... WHAT THE HELL ARE YOU *DOING?!*

THIS *PIN,* I KEEP IT IN MY CHEEK, GENERAL.

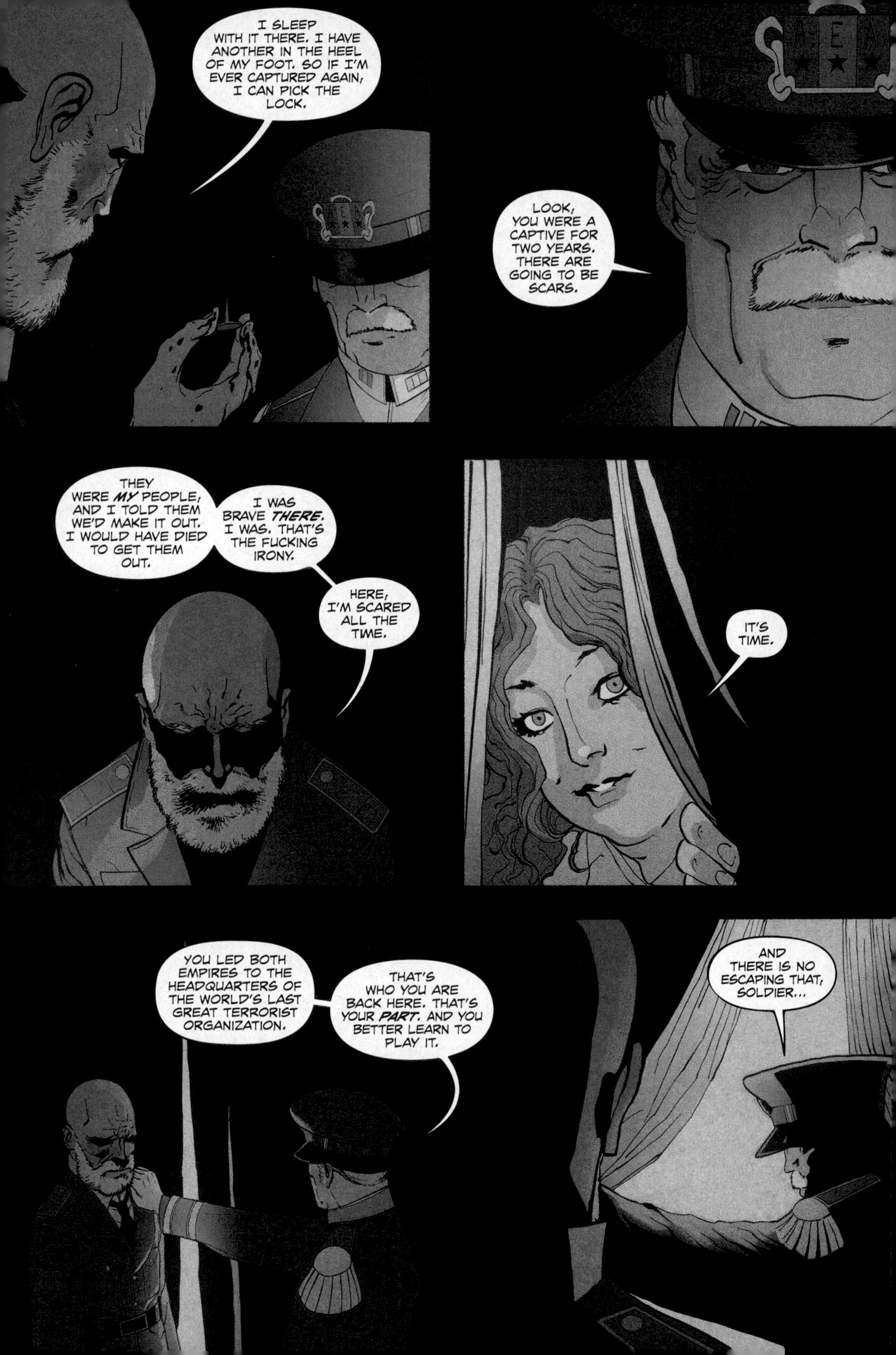
I SLEEP WITH IT THERE. I HAVE ANOTHER IN THE HEEL OF MY FOOT. SO IF I'M EVER CAPTURED AGAIN, I CAN PICK THE LOCK.
LOOK, YOU WERE A CAPTIVE FOR TWO YEARS. THERE ARE GOING TO BE SCARS.
THEY WERE *MY* PEOPLE, AND I TOLD THEM WE'D MAKE IT OUT. I WOULD HAVE DIED TO GET THEM OUT.
I WAS BRAVE ***THERE***. I WAS. THAT'S THE FUCKING IRONY.
HERE, I'M SCARED ALL THE TIME.
IT'S TIME.
YOU LED BOTH EMPIRES TO THE HEADQUARTERS OF THE WORLD'S LAST GREAT TERRORIST ORGANIZATION.
THAT'S WHO YOU ARE BACK HERE. THAT'S YOUR ***PART***. AND YOU BETTER LEARN TO PLAY IT.
AND THERE IS NO ESCAPING THAT, SOLDIER...

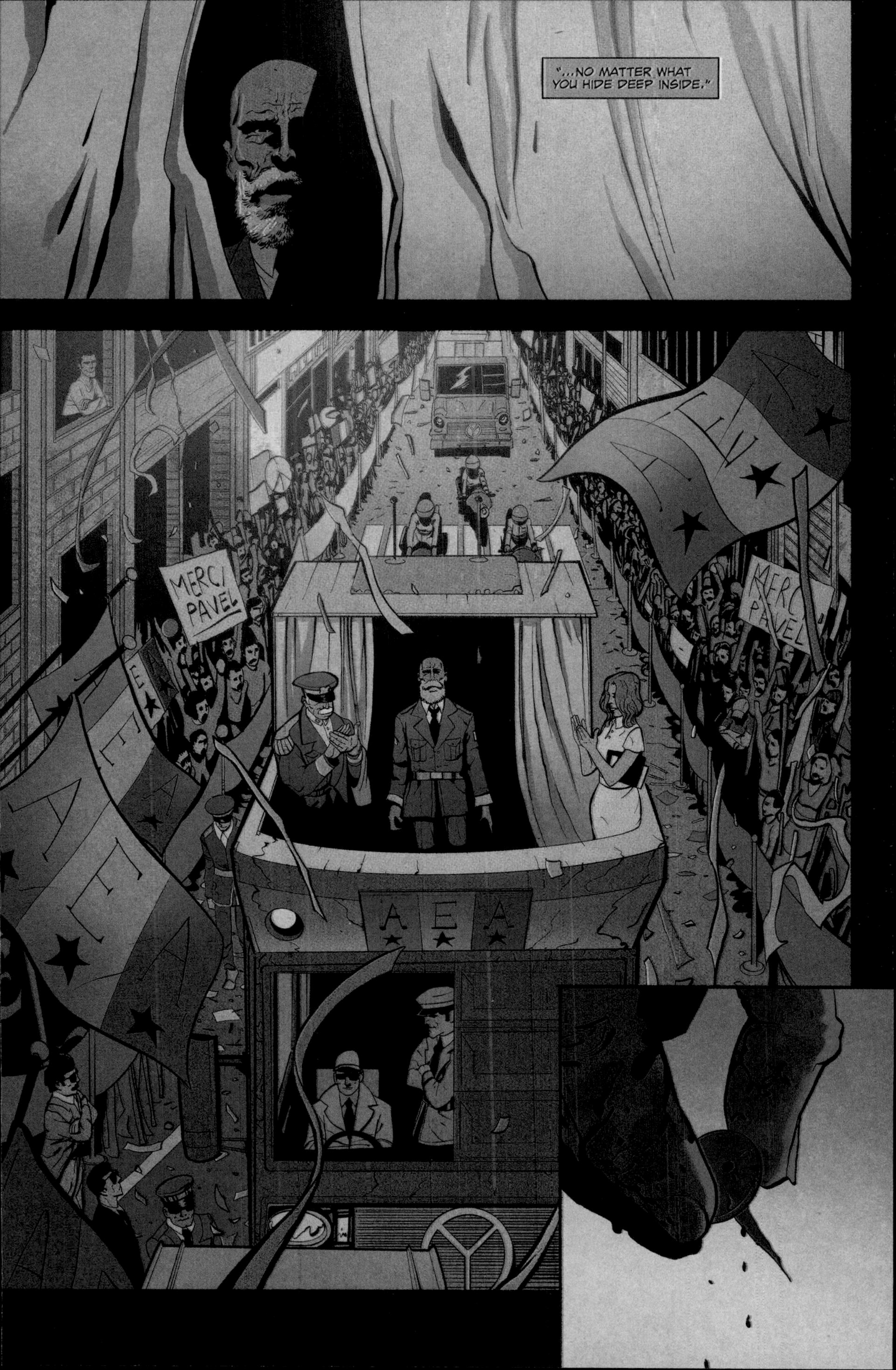
"...NO MATTER WHAT YOU HIDE DEEP INSIDE."
MERCI PAVEL
MERCI PAVEL
A E A

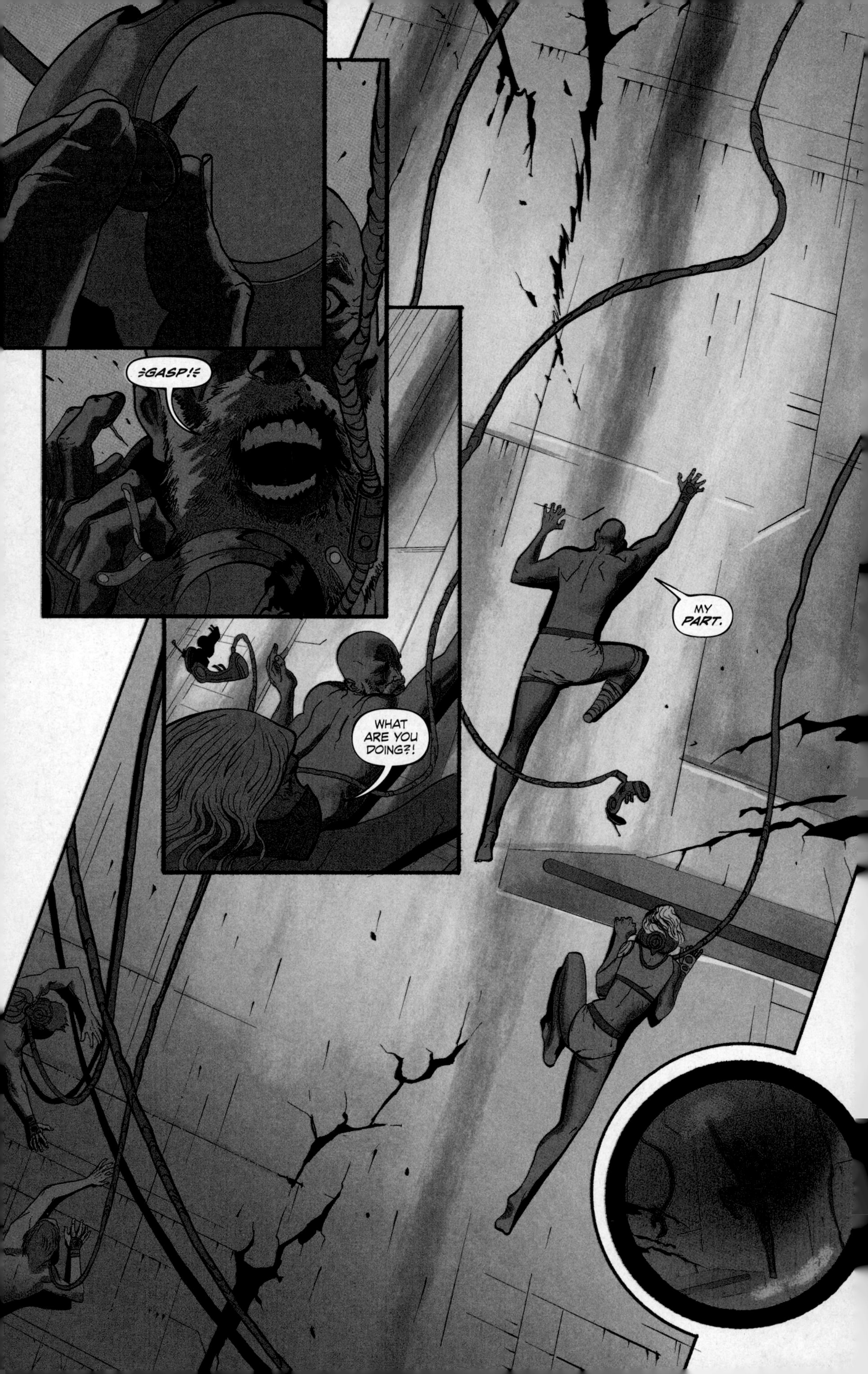
GASP!
WHAT ARE YOU DOING?!
MY PART.

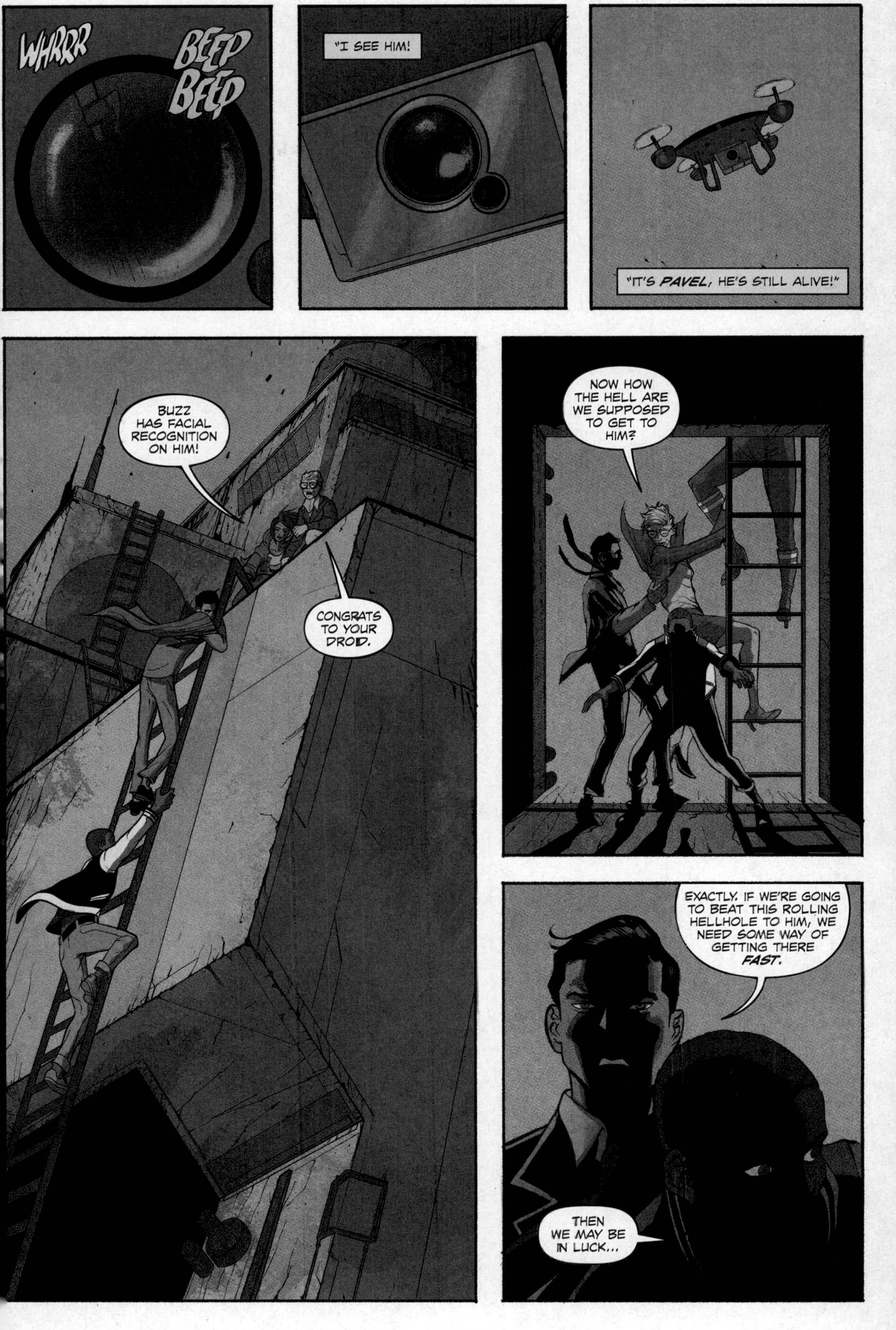
WHRRR
BEEP BEEP
"I SEE HIM!
"IT'S PAVEL, HE'S STILL ALIVE!"
BUZZ HAS FACIAL RECOGNITION ON HIM!
CONGRATS TO YOUR DROID.
NOW HOW THE HELL ARE WE SUPPOSED TO GET TO HIM?
EXACTLY. IF WE'RE GOING TO BEAT THIS ROLLING HELLHOLE TO HIM, WE NEED SOME WAY OF GETTING THERE FAST.
THEN WE MAY BE IN LUCK...

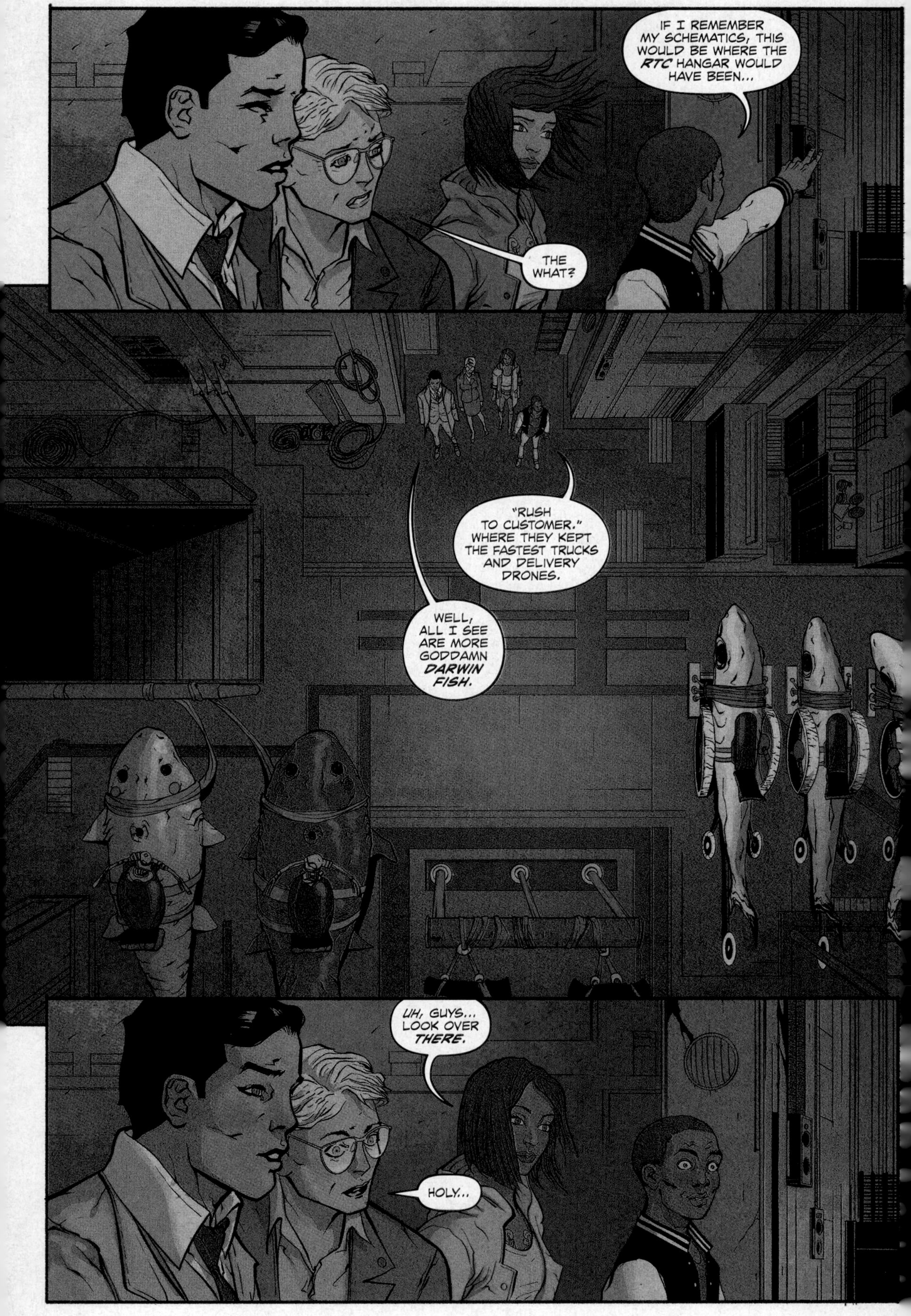

IF I REMEMBER MY SCHEMATICS, THIS WOULD BE WHERE THE RTC HANGAR WOULD HAVE BEEN...
THE WHAT?
"RUSH TO CUSTOMER." WHERE THEY KEPT THE FASTEST TRUCKS AND DELIVERY DRONES.
WELL, ALL I SEE ARE MORE GODDAMN DARWIN FISH.
UH, GUYS... LOOK OVER THERE.
HOLY...

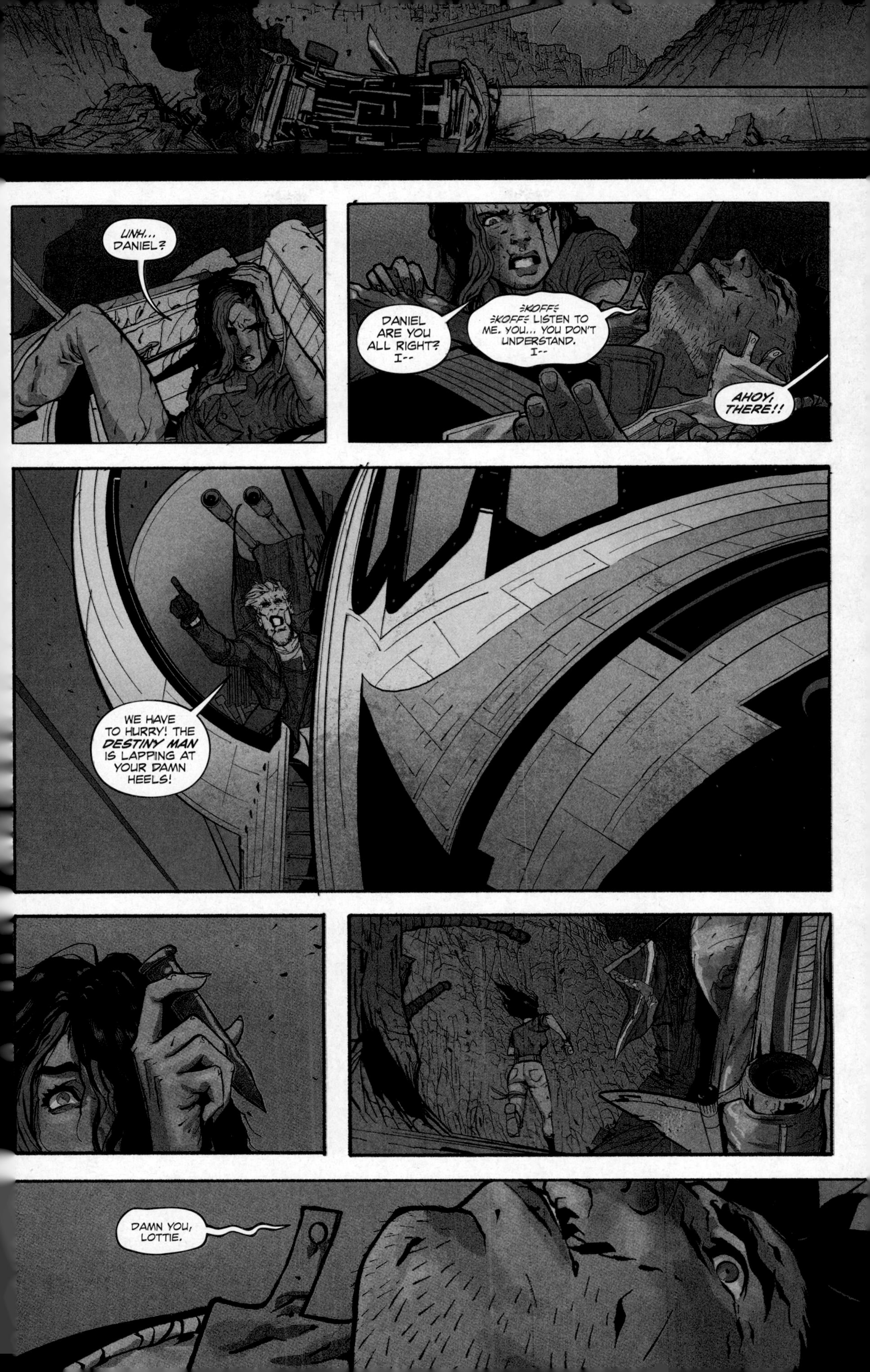
UNH... DANIEL?
DANIEL ARE YOU ALL RIGHT? I--
KOFF KOFF LISTEN TO ME. YOU... YOU DON'T UNDERSTAND. I--
AHOY, THERE!!
WE HAVE TO HURRY! THE DESTINY MAN IS LAPPING AT YOUR DAMN HEELS!
DAMN YOU, LOTTIE.

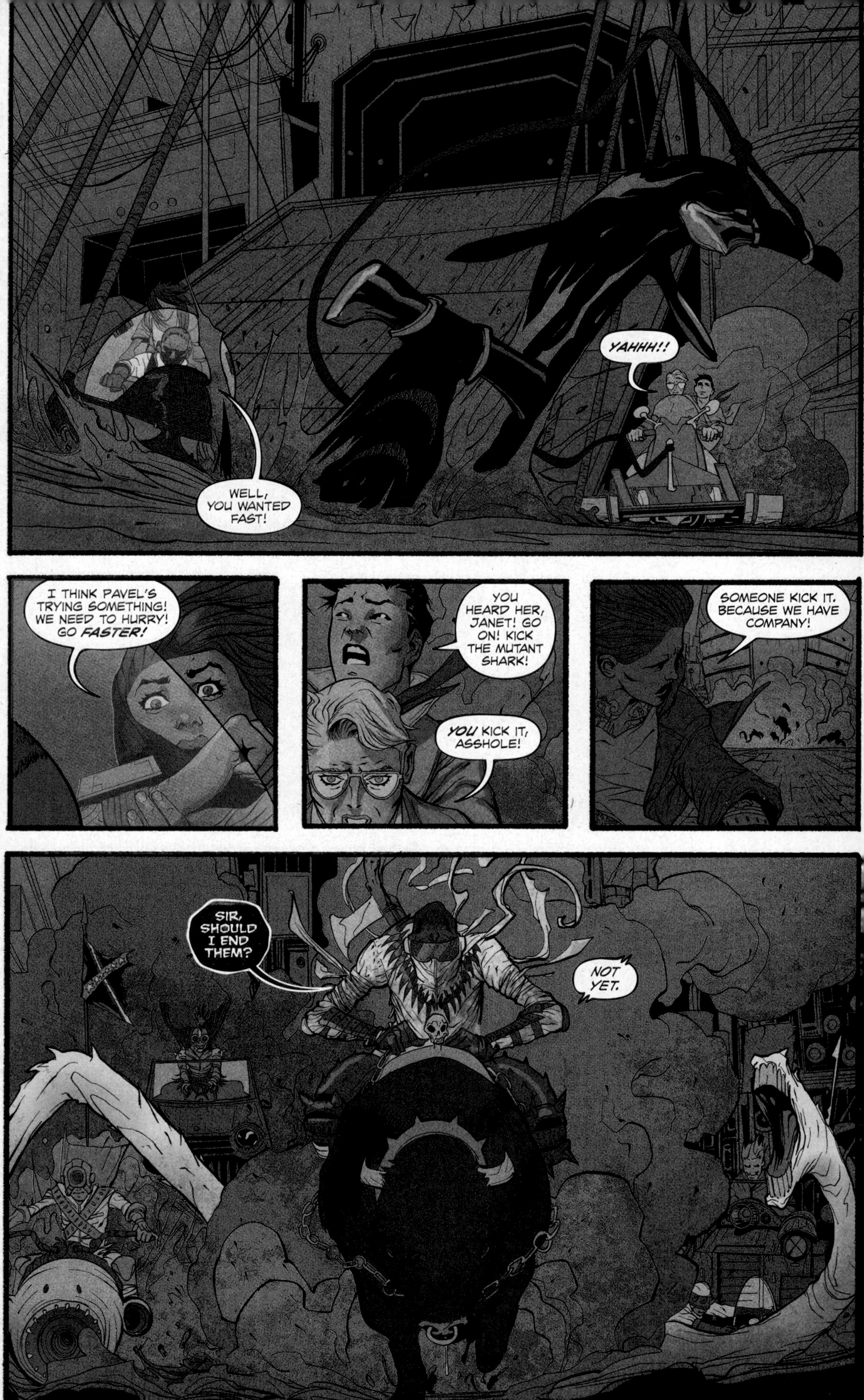
YAHHH!!
WELL, YOU WANTED FAST!
I THINK PAVEL'S TRYING SOMETHING! WE NEED TO HURRY! GO FASTER!
YOU HEARD HER, JANET! GO ON! KICK THE MUTANT SHARK!
YOU KICK IT, ASSHOLE!
SOMEONE KICK IT. BECAUSE WE HAVE COMPANY!
SIR, SHOULD I END THEM?
NOT YET.

TAKE THEM AT THE WALL.
YES, SIR.
I'LL MEET YOU THERE MYSELF.
AND THEN...
...SHE WILL OPEN THE DOOR FOR US, AND WE WILL WALK UNTO HER GLORY.

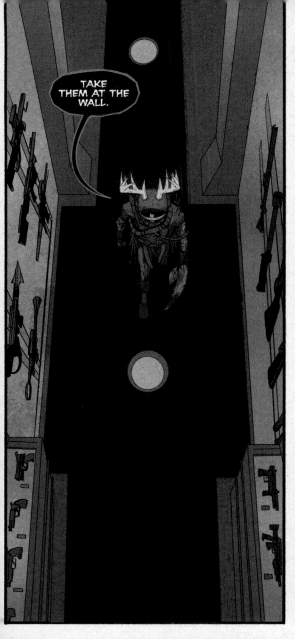

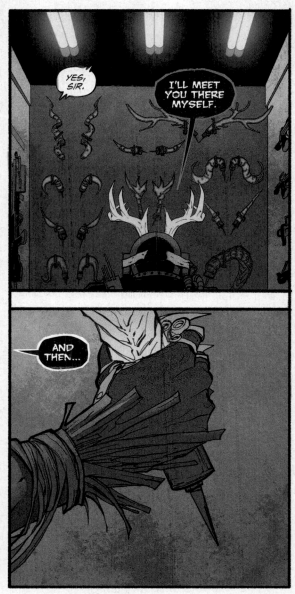

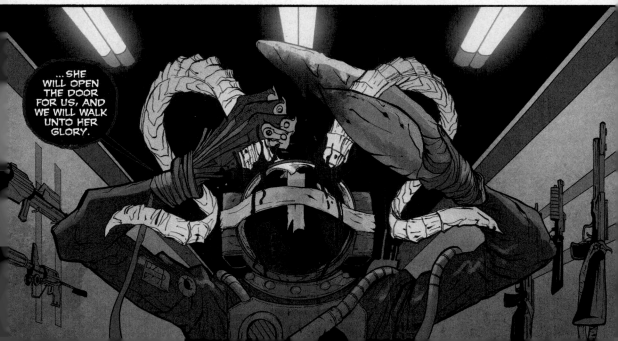

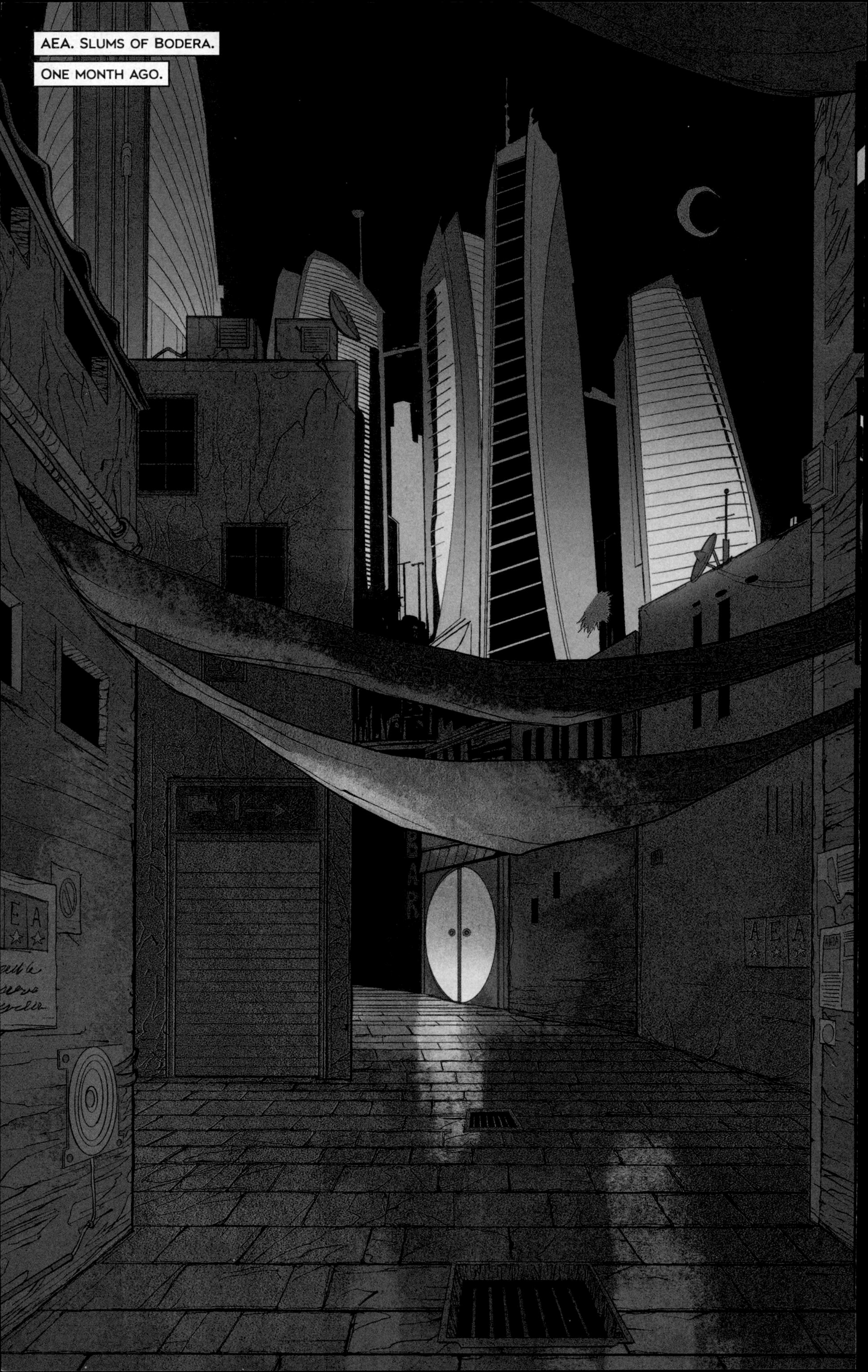
AEA. SLUMS OF BODERA.
ONE MONTH AGO.

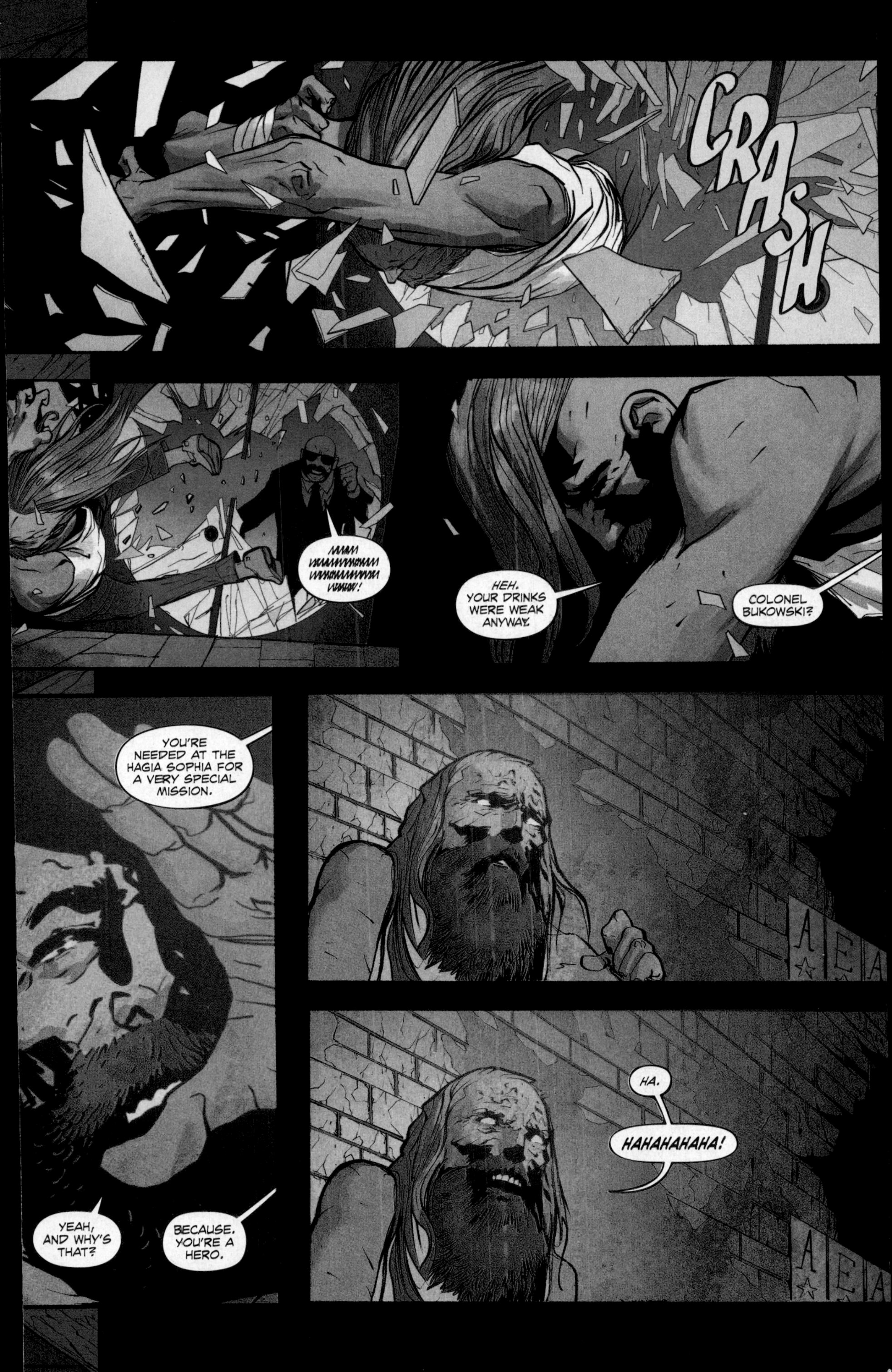
CRASH
MMMM WAAAAAAAAAAAAAAAAAAAAAAAAAA!
HEH. YOUR DRINKS WERE WEAK ANYWAY.
COLONEL BUKOWSKI?
YOU'RE NEEDED AT THE HAGIA SOPHIA FOR A VERY SPECIAL MISSION.
YEAH, AND WHY'S THAT?
BECAUSE. YOU'RE A HERO.
HA.
HAHAHAHAHA!

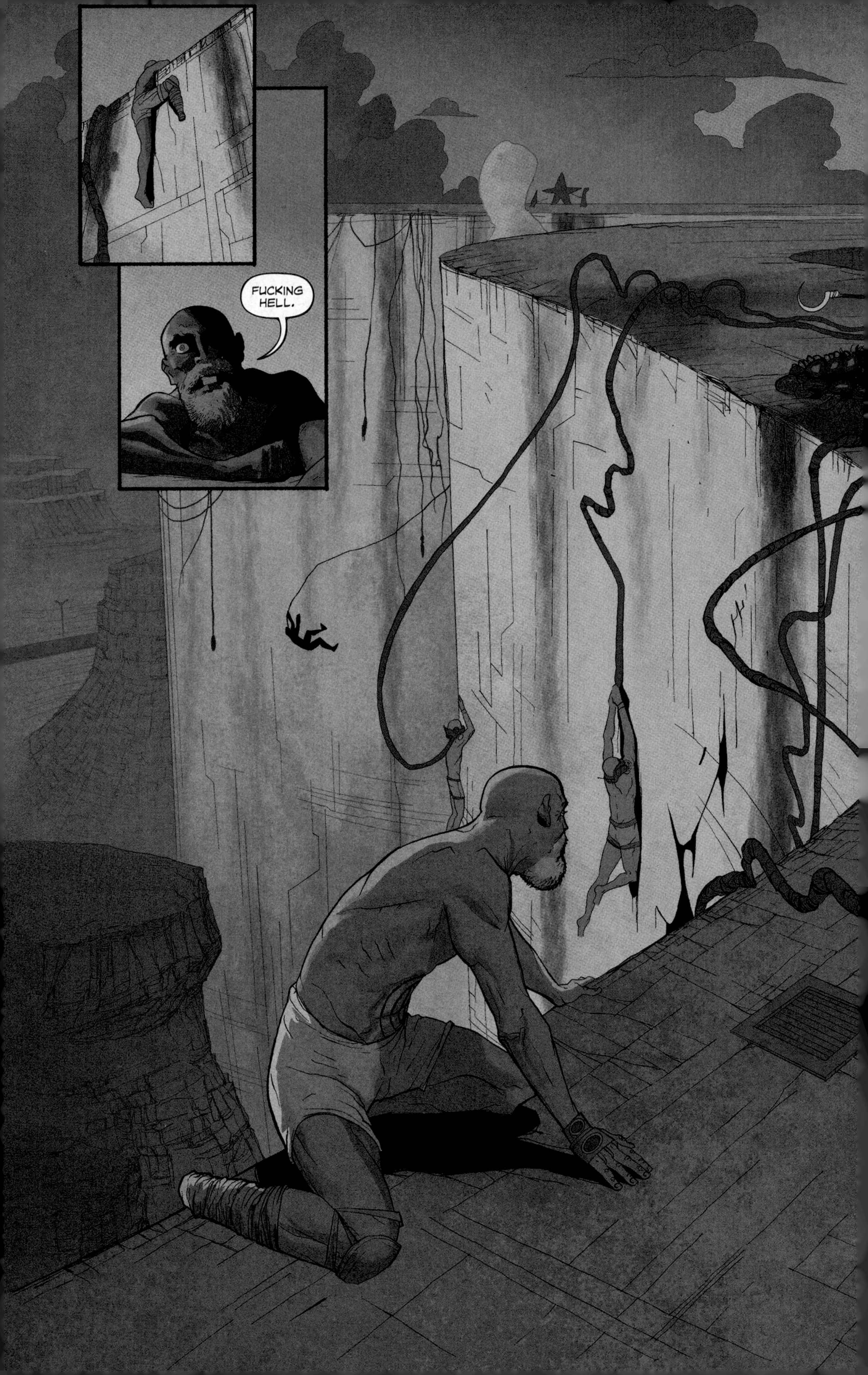
FUCKING HELL.

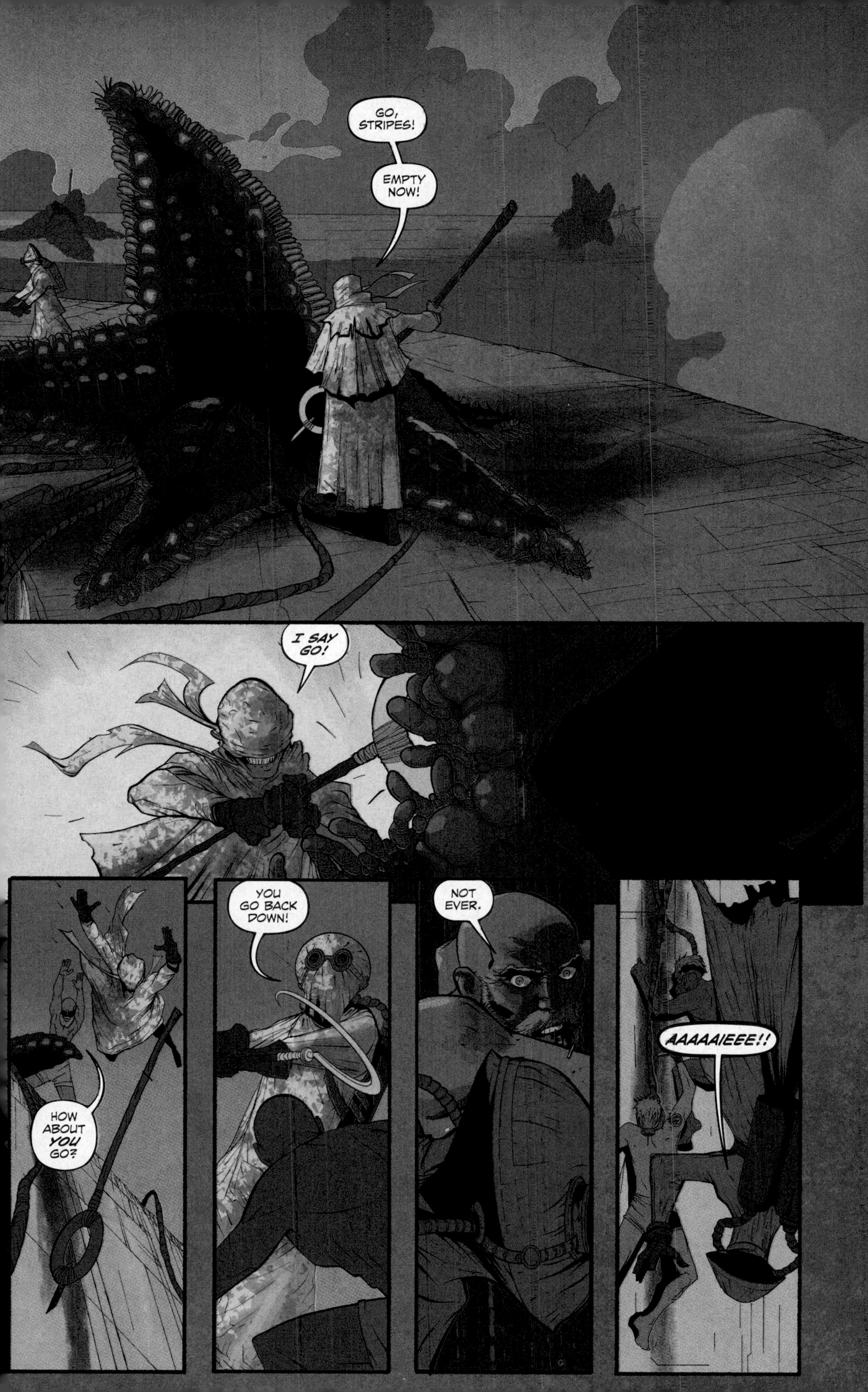
GO, STRIPES!
EMPTY NOW!
I SAY GO!
HOW ABOUT YOU GO?
YOU GO BACK DOWN!
NOT EVER.
AAAAAIEEE!!

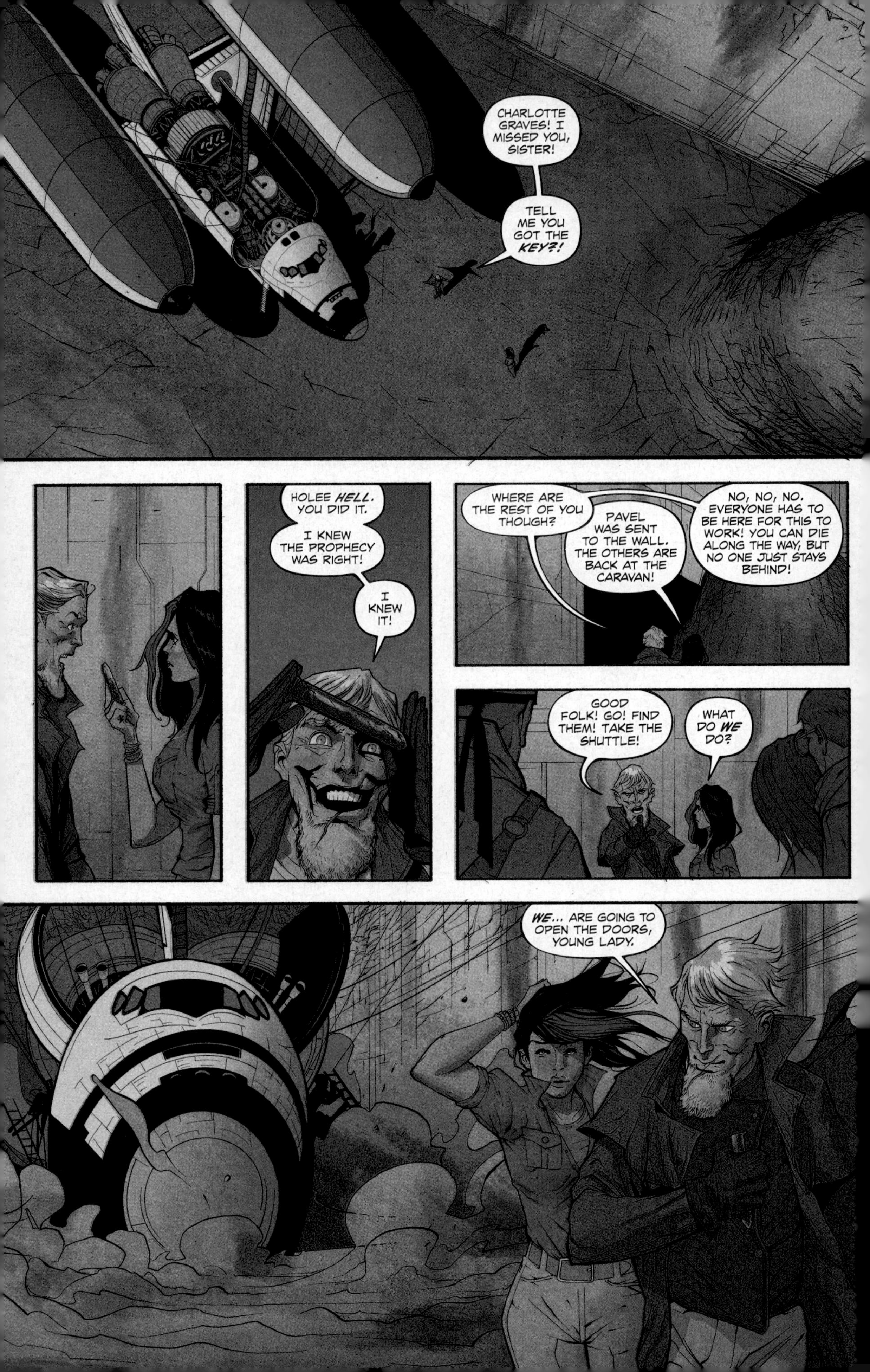
CHARLOTTE GRAVES! I MISSED YOU, SISTER!
TELL ME YOU GOT THE *KEY?!*
HOLEE *HELL*. YOU DID IT.
I KNEW THE PROPHECY WAS RIGHT!
I KNEW IT!
WHERE ARE THE REST OF YOU THOUGH?
PAVEL WAS SENT TO THE WALL. THE OTHERS ARE BACK AT THE CARAVAN!
NO, NO, NO. EVERYONE HAS TO BE HERE FOR THIS TO WORK! YOU CAN DIE ALONG THE WAY, BUT NO ONE JUST STAYS BEHIND!
GOOD FOLK! GO! FIND THEM! TAKE THE SHUTTLE!
WHAT DO *WE* DO?
WE... ARE GOING TO OPEN THE DOORS, YOUNG LADY.

BECAUSE I SET THEM *MYSELF* DECADES AGO, THE LAST TIME I SAW YOUR PARENTS.

BUT THIS IS *NOWHERE NEAR* THE WALL. YOU SAID THE KEYHOLE WAS IN--

I SAID THE DESTINY MAN *THINKS* IT'S IN THE WALL. BUT A KEYHOLE CAN BE ANYWHERE INSIDE A TERRITORY.

THERE'S NOTHING HERE, THOUGH. HOW DO YOU KNOW YOUR COORDINATES ARE RIGHT?

MY PARENTS? SO YOU *ARE* SAM ELGIN?

WE ALL ARE. WE'LL HAVE TIME FOR ALL THAT LATER. NOW, WE NEED TO MOVE.

THE SPIRAL AWAITS, AND BEYOND IT, *AURORA.* BUT FIRST, PASSAGE.

PASSAGE FROM THIS INTRODUCTORY PLACE TO THE FIRST TRUE ZONE.

SO THE ROCK JUST PARTS AND WE WALK THROUGH?

HEH. CHARLOTTE, MY DEAR...

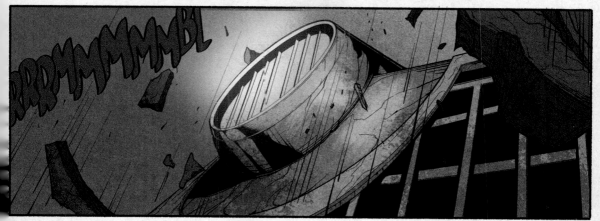

BBRROOMMMMMBL

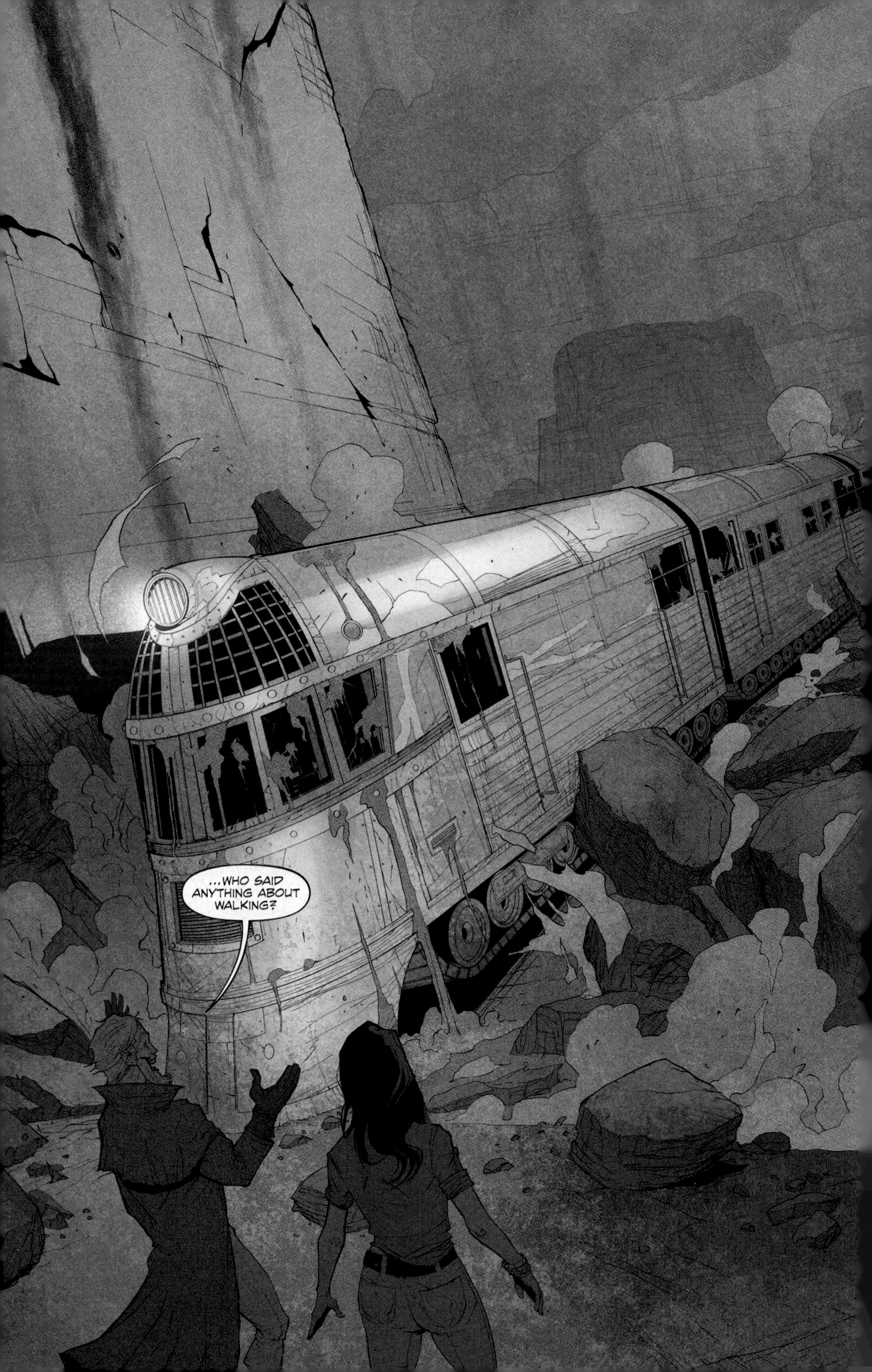
...WHO SAID ANYTHING ABOUT WALKING?

"I've been fighting since I was eighteen years old. My country's been tossed back and forth between the Freaks and Zoners so many times I can't remember who invaded us first. One war after another, and in the years here and there we weren't being occupied, we fought amongst ourselves. Guess we just got used to it. They say the world was different before the Sealing. That America kept the peace. I don't even know what that word even means."

—Abdul Hafiz Abadi, 29, soldier, Mecca, Conflicted Territory of Saudi Arabia

"We were playing an exhibition match in Korea when it all went down. Nothing that unusual. We should have been back State-side in a few days. Then, the Sealing, and, well... that's how we ended up becoming the Seoul Celtics. World Champions the next six years in a row. No surprise there."

—Andrew Jenkins, 52, former professional athlete, Pyongyang, Pan-Asian Prosperity Zone

Quotes from *The New World: An Oral History of the Sealing* by Valentina Sandoval.

CHAPTER SIX

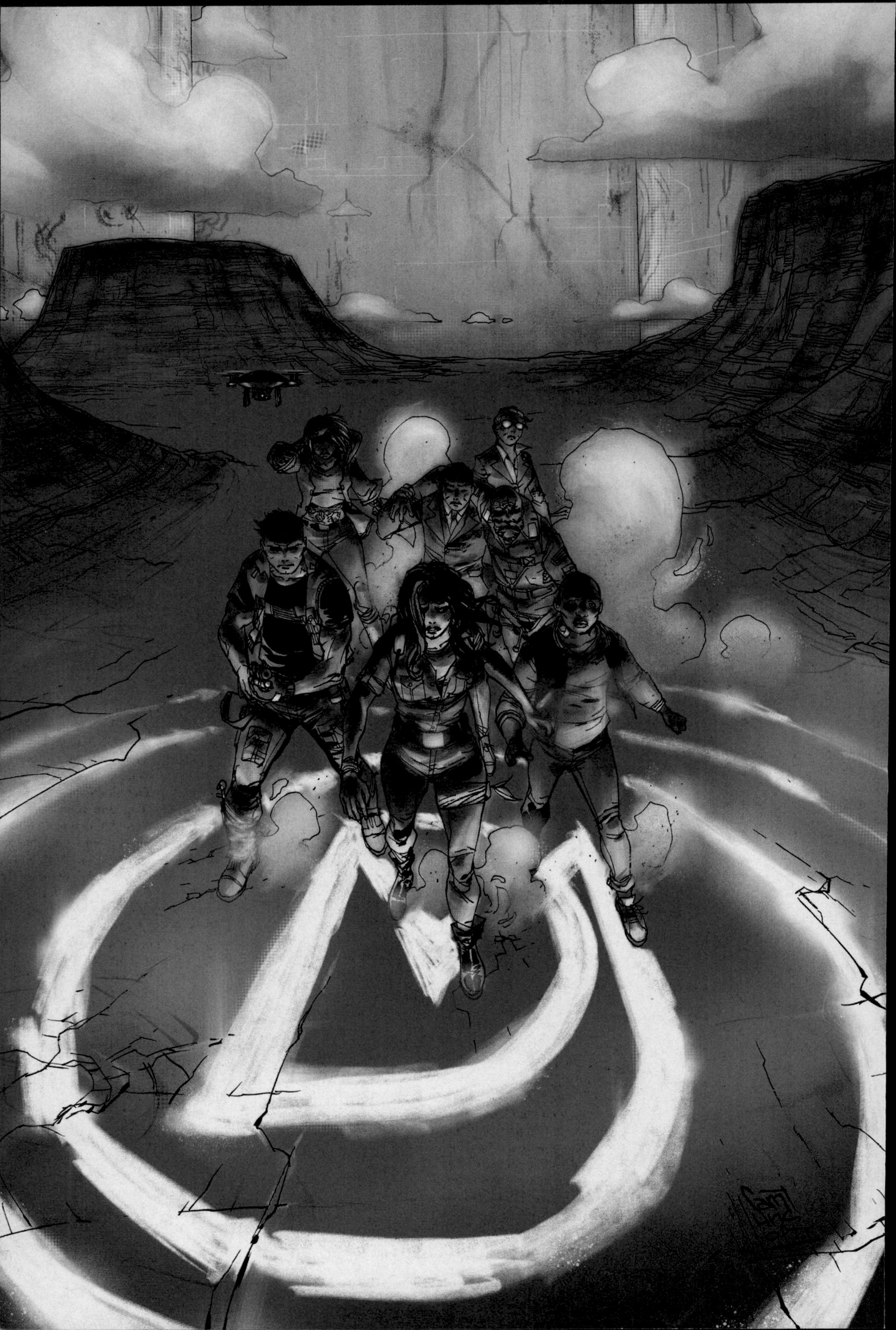

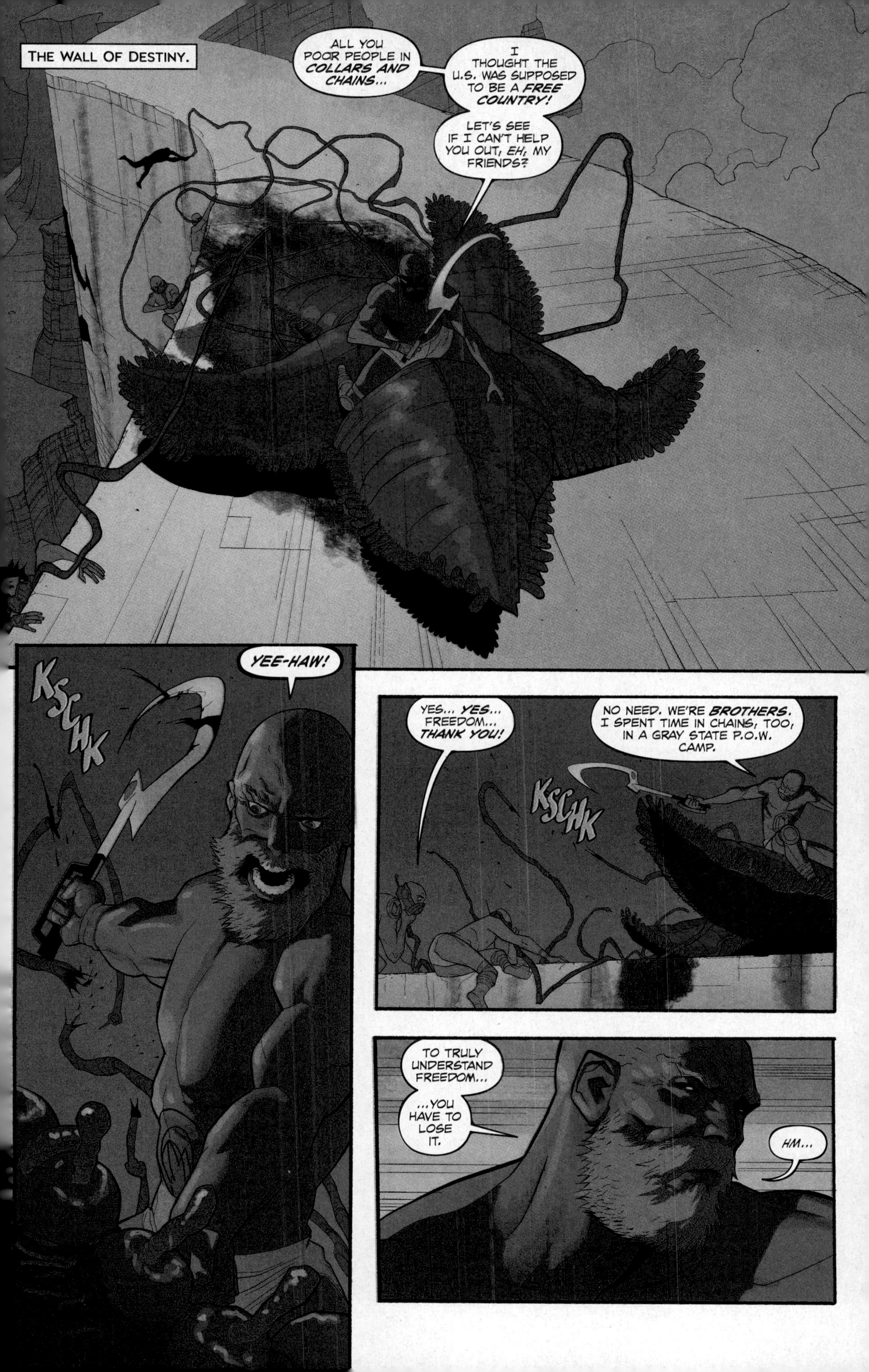
THE WALL OF DESTINY.
ALL YOU POOR PEOPLE IN COLLARS AND CHAINS...
I THOUGHT THE U.S. WAS SUPPOSED TO BE A FREE COUNTRY!
LET'S SEE IF I CAN'T HELP YOU OUT, EH, MY FRIENDS?
KSCHK
YEE-HAW!
YES... YES... FREEDOM... THANK YOU!
NO NEED. WE'RE BROTHERS. I SPENT TIME IN CHAINS, TOO, IN A GRAY STATE P.O.W. CAMP.
KSCHK
TO TRULY UNDERSTAND FREEDOM...
...YOU HAVE TO LOSE IT.
HM...

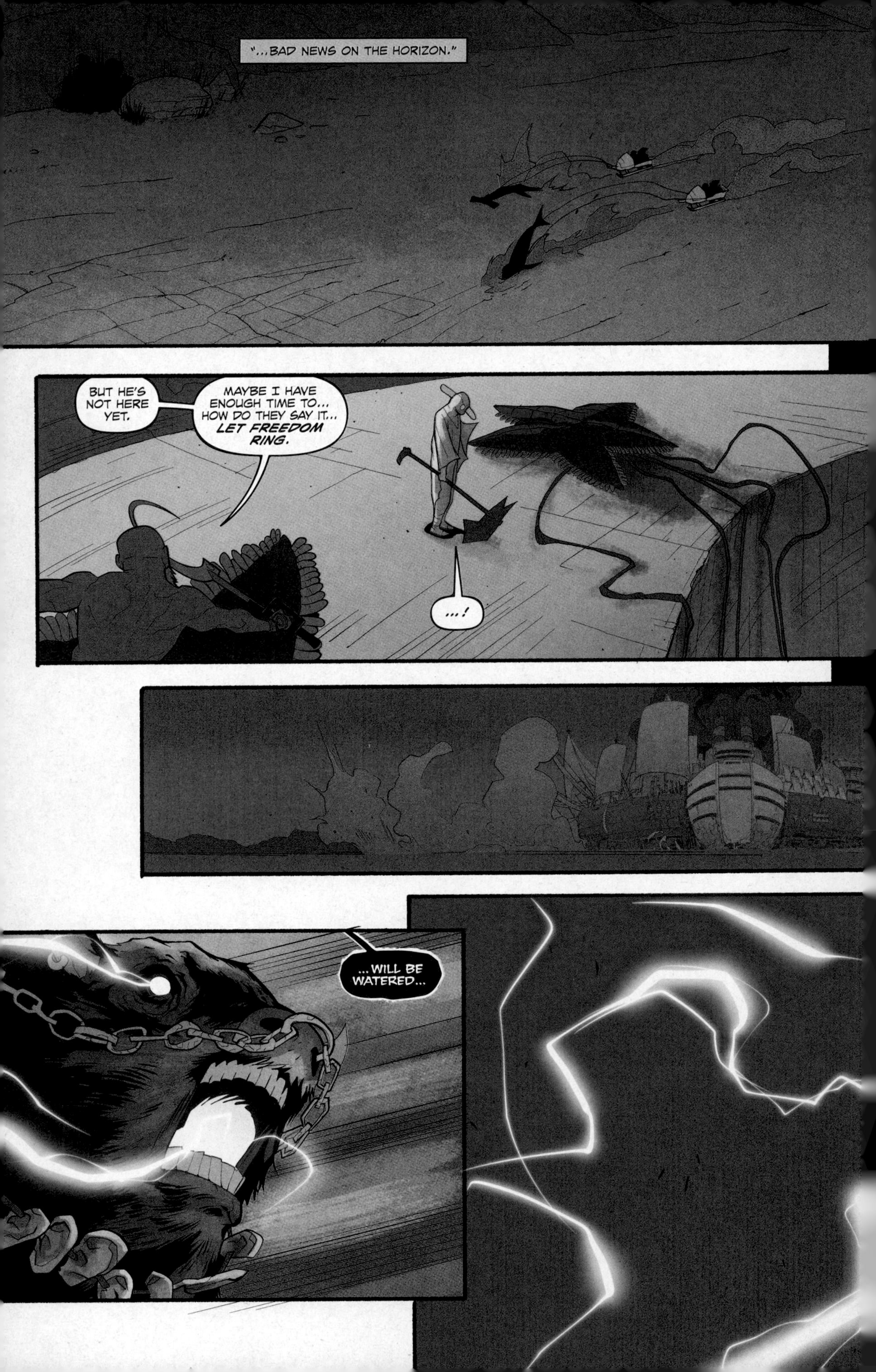
"...BAD NEWS ON THE HORIZON."
BUT HE'S NOT HERE YET.
MAYBE I HAVE ENOUGH TIME TO... HOW DO THEY SAY IT... LET FREEDOM RING.
...!
...WILL BE WATERED...

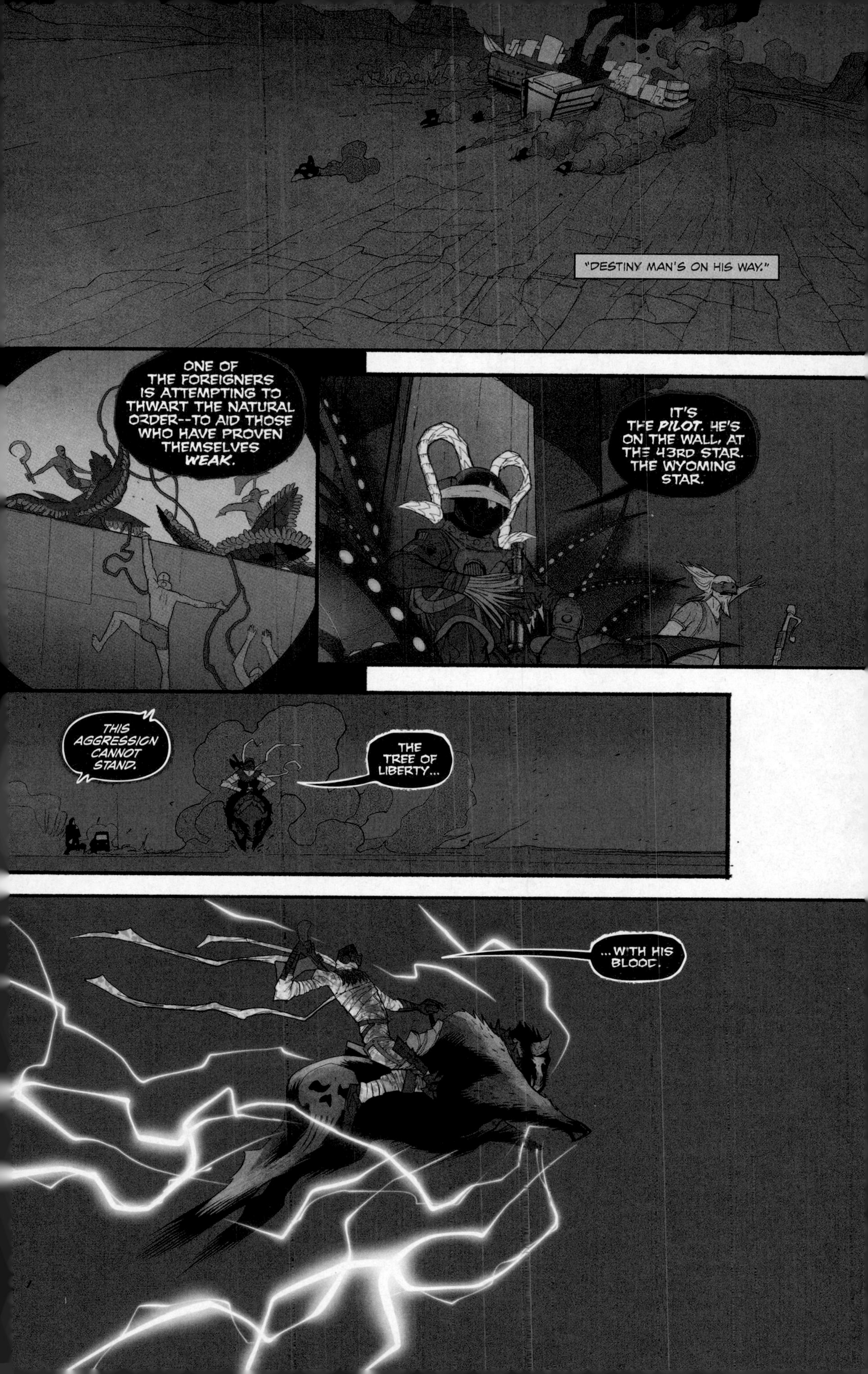

"DESTINY MAN'S ON HIS WAY."
ONE OF THE FOREIGNERS IS ATTEMPTING TO THWART THE NATURAL ORDER--TO AID THOSE WHO HAVE PROVEN THEMSELVES *WEAK*.
IT'S THE *PILOT*. HE'S ON THE WALL, AT THE 43RD STAR. THE WYOMING STAR.
THIS AGGRESSION CANNOT STAND.
THE TREE OF LIBERTY...
...WITH HIS BLOOD.

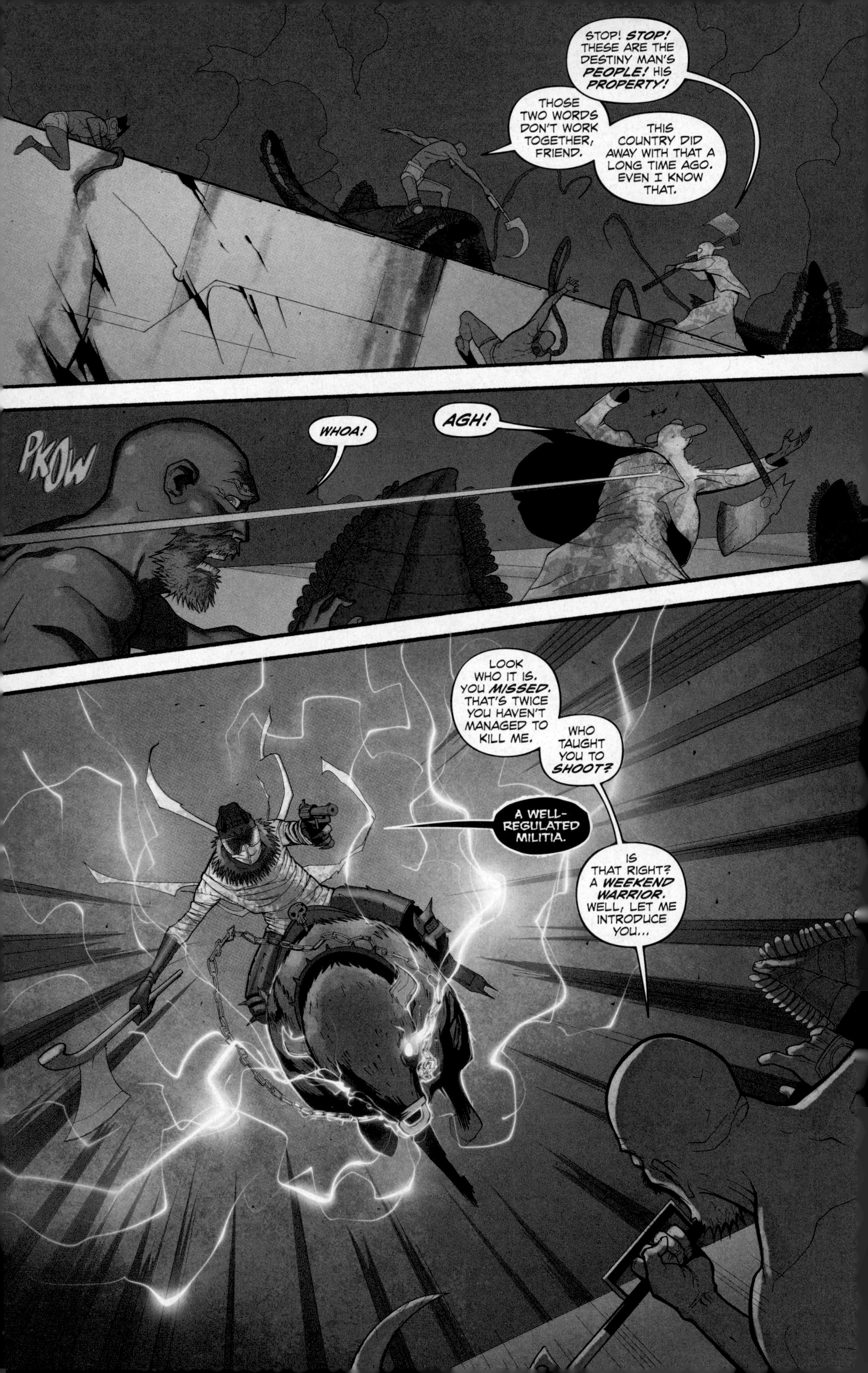
STOP! STOP! THESE ARE THE DESTINY MAN'S PEOPLE! HIS PROPERTY!
THOSE TWO WORDS DON'T WORK TOGETHER, FRIEND.
THIS COUNTRY DID AWAY WITH THAT A LONG TIME AGO. EVEN I KNOW THAT.
PKOW
WHOA!
AGH!
LOOK WHO IT IS. YOU MISSED. THAT'S TWICE YOU HAVEN'T MANAGED TO KILL ME.
WHO TAUGHT YOU TO SHOOT?
A WELL-REGULATED MILITIA.
IS THAT RIGHT? A WEEKEND WARRIOR. WELL, LET ME INTRODUCE YOU...

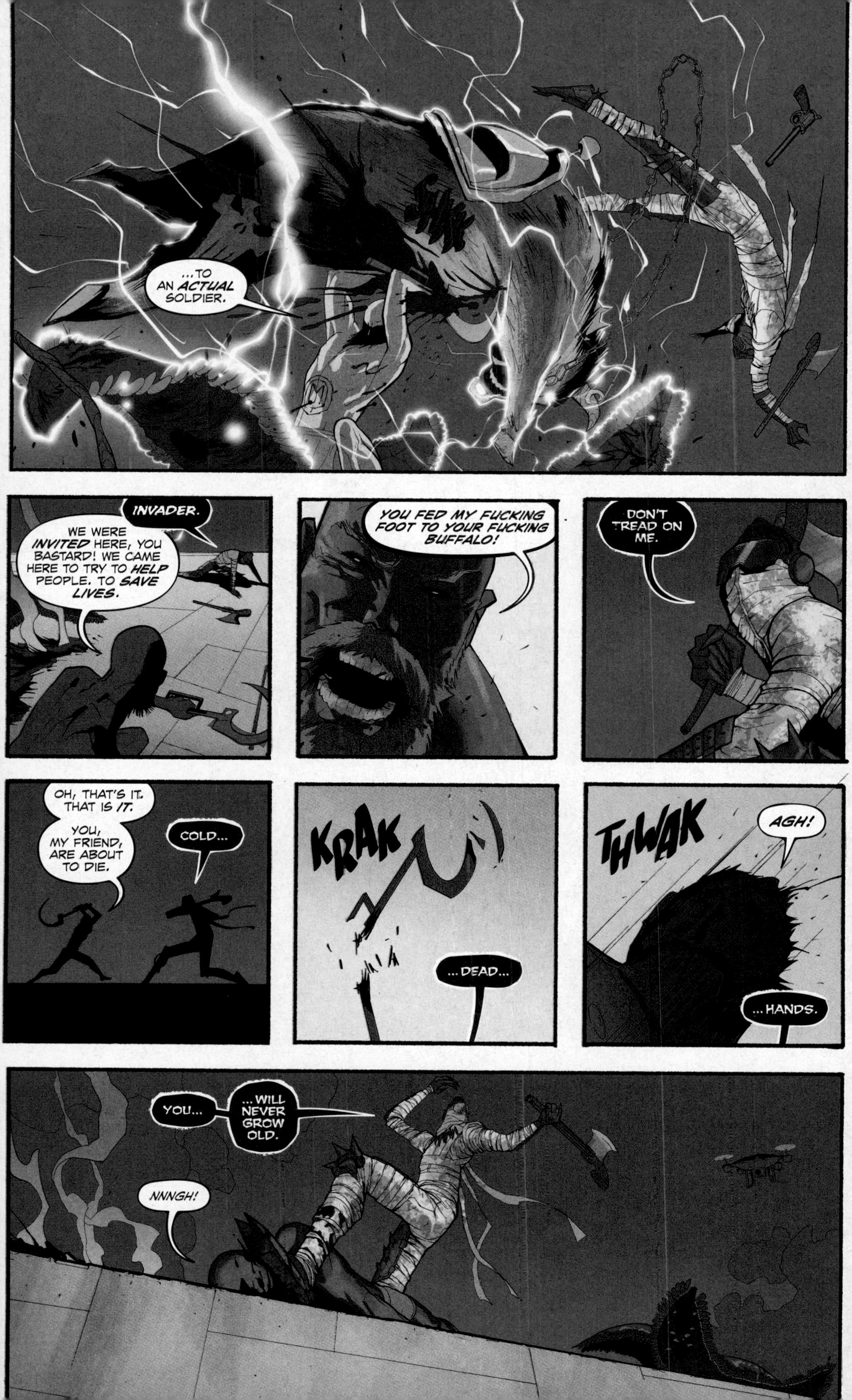
...TO AN ACTUAL SOLDIER.
INVADER.
WE WERE INVITED HERE, YOU BASTARD! WE CAME HERE TO TRY TO HELP PEOPLE. TO SAVE LIVES.
YOU FED MY FUCKING FOOT TO YOUR FUCKING BUFFALO!
DON'T TREAD ON ME.
OH, THAT'S IT. THAT IS IT.
YOU, MY FRIEND, ARE ABOUT TO DIE.
COLD...
KRAK
...DEAD...
THWAK
AGH!
...HANDS.
YOU...
...WILL NEVER GROW OLD.
NNNGH!

FWSSH

AGH!

MY EYES! THE ROCKETS' RED--

COME ON, MY STARRY FRIEND, YOU CAN DO IT... GET THAT BAD STUFF OUT OF YOU, YOU KNOW YOU WANT TO...

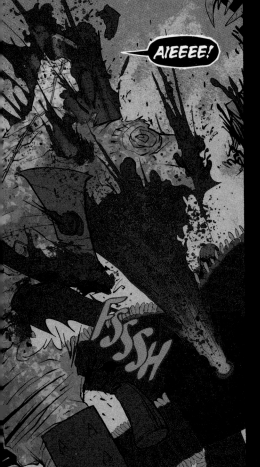

AIEEEE!

FSSSH

YIPPEE-KI-YAY, MOTHERF--

PAVEL!

...MS. SANDOVAL? IS THAT YOU, VALENTINA?

THANK YOU FOR THE ASSIST.

WHERE THE HELL ARE YOU?

ARE YOU ALL RIGHT?

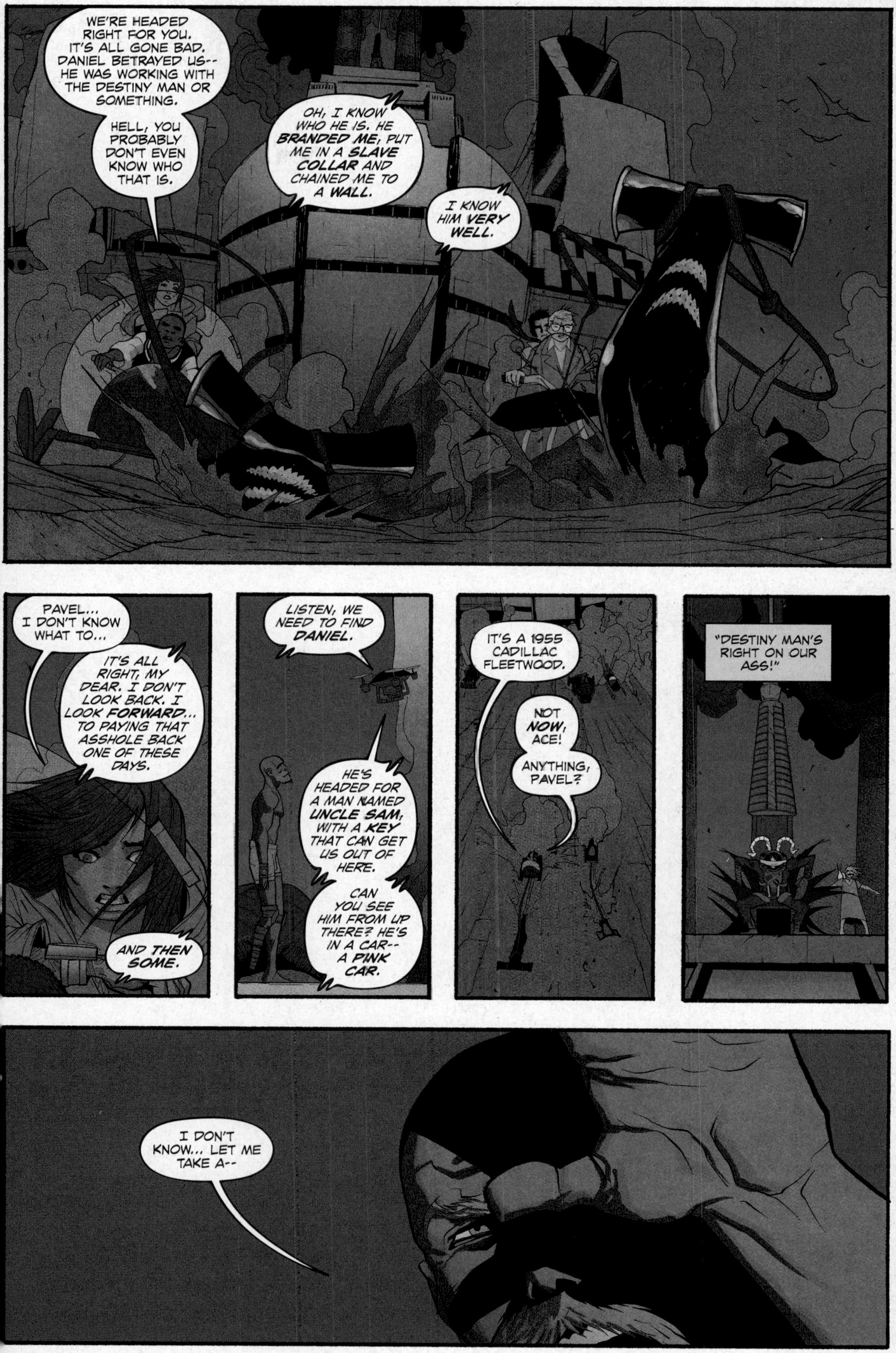
WE'RE HEADED RIGHT FOR YOU. IT'S ALL GONE BAD. DANIEL BETRAYED US-- HE WAS WORKING WITH THE DESTINY MAN OR SOMETHING.
HELL, YOU PROBABLY DON'T EVEN KNOW WHO THAT IS.
OH, I KNOW WHO HE IS. HE BRANDED ME, PUT ME IN A SLAVE COLLAR AND CHAINED ME TO A WALL.
I KNOW HIM VERY WELL.
PAVEL... I DON'T KNOW WHAT TO...
IT'S ALL RIGHT, MY DEAR. I DON'T LOOK BACK. I LOOK FORWARD... TO PAYING THAT ASSHOLE BACK ONE OF THESE DAYS.
AND THEN SOME.
LISTEN, WE NEED TO FIND DANIEL.
HE'S HEADED FOR A MAN NAMED UNCLE SAM, WITH A KEY THAT CAN GET US OUT OF HERE.
CAN YOU SEE HIM FROM UP THERE? HE'S IN A CAR-- A PINK CAR.
IT'S A 1955 CADILLAC FLEETWOOD.
NOT NOW, ACE!
ANYTHING, PAVEL?
"DESTINY MAN'S RIGHT ON OUR ASS!"
I DON'T KNOW... LET ME TAKE A--

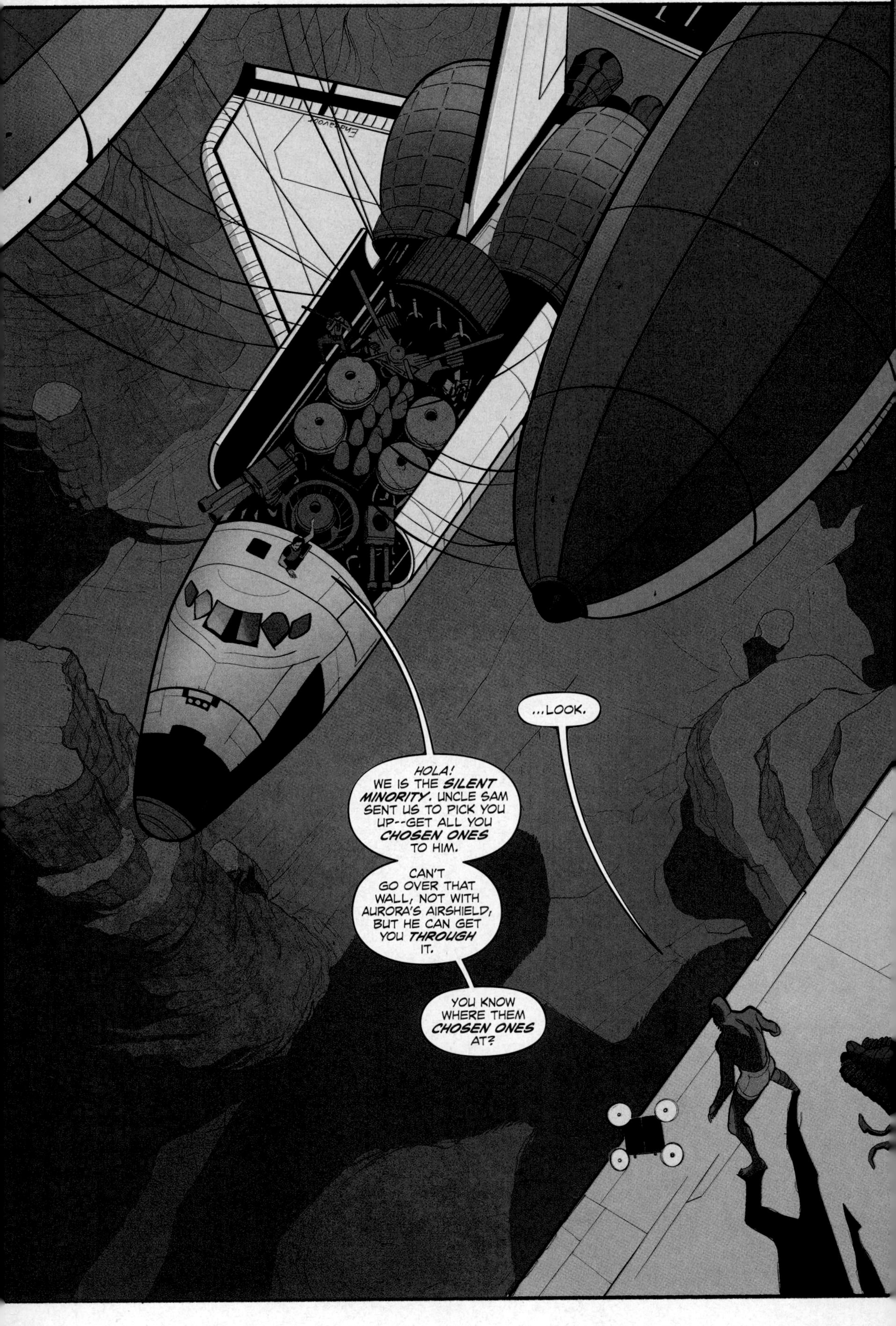

...LOOK.
HOLA! WE IS THE SILENT MINORITY. UNCLE SAM SENT US TO PICK YOU UP--GET ALL YOU CHOSEN ONES TO HIM.
CAN'T GO OVER THAT WALL, NOT WITH AURORA'S AIRSHIELD, BUT HE CAN GET YOU THROUGH IT.
YOU KNOW WHERE THEM CHOSEN ONES AT?

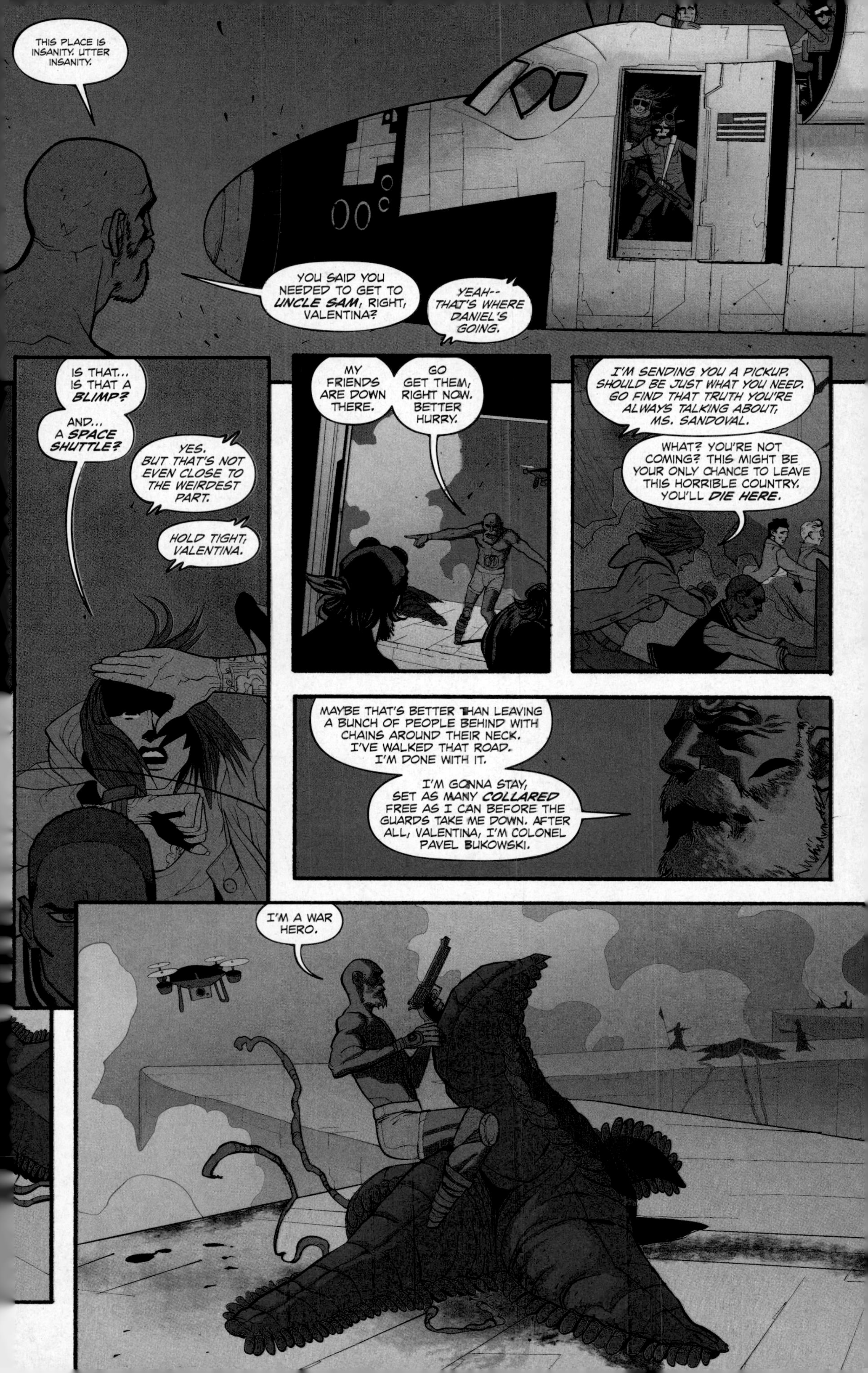
THIS PLACE IS INSANITY. UTTER INSANITY.
YOU SAID YOU NEEDED TO GET TO UNCLE SAM, RIGHT, VALENTINA?
YEAH--THAT'S WHERE DANIEL'S GOING.
IS THAT... IS THAT A BLIMP?
AND... A SPACE SHUTTLE?
YES. BUT THAT'S NOT EVEN CLOSE TO THE WEIRDEST PART.
HOLD TIGHT, VALENTINA.
MY FRIENDS ARE DOWN THERE.
GO GET THEM, RIGHT NOW. BETTER HURRY.
I'M SENDING YOU A PICKUP. SHOULD BE JUST WHAT YOU NEED. GO FIND THAT TRUTH YOU'RE ALWAYS TALKING ABOUT, MS. SANDOVAL.
WHAT? YOU'RE NOT COMING? THIS MIGHT BE YOUR ONLY CHANCE TO LEAVE THIS HORRIBLE COUNTRY. YOU'LL DIE HERE.
MAYBE THAT'S BETTER THAN LEAVING A BUNCH OF PEOPLE BEHIND WITH CHAINS AROUND THEIR NECK. I'VE WALKED THAT ROAD. I'M DONE WITH IT.
I'M GONNA STAY, SET AS MANY COLLARED FREE AS I CAN BEFORE THE GUARDS TAKE ME DOWN. AFTER ALL, VALENTINA, I'M COLONEL PAVEL BUKOWSKI.
I'M A WAR HERO.

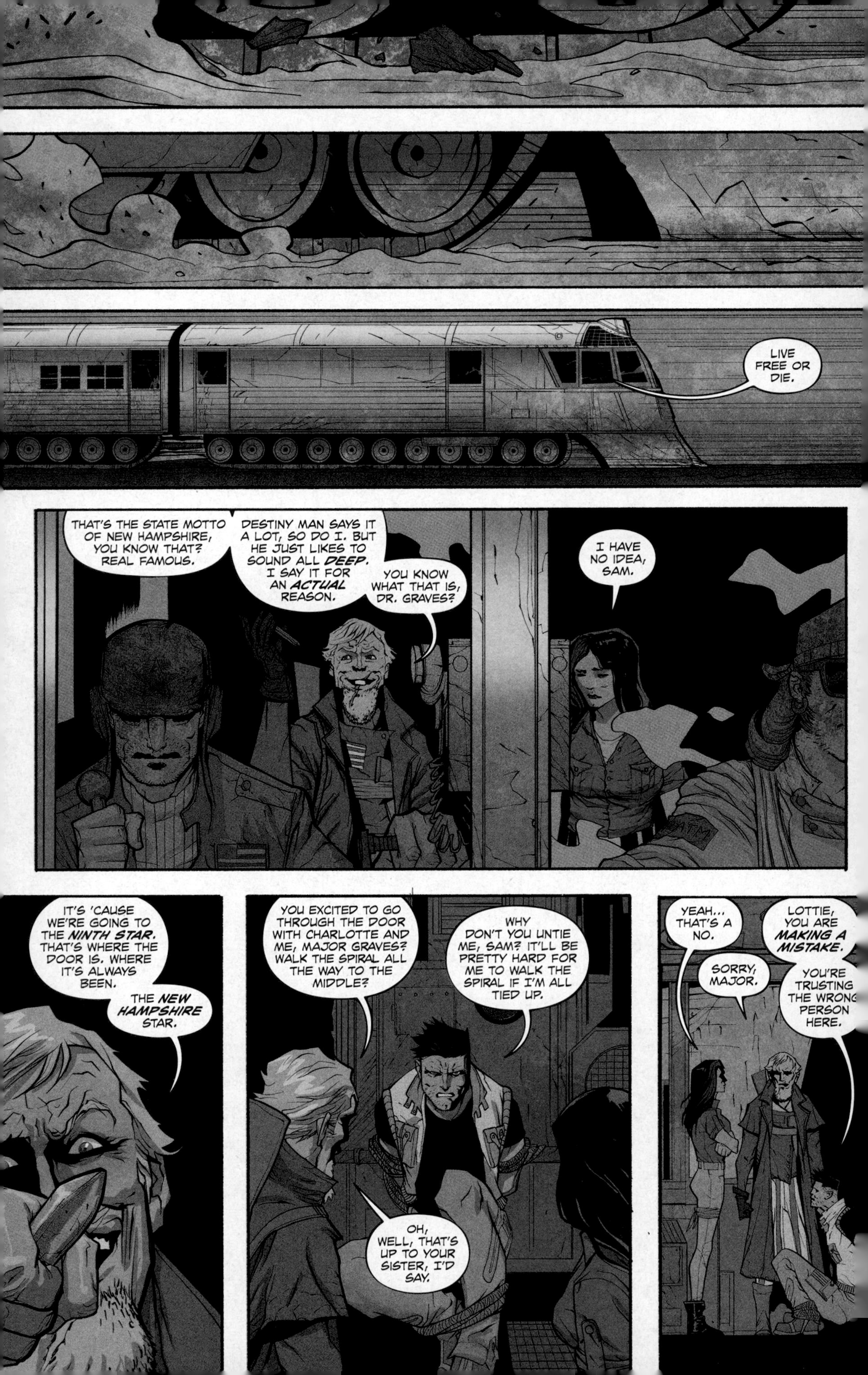
LIVE FREE OR DIE.
THAT'S THE STATE MOTTO OF NEW HAMPSHIRE, YOU KNOW THAT? REAL FAMOUS.
DESTINY MAN SAYS IT A LOT, SO DO I. BUT HE JUST LIKES TO SOUND ALL DEEP. I SAY IT FOR AN ACTUAL REASON.
YOU KNOW WHAT THAT IS, DR. GRAVES?
I HAVE NO IDEA, SAM.
IT'S 'CAUSE WE'RE GOING TO THE NINTH STAR. THAT'S WHERE THE DOOR IS. WHERE IT'S ALWAYS BEEN.
THE NEW HAMPSHIRE STAR.
YOU EXCITED TO GO THROUGH THE DOOR WITH CHARLOTTE AND ME, MAJOR GRAVES? WALK THE SPIRAL ALL THE WAY TO THE MIDDLE?
WHY DON'T YOU UNTIE ME, SAM? IT'LL BE PRETTY HARD FOR ME TO WALK THE SPIRAL IF I'M ALL TIED UP.
OH, WELL, THAT'S UP TO YOUR SISTER, I'D SAY.
YEAH... THAT'S A NO.
SORRY, MAJOR.
LOTTIE, YOU ARE MAKING A MISTAKE.
YOU'RE TRUSTING THE WRONG PERSON HERE.

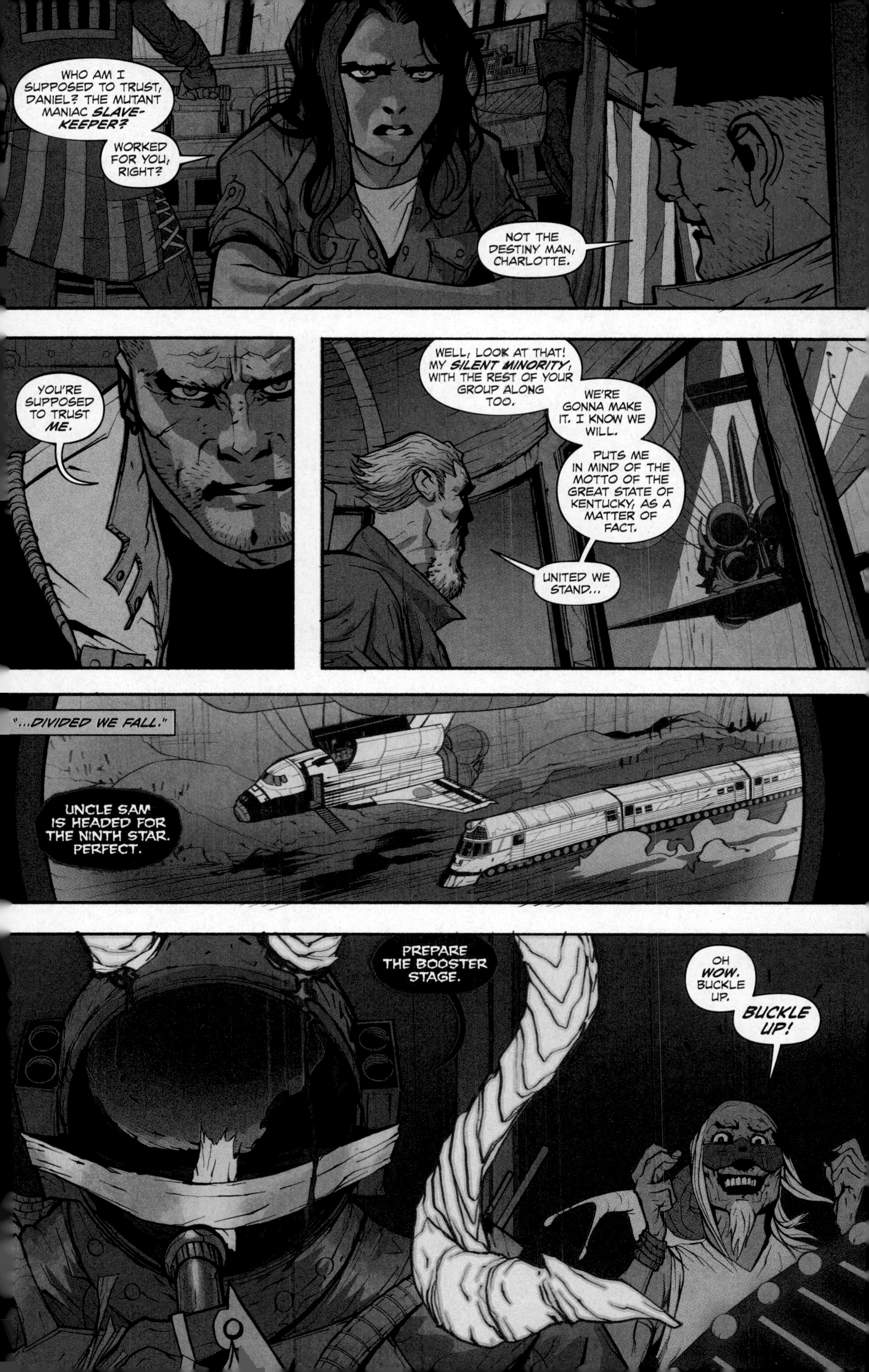
WHO AM I SUPPOSED TO TRUST, DANIEL? THE MUTANT MANIAC SLAVE-KEEPER?
WORKED FOR YOU, RIGHT?
NOT THE DESTINY MAN, CHARLOTTE.
YOU'RE SUPPOSED TO TRUST ME.
WELL, LOOK AT THAT! MY SILENT MINORITY, WITH THE REST OF YOUR GROUP ALONG TOO.
WE'RE GONNA MAKE IT. I KNOW WE WILL.
PUTS ME IN MIND OF THE MOTTO OF THE GREAT STATE OF KENTUCKY, AS A MATTER OF FACT.
UNITED WE STAND...
"...DIVIDED WE FALL."
UNCLE SAM IS HEADED FOR THE NINTH STAR. PERFECT.
PREPARE THE BOOSTER STAGE.
OH WOW. BUCKLE UP.
BUCKLE UP!

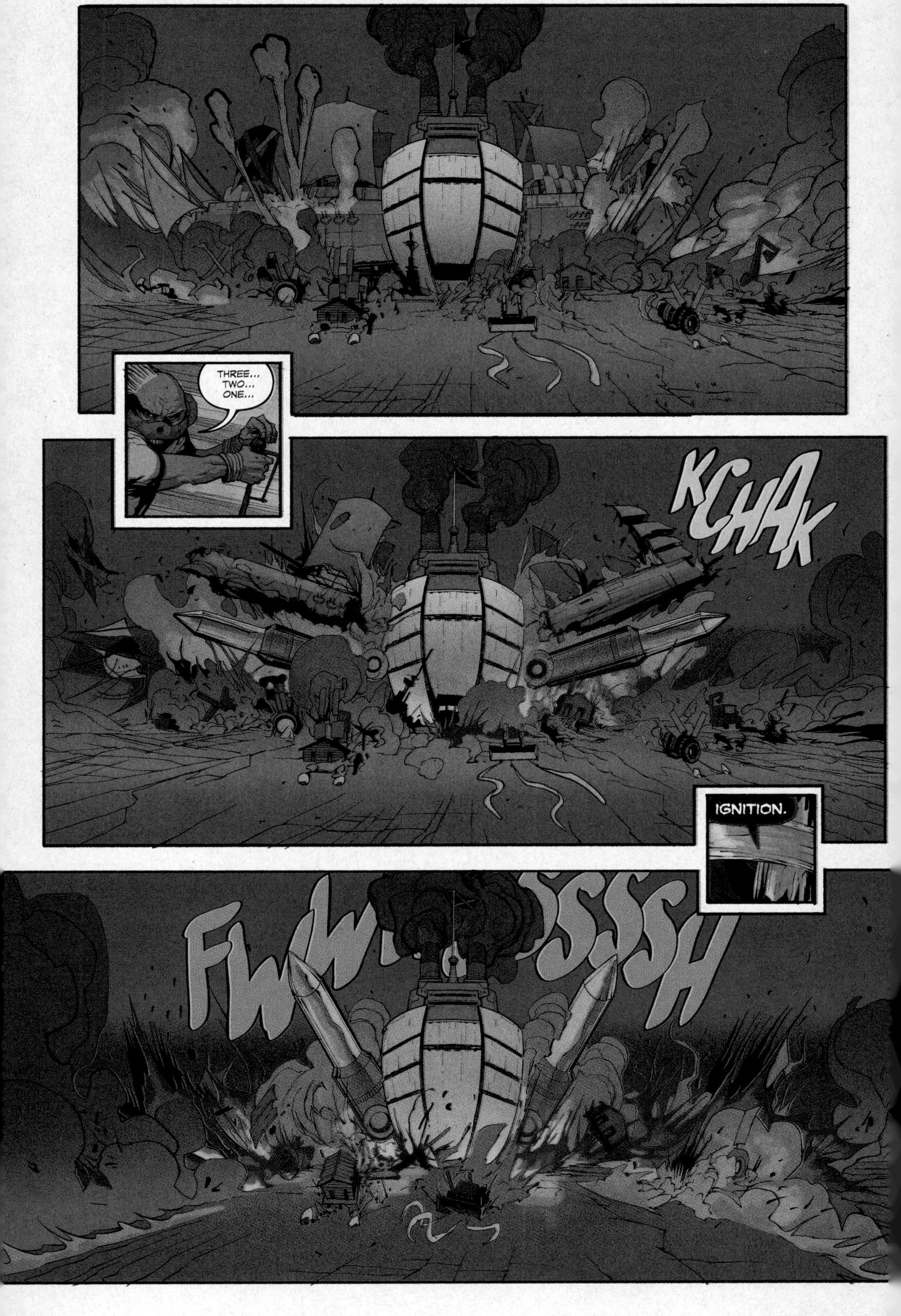
THREE... TWO... ONE...
KCHAK
IGNITION.
FWWSSSSH

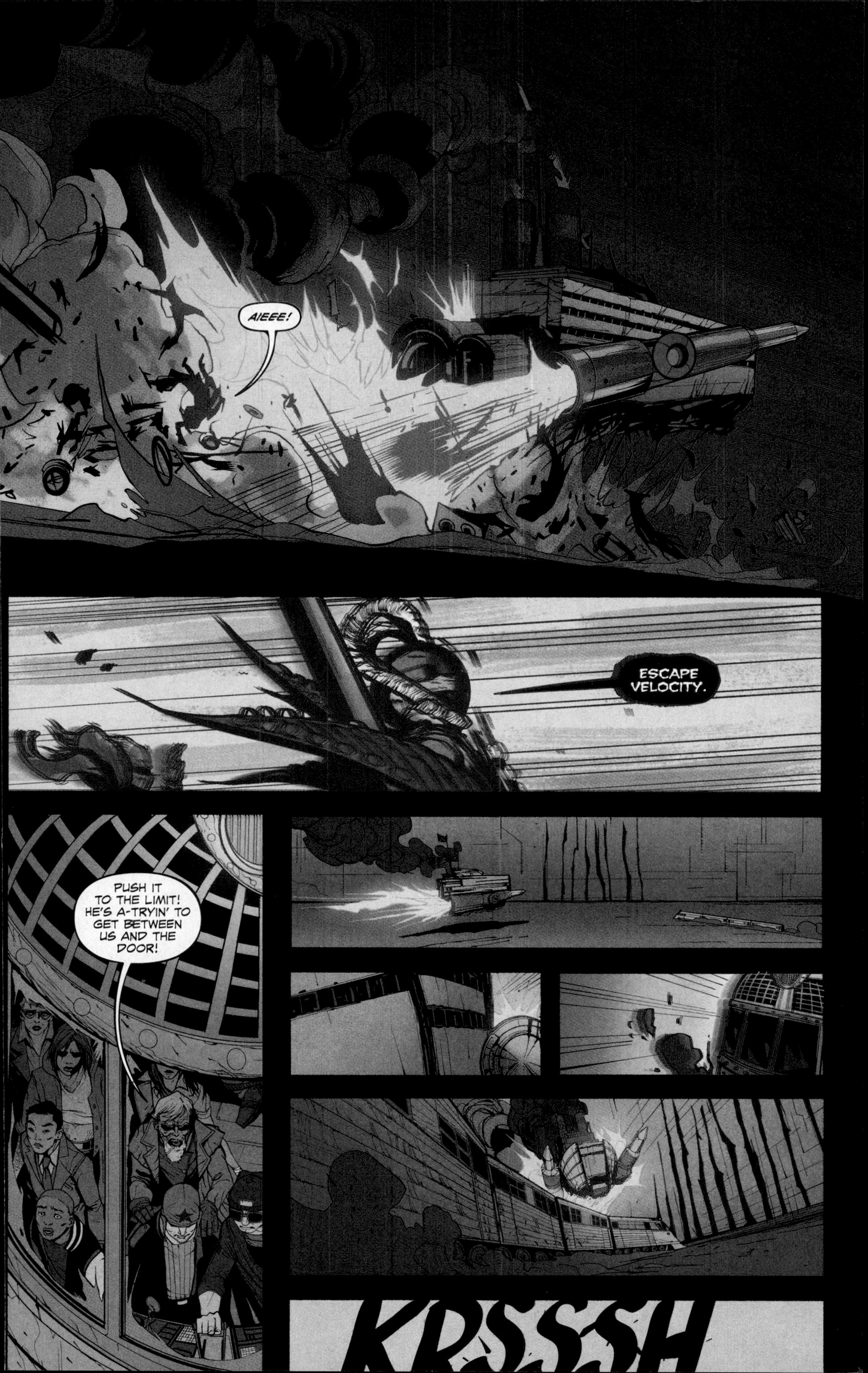

AIEEE!
ESCAPE VELOCITY.
PUSH IT TO THE LIMIT! HE'S A-TRYIN' TO GET BETWEEN US AND THE DOOR!
KRSSSH

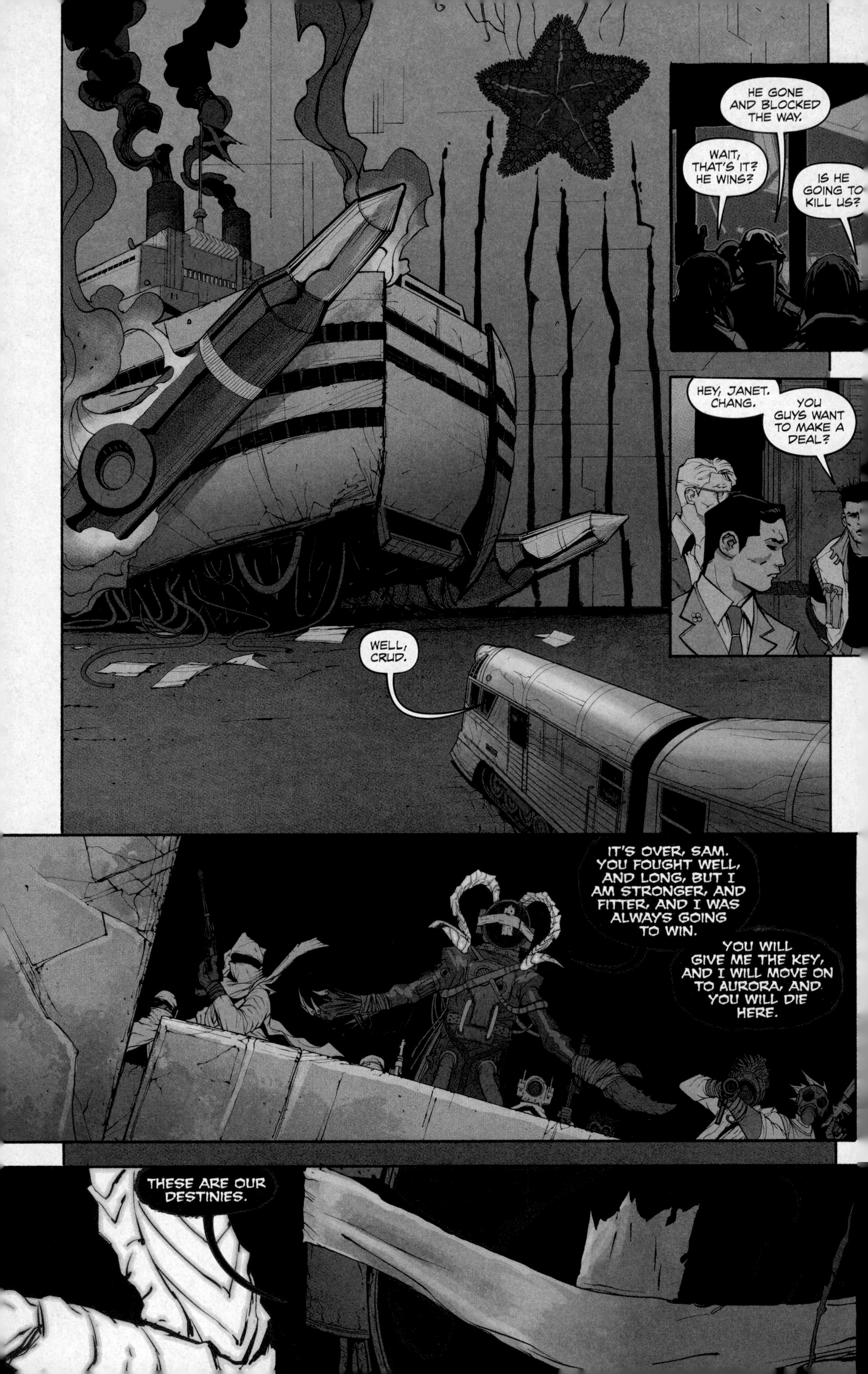
HE GONE AND BLOCKED THE WAY.
WAIT, THAT'S IT? HE WINS?
IS HE GOING TO KILL US?
HEY, JANET. CHANG.
YOU GUYS WANT TO MAKE A DEAL?
WELL, CRUD.
IT'S OVER, SAM. YOU FOUGHT WELL, AND LONG, BUT I AM STRONGER, AND FITTER, AND I WAS ALWAYS GOING TO WIN.
YOU WILL GIVE ME THE KEY, AND I WILL MOVE ON TO AURORA, AND YOU WILL DIE HERE.
THESE ARE OUR DESTINIES.

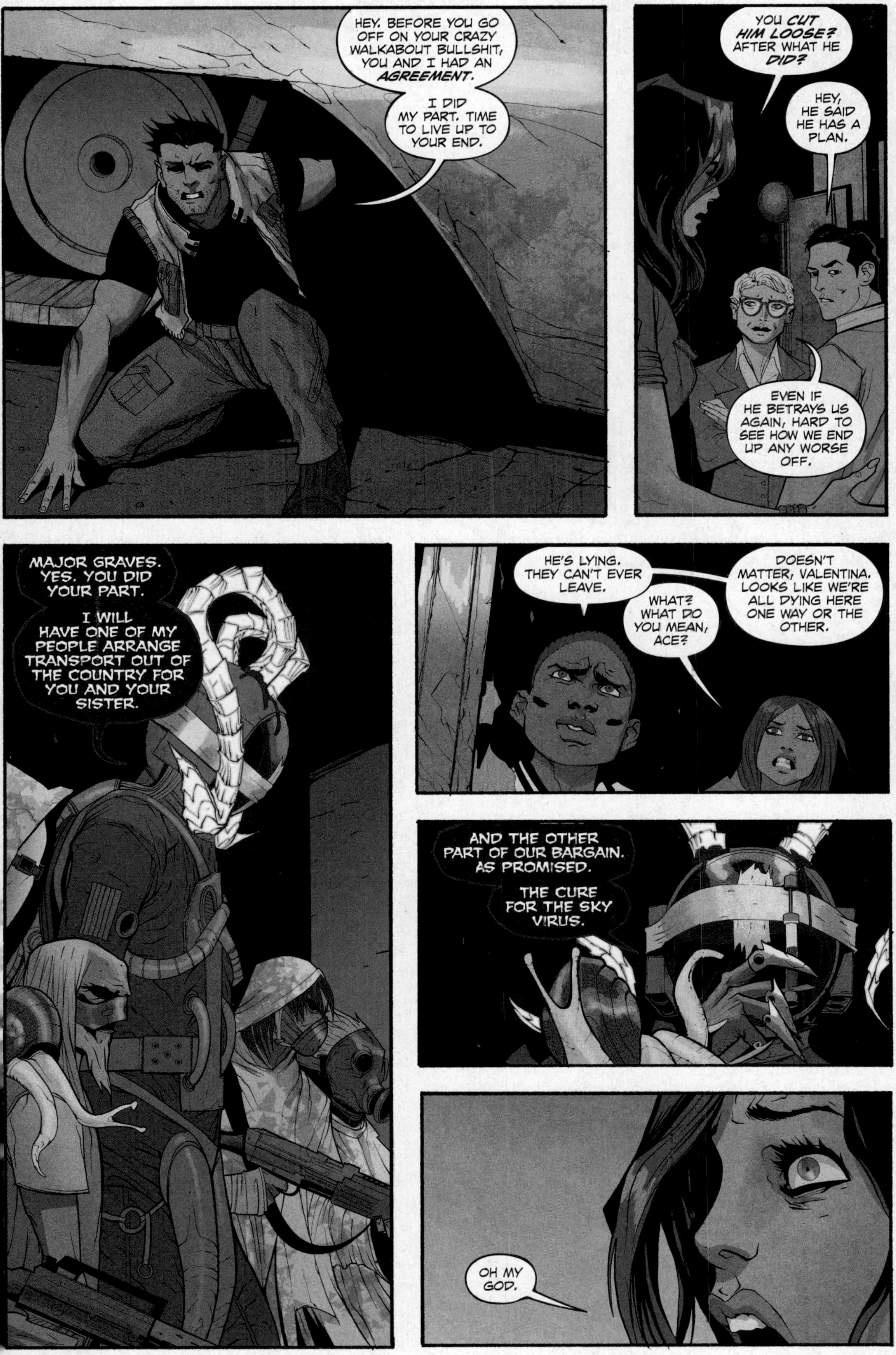
HEY. BEFORE YOU GO OFF ON YOUR CRAZY WALKABOUT BULLSHIT, YOU AND I HAD AN *AGREEMENT*.
I DID MY PART. TIME TO LIVE UP TO YOUR END.
YOU *CUT HIM LOOSE?* AFTER WHAT HE *DID?*
HEY, HE SAID HE HAS A PLAN.
EVEN IF HE BETRAYS US AGAIN, HARD TO SEE HOW WE END UP ANY WORSE OFF.
MAJOR GRAVES. YES. YOU DID YOUR PART.
I WILL HAVE ONE OF MY PEOPLE ARRANGE TRANSPORT OUT OF THE COUNTRY FOR YOU AND YOUR SISTER.
HE'S LYING. THEY CAN'T EVER LEAVE.
WHAT? WHAT DO YOU MEAN, ACE?
DOESN'T MATTER, VALENTINA. LOOKS LIKE WE'RE ALL DYING HERE ONE WAY OR THE OTHER.
AND THE OTHER PART OF OUR BARGAIN. AS PROMISED.
THE CURE FOR THE SKY VIRUS.
OH MY GOD.

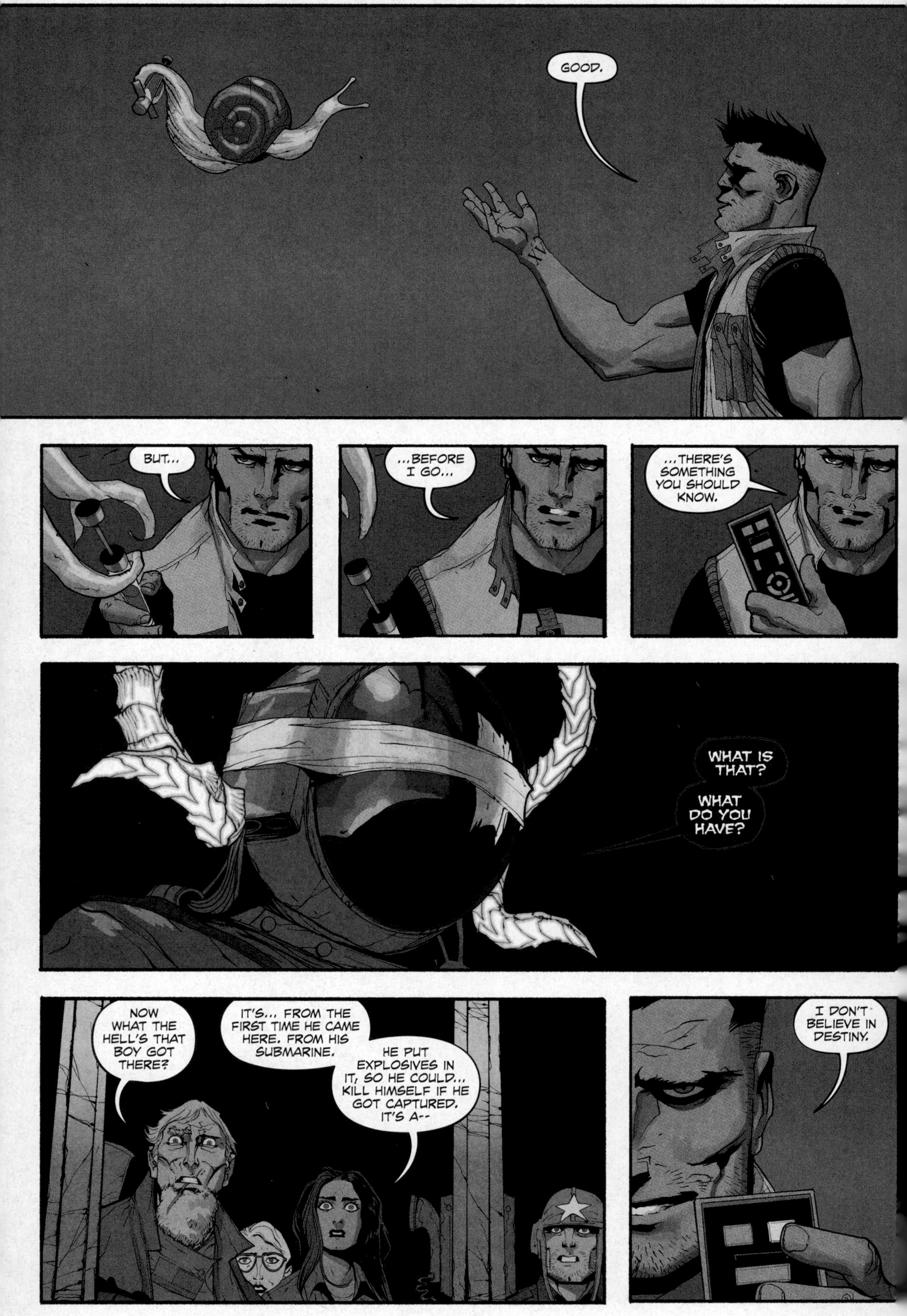
GOOD.
BUT...
...BEFORE I GO...
...THERE'S SOMETHING YOU SHOULD KNOW.
WHAT IS THAT?
WHAT DO YOU HAVE?
NOW WHAT THE HELL'S THAT BOY GOT THERE?
IT'S... FROM THE FIRST TIME HE CAME HERE. FROM HIS SUBMARINE.
HE PUT EXPLOSIVES IN IT, SO HE COULD... KILL HIMSELF IF HE GOT CAPTURED. IT'S A--
I DON'T BELIEVE IN DESTINY.

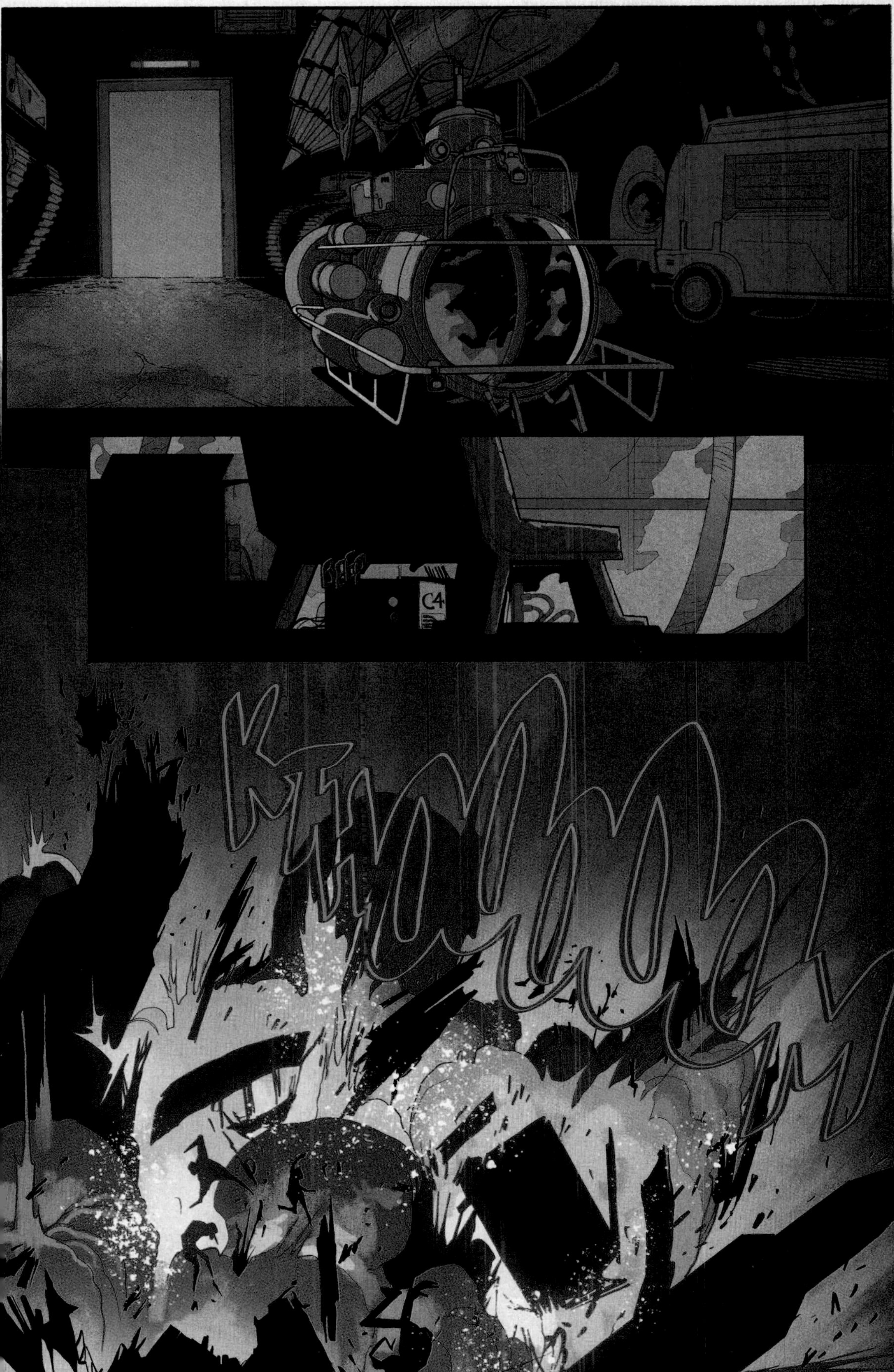
BEEP
C4
KTHOOOOM

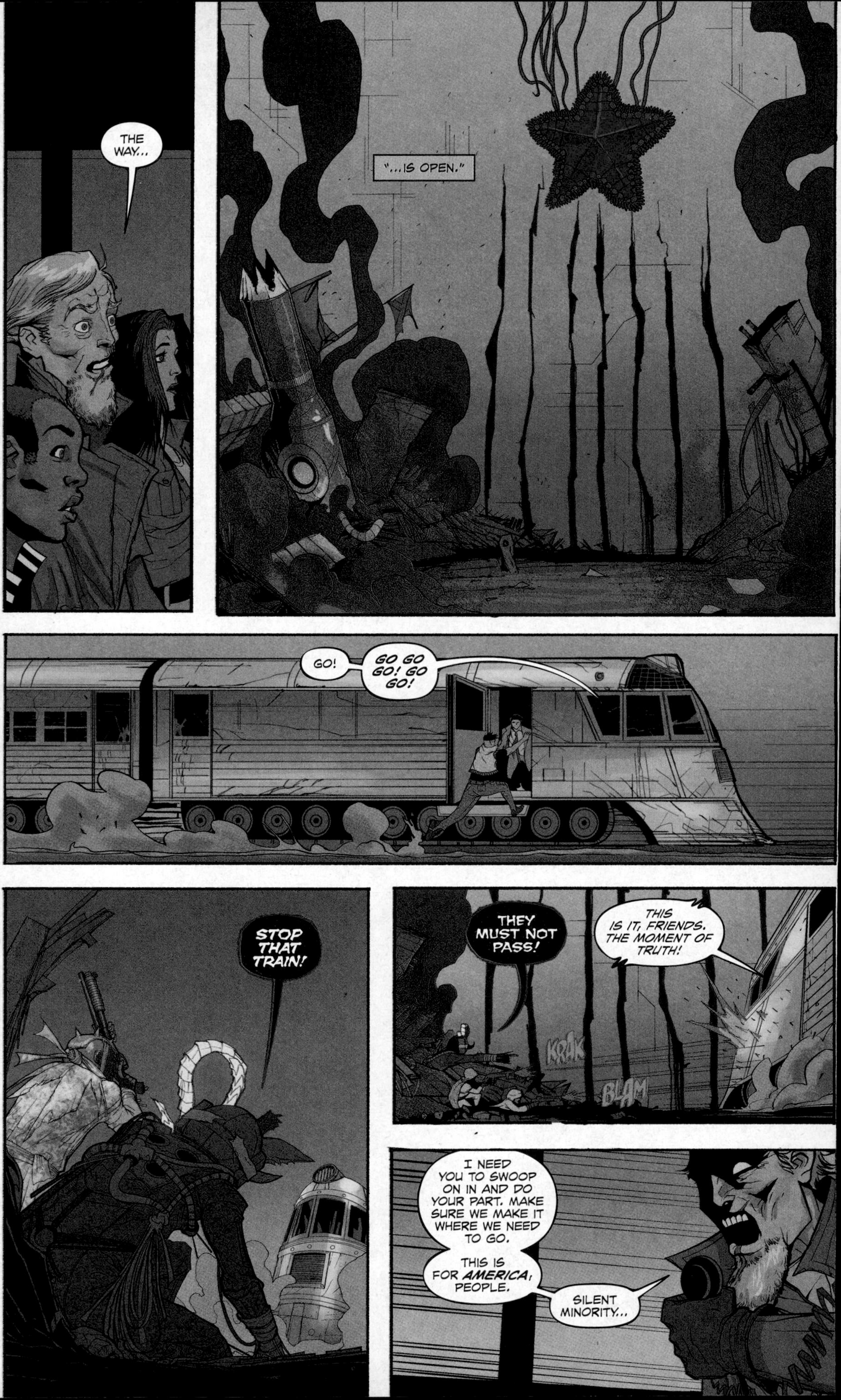
THE WAY...
"...IS OPEN."
GO!
GO GO GO! GO GO!
STOP THAT TRAIN!
THEY MUST NOT PASS!
THIS IS IT, FRIENDS. THE MOMENT OF TRUTH!
KRAK
BLAM
I NEED YOU TO SWOOP ON IN AND DO YOUR PART. MAKE SURE WE MAKE IT WHERE WE NEED TO GO.
THIS IS FOR AMERICA, PEOPLE.
SILENT MINORITY...

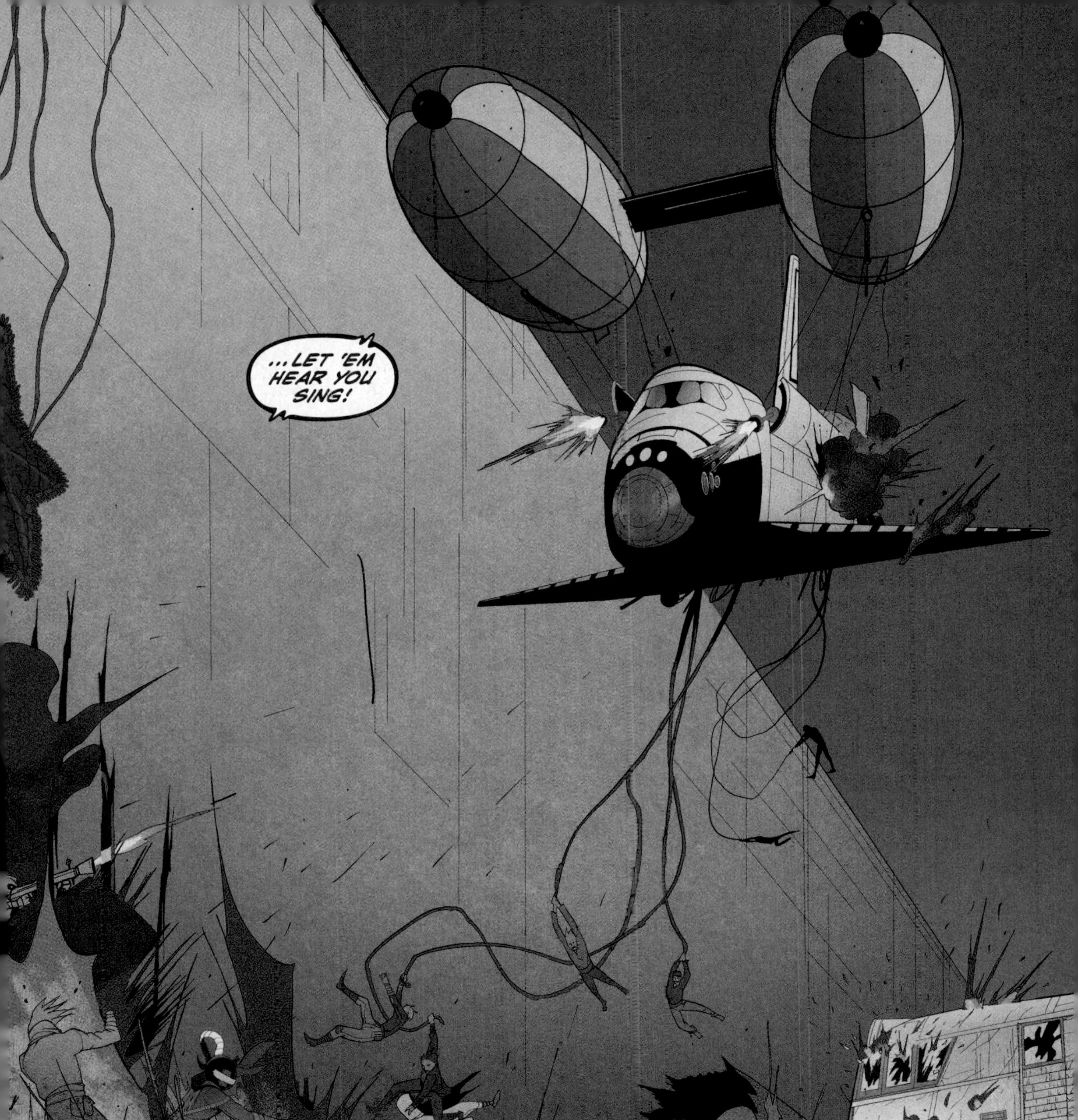
...LET 'EM HEAR YOU SING!

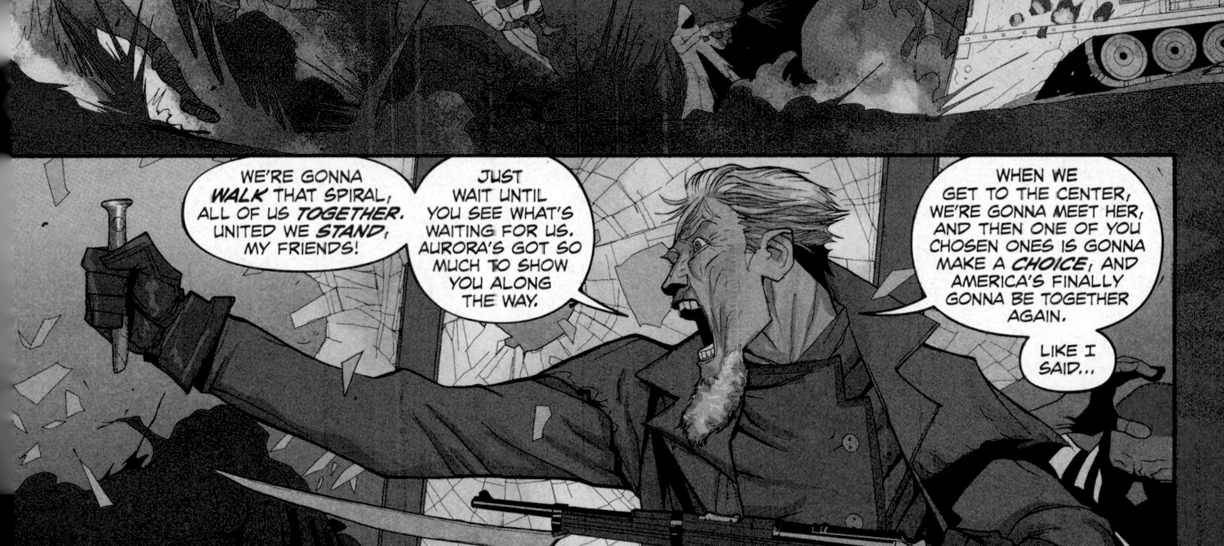
WE'RE GONNA WALK THAT SPIRAL, ALL OF US TOGETHER. UNITED WE STAND, MY FRIENDS!
JUST WAIT UNTIL YOU SEE WHAT'S WAITING FOR US. AURORA'S GOT SO MUCH TO SHOW YOU ALONG THE WAY.
WHEN WE GET TO THE CENTER, WE'RE GONNA MEET HER, AND THEN ONE OF YOU CHOSEN ONES IS GONNA MAKE A CHOICE, AND AMERICA'S FINALLY GONNA BE TOGETHER AGAIN.
LIKE I SAID...

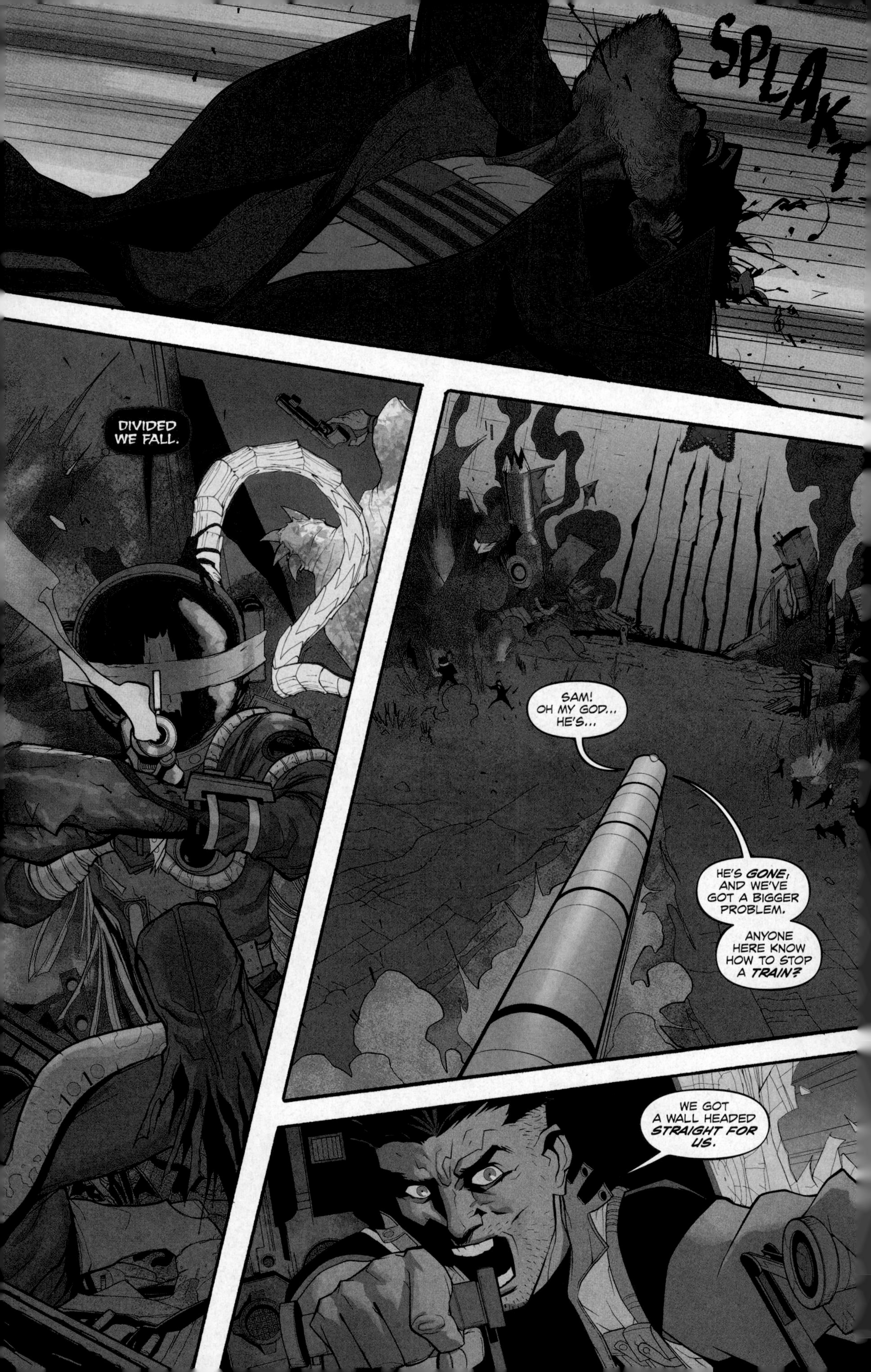
SPLAKT
DIVIDED WE FALL.
SAM! OH MY GOD... HE'S...
HE'S GONE; AND WE'VE GOT A BIGGER PROBLEM.
ANYONE HERE KNOW HOW TO STOP A TRAIN?
WE GOT A WALL HEADED STRAIGHT FOR US.

KLK

KSHK

ARE THOSE... GUNS?

VERY *BIG* GUNS.

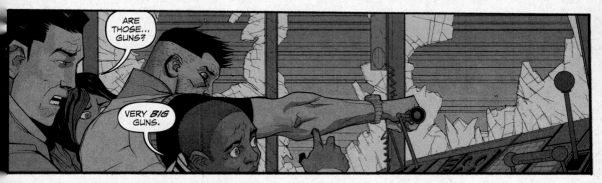

BRAKKA BRAKKA BRAKKA

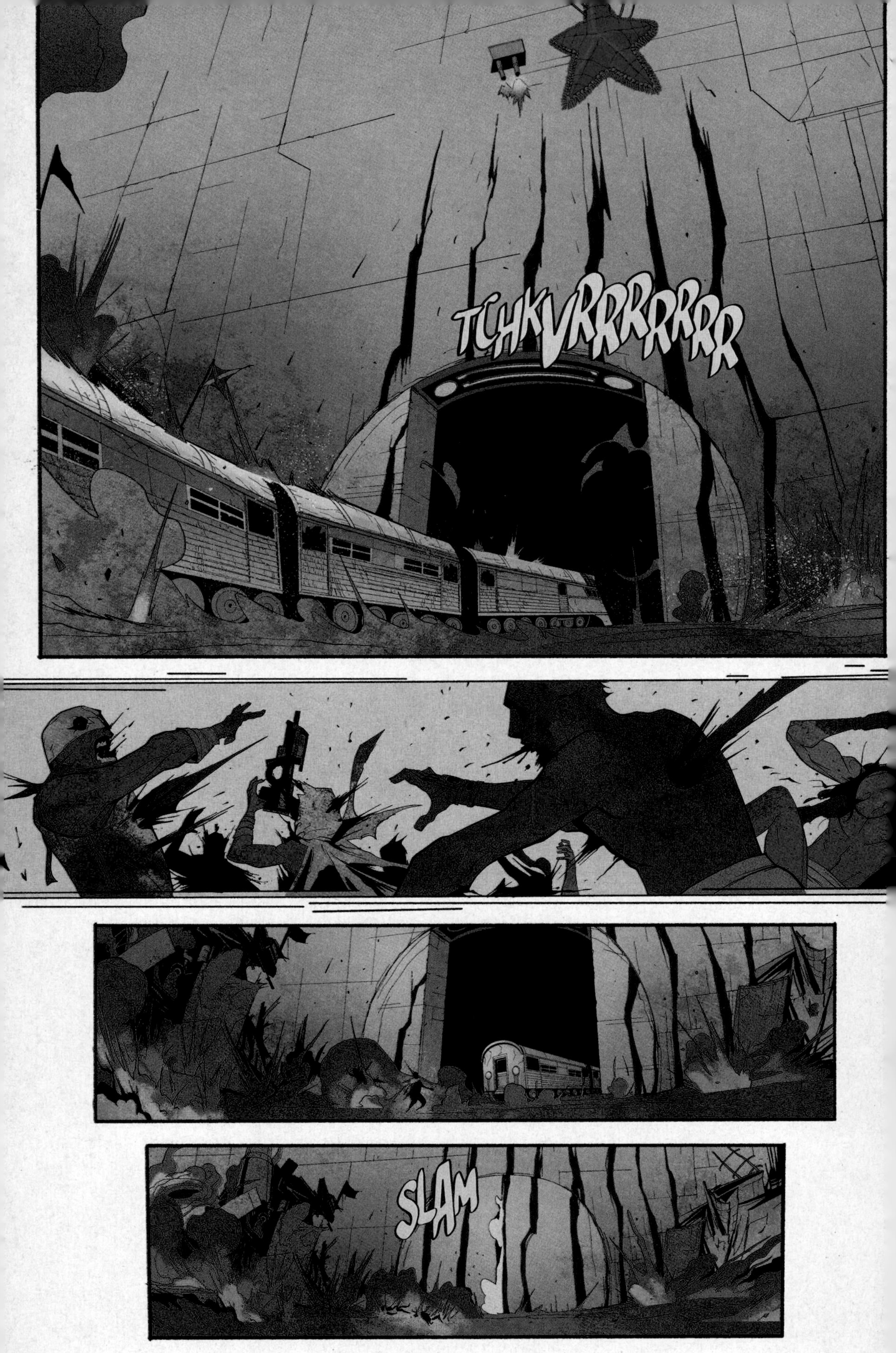
TCHKVRRRRRRRR
SLAM

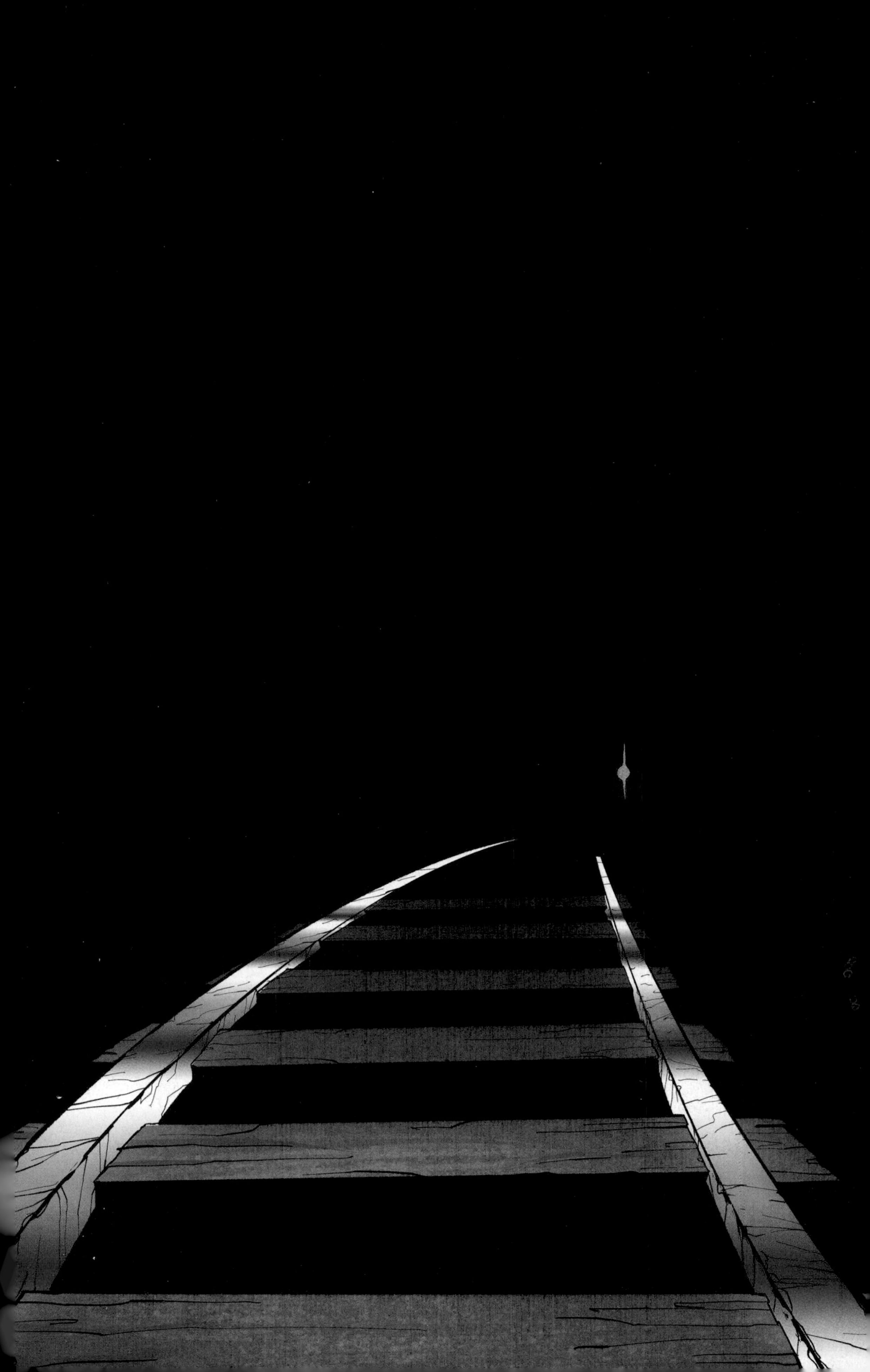

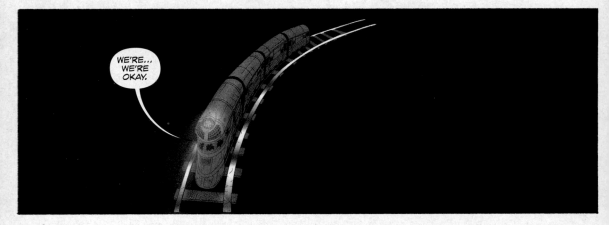

WE'RE... WE'RE OKAY.

NOT *ALL* OF US.

SAM'S *DEAD.*

AND *EVERYONE ELSE,* IT LOOKED LIKE.

WHERE DID THOSE *GUNS* COME FROM? WHO WAS *FIRING THEM?*

OR, TO PUT IT ANOTHER WAY...

...WHAT THE FUCK ARE WE SUPPOSED TO DO NOW?

WE WALK THE SPIRAL, CHANG. WE DON'T HAVE A CHOICE.

WE NEVER DID.

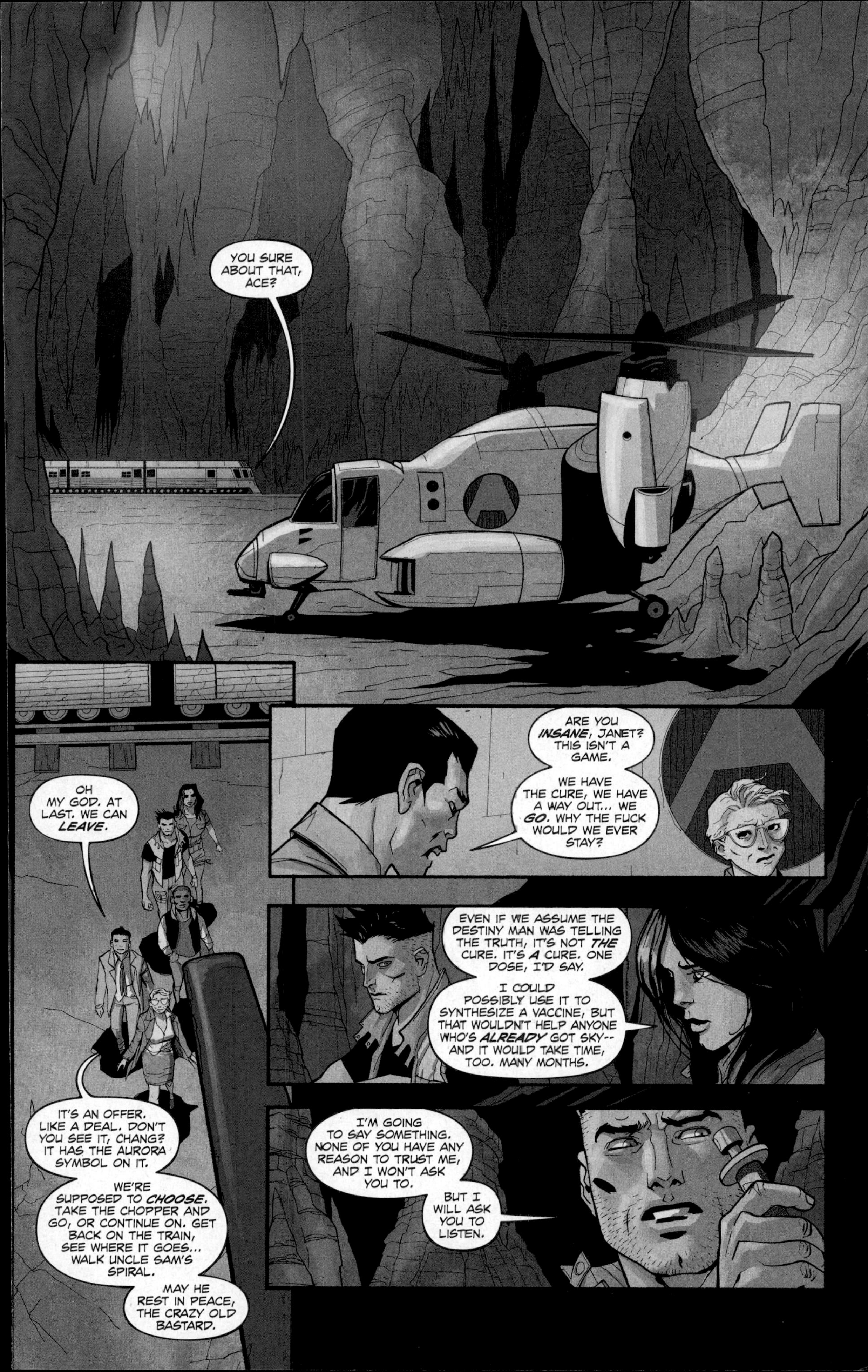
YOU SURE ABOUT THAT, ACE?
OH MY GOD. AT LAST. WE CAN *LEAVE*.
ARE YOU *INSANE*, JANET? THIS ISN'T A GAME.
WE HAVE THE CURE, WE HAVE A WAY OUT... WE *GO*. WHY THE FUCK WOULD WE EVER STAY?
EVEN IF WE ASSUME THE DESTINY MAN WAS TELLING THE TRUTH, IT'S NOT *THE* CURE. IT'S *A* CURE. ONE DOSE, I'D SAY.
I COULD POSSIBLY USE IT TO SYNTHESIZE A VACCINE, BUT THAT WOULDN'T HELP ANYONE WHO'S *ALREADY* GOT SKY-- AND IT WOULD TAKE TIME, TOO. MANY MONTHS.
IT'S AN OFFER. LIKE A DEAL. DON'T YOU SEE IT, CHANG? IT HAS THE AURORA SYMBOL ON IT.
WE'RE SUPPOSED TO *CHOOSE*. TAKE THE CHOPPER AND GO, OR CONTINUE ON. GET BACK ON THE TRAIN, SEE WHERE IT GOES... WALK UNCLE SAM'S SPIRAL.
MAY HE REST IN PEACE, THE CRAZY OLD BASTARD.
I'M GOING TO SAY SOMETHING. NONE OF YOU HAVE ANY REASON TO TRUST ME, AND I WON'T ASK YOU TO.
BUT I WILL ASK YOU TO LISTEN.

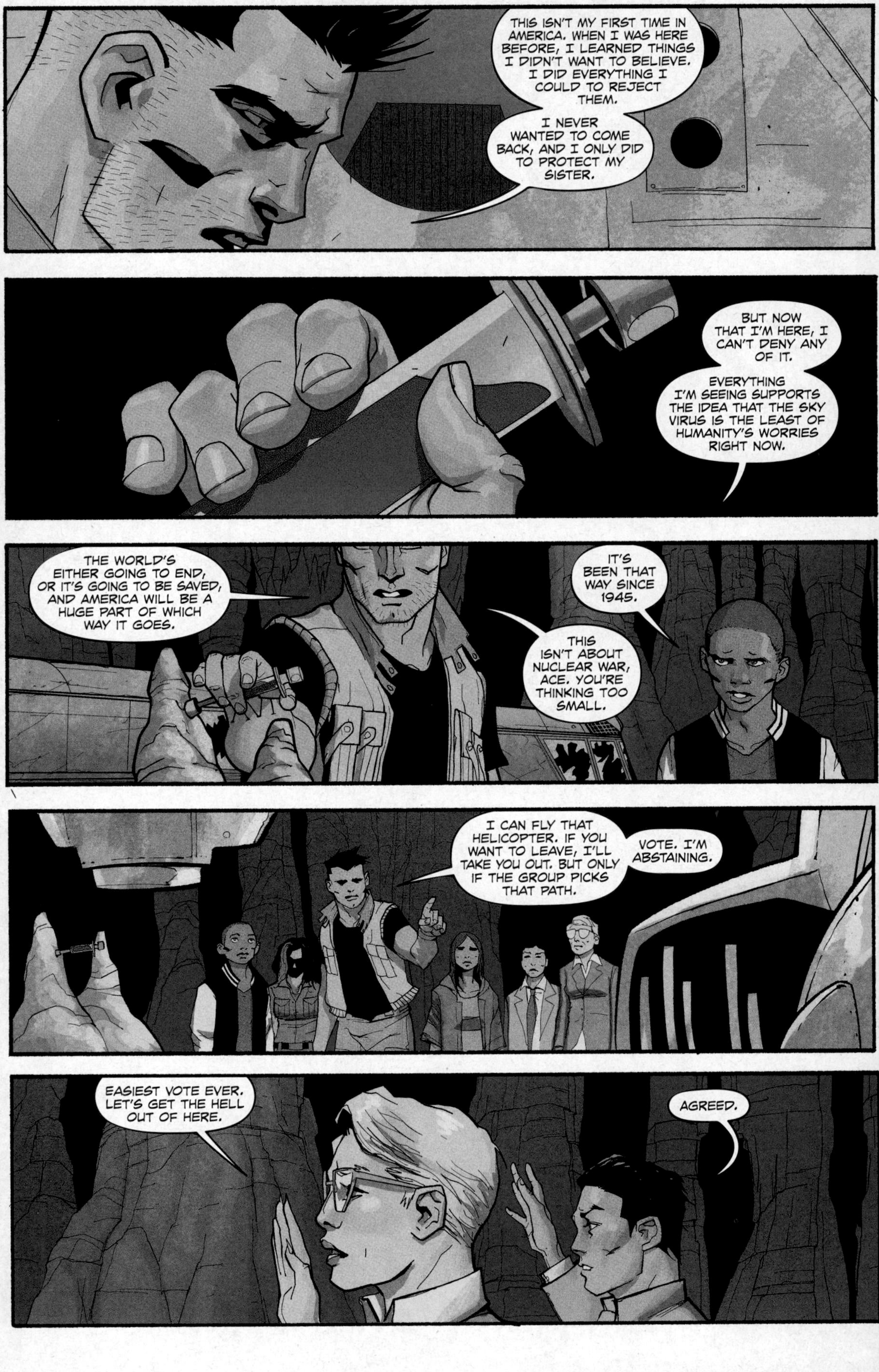
THIS ISN'T MY FIRST TIME IN AMERICA. WHEN I WAS HERE BEFORE, I LEARNED THINGS I DIDN'T WANT TO BELIEVE. I DID EVERYTHING I COULD TO REJECT THEM.
I NEVER WANTED TO COME BACK, AND I ONLY DID TO PROTECT MY SISTER.
BUT NOW THAT I'M HERE, I CAN'T DENY ANY OF IT.
EVERYTHING I'M SEEING SUPPORTS THE IDEA THAT THE SKY VIRUS IS THE LEAST OF HUMANITY'S WORRIES RIGHT NOW.
THE WORLD'S EITHER GOING TO END, OR IT'S GOING TO BE SAVED, AND AMERICA WILL BE A HUGE PART OF WHICH WAY IT GOES.
IT'S BEEN THAT WAY SINCE 1945.
THIS ISN'T ABOUT NUCLEAR WAR, ACE. YOU'RE THINKING TOO SMALL.
I CAN FLY THAT HELICOPTER. IF YOU WANT TO LEAVE, I'LL TAKE YOU OUT. BUT ONLY IF THE GROUP PICKS THAT PATH.
VOTE. I'M ABSTAINING.
EASIEST VOTE EVER. LET'S GET THE HELL OUT OF HERE.
AGREED.

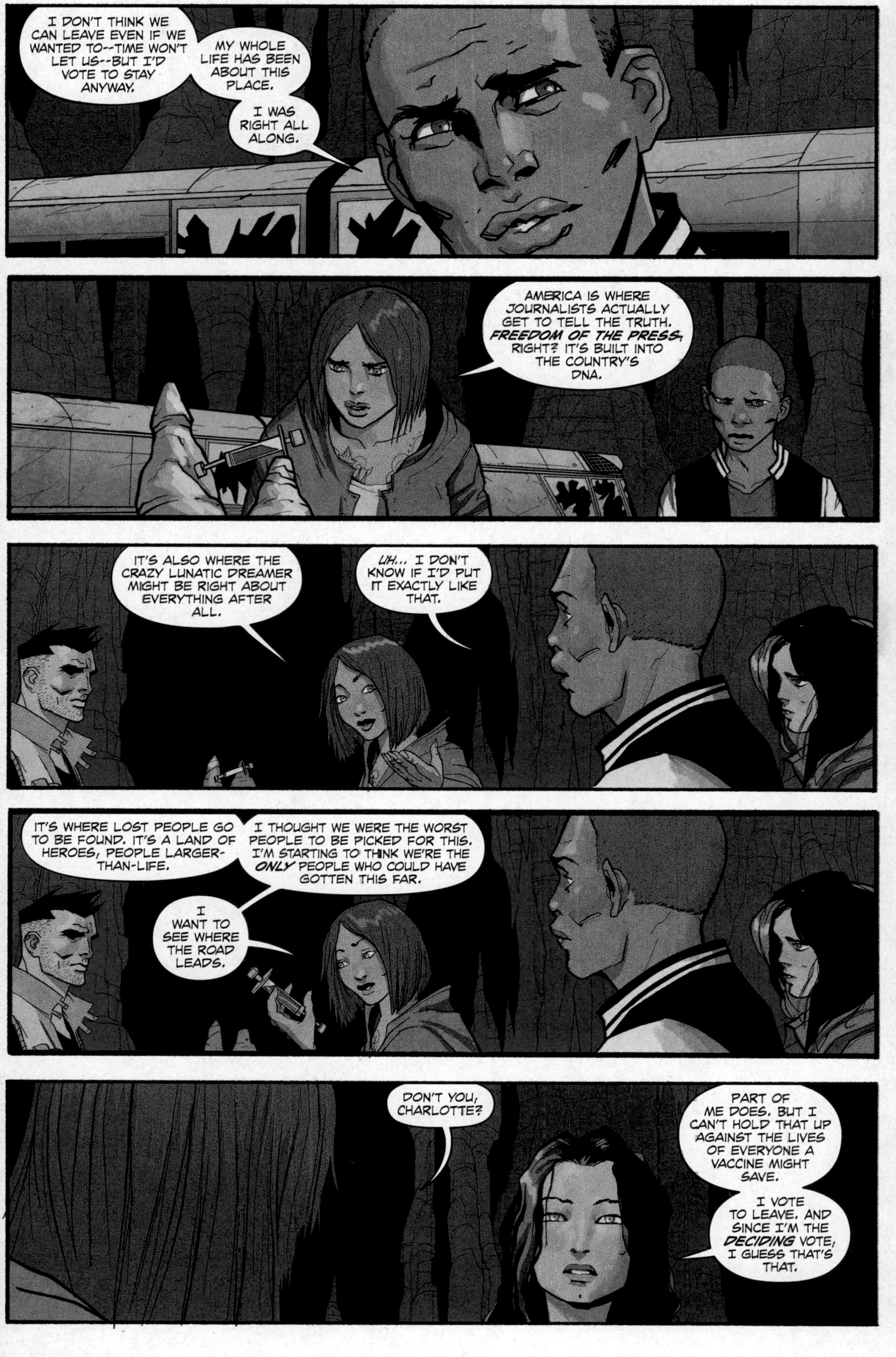
I DON'T THINK WE CAN LEAVE EVEN IF WE WANTED TO--TIME WON'T LET US--BUT I'D VOTE TO STAY ANYWAY.
MY WHOLE LIFE HAS BEEN ABOUT THIS PLACE.
I WAS RIGHT ALL ALONG.
AMERICA IS WHERE JOURNALISTS ACTUALLY GET TO TELL THE TRUTH. FREEDOM OF THE PRESS, RIGHT? IT'S BUILT INTO THE COUNTRY'S DNA.
IT'S ALSO WHERE THE CRAZY LUNATIC DREAMER MIGHT BE RIGHT ABOUT EVERYTHING AFTER ALL.
UH... I DON'T KNOW IF I'D PUT IT EXACTLY LIKE THAT.
IT'S WHERE LOST PEOPLE GO TO BE FOUND. IT'S A LAND OF HEROES, PEOPLE LARGER-THAN-LIFE.
I THOUGHT WE WERE THE WORST PEOPLE TO BE PICKED FOR THIS. I'M STARTING TO THINK WE'RE THE ONLY PEOPLE WHO COULD HAVE GOTTEN THIS FAR.
I WANT TO SEE WHERE THE ROAD LEADS.
DON'T YOU, CHARLOTTE?
PART OF ME DOES. BUT I CAN'T HOLD THAT UP AGAINST THE LIVES OF EVERYONE A VACCINE MIGHT SAVE.
I VOTE TO LEAVE. AND SINCE I'M THE DECIDING VOTE, I GUESS THAT'S THAT.

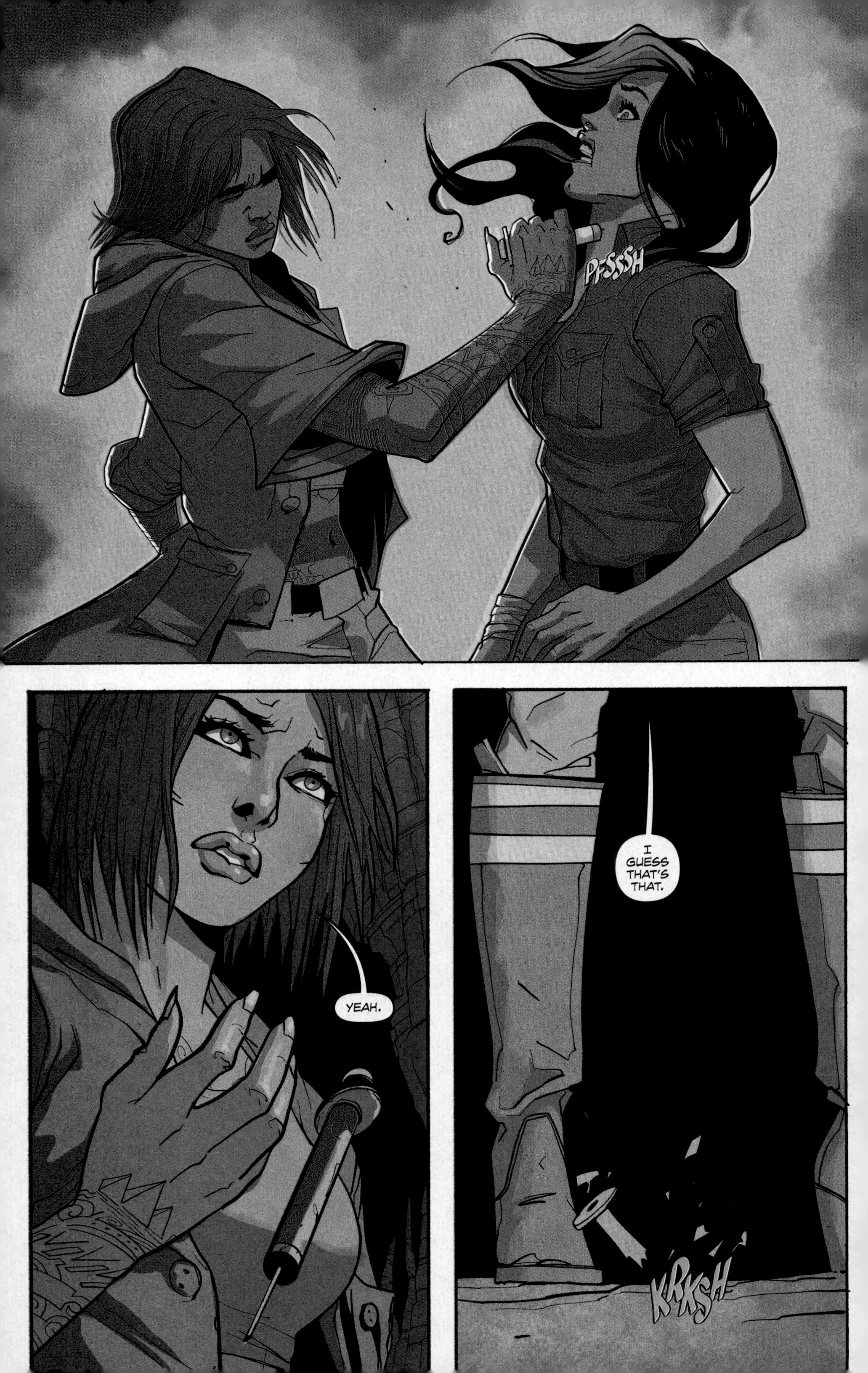

PFSSSH
YEAH.
I GUESS THAT'S THAT.
KRKSH

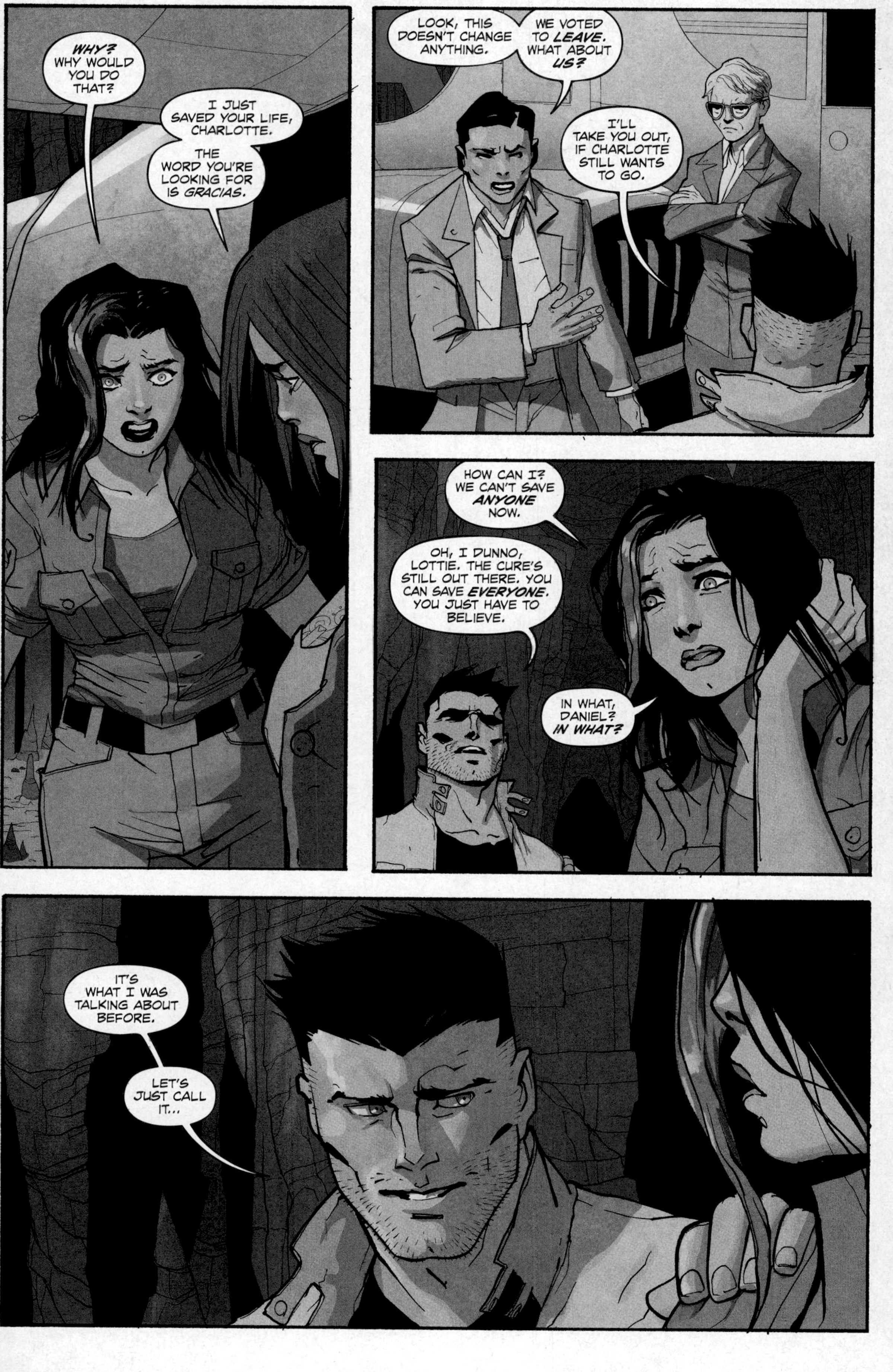
WHY? WHY WOULD YOU DO THAT?
I JUST SAVED YOUR LIFE, CHARLOTTE.
THE WORD YOU'RE LOOKING FOR IS GRACIAS.
LOOK, THIS DOESN'T CHANGE ANYTHING.
WE VOTED TO LEAVE. WHAT ABOUT US?
I'LL TAKE YOU OUT, IF CHARLOTTE STILL WANTS TO GO.
HOW CAN I? WE CAN'T SAVE ANYONE NOW.
OH, I DUNNO, LOTTIE. THE CURE'S STILL OUT THERE. YOU CAN SAVE EVERYONE. YOU JUST HAVE TO BELIEVE.
IN WHAT, DANIEL? IN WHAT?
IT'S WHAT I WAS TALKING ABOUT BEFORE.
LET'S JUST CALL IT...

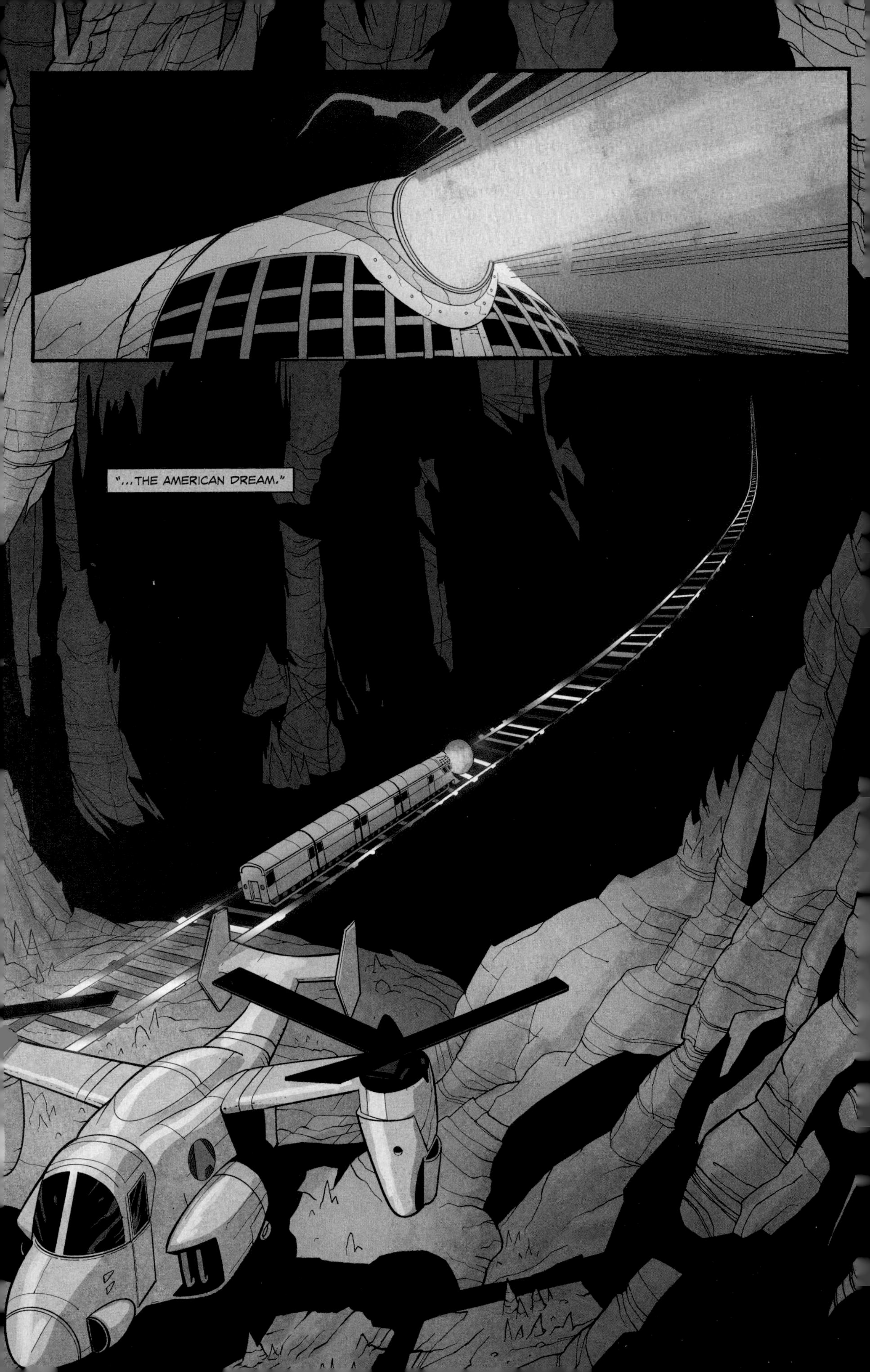
"...THE AMERICAN DREAM."

EPILOGUE.

PLEASE.

PLEASE.

I DID *EVERYTHING* FOR YOU. I TOOK THIS ZONE AND I MADE IT MINE. I TESTED MY THEORIES.

I'M RIGHT. THIS IS THE WAY. I'M SURE OF IT. I CAN SHOW YOU. JUST... LET ME TRY AGAIN.

I'LL WALK THE SPIRAL. I'LL DO *ANYTHING*. JUST LET ME PROVE I'M WORTHY.

AURORA... ONE MORE CHANCE. I'M *BEGGING* YOU.

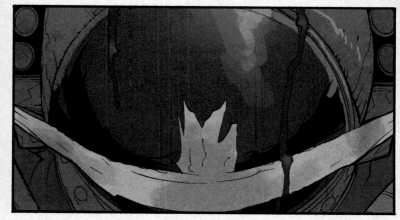

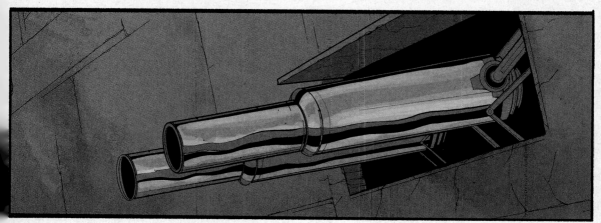

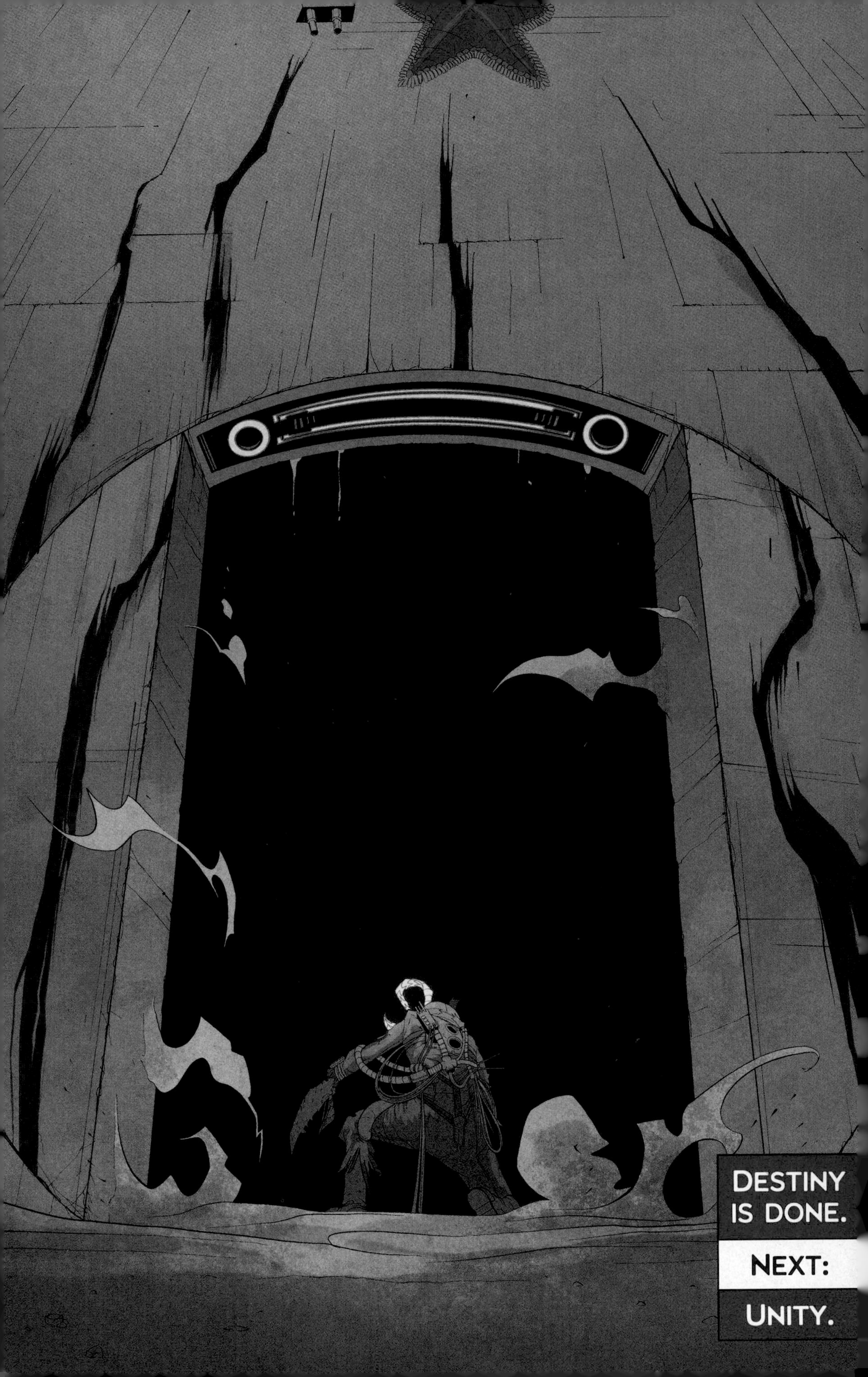
DESTINY IS DONE.
NEXT:
UNITY.

"A lot of people ask me about the United States of America before the Sealing - I'm one of the leading experts on its history, culture, and what the loss of that country did to the world. But the question I'm more concerned with—and we all should be— is this: what the hell have they been doing since?"

—Dr. Warren Gaines, 63, Professor Emeritus of American History, Oxford University and current chairman of the Lafayette Group, London, Alliance Euro-Afrique

"God Bless America."

—Elizabeth Arch, 102, the oldest living citizen of the former United States, Bangkok, Pan-Asian Prosperity Zone

Quotes from *The New World: An Oral History of the Sealing* by Valentina Sandoval.

ORIGINS

Originally published in **UNDISCOVERED COUNTRY** #1, November 2019.

First of all, Charles and I wanted to say THANK YOU so much for embarking on this weird, wild journey with us. And UNDISCOVERED COUNTRY will be a journey—a crazy trek through strange, transformed landscapes, peopled with characters (human and otherwise) who've captured our imaginations. The truth is, this book is a passion project for us both. It touches on everything we love to write about; it's high adventure, but it's also rooted in urgent fears. It's bombastic but deeply personal. It's SO many things to us that we figured that once in a while, we'd try and take this space in the back of the book to explore how some of the series' wilder elements came to be. For this first piece, though, we thought it'd only be appropriate to apply that idea to the entire project and give you the origin story of the series itself.

So how did UNDISCOVERED COUNTRY actually come to be?

The truth is, just like the expedition undertaken by our characters, UC began with a simple, unexpected invitation. This was all the way back in about 2012. I was finishing a run on Swamp Thing for DC and a writer named Charles Soule had just been hired to take over the book. We were both at a con in Chicago and Charles wrote me saying he'd seen my posts about running. He went on to suggest we go running together before the con started. We didn't know each other at all at this point—we'd exchanged a few friendly emails about old Swampy, but that was it, so I was hesitant at first. Cons are huge fun—meeting fans, seeing friends—but they're also a lot of work. Running for me was always a way to just take a moment before the con to get ready and prepare. So running with someone else didn't hold much appeal—and who was this Charles guy, anyway? His bio said he was a lawyer? Really? So we planned a tight course, hugging the convention center so we could come back at any point.

The funny thing was though, from the moment we started running together, we just hit it off. We're very different people Charles and I—almost opposites—but so many of our interests overlapped. We got so lost in conversation about the comics that inspired us that we ended up getting lost in earnest. Before we knew it, we'd gone way off course and we were standing on the coast of Lake Michigan, far from the convention center. The sight was something else, though. The sun was just coming up over the lake, sparks of light on iron gray water, like coming upon a foundry where day was being forged.

We had to rush back to the con to be there in time, but we agreed to make it a habit to run together at any con we were both attending. So it went. Later that year, we ran together in Vegas by the edge of the purple desert. We ran in Florida and saw a gator or two. More and more, the point became exploring together, or getting lost. Wandering far enough to see something inspiring, something new, something unexpected.

Something to know is that we became real friends on these runs. Many of you have seen the pics over the years of us running together and remarked on it. But along the way, our talks became more personal. We started trading scripts and story ideas, helping each other to craft plots and create characters. Our families became friends as well—our wives, our kids. We became family. Soon Charles and started talking about doing a book together someday, when the Marvel and DC stuff quieted down. Something big and epic that reflected all the things we both loved to write about...something that had to do with American history, with elements of adventure, like our favorite old shows and pulps, but we didn't have the core concept yet.

Finally, about three years ago, we got serious. We both had series ending, we were both at points in our careers and lives where, above all, we wanted a new challenge, something that would push us out of our creative comfort zones and force us to flex new creative muscles. We had lots of ideas, but none seemed quite big enough, wild enough.

So, that spring, in hopes of finding the right idea, we decided to accept another invitation. Over the years, doing research for Batman and Daredevil, we'd come into contact with a man who'd worked in the CIA for a number of years and was still an active consultant on matters of national security. We'd all become friends and, on a few occasions, he'd invited Charles and me down to visit the CIA with him and even meet some folks from various departments of DARPA, the Defense Advanced Research Projects Agency, the department responsible for the development of advanced technologies for the military.

The CIA visit was wild; we learned about secret, dangerous moments in the cold war, how close America and the Soviet Union came to all out hostility. And we learned about gadgets and missions, operations straight out of fiction. We learned about incredible acts of service performed by men and women whose names will forever remain unknown but whose sacrifices will never be forgotten.

We went to DARPA soon after, where we got to meet with department heads from all different branches of research. We learned about vehicles with smart armor, drones that swarm an enemy, we learned about nano space warfare, cyber-warfare... All sorts of technologies being developed to help America defend itself and stay prepared in a changing global landscape.

Above all, what we came away from the visits with was an appreciation of service and sacrifice, an awe for the blood sweat and tears shed for dedication to a belief, an ideal, a faith in what America could and should stand for.

Our heads swimming with all this, we decided to go for a run in the National Mall. We figured seeing the monuments, the huge classic iconography might bring it all together for us. The Washington Monument, the Lincoln Memorial. It was chilly, and few people were out. The trees were bare. We ran around and around the reflecting pool, throwing ideas back and forth. What if one of those technologies ran amok? What if one of those missions we'd heard about had failed...? What if...? We came up with dozens of ideas we liked but none quite big enough for the kind of project we wanted this to be. We stopped running the loop and turned, cutting a different path, and suddenly came upon—of all things—the Ferris Bueller 961 Ferrari being set up on display for tourists. So, taking a break, we started talking about that movie, about how it's a favorite of our kids. This led to a conversation about how differently our children consume entertainment from the ways we had as kids, how much of their experience now is theirs to choose.

We talked about how they'll be able to completely choose the politics they consume, the entertainment, how great and horrible it all is, that total agency. How almost everything they don't want to hear or see will be avoidable. How they will be able to insulate themselves in their own interests—whatever those may be—more singularly than any generation before. Will our kids be less likely to look outside themselves, outside their own comfort zones? Will they NEVER want to be challenged, to explore, to just... get lost?

And soon we started talking about how, on a global scale, the same tensions between collectivism and solipsism seem to be playing out everywhere, so many countries teetering between a total retreat from the global stage and some desperate call for multi-lateral action. Do we recoil from the world, as individuals, as communities, as nations, or do we join together to face all the daunting world-threatening problems out there? Are we in it as one, or are should we look out for ours and ours alone?

And then it came to us—not from the looming monuments, but as always, from the unexpected angle, from the weird discovery—an idea borne of all of these things we'd been thinking about and circling, from the personal to the speculative:

What if the US suddenly sealed itself off entirely from the rest of the world, became a black box, and stayed that way for thirty years, until one day, the doors opened,

just a crack...and invited one special team of people to visit... What if?

And from that moment on, we *never* stopped talking about it.

That was 2017, and ever since we've been tinkering with this one, building it, character by character, territory by territory. We'd call each other up just to talk new ideas, new zones the team might cross through, each a comic book extension of a real scientific possibility. Those bacteria-resistant fish we learned about, the ones grown to be larger, more adaptable—they became the fauna of this first zone. And the advanced foil shielding for UV rays we'd learned about became the material of the robes worn by the Destiny Man's tribe. We spoke again with our friend at the CIA and he informed us that the idea of an independent America was something he and his partners had been war-gaming for years in think tanks—how a wall might be built, literally and figuratively, how a new currency might be developed, how communication could be shut down... all of it. Every fact led to a new idea, a new territory. A prehistoric zone! An oceanic zone! And on and on and now here we are.

So what to make of all this? In the end, the point of this essay is simple: every aspect of this book—from its very creation to its entire narrative world—was borne from the wonder and terror of allowing yourself to get lost with someone else. That's what UC is at its core: an excursion that started as a tightly scripted path and ended up being a journey into places unexplored. A "getting lost" in the best way.

I'd be remiss if I didn't talk about our other expedition members here, too: Giuseppe Camuncoli, "Cammo," is more than just our artist on this endeavor — he's our co-creator and partner, and we couldn't be more grateful for his leadership. He and inker Daniele Orlandini add to every idea and elevate every moment with their sharp, emotive style. Matt Wilson brings the world of UNDISCOVERED COUNTRY to life in stunning, vibrant color like no one else can, and a big thanks to letterer Crank! for giving voice to the characters (human and otherwise!) with real visual flair. Finally, editor Will Dennis is our navigator on this one, and we'd be really lost without his expert guidance.

So that's our team and this is UNDISCOVERED COUNTRY. It's a big, sprawling book about who we are and who we could become, a true ongoing, filled with twists, turns, crazy adventures and heartbreaking moments.

And now, finally, this is us, Charles and me, inviting you, reader, to come with us and get lost together in this strange, wild, new land.

Thanks again.

Scott and Charles

TIMELINE OF THE SEALING OF THE UNITED

The following events, when viewed through the lens of history, paint a clear picture of a nation preparing to close itself off from the world. Pressures internal and external created a scenario that was at the time unthinkable, but now seems all but inevitable. July 20, 2029... 0-Day, The Sealing, the day the borders closed. The day the world lost America, perhaps forever. One day, one single act by the country's leaders—but the seeds of that catastrophe had been sown many years before.

-8 YEARS

In retaliation for an endless series of escalating tariffs and trade wars that crossed multiple administrations, China called in its outstanding US-currency debt, causing an immediate devaluation of the dollar, inflation, and a brutal global recession whose effects were disproportionately felt inside the United States.

-7 YEARS, 5 MONTHS

The United States national power grid experiences a cascading failure, causing a blackout across more than a third of the country. The power is not fully restored for over three weeks, and the event comes to be known as The Smokeout due to much of the population using all available sources of fuel for fires to remain warm during frigid February temperatures.

-4 YEARS, 2 MONTHS

Exports of consumer goods containing yttrium, promethium, cerium and similar rare earth materials are prohibited. The mineral mines located at Mountain Pass, CA are nationalized, as are all privately held stockpiles of rare earth materials within the borders of the United States.

-5 YEARS, 3 MONTHS

The Occupation of Raleigh ends with the deployment of the 120th Infantry Regiment of the North Carolina National Guard.

Project Aurora begins, in a facility just outside Leadville, Colorado, located at the highest elevation of any city in the United States.

-7 YEARS

The first tests of "Air Wall" force-shield technology, developed by the Defense Advanced Research Projects Agency (DARPA) in conjunction with Bell Labs, are conducted in Arlington, Virginia.

-7 YEARS, 10 MONTHS

Congress approves $20 billion for construction of sea walls around much of the nation's coasts to mitigate effects of rising sea levels.

-6 YEARS

All private leases allowing drilling and removal from the National Petroleum Reserve (Alaska) are terminated, with exploitation of the region's oil and natural gas reserves taken over by the US government and dramatically accelerated.

-5 YEARS

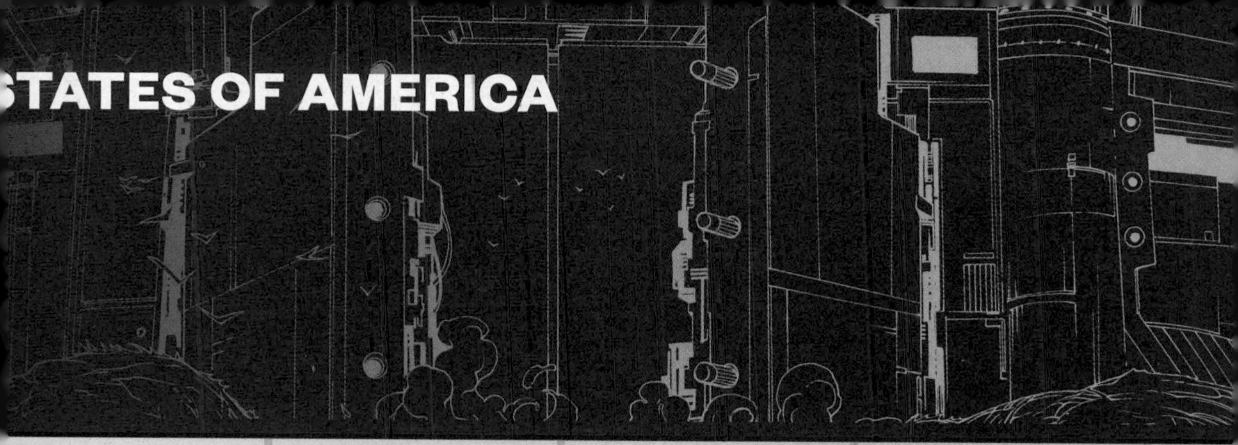

STATES OF AMERICA

-3 YEARS, 4 MONTHS

Comprehensive withdrawal of US military forces from overseas deployment begins, including Ramstein Air Base in Rhineland-palatinate, Germany and United States forces Korea.

-2 YEARS, 11 MONTHS

Members of Project Aurora offer closed session testimony to the Senate Armed Services committee.

-2 YEARS, 8 MONTHS

The Marine Access Zone Exclusion Act, or "MAZE," is passed by majority vote of congress and signed into law. The MAZE act extends the United States maritime border from twelve nautical miles to one hundred, and claims these areas as sovereign territorial seas.

-2 YEARS

The United States Citizenship and Immigration Service discontinues the acceptance of new immigration-based visa applications in all employment- and family-based categories, though "extraordinary ability" petitions for highly skilled foreign parties continue to be handled on a case-by-case basis.

-1 YEAR, 6 MONTHS

Experiments in gravitational lensing at a Project Aurora facility outside Pittsburgh, Pennsylvania result in a patch of farmland aging an apparent century, resulting in the area returning from plowed field to old-growth forest in a matter of minutes

-7 MONTHS

The final section of wall along the country's northern border is completed approximately two miles north of Pembina, North Dakota.

-5 DAYS

The President of the United States addresses the nation and the world, indicating that in five days all US borders and ports of entry will be closed, and all communication, trade, treaty observance, diplomacy and further interaction with the outer world will cease until further notice. Everyone inside the borders at that point will be allowed to stay, no matter their country of origin. Anyone outside will not be allowed back in. These new policies of the American government will be enforced with the full power of the nation's military.

THE SEALING

COVER VARIANTS

Issue 1, Cover B
Art by Jock

Issue 1, 2nd Printing
Art by Giuseppe Camuncoli & Daniele Orlandini
Colors by Matt Wilson

Issue 1, 4th Printing
Art by Giuseppe Camuncoli
Colors by Matt Wilson

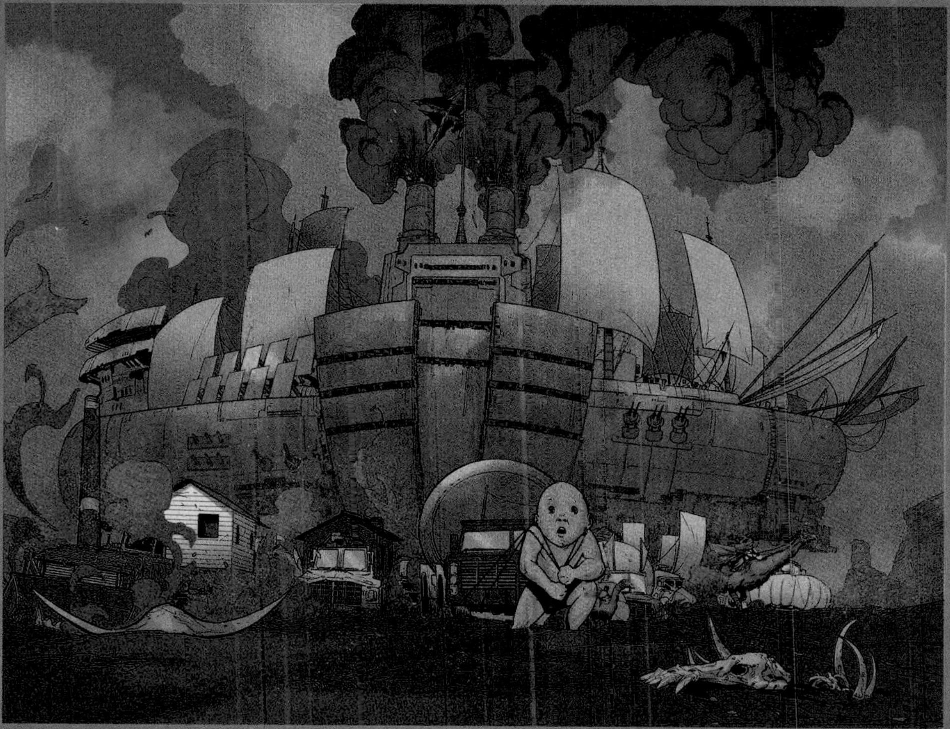

Issue 1, 3rd Printing
Art by Giuseppe Camuncoli & Daniele Orlandini
Colors by Matt Wilson

Issue 2, Cover B
Art by Francis Manapul

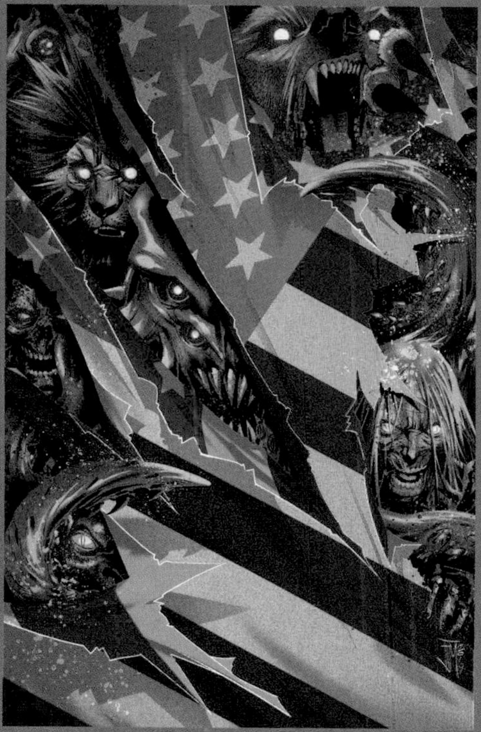

Issue 2, 2nd Printing
Art by Giuseppe Camuncoli
Colors by Matt Wilson

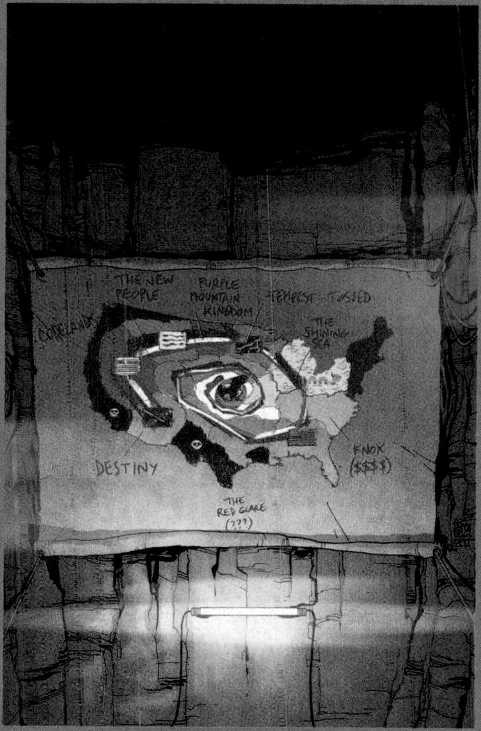
THE NEW PEOPLE
PURPLE MOUNTAIN KINGDOM
TEMPEST-TOSSED
THE SHINING SEA
DESTINY
KNOX ($$$$)
THE RED GLARE (???)

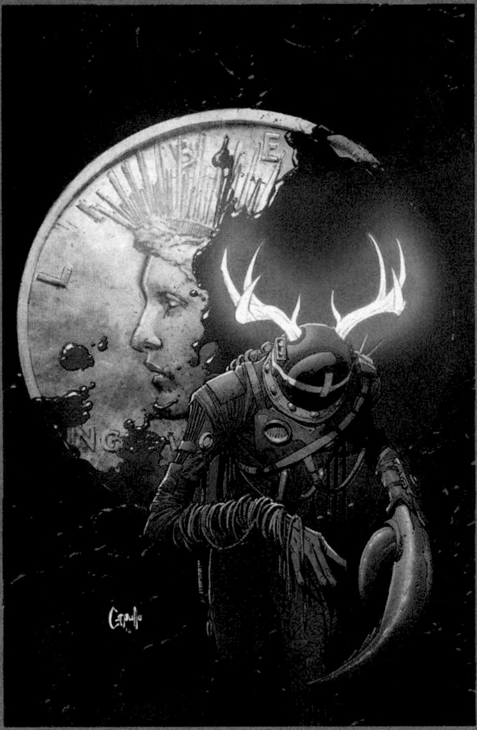

Issue 3, Cover B
Art by Greg Capullo
Colors by FCO Plascencia

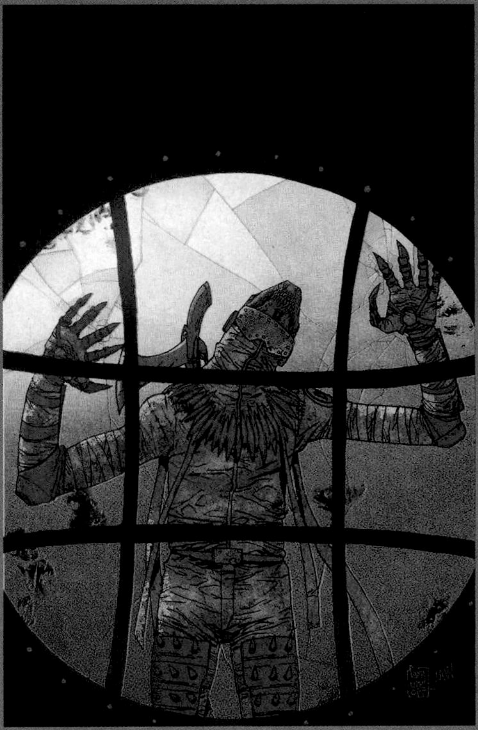

Issue 3, 2nd Printing
Art by Giuseppe Camuncoli
Colors by Matt Wilson

Issue 4, Cover B
Art by Jamie McKelvie

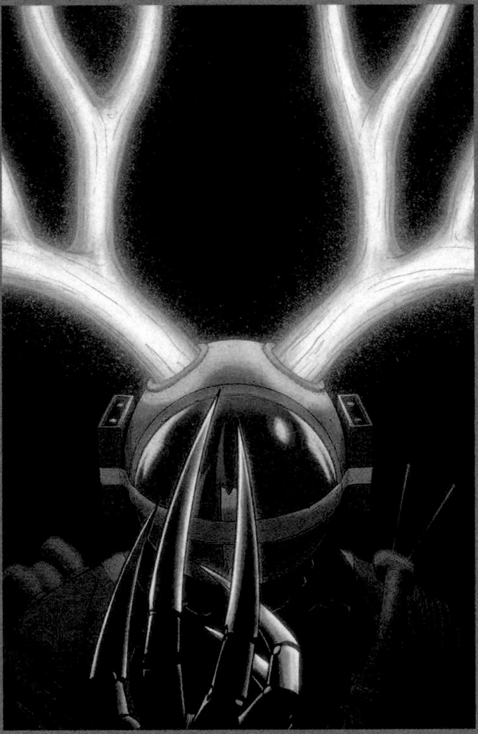

Issue 5, Cover B
Art by Phil Noto

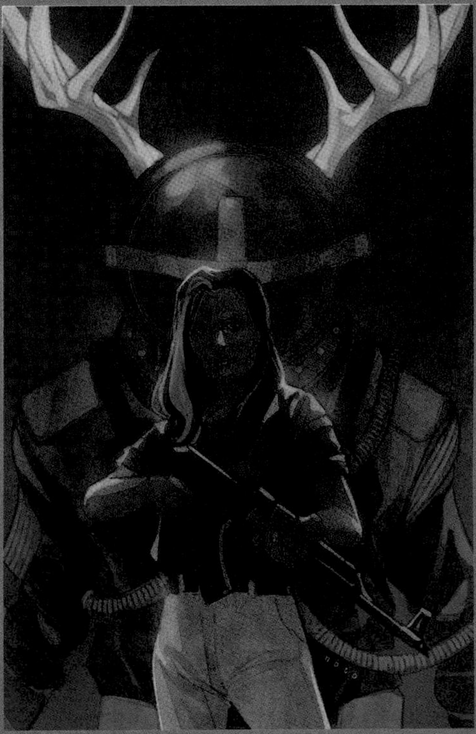

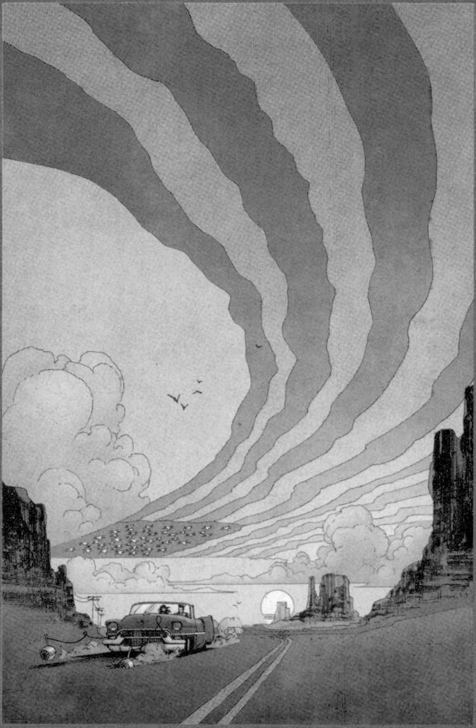

Issue 6, Cover B
Art by Sean Murphy
Colors by Matt Hollingsworth

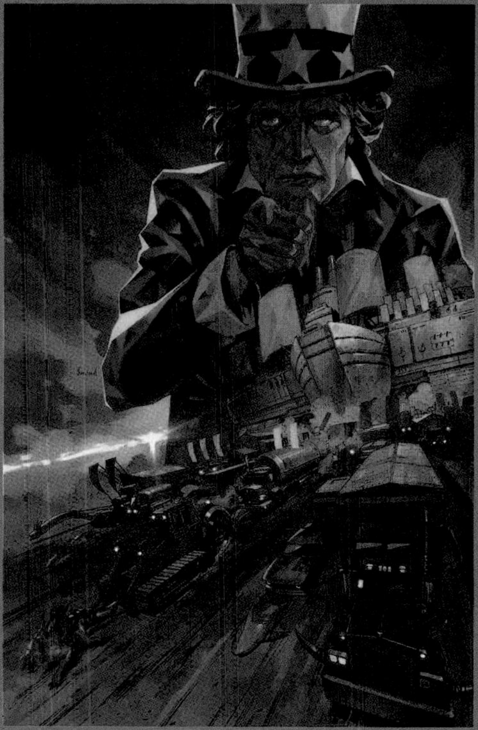

Issue 1, Cover C
Art by Kael Ngu

Issue 1, Cover D
Art by Johnny Desjardins

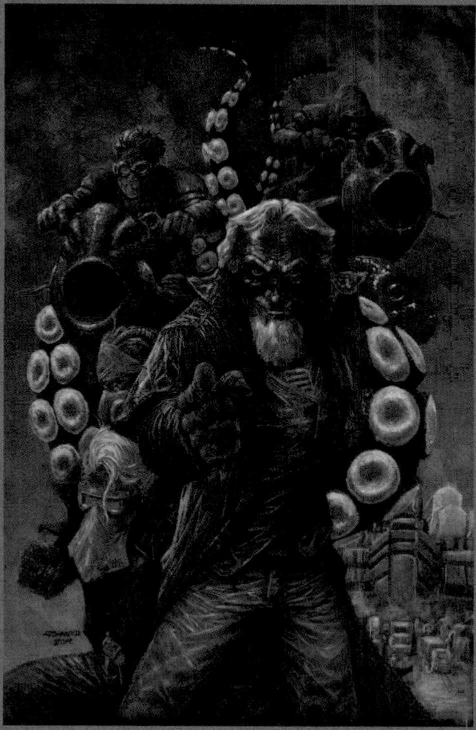

Issue 1, Cover G
Art by Steven Segovia

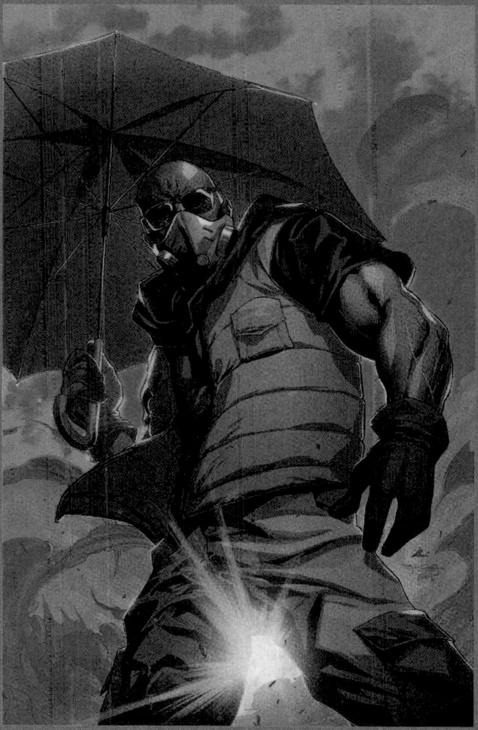

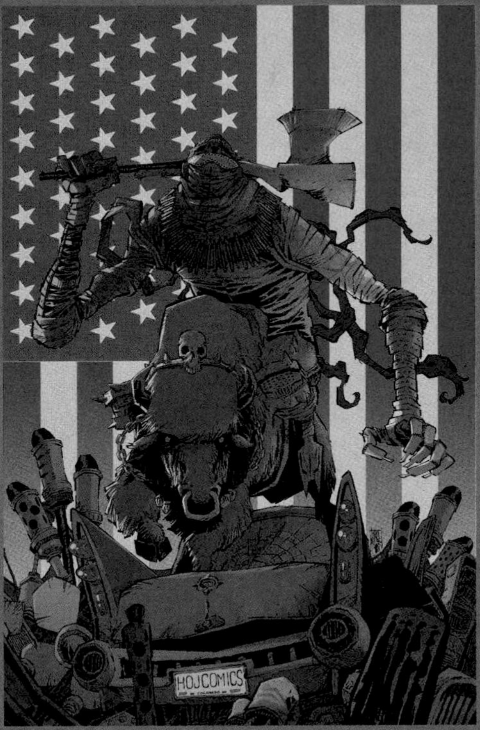
HOJCOMICS

Issue 1, Cover H
Art by Jorge Corona

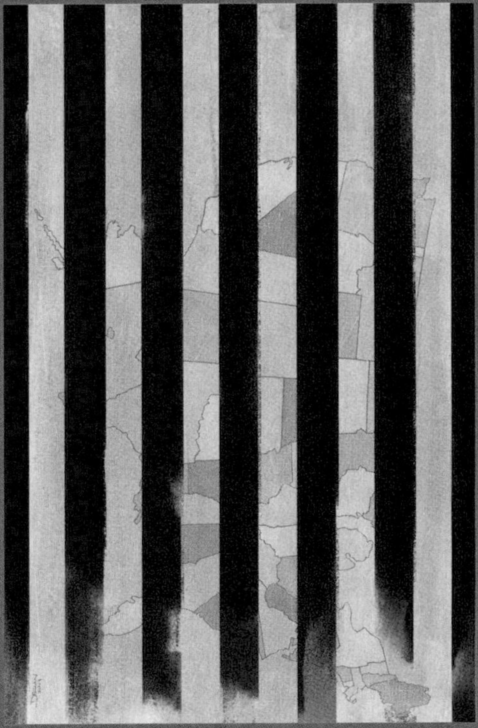

Issue 1, Cover I
Art by Declan Shalvey

Ilssue 1, Cover J
Art by John Gallagher

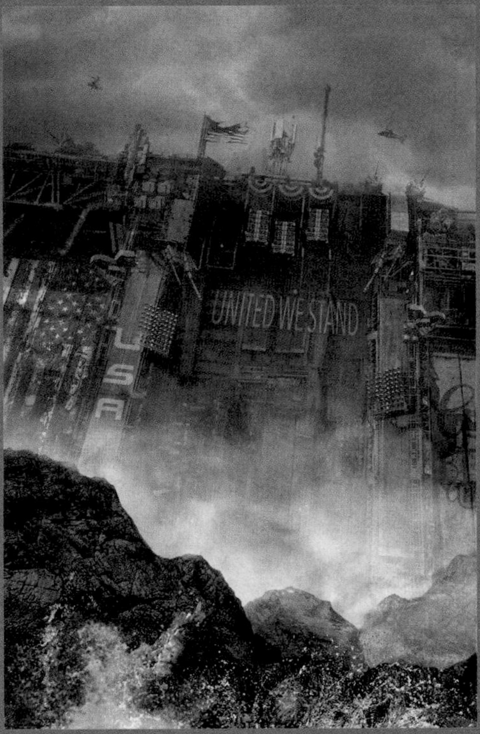
UNITED WE STAND
USA

Issue 1, Cover K
Art by Joseph Shmalke

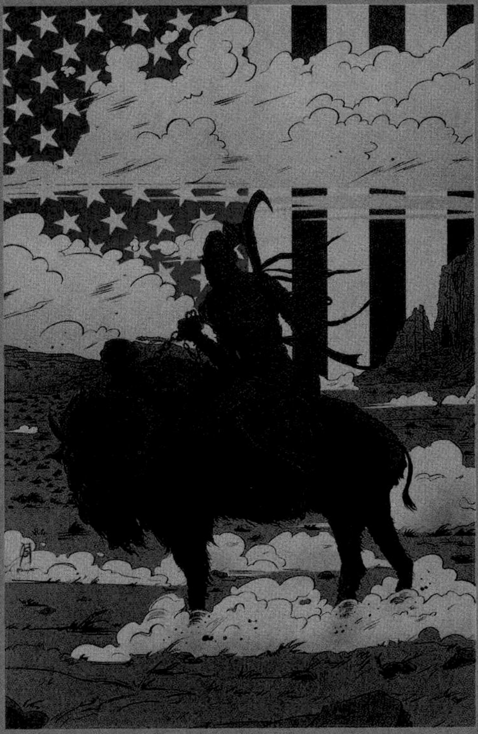

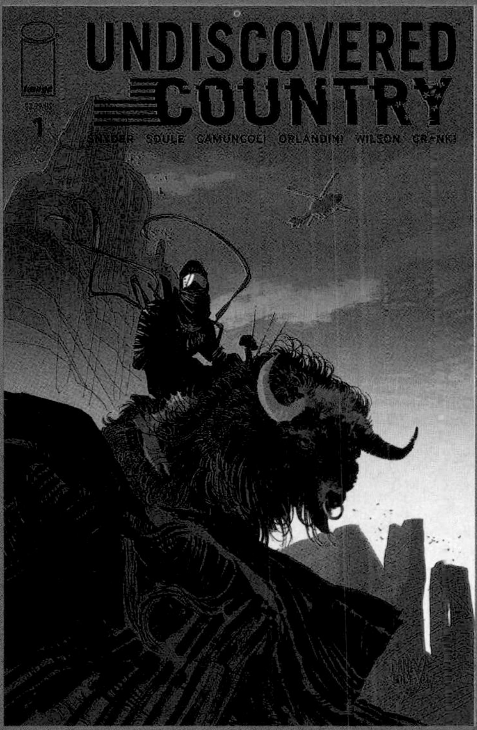
UNDISCOVERED
COUNTRY
1
SNYDER SOULE CAMUNCOLI ORLANDINI WILSON

Issue 1, Cover L
Art by Dani

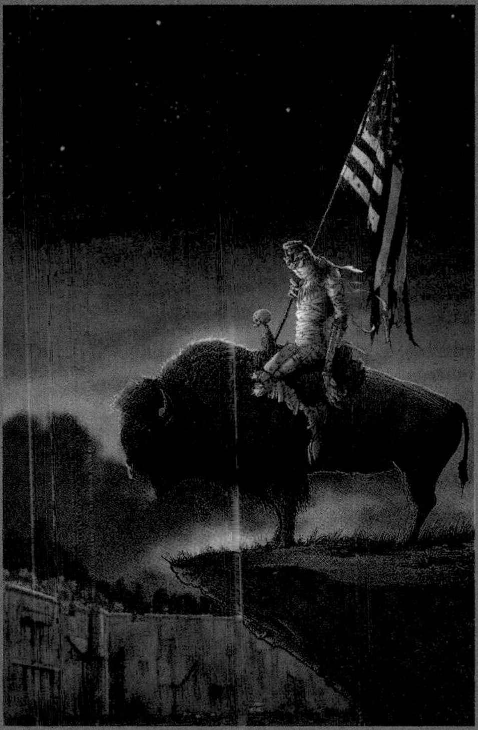

Issue 1, Cover N
Art by Stan Yak

Issue 1, Cover M
Art by Tom Whalen

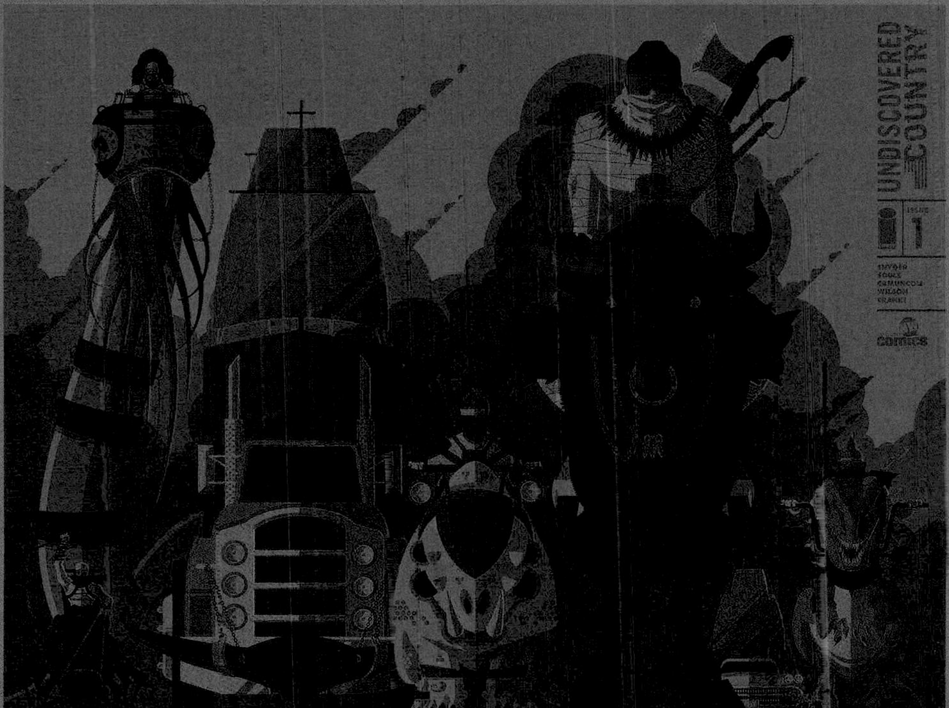
UNDISCOVERED
COUNTRY
ISSUE
1

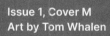

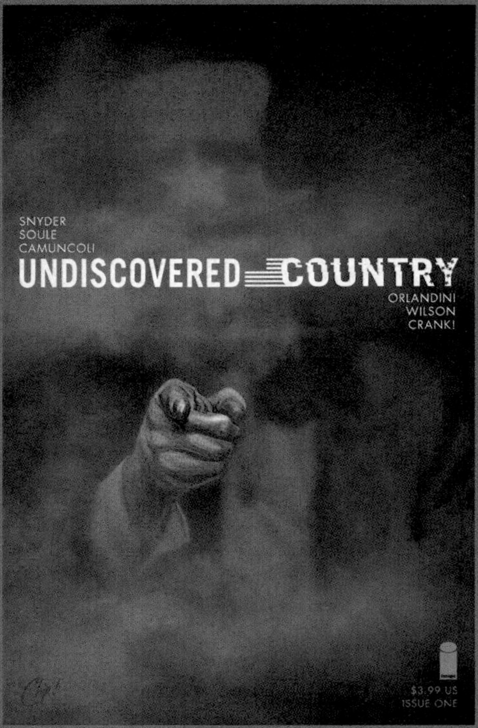
SNYDER
SOULE
CAMUNCOLI
UNDISCOVERED COUNTRY
ORLANDINI
WILSON
CRANK!
$3.99 US
ISSUE ONE

Issue 1, Cover O
Art by Chip Zdarsky

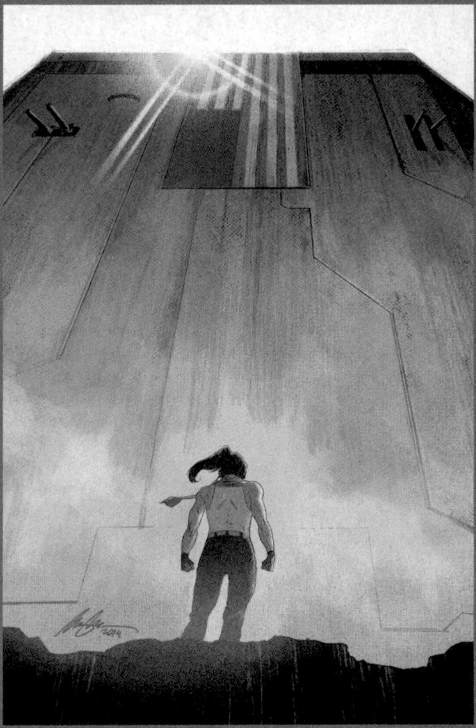

Issue 1, Cover Q
Art by Rafael Albuquerque

Issue 1, Cover R
Art by Dexter Soy

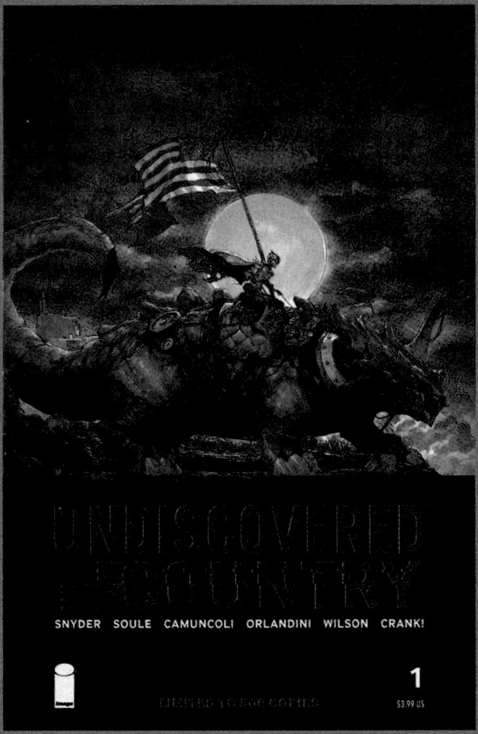
UNDISCOVERED
COUNTRY
SNYDER SOULE CAMUNCOLI ORLANDINI WILSON CRANK!
1
$3.99 US

Issue 1, Cover S
Art by Monte Michael Moore

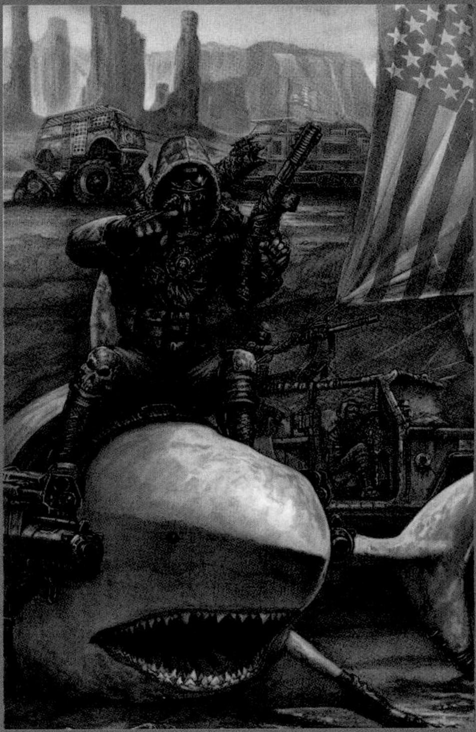

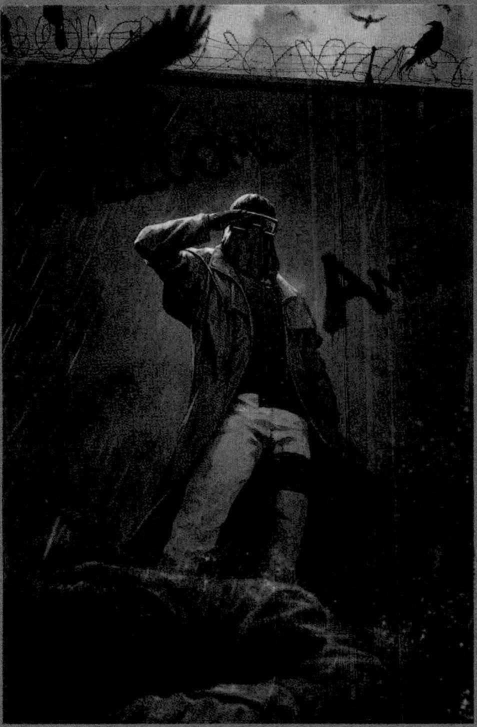

Issue 1, Cover T
Art by Skan

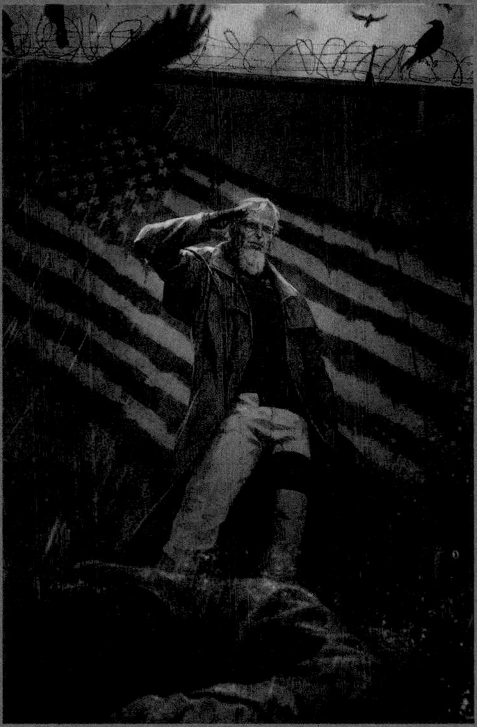

Issue 1, Cover U
Art by Skan

Issue 1, Cover V
Art by Stephanie Hans

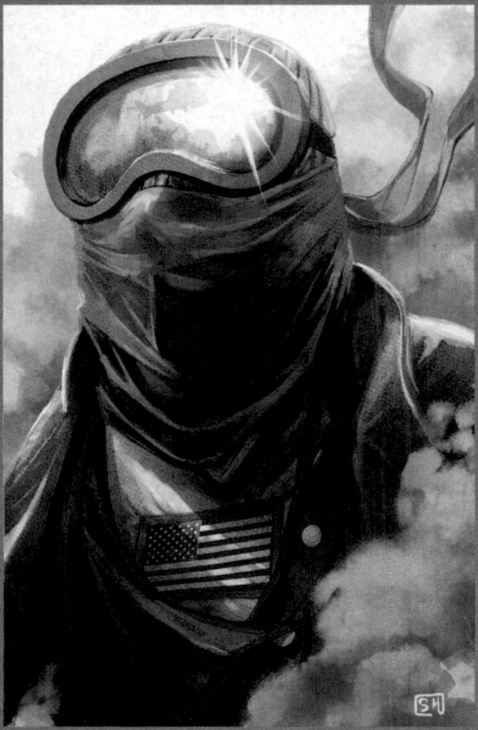

Issue 1, Cover W
Art by Julius Ohta

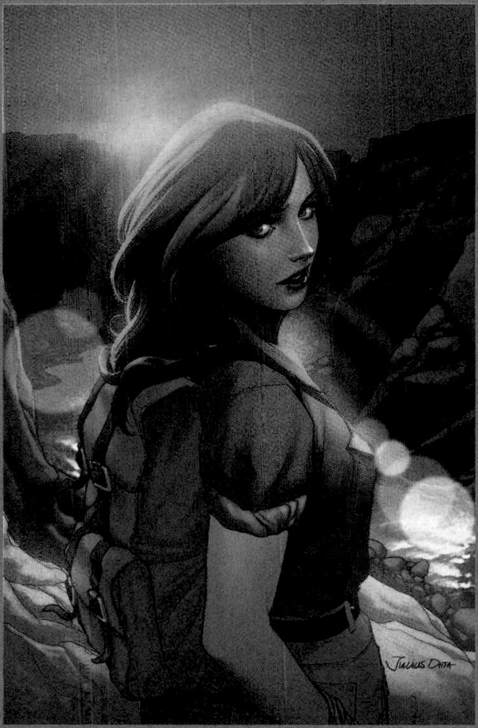
JULIUS OHTA

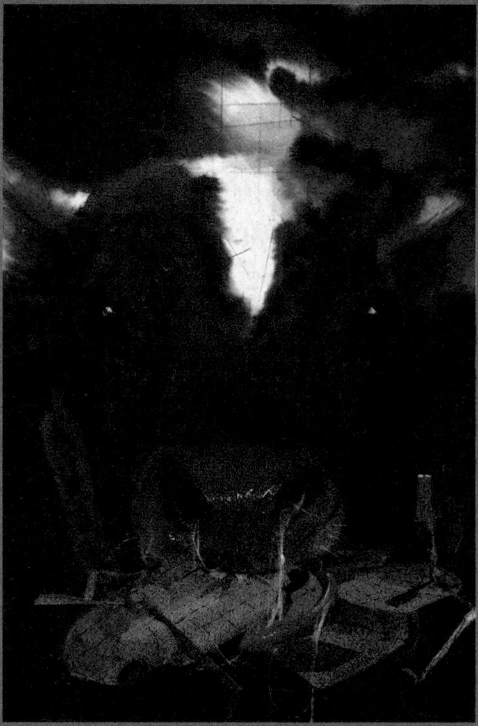

Issue 1, Cover X
Art by Anand Radhakrishnan

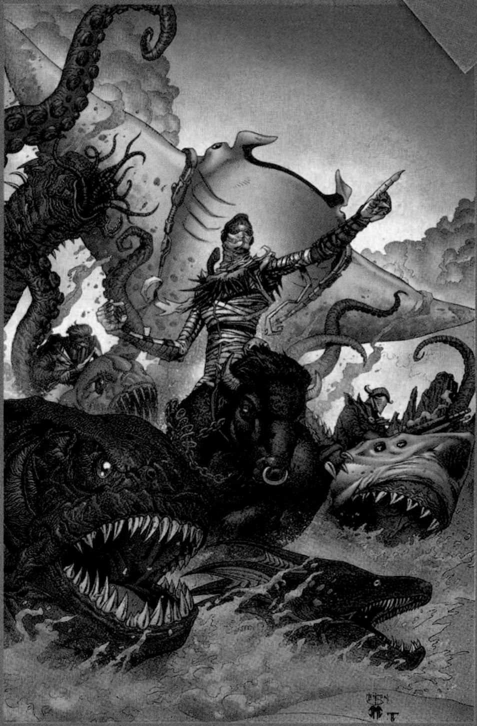

Issue 1, Cover Y
Art by Eric Henson

Issue 1, Cover Z
Art by Eric Henson

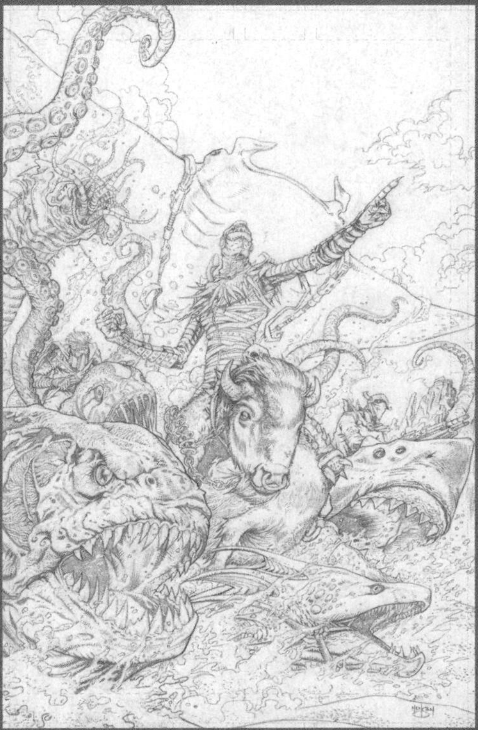

GalaxyCon Exclusive
Art by Giuseppe Camuncoli

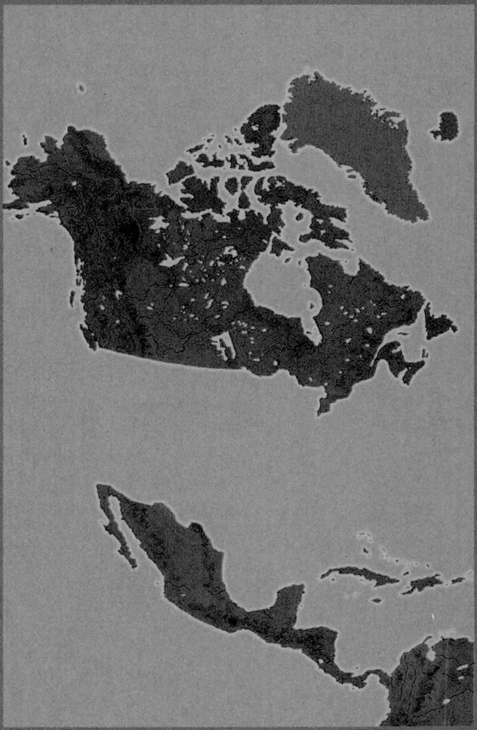